AGENT ZERO

Jack Mars is the USA Today bestselling author of the LUKE STONE thriller series, which includes seven books. He is also the author of the new FORGING OF LUKE STONE prequel series, comprising three books (and counting); and of the AGENT ZERO spy thriller series, comprising six books (and counting).

ANY MEANS NECESSARY (book #1), which has over 800 five star reviews, is available as a free download on Amazon!

Jack loves to hear from you, so please feel free to visit www. Jackmarsauthor.com to join the email list, receive a free book, receive free giveaways, connect on Facebook and Twitter, and stay in touch!

AGENT ZERO

(An Agent Zero Spy Thriller—Book #1)

JACK MARS

CONTENTS

"The life of the dead is placed in the memory of the living."
—Marcus Tullius Cicero

CHAPTER ONE

The first class of the day was always the toughest. Students shuffled into the lecture hall at Columbia University like shiftless, dead-eyed zombies, their senses dulled by all-night study sessions or hangovers or some combination thereof. They wore sweatpants and yesterday's T-shirts and clutched Styrofoam cups of soy mocha lattes or artisanal blonde roasts or whatever it was the kids were drinking these days.

Professor Reid Lawson's job was to teach, but he also recognized the need for a morning boost—a mental stimulant to supplement the caffeine. Lawson gave them a moment to find their seats and get comfortable while he took off his tweed sport coat and draped it over his chair.

"Good morning," he said loudly. The announcement jarred several students, who looked up suddenly as if they hadn't realized they'd wandered into a classroom. "Today, we're going to talk about pirates."

That got some attention. Eyes looked forward, blinking through the slush of sleep deprivation and trying to determine if he had really said "pirates" or not.

"Of the Caribbean?" joked a sophomore in the front row.

"Of the Mediterranean, actually," Lawson corrected. He paced slowly with his hands clasped behind his back. "How many of you have taken Professor Truitt's class on ancient empires?" About a third of the class raised their hands. "Good. Then you know that the Ottoman Empire was a major world power for, oh, almost six hundred years. What you may *not* know is that the Ottoman corsairs, or more colloquially, the Barbary pirates, stalked the seas for much of that time, from the coast of Portugal, through the Strait of Gibraltar, and much of the Mediterranean. What do you think they were after? Anyone? I know you're alive out there."

"Money?" asked a girl in the third row.

"Treasure," said the sophomore from the front.

"Rum!" came a shout from a male student in the back of the room, eliciting a chuckle from the class. Reid grinned too. There was some life in this crowd after all.

"All good guesses," he said. "But the answer is 'all of the above.' See, the Barbary pirates mostly targeted European merchant vessels, and they would take everything—and I mean *everything*. Shoes, belts, money, hats, goods, the ship itself... and its crew. It's believed that in the two-century span from 1580 to 1780, the Barbary pirates captured and enslaved more than two *million* people. They would take it all back to their North African kingdom. This went on for centuries. And what do you think the European nations did in return?"

"Declared war!" shouted the student in the back.

A mousy girl in horn-rimmed glasses raised her hand slightly and asked, "Did they broker a treaty?"

"In a way," Lawson replied. "The powers of Europe agreed to pay tribute to the Barbary nations, in the form of huge sums of money and goods. I'm talking Portugal, Spain, France, Germany, England, Sweden, the Netherlands... they were all paying the pirates to keep away from their boats. The rich got richer, and the pirates backed off—mostly. But then, between the late eighteenth and early nineteenth century, something happened. An event occurred that would be a catalyst to the end of the Barbary pirates. Anyone want to venture a guess?"

No one spoke. To his right, Lawson spotted a kid scrolling on his phone.

"Mr. Lowell," he said. The kid snapped to attention. "Any guess?"

"Um... America happened?"

Lawson smiled. "Are you asking me, or telling me? Be confident in your answers, and the rest of us will at least *think* you know what you're talking about."

"America happened," he said again, more emphatically this time.

"That's right! America happened. But, as you know, we were just a fledgling nation then. America was younger than most of you are. We had to establish trade routes with Europe to boost our economy, but the Barbary pirates started taking our ships. When we said, 'What the hell, guys?' they demanded tribute. We barely had a treasury, let alone anything in it. Our piggy bank was empty. So what choice did we have? What could we do?"

"Declare war!" came a familiar shout from the rear of the hall.

"Precisely! We had no choice but to declare war. Now, Sweden had already been fighting the pirates for a year, and together, between 1801 and 1805, we took Tripoli Harbor and captured the city of Derne, effectively ending the conflict." Lawson leaned against the edge of his desk and folded his hands in front of him. "Of course, that's glossing over a lot of details, but this is a European history class, not American history. If you get the chance, you should do some reading on Lieutenant Stephen Decatur and the USS *Philadelphia*. But I digress. Why are we talking about pirates?"

"Because pirates are cool?" said Lowell, who had since put away his phone.

Lawson chuckled. "I can't disagree. But no, that's not the point. We're talking about pirates because the Tripolitan War represents something rarely seen in the annals of history." He stood up straight, scanning the room and making eye contact with several students. At least now Lawson could see light in their eyes, a glimpse that most students were alive this morning, if not attentive. "For literal centuries, none of the European powers wanted to stand up to the Barbary nations. It was easier to just pay them. It took America—which was, back then, a joke to most of the developed world—to be the change. It took an act of desperation from a nation that was hilariously and hopelessly outgunned to bring about a shift in the power dynamic of the world's most valuable trade route at the time. And therein lies the lesson."

"Don't mess with America?" someone offered.

Lawson smiled. "Well, yes." He stuck a finger in the air to punctuate his point. "But moreover, that desperation and an utter lack of viable choices can and has, historically, led to some of the biggest triumphs the world has ever seen. History has taught us, again and again, that there is no regime too big to topple, no country too small or weak to make a real difference." He winked. "Think about that next time you're feeling like little more than a speck in this world."

By the end of class, there was a marked difference between the dragging, weary students who had entered and the laughing, chatting group that filed out of the lecture hall. A pink-haired girl paused by his desk on the way out to smile and comment, "Great talk, Professor. What was the name of that American lieutenant you mentioned?"

"Oh, that was Stephen Decatur."

"Thanks." She jotted it down and hurried out of the hall.

"Professor?"

Lawson glanced up. It was the sophomore from the front row. "Yes, Mr. Garner? What can I do for you?"

"Wondering if I can ask a favor. I'm applying for an internship at the Museum of Natural History, and uh, I could use a letter of recommendation."

"Sure, no problem. But aren't you an anthropology major?"

"Yeah. But, uh, I thought a letter from you might carry a bit more weight, you know? And, uh..." The kid looked at his shoes. "This is kind of my favorite class."

"Your favorite class so far." Lawson smiled. "I'd be happy to. I'll have something for you tomorrow—oh, actually, I have an important engagement tonight that I can't miss. How's Friday?"

"No rush. Friday would be great. Thanks, Professor. See ya!" Garner hurried out of the hall, leaving Lawson alone.

He glanced around the empty auditorium. This was his favorite time of day, between classes—the present satisfaction of the previous mingled with the anticipation of the next.

His phone chimed. It was a text from Maya. *Home by 5:30?*

Yes, he replied. *Wouldn't miss it.* The "important engagement" that evening was game night at the Lawson house. He cherished his quality time with his two girls.

Good, his daughter texted back. *I have news.*

What news?

Later was her reply. He frowned at the vague message. Suddenly the day was going to feel very long.

Lawson packed up his messenger bag, pulled on his downy winter coat, and hurried to the parking lot as his teaching day came to an end. February in New York was typically bitter cold, and lately it had been even worse. The slightest bit of wind was downright blistering.

He started the car and let it warm for a few minutes, cupping his hands over his mouth and blowing warm breath over his frozen fingers. This was his second winter in New York, and it didn't seem like he was acclimating to the colder climate. In Virginia he had thought forty degrees in February was frigid. *At least it isn't snowing,* he thought. *Silver linings.*

The commute from the Columbia campus to home was only seven miles, but traffic at this time of day was heavy and fellow commuters were generally irritating. Reid mitigated that with audiobooks, which his older daughter had recently turned him on to. He was currently working his way through Umberto Eco's *The Name of the Rose,* though today he barely heard the words. He was thinking about Maya's cryptic message.

The Lawson home was a brown-bricked, two-story bungalow in Riverdale in the northern end of the Bronx. He loved the bucolic, suburban neighborhood—the proximity to the city and the university, the winding streets that gave way to wide boulevards to the south. The girls loved it too, and if Maya was accepted to Columbia, or even her safety school of NYU, she wouldn't have to leave home.

Reid immediately knew something was different when he entered the house. He could smell it in the air, and he heard the hushed voices coming from the kitchen down the hall. He set down his messenger bag and slid quietly out of his sport coat before carefully tiptoeing from the foyer.

"What in the world is going on here?" he asked by way of greeting.

"Hi, Daddy!" Sara, his fourteen-year-old, bounced on the balls of her feet as she watched Maya, her older sister, perform some suspicious ritual over a Pyrex baking dish. "We're making dinner!"

"*I'm* making dinner," Maya murmured, not looking up. "*She* is a spectator."

Reid blinked in surprise. "Okay. I have questions." He peered over Maya's shoulder as she applied a purplish glaze to a neat row of pork chops. "Starting with ... *huh?*"

Maya still didn't glance up. "Don't give me that look," she said. "If they're going to make home ec a required course, I'm going to put it to some use." Finally she looked up at him and smiled thinly. "And *don't* get used to it."

Reid put his hands up defensively. "By all means."

Maya was sixteen, and dangerously smart. She had clearly inherited her mother's intellect; she would be a senior that coming school year by virtue of having skipped the eighth grade. She had Reid's dark hair, pensive smile, and flair for the dramatic. Sara, on the other hand, got her looks entirely from Kate. As she grew into a teenager, it sometimes pained Reid to look at her face, though he never let on. She'd also acquired Kate's fiery temper. Most of the time, Sara was a total sweetheart, but every now and then she would detonate, and the fallout could be devastating.

Reid watched in astonishment as the girls set the table and served dinner. "This looks amazing, Maya," he commented.

"Oh, wait. One more thing." She retrieved something from the fridge—a brown bottle. "Belgian is your favorite, right?"

Reid narrowed his eyes. "How did you ...?"

"Don't worry, I had Aunt Linda buy it." She popped the cap and poured the beer into a glass. "There. Now we can eat."

Reid was extremely grateful to have Kate's sister, Linda, only a few minutes away. Gaining his associate professorship while raising two girls into teenagers would have been an impossible task without her. It was one of the primary motivators for the move to New York, for the girls to have a positive female influence close by. (Though he had to admit, he wasn't crazy about Linda buying his teenage daughter beer, regardless of who it was for.)

"Maya, this is amazing," he gushed after the first bite.

"Thank you. It's a chipotle glaze."

He wiped his mouth, set down his napkin, and asked, "Okay, I'm suspicious. What did you do?"

"What? Nothing!" she insisted.

"What'd you break?"

"I didn't..."

"You get suspended?"

"Dad, come on..."

Reid melodramatically gripped the table with both hands. "Oh God, don't tell me you're pregnant. I don't even own a shotgun."

Sara giggled.

"Would you stop?" Maya huffed. "I'm allowed to be nice, you know." They ate in silence for a minute or so before she casually added, "But since you mention it..."

"Oh, boy. Here it comes."

She cleared her throat and said, "I sort of have a date. For Valentine's Day."

Reid nearly choked on his pork chop.

Sara smirked. "I *told* you he'd be weird about it."

He recovered and held up a hand. "Wait, wait. I'm not being weird. I just didn't think... I didn't know you were, uh... Are you dating?"

"No," Maya said quickly. Then she shrugged and looked down at her plate. "Maybe. I don't know yet. But he's a nice guy, and he wants to take me to dinner in the city..."

"In the city," Reid repeated.

"Yes, Dad, in the city. And I'd need a dress. It's a fancy place. I don't really have anything to wear."

There were many times when Reid desperately wished Kate was there, but this might have topped them. He had always assumed that his daughters would date at some point, but he was hoping that it wouldn't be until they were twenty-five. It was times like this that he resorted to his favored parenting acronym, WWKS—what would Kate say? As an artist and a decidedly free spirit, she probably would have handled the situation much differently than he would, and he tried to stay cognizant of that.

He must have looked particularly troubled, because Maya laughed a little and put her hand on his. "Are you okay, Dad? It's just a date. Nothing's going to happen. It's not a big deal."

"Yeah," he said slowly. "You're right. Of course it's no big deal. We can see if Aunt Linda can take you to the mall this weekend and—"

"I want you to take me."

"You do?"

She shrugged. "I mean, I wouldn't want to get anything you weren't okay with."

A dress, dinner in the city, and some boy… this wasn't anything he'd actually considered having to deal with before.

"All right then," he said. "We'll go on Saturday. But I have a condition—I get to pick tonight's game."

"Hmm," said Maya. "You drive a hard bargain. Let me consult with my associate." Maya turned to her sister.

Sara nodded. "Fine. As long as it's not Risk."

Reid scoffed. "You don't know what you're talking about. Risk is the best."

After dinner, Sara cleared the dishes while Maya made hot chocolate. Reid set up one of their favorites, Ticket to Ride, a classic game about building train routes across America. As he set out cards and plastic train cars, he found himself wondering when this had happened. When had Maya grown up so quickly? For the last two years, ever since Kate passed, he had played the parts of both parents (with some much-appreciated help from their Aunt Linda). They both still needed him, or so it seemed, but it wouldn't be long until they were off to college, and then careers, and then …

"Dad?" Sara entered the dining room and took a seat across from him. As if reading his mind, she said, "Don't forget, I have an art show at school next Wednesday night. You'll be there, right?"

He smiled. "Of course, honey. Wouldn't miss it." He clapped his hands together. "Now! Who's ready to get demolished—I mean, who's ready to play a family-friendly game?"

"Bring it on, old man," Maya called from the kitchen.

"Old man?" Reid said indignantly. "I'm thirty-eight!"

"I stand by it." She laughed as she entered the dining room. "Oh, the train game." Her grin dissolved to a thin smile. "This was Mom's favorite, wasn't it?"

"Oh … yeah." Reid frowned. "It was."

"I'm blue!" Sara announced, grabbing at pieces.

"Orange," said Maya. "Dad, what color? Dad, hello?"

"Oh." Reid snapped out of his thoughts. "Sorry. Uh, green."

Maya pushed some pieces his way. Reid forced a smile, though his thoughts were troubled.

After two games, both of which Maya had won, the girls went to bed and Reid retired to his study, a small room on the first floor, just off the foyer.

Riverdale was not a cheap area, but it was important to Reid to ensure that his girls had a safe and happy environment. There were only two bedrooms, so he had claimed the den on the first floor as his office. All of his books and memorabilia were crammed into nearly every available inch of the ten-by-ten first-floor room. With his desk and a leather armchair, only a small patch of well-worn carpet was still visible.

He fell asleep often in that armchair, after late nights of taking notes, preparing lectures, and rereading biographies. It was starting to give him back problems. Yet if he was being honest with himself, it wasn't getting any easier to sleep in his own bed. The location might have changed—he and the girls moved to New York shortly after Kate passed—but he still had the king-sized mattress and frame that had been *theirs*, his and Kate's.

He would have thought that by now the pain of losing Kate might have waned, at least slightly. Sometimes it did, temporarily, and then he would pass her favorite restaurant or catch a glimpse of one of her favorite movies on TV and it would come roaring back, as fresh as if it had happened yesterday.

If either of the girls experienced the same, they didn't talk about it. In fact, they often spoke about her openly, something that Reid still hadn't been able to do.

There was a picture of her on one of his bookshelves, taken at a friend's wedding a decade earlier. Most nights the frame was turned backward, or else he would spend the entire evening staring at it.

How stunningly unfair the world could be. One day, they had everything—a nice home, wonderful kids, great careers. They were living in McLean, Virginia; he was working as an adjunct professor at the nearby George Washington University. His job had him traveling a lot, to seminars and summits and as a guest lecturer on European history to schools all over the country. Kate was in the restorations department at the Smithsonian American Art Museum. Their girls were thriving. Life was perfect.

But as Robert Frost famously said, nothing gold can stay. One wintry afternoon Kate fainted at work—at least that's what her coworkers believed it to be when she suddenly went limp and fell out of her chair. They called an ambulance, but it was already too late. She was announced DOA at the hospital. An embolism, they had said. A blood clot had traveled to her brain and caused an ischemic stroke. The doctors used barely comprehensible medical terms wherever possible in their explanation, as if it would somehow soften the blow.

Worst of all, Reid had been away when it happened. He was at an undergraduate seminar in Houston, Texas, giving talks about the Middle Ages when he got the call.

That was how he discovered his wife had died. A phone call, just outside a conference room. Then came the flight home, the attempts to console his daughters in the midst of his own devastating grief, and the eventual move to New York.

He pushed himself up from the chair and spun the photo around. He didn't like thinking about all that, the end and the aftermath. He wanted to remember her like this, in the photo, Kate at her brightest. That's what he chose to remember.

There was something else, something right at the edge of his consciousness—some sort of hazy memory attempting to surface as he stared at the picture. It almost felt like déjà vu, but not of the present moment. It was as if his subconscious was trying to push something through.

A sudden knock at the door startled him back to reality. Reid hesitated, wondering who it could be. It was nearly midnight; the girls had been in bed for a couple of hours. The brisk knock came again. Fearing it might wake the kids, he hurried to answer it. After all, he lived in a safe neighborhood and had no reason to fear opening his door, midnight or not.

The harsh winter wind was not what froze him in his tracks. He stared in surprise at the three men on the other side. They were decidedly Middle Eastern, each with dark skin, a dark beard, and deep-set eyes, dressed in thick black jackets and boots. The two that flanked either side of the exit were tall and lanky; the third, behind them, was broad-shouldered and hulking, with an assumedly perpetual scowl.

"Reid Lawson," said the tall man to the left. "Is that you?" His accent sounded Iranian, but it was not thick, suggesting he had spent a decent amount of time stateside.

Reid's throat felt dry as he noticed, over their shoulders, a gray van idling at the curb, its headlights turned off. "Um, I'm sorry," he told them. "You must have the wrong house."

The tall man to the right, without taking his eyes off Reid, held up a cell phone for his two associates to see. The man to the left, the one asking the question, nodded once.

Without warning, the hulking man lurched forward, deceptively fast for his size. One meaty hand reached for Reid's throat. Reid accidentally twisted away, just out of reach, by stumbling backward and nearly tripping over his own feet. He recovered, touching down with his fingertips on the tiled floor.

As he skittered backward to regain his balance, the three men entered his house. He panicked, thinking only of the girls asleep in their beds upstairs.

He turned and ran through the foyer, into the kitchen, and skirted around the island. He glanced over his shoulder—the men gave chase. *Cell phone*, he thought desperately. It was on his desk in the study, and his assailants blocked the way.

He had to lead them away from the house, and away from the girls. To his right was the door to the backyard. He threw it open and ran out onto the deck. One of the men cursed in a foreign tongue—Arabic, he guessed—as they ran after him. Reid vaulted over the railing of the deck and landed in the small backyard. A bolt of pain shot up through his ankle with the impact, but he ignored it. He rounded the corner of the house and flattened himself against the brick façade, trying desperately to quiet his ragged breathing.

The brick was icy to the touch and the slight winter breeze cut through him like a knife. His toes were already numb—he'd run out of the house in only his socks. Goose bumps prickled up and down his limbs.

He could hear the men whispering to each other, hoarsely and urgently. He counted the distinct voices—one, two, and then three. They were out of the house. Good; that meant they were only after him, and not the kids.

He needed to get to a phone. He couldn't go back into the house without endangering his girls. He couldn't very well bang on a neighbor's door. Wait—there was a yellow emergency call box mounted on a telephone pole down the block. If he could get there ...

He took a deep breath and sprinted across the dark yard, daring to enter the halo of light cast from the streetlamps above. His ankle throbbed in protest and the shock of the cold sent stings up his feet, but he forced himself to move as fast as he could.

Reid glanced over his shoulder. One of the tall men had spotted him. He shouted to his cohorts, but did not chase after him. Strange, Reid thought, but he didn't stop to question it.

He reached the yellow emergency call box, tore it open, and jammed his thumb against the red button, which would send an alert to the local 911 dispatch. He looked over his shoulder again. He couldn't see any of them.

"Hello?" he hissed into the intercom. "Can anyone hear me?" Where was the light? There was supposed to be a light when the call button was pushed. Was this even working? "My name is Reid Lawson, there are three men after me, I live at—"

A strong hand grabbed a fistful of Reid's short brown hair and yanked backward. His words caught in his throat and escaped as little more than a hoarse wheeze.

Next thing he knew, there was rough fabric over his face, blinding him—a bag on his head—and at the same time, his arms were forced behind his back and locked into cuffs. He tried to struggle, but the strong hands held him firmly, twisting his wrists nearly to the point of breaking.

"Wait!" he managed to cry out. "Please..." An impact struck his abdomen so hard that the air rushed out of his lungs. He couldn't breathe, let alone speak. Dizzying colors swam in his vision as he nearly passed out.

Then he was being dragged, his socks scraping the pavement of the sidewalk. They shoved him into the van and slid the door shut behind him. The three men exchanged guttural foreign words with each other that sounded accusatory.

"Why...?" Reid finally managed to choke out.

He felt the sharp sting of a needle in his upper arm, and then the world fell away.

CHAPTER TWO

B lind. Cold. Rumbling, deafening, jostling, aching.

The first thing Reid noticed as he woke was that the world was black—he could not see. The acrid scent of fuel filled his nostrils. He tried to move his throbbing limbs, but his hands were bound behind him. He was freezing, but there was no breeze; just cold air, as if he were sitting in a refrigerator.

Slowly, as if through a fog, the memory of what had occurred floated back to him. The three Middle Eastern men. A bag over his head. A needle in his arm.

He panicked, yanking at his bonds and flailing his legs. Pain seared through his wrists where the metal of the cuffs dug into his skin. His ankle pulsed, sending shockwaves up his left leg. There was an intense pressure in his ears, and he could not hear anything other than a roaring engine.

For just a split second, he felt a dropping sensation in his stomach—a result of negative vertical acceleration. He was on a plane. And by the sound of it, this was no ordinary passenger plane. The rumbling, the intensely loud engine, the smell of fuel… he realized he must on a cargo plane.

How long had he been unconscious? What did they shoot him with? Were the girls safe? *The girls.* Tears stung his eyes as he hoped against hope that they were safe, that the police had heard enough of his message, and that authorities had been sent to the house…

He squirmed in his metal seat. Despite the pain and hoarseness in his throat, he ventured to speak.

"H-hello?" It came out as barely a whisper. He cleared his throat and tried again. "Hello? Anyone…?" He realized then that the noise of the engine would drown him out to anyone who wasn't seated beside him. "Hello!" he tried to shout. "Please…someone tell me what's—"

A harsh male voice hissed at him in Arabic. Reid flinched; the man was close, no more than a few feet away.

"Please, just tell me what's going on," he pleaded. "What's happening? Why are you doing this?"

Another voiced shouted threateningly in Arabic, this time to his right. Reid winced at the sharp reprimand. He hoped that the rumbling of the plane masked the trembling in his limbs.

"You have the wrong person," he said. "What is it you want? Money? I don't have much, but I can—wait!" A strong hand closed around his upper arm in a viselike grip, and an instant later he was ripped from his seat. He staggered, trying to stand, but the unsteadiness of the plane and the pain in his ankle won out. His knees buckled and he fell on his side.

Something solid and heavy struck him in the midsection. Pain spider-webbed through his torso. He tried to protest, but his voice only came out in unintelligible sobs.

Another boot kicked him in the back. Yet another, in the chin.

Despite the horrifying situation, a bizarre thought struck Reid. These men, their voices, these blows all suggested a personal vendetta. He did not just feel attacked. He felt *loathed*. These men were angry—and their anger was directed at him like the pinpoint of a laser.

The pain subsided, slowly, and gave way to a cold numbness that engulfed his body as he passed out.

Pain. Searing, throbbing, aching, burning.

Reid woke again. The memories of the past…he didn't even know how long it had been, nor did he know if it was day or night, and where he was that it might be day or night. But the memories came again, disjointed, like single frames cut from a film reel and left on the floor.

Three men.

The emergency box.

The van.

The plane.

And now...

Reid dared to open his eyes. It was difficult. The lids felt as if they were glued shut. Even behind the thin skin he could tell that there was a bright, harsh light waiting on the other side. He could feel the heat of it on his face, and see the network of tiny capillaries through his lids.

He squinted. All he could see was the unforgiving light, bright and white and searing into his head. God, his head hurt. He tried to groan and found, through an electric dose of new pain, that his jaw hurt as well. His tongue felt fat and dry, and he tasted a mouthful of pennies. Blood.

His eyes, he realized—they had been difficult to open because they were, in fact, glued shut. The side of his face felt hot and sticky. Blood had run down his forehead and into his eyes, no doubt from being relentlessly kicked to unconsciousness on the plane.

But he could see the light. The bag had been removed from his head. Whether or not that was a good thing remained to be seen.

As his eyes adjusted, he tried again in vain to move his hands. They were still bound, but this time, not by handcuffs. Thick, coarse ropes held him in place. His ankles, too, were lashed to the legs of a wooden chair.

Finally his eyes adjusted to the harshness of the light and hazy outlines formed. He was in a small windowless room with uneven concrete walls. It was hot and humid, enough for sweat to prickle on the back of his neck, though his body felt cold and partially numb.

He could not fully open his right eye and it stung to try. Either he had been kicked there, or his captors had beaten him further while he was unconscious.

The bright light was coming from a thin procedure lamp on a tall, thin wheeled base, adjusted to about his height and shining downward in his face. The halogen bulb shined fiercely. If there was anything behind that lamp, he couldn't see it.

He flinched as a heavy *chink* echoed through the small room—the sound of a deadbolt sliding aside. Hinges groaned, but Reid could not see a door. It closed again with a dissonant clang.

A silhouette blocked the light, bathing him in its shadow as it stood over him. He trembled, not daring to look up.

"Who are you?" The voice was male, slightly higher pitched than that of his previous captors, but still heavily tinged with a Middle Eastern accent.

Reid opened his mouth to speak—to tell them he was nothing more than a history professor, that they had the wrong guy—but he quickly recalled that the last time he tried to do so, he was kicked into submission. Instead, a small whimper escaped his lips.

The man sighed and retreated away from the light. Something scraped against the concrete floor; the legs of a chair. The man adjusted the lamp so that it faced slightly away from Reid, and then sat across from him in the chair so that their knees were nearly touching.

Reid slowly looked up. The man was young, thirty at best, with dark skin and a neatly trimmed black beard. He wore round, silver eyeglasses and a white *kufi*, a brimless, rounded cap.

Hope blossomed within Reid. This young man appeared to be an intellectual, not like the savages who had attacked him and torn him from his home. Perhaps he could negotiate with this man. Perhaps he was in charge…

"We will start simple," the man said. His voice was soft and casual, the way a psychologist might speak with a patient. "What is your name?"

"L…Lawson." His voice cracked on his first try. He coughed, and was slightly alarmed to see specks of blood hit the floor. The man before him wrinkled his nose distastefully. "My name is…Reid Lawson." Why did they keep asking his name? He'd told them already. Did he unwittingly wrong someone?

The man sighed slowly, in and out through his nose. He propped his elbows against his knees and leaned forward, lowering his voice further. "There are many people who would like to be in this room right now. Lucky for you, it is just you and I. However, if you are not honest with me, I will have no choice but to invite … others. And they tend to lack my compassion." He sat up straight. "So I ask you again. What … is … your … name?"

How could he convince them that he was who he said he was? Reid's heart rate doubled as a stark realization struck him like a blow to the head. He might very well die in this room. "I'm telling you the truth!" he insisted. Suddenly the words flowed from him like a burst dam. "My name is Reid Lawson. Please, just tell me why I'm here. I don't know what's happening. I haven't done anything—"

The man backhanded Reid across the mouth. His head jerked wildly. He gasped as the sting radiated through his freshly split lip.

"Your name." The man wiped blood from the gold ring on his hand.

"I t-told you," he stammered. "M-my name is Lawson." He choked back a sob. "Please."

He dared to look up. His interrogator stared back impassively, coldly. "Your name."

"Reid Lawson!" Reid felt heat rise in his face as the pain congealed into anger. He didn't know what else to say, what they wanted him to say. "Lawson! It's Lawson! You can check my … my …" No, they couldn't check his identification. He didn't have his wallet on him when the trio of Muslim men took him.

His interrogator tut-tutted, and then drove his bony fist into Reid's solar plexus. The air was again forced from his lungs. For a full minute, Reid could not draw a breath; it finally came again in a ragged gasp. His chest burned fiercely. Sweat dripped down his cheeks and burned his split lip. His head hung limp, his chin between his collarbones, as he fought off a wave of nausea.

"Your name," the interrogator repeated calmly.

"I … I don't know what you want me to tell you," Reid whispered. "I don't know what you're looking for. But it's not me." Was he losing his mind? He was certain he hadn't done anything to deserve this sort of treatment.

The man in the *kufi* leaned forward again, this time taking Reid's chin gently with two fingers. He lifted his head, forcing Reid to look him in the eyes. His thin lips stretched into a half smirk.

"My friend," he said, "this will get much, much worse before it gets better."

Reid swallowed and tasted copper at the back of his throat. He knew that blood was an emetic; about two cups' worth would cause him to vomit, and he already felt nauseous and dizzy. "Listen to me," he implored. His voice sounded tremulous and timid. "The three men that took me, they came to 22 Ivy Lane, my home. My name is Reid Lawson. I am a professor of European history at Columbia University. I am a widower, with two teen..." He stopped himself. So far his captors had not given any indication that they knew about his girls. "If that's not what you're looking for, I cannot help you. Please. That's the truth."

The interrogator stared for a long, unblinking moment. Then he barked something sharply in Arabic. Reid flinched at the sudden outburst.

The deadbolt slid back again. Over the man's shoulder, Reid could see just an outline of the thick door as it swung open. It appeared to be made of some kind of metal, iron or steel.

This room, he realized, was built to be a prison cell.

A silhouette appeared in the doorway. The interrogator shouted something else in his native tongue, and the silhouette vanished. He smirked at Reid. "We will see," he said simply.

There was a telltale squeak of wheels, and the silhouette reappeared, this time pushing a steel cart into the small concrete room. Reid recognized the conveyor as the quiet, hulking brute who had come to his home, still wearing the perpetual scowl.

Upon the cart was an archaic machine, a brown box with a dozen knobs and dials and thick black wires plugged into one side. From the opposite end trailed a scroll of white paper with four thin needles pressed against it.

It was a polygraph machine—probably nearly as old as Reid was, but a lie detector nonetheless. He breathed a sigh of half-relief. At least they would know that he was telling the truth.

What they might do with him afterward...he didn't want to think about that.

The interrogator set about wrapping the Velcro sensors around two of Reid's fingers, a cuff around his left bicep, and two cords around his chest. He took a seat again, produced a pencil from his pocket, and stuck the pink eraser end in his mouth.

"You know what this is," he said simply. "You know how this works. If you say anything other than the answers to my questions, we will hurt you. Do you understand?"

Reid nodded once. "Yes."

The interrogator flicked a switch and fiddled with the knobs of the machine. The scowling brute stood over his shoulder, blocking the light from the procedure lamp and staring down at Reid.

The thin needles danced slightly against the scroll of white paper, leaving four black trails. The interrogator marked the sheet with a scribble, and then turned his cool gaze back to Reid. "What color is my hat?"

"White," Reid answered quietly.

"What species are you?"

"Human." The interrogator was establishing a baseline for the questions to come—usually four or five known truths so that he could monitor for potential lies.

"In what city do you dwell?"

"New York."

"Where are you now?"

Reid almost scoffed. "In a...in a chair. I don't know."

The interrogator made intermittent marks on the paper. "What is your name?"

Reid did his best to keep his voice steady. "Reid. Lawson."

All three of them were eyeing the machine. The needles continued unperturbed; there were no significant crests or valleys in the scrawling lines.

"What is your occupation?" the interrogator asked.

"I am a professor of European history at Columbia University."

"How long have you been a university professor?"

"Thirteen years," Reid answered honestly. "I was an assistant professor for five and an adjunct professor in Virginia for another six. I've been an associate professor in New York for the past two years."

"Have you ever been to Tehran?"

"No."

"Have you ever been to Zagreb?"

"No!"

"Have you ever been to Madrid?"

"N—yes. Once, about four years ago. I was there for a summit, on behalf of the university."

The needles remained steady.

"Don't you see?" As much as Reid wanted to shout, he fought to remain calm. "You have the wrong person. Whoever you're looking for, it's not me."

The interrogator's nostrils flared, but otherwise there was no reaction. The brute clasped his hands in front of him, his veins standing stark against his skin.

"Have you ever met a man named Sheikh Mustafar?" the interrogator asked.

Reid shook his head. "No."

"He's lying!" A tall, lanky man entered the room—one of the other two men who had assaulted his home, the same one who had first asked him his name. He swept in with long strides, his hostile gaze directed at Reid. "This machine can be beaten. We know this."

"There would be some sign," the interrogator replied calmly. "Body language, sweat, vitals…Everything here suggests he is telling the truth." Reid couldn't help but think they were speaking in English for his benefit.

The tall man turned away and paced the length of the concrete room, muttering angrily in Arabic. "Ask him about Tehran."

"I did," the interrogator answered.

The tall man spun on Reid, fuming. Reid held his breath, waiting to be struck again.

Instead, the man resumed his pacing. He said something rapidly in Arabic. The interrogator responded. The brute stared at Reid.

"Please!" he said loudly over their chattering. "I'm not whoever you think I am. I have no memory of anything you're asking..."

The tall man fell silent, and his eyes widened. He almost smacked himself in the forehead, and then spoke excitedly to the interrogator. The impassive man in the *kufi* stroked his chin.

"Possible," he said in English. He stood and took Reid's head in both his hands.

"What is this? What are you doing?" Reid asked. The man's fingertips felt slowly up and down his scalp.

"Quiet," the man said flatly. He probed Reid's hairline, his neck, his ears—"Ah!" he said sharply. He jabbered to his cohort, who dashed over and violently yanked Reid's head to one side.

The interrogator ran a finger along Reid's left mastoid process, the small section of temporal bone just behind the ear. There was an oblong lump beneath the skin, barely larger than a grain of rice.

The interrogator barked something at the tall man, and the latter quickly swept out of the room. Reid's neck ached from the strange angle at which they were holding his head.

"What? What's going on?" he asked.

"This lump, here," the interrogator said, running his finger over it again. "What is this?"

"It's...it's just a bone spur," said Reid. "I've had it since a car accident, in my twenties."

The tall man returned quickly, this time with a plastic tray. He set it down on the cart, next to the polygraph machine. Despite the dim light and the odd angle of his head, Reid could clearly see what was inside the tray. A knot of fear tightened in his stomach.

The tray was home to a number of sharp, silver implements.

"What are those for?" His voice was panicked. He squirmed against his bonds. "What are you doing?"

The interrogator snapped a short command to the brute. He stepped forward, and the sudden brightness of the procedure lamp nearly blinded Reid.

"Wait...wait!" he shouted. "Just tell me what you want to know!"

The brute seized Reid's head in his large hands and gripped it tightly, forcing him still. The interrogator chose a tool—a thin-bladed scalpel.

"Please don't...please don't..." Reid's breath came in short gasps. He was nearly hyperventilating.

"Shh," said the interrogator calmly. "You will want to remain still. I would not want to cut off your ear. At least, not by accident."

Reid screamed as the blade sliced into the skin behind his ear, but the brute held him still. Every muscle in his limbs went taut.

A strange sound reached his ears—a soft melody. The interrogator was singing a tune in Arabic as he cut into Reid's head.

He dropped the bloody scalpel into the tray as Reid hissed shallow breaths through his teeth. Then the interrogator reached for a pair of needle-nose pliers.

"I'm afraid that was just the beginning," he whispered in Reid's ear. "This next part will actually hurt."

The pliers gripped something in Reid's head—was it his bone?—and the interrogator tugged. Reid screamed in agony as white-hot pain shot through his brain, pulsing out into nerve endings. His arms trembled. His feet slapped against the floor.

The pain crescendoed until Reid thought he couldn't possibly take any more. Blood pounded in his ears, and his own screams sounded as if they were far away. Then the procedure lamp dimmed, and the edges of his vision darkened as he slipped into unconsciousness.

CHAPTER THREE

When Reid was twenty-three, he was in a car accident. The stoplight had turned green and he eased into the intersection. A pickup truck jumped the light and smashed into his front passenger side. His head struck the window. He was unconscious for several minutes.

His only injury was a cracked temporal bone in his skull. It healed fine; the only evidence of the accident was a small lump behind his ear. The doctor told him it was a bone spur.

The funny thing about the accident was that while he could recall the event, he couldn't recall any pain—not when it happened, and not afterward, either.

But he could feel it now. As he regained consciousness, the small patch of bone behind his left ear thrummed torturously. The procedure lamp was again shining in his eyes. He squinted and moaned slightly. Moving his head the slightest amount sent a fresh sting up his neck.

Suddenly his mind flashed onto something. The bright light in his eyes was not the lamp at all.

The afternoon sun blazes against a blue cloudless sky. An A-10 Warthog flies overhead, banking right and dipping in altitude over the flat, drab rooftops of Kandahar.

The vision was not fluid. It came in flashes, like several still photographs in sequence; like watching someone dance under a strobe light.

You stand on the beige rooftop of a partially destroyed building, a third of it blasted away. You bring the stock to your shoulder, eye the scope, and sight in on a man below…

Reid jerked his head and groaned. He was in the concrete room, under the discerning eye of the procedure lamp. His fingers trembled and his limbs felt cold. Sweat trickled down his brow. He was likely going into shock. In his periphery, he could see that the left shoulder of his shirt was soaked in blood.

"Bone spur," said the interrogator's placid voice. Then he chuckled sardonically. A slender hand appeared in Reid's field of vision, gripping the pair of needle-nose pliers. Pinched between its teeth was something tiny and silver, but Reid couldn't make out details. His vision was fuzzy and the room tilted slightly. "Do you know what this is?"

Reid shook his head slowly.

"I admit, I have only ever seen this once before," said the interrogator. "A memory suppression chip. It is a very useful tool for people in your unique situation." He dropped the bloody pliers and the small silver grain into the plastic tray.

"No," Reid grunted. "Impossible." The last word came out as little more than a murmur. Memory suppression? That was science fiction. For that to work, it would have to affect the entire limbic system of the brain.

The fifth floor of the Ritz Madrid. You adjust your black tie before you kick in the door with a solid heel just above the doorknob. The man inside is caught off guard; he leaps to his feet and snatches a pistol from the bureau. But before the man can level it at you, you grab his gun hand and twist it down and away. The force snaps the wrist easily...

Reid shook the muddled sequence from his brain as the interrogator took a seat in the chair across from him.

"You did something to me," he muttered.

"Yes," the interrogator agreed. "We have liberated you from a mental prison." He leaned forward with his tight smirk, searching Reid's eyes for something. "You're remembering. This is fascinating to watch. You're confused. Your pupils are abnormally dilated, despite the light. What is real, 'Professor Lawson'?"

The sheikh. By any means necessary.

"When our memories fail us..."

Last known whereabouts: Safe house in Tehran.

"Who are we?"

A bullet sounds the same in every language... Who said that?

"Who do we become?"

You said that.

Reid felt himself slipping again into the void. The interrogator slapped him twice, jarring him back to the concrete room. "Now we may continue in earnest. So I ask you again. What ... is ... your ... name?"

You enter the interrogation room alone. The suspect is cuffed to a looped bolt in the table. You reach into your inner suit pocket and produce a leather-bound ID badge and open it...

"Reid. Lawson." His voice was uncertain. "I'm a professor ... of European history ..."

The interrogator sighed disappointedly. He beckoned with one finger to the brutish, scowling man. A heavy fist plowed into Reid's cheek. A molar bounced across the floor in a wake of fresh blood.

For a moment, there was no pain; his face was numb, pulsing with the impact. Then a fresh, nebulous agony took over.

"Nnggh..." He tried to form words, but his lips would not move.

"I ask you again," said the interrogator. "Tehran?"

The sheikh was holed up in a safe house disguised as an abandoned textile factory.

"Zagreb?"

Two Iranian men are apprehended on a private airstrip, about to board a chartered plane to Paris.

"Madrid?"

The Ritz, fifth floor: an activated sleeper cell with a suitcase bomb. Suspected destination: the Plaza de Cibeles.

"Sheikh Mustafar?"

He bargained for his life. Gave us everything he knew. Names, locations, plans. But he only knew so much...

"I know you are remembering," said the interrogator. "Your eyes betray you ... Zero."

Zero. An image flashed in his head: *A man in aviator sunglasses and a dark motorcycle jacket. He stands on the street corner in some European city. Moves with the crowd. No one is aware. No one knows he's there.*

Reid tried again to shake the visions from his head. What was happening to him? The images danced in his head like stop-motion sequences, but he refused to acknowledge them as memories. They were false. Implanted, somehow. He was a university professor, with two teenage girls and a humble home in the Bronx...

"Tell us what you know of our plans," the interrogator demanded flatly.

We don't talk. Ever.

The words echoed through the cavern of his mind, over and over. *We don't talk. Ever.*

"This is taking too long!" shouted the tall Iranian man. "Coerce him."

The interrogator sighed. He reached for the metal cart—but not to turn on the polygraph machine. Instead, his fingers lingered over the plastic tray. "I am generally a patient man," he told Reid. "But I admit, my associate's frustration is somewhat contagious." He plucked up the bloody scalpel, the tool he had used to cut the small silver grain from his head, and he gently pressed the tip of the blade against Reid's denim jeans, about four inches above the knee. "All we want to know is what you know. Names. Dates. Who you've told about what you know. The identities of your fellow agents in the field."

Morris. Reidigger. Johansson. Names flashed across his mind, and with each came a face that he had never seen before. A younger man with dark hair and a cocky smile. A round-faced, friendly-look-ing guy in a starched white shirt. A woman with flowing blonde hair and steely, gray eyes.

"And what became of the sheikh."

Somehow Reid was suddenly aware that the sheikh in question had been detained and taken to a black site in Morocco. It wasn't a vision. He simply knew.

We don't talk. Ever.

A cold chill ran down Reid's spine as he struggled to maintain some semblance of sanity.

"Tell me," the interrogator insisted.

"I don't know." The words felt strange rolling from his swollen tongue. He glanced up in alarm and saw the other man smirking back at him.

He had understood the foreign demand…and answered back in flawless Arabic.

The interrogator pushed the tip of the scalpel into Reid's leg. He screamed as the knife penetrated the muscle of his thigh. He instinctively tried to pull his leg away, but his ankles were bound to the chair legs.

He clenched his teeth hard, his jaw aching in protest. The wound in his leg burned fiercely.

The interrogator smirked and cocked his head slightly. "I will admit, you're tougher than most, Zero," he said in English. "Unfortunately for you, I am a professional." He reached down and slowly tugged off one of Reid's now-filthy socks. "I don't get to resort to this tactic often." He straightened and stared Reid directly in the eye. "Here is what is going to happen next: I am going to cut off small pieces of you, and show you each one. We will begin with your toes. Then the fingers. After that…we will see where we stand." The interrogator knelt and pressed the blade against the smallest toe of his right foot.

"Wait," Reid pleaded. "Please, just wait."

The other two men in the room gathered on either side, watching with interest.

Desperate, Reid fingered the ropes that held his wrists in place. It was an inline knot with two opposing loops tied with half hitches…

An intense shiver ran from the base of his spine to his shoulders. He knew. Somehow he just *knew*. He had an intense feeling of déjà vu, as if he had been in this situation before—or rather, these insane visions somehow implanted in his head told him he had.

But most importantly, he knew what he had to do.

"I'll tell you!" Reid panted. "I'll tell you what you want to know."

The interrogator glanced up. "Yes? Good. First, however, I am still going to remove this toe. I would not want you to believe that I was bluffing."

Behind the chair, Reid gripped his left thumb in his opposite hand. He held his breath and jerked hard. He felt the pop as the thumb dislocated. He waited for the sharp, intense pain to come, but it was little more than a dull throb.

A new realization struck him—this was not the first time that had happened to him.

The interrogator sliced into the skin of his toe and he yelped. With his thumb opposite its normal angle, he slipped his hand free of its bonds. With one loop open, the other gave way.

His hands were free. But he had no idea what to do with them.

The interrogator glanced up and his brow furrowed in confusion. "What…?"

Before he could utter another word, Reid's right hand shot out and grabbed the first implement it closed on—a black-handled precision knife. As the interrogator tried to stand, Reid pulled his hand back. The blade raked across the man's carotid.

Both hands flew to his throat. Blood eked between his fingers as the wide-eyed interrogator collapsed to the floor.

The hulking brute roared in fury as he lunged forward. He wrapped both meaty hands around Reid's throat and squeezed. Reid tried to think, but fear gripped him.

Next thing he knew, he lifted the precision knife again and jammed it into the brute's inner wrist. He twisted his shoulders as he pushed, and opened an avenue up the length of the man's forearm. The brute screamed and fell, clutching his grievous injury.

The tall, thin man stared in disbelief. Much like before, on the street in front of Reid's house, he seemed hesitant to approach him. Instead, he fumbled for the plastic tray and a weapon. He grabbed a curved blade and stabbed straight for Reid's chest.

Reid threw his body weight backward, toppling the chair and narrowly avoiding the knife. At the same time, he forced his legs outward as hard as he could. As the chair hit the concrete, the legs broke off from the frame. Reid stood and nearly stumbled, his legs weak.

The tall man shouted for help in Arabic, and then slashed the air indiscriminately with the knife, back and forth in wide sweeps to keep Reid at bay. Reid kept his distance, watching the silver blade swing hypnotically. The man swept right, and Reid lunged, trapping the arm—and the knife—between their bodies. His momentum drove them forward, and as the Iranian toppled, Reid twisted and neatly sliced through the femoral artery on the back of his thigh. He planted a foot and swished the knife the opposite way, piercing the jugular.

He didn't know how he knew, but he knew that the man had about forty-seven seconds of life left.

Feet pounded a staircase from nearby. Fingers shaking, Reid dashed to the open doorway and flattened himself against one side. The first thing through was a gun—he immediately identified it as a Beretta 92 FS—and an arm followed, and then a torso. Reid spun, caught the gun in the crook of his elbow, and slid the precision knife sideways between two ribs. The blade pierced the man's heart. A cry caught on his lips as he slid to the floor.

Then there was only silence.

Reid staggered backward. His breathing came in shallow gulps. "Oh god," he breathed. "Oh god."

He had just killed—no, he had just *murdered* four men in the span of several seconds. Even worse was that it was kneejerk, reflexive, like riding a bike. Or suddenly speaking Arabic. Or knowing the sheikh's fate.

He was a professor. He had memories. He had children. A career. But clearly his body knew how to fight, even if he didn't. He knew how to escape from bonds. He knew where to deliver a lethal blow.

"What is happening to me?" he gasped.

He covered his eyes briefly as a roiling wave of nausea washed over him. There was blood on his hands—literally. Blood on his shirt. As the adrenaline subsided, the aches permeated through his limbs from being stationary for so long. His ankle still throbbed from leaping off his deck. He'd been stabbed in the leg. He had an open wound behind his ear.

He didn't even want to *think* about how his face might look.

Get out, his brain screamed at him. *More may come.*

"Okay," Reid said aloud, as if he were assenting to someone else in the room. He calmed his breathing as best he could and scanned his surroundings. His unfocused eyes fell on certain details—the Beretta. A rectangular lump in the interrogator's pocket. A strange mark on the neck of the brute.

He knelt beside the hulking man and stared at the scar. It was near the jaw line, partially obscured by beard, and no bigger than a dime. It appeared to be some sort of brand, burned into the skin, and looked similar to a glyph, like some letter in another alphabet. But he didn't recognize it. Reid examined it for several seconds, etching it into his memory.

He quickly rifled through the dead interrogator's pocket and found an ancient brick of a cell phone. *Likely a burner,* his brain told him. In the tall man's back pocket he found a scrap of torn white paper, one corner stained with blood. In a scrawling, nearly illegible hand was a long series of digits that began with 963—the country code to make an international call to Syria.

None of the men had any identification, but the would-be shooter had a thick billfold of euro banknotes, easily a few thousand. Reid pocketed that as well, and then lastly, he took the Beretta. The pistol's weight felt oddly natural in his hands. *Nine-millimeter caliber. Fifteen-round magazine. One-hundred-twenty-five-millimeter barrel.*

His hands expertly ejected the clip in a fluid motion, as if someone else were controlling them. Thirteen rounds. He pushed it back in and cocked it.

Then he got the hell out of there.

Outside the thick steel door was a dingy hall that ended in a staircase going up. At the top of it was evidence of daylight. Reid climbed the stairs carefully, the pistol aloft, but he heard nothing. The air grew cooler as he ascended.

He found himself in a small, filthy kitchen, the paint peeling from the walls and dishes caked in grime piled high in the sink. The windows were translucent; they had been smeared with grease. The radiator in the corner was cold to the touch.

Reid cleared the rest of the small house; there was no one besides the four dead men in the basement. The single bathroom was in far worse shape than the kitchen, but Reid found a seemingly ancient first-aid kit. He didn't dare look at himself in the mirror as he washed as much blood as he could from his face and neck. Everything from head to toe stung, ached, or burned. The tiny tube of antiseptic ointment had expired three years earlier, but he used it anyway, wincing as he pressed bandages over his open cuts.

Then he sat on the toilet and held his head in his hands, taking a brief moment to get a grip. *You could leave*, he told himself. *You have money. Go to the airport. No, you don't have a passport. Go to the embassy. Or find a consulate. But...*

But he had just killed four men, and his own blood was all over the basement. And there was the other, clearer problem.

"I don't know who I am," he murmured aloud.

Those flashes, those visions that stalked his mind, they were from his perspective. His point of view. But he had never, *would* never do anything like that. Memory suppression, the interrogator had said. Was that even possible? He thought again of his girls. Were they safe? Were they scared? Were they... his?

That notion jarred him to his core. What if, somehow, what he thought was real wasn't real at all?

No, he told himself adamantly. They were his daughters. He was there for their birth. He raised them. None of these bizarre, intrusive visions contradicted that. And he needed to find a way to contact them, to make sure they were all right. That was his top priority. There was no way he would use the burner phone to contact his family; he didn't know if it was being traced or who might be listening in.

He suddenly remembered the slip of paper with the phone number on it. He stood and pulled it out of his pocket. The bloodstained paper stared back at him. He didn't know what this was about or why they thought he was anyone different than who he said he was, but there was a shade of urgency beneath the surface of his subconscious, something telling him that he was now unwillingly involved in something that was much, much bigger than him.

His hands shaking, he dialed the number on the burner.

A gruff male voice answered on the second tone. "Is it done?" he asked in Arabic.

"Yes," Reid replied. He tried to mask his voice as best he could and affect an accent.

"You have the information?"

"Mm."

The voice was silent for a long moment. Reid's heart pounded in his chest. Had they realized it wasn't the interrogator?

"187 Rue de Stalingrad," the man said finally. "Eight p.m." And he hung up.

Reid ended the call and took a deep breath. *Rue de Stalingrad?* he thought. *In France?*

He wasn't sure what he was going to do yet. His mind felt like he had broken through a wall and discovered a whole other chamber on the other side. He couldn't return home without knowing what was happening to him. Even if he did, how long would it be until they found him, and the girls, again? He had only one lead. He had to follow it.

He stepped out of the small house and found himself in a narrow alley, the mouth of which opened onto a street called Rue Marceau. He immediately knew where he was—a suburb of Paris, mere blocks from the Seine. He almost laughed. He thought he would be stepping out into the war-torn streets of a Middle Eastern city. Instead, he found a boulevard lined with shops and row homes, unassuming passersby enjoying their casual afternoon, bundled against the chilly February breeze.

He tucked the pistol into the waistband of his jeans and stepped out onto the street, blending in with the crowd and trying not to draw any attention to his blood-stained shirt, bandages, or obvious bruises. He hugged his arms close to him—he would need some new clothes, a jacket, something warmer than just his shirt.

He needed to make sure his girls were safe.

Then he would get some answers.

CHAPTER FOUR

Walking the streets of Paris felt like a dream—just not in the way that anyone would expect or even desire. Reid reached the intersection of Rue de Berri and Avenue des Champs-Élysées, ever the tourist hotspot despite the chilly weather. The Arc de Triomphe loomed several blocks away to the northwest, the centerpiece of Place Charles de Gaulle, but its grandeur was lost on Reid. A new vision flashed across his mind.

I've been here before. I've stood in this spot and looked up at this street sign. Wearing jeans and a black motorcycle jacket, the colors of the world muted by polarized sunglasses...

He turned right. He wasn't sure what he would find this way, but he had the eerie suspicion that he would recognize it as he saw it. It was an incredibly bizarre sensation to not know where he was going until he got there.

It felt as if every new sight brought on some vignette of vague recollection, each disconnected from the next, yet still somehow congruent. He knew that the café on the corner served the best pastis he would ever taste. The sweet scent of the patisserie across the street made his mouth water for savory palmiers. He had never tasted palmiers before. Had he?

Even sounds jarred him. Passersby chattered idly to one another as they strolled the boulevard, occasionally stealing glances at his bandaged, bruised face.

"I would hate to see the other guy," a young Frenchman muttered to his girlfriend. They both chuckled.

Okay, don't panic, Reid thought. *Apparently you know Arabic and French.* The only other language that Professor Lawson spoke was German and a few phrases in Spanish.

There was something else too, something harder to define. Beneath his rattling nerves and instinct to run, to go home, to hide somewhere, beneath all of that there was a cold, steely reserve. It was like having the heavy hand of an older brother on his shoulder, a voice in the back of his mind saying, *Relax. You know all of this.*

While that voice ushered him softly from the back of his mind, on the forefront was his girls and their safety. Where were they? What were they thinking right then? What would it mean for them if they lost both parents?

He had never stopped thinking about them. Even as he was being beaten in the dingy basement prison, even as these flashes of visions were intruding on his mind, he had been thinking about the girls—particularly that last question. What would happen to them if he had died down there in that basement? Or if he died doing the very foolhardy thing that he was about to do?

He had to make sure. He had to reach out somehow.

But first, he needed a jacket, and not just to cover his blood-stained shirt. The February weather was approaching fifty degrees, but still too chilly for just a shirt. The boulevard acted as a wind tunnel and the breeze was brisk. He ducked into the next clothing boutique and chose the first coat that caught his eye—a dark brown bomber jacket, leather with a fleece lining. Strange, he thought. He would never have picked a jacket like this before, what with his tweed and plaid fashion sense, but he was drawn to it.

The bomber jacket was two hundred and forty euros. No matter; he had a pocketful of money. He picked out a new shirt as well, a slate-gray tee, and then a pair of jeans, new socks, and sturdy brown boots. He brought all his purchases up to the counter and paid in cash.

There was a thumbprint of blood on one of the bills. The thin-lipped clerk pretended not to notice. A strobe-like flash in his mind—

36

"A guy walks into a gas station covered in blood. He pays for his fuel and starts to leave. The bewildered attendant calls out, 'Hey, man, are you okay?' The guy smiles. 'Oh yeah, I'm fine. It's not my blood.'"

I've never heard that joke before.

"May I use your changing room?" Reid asked in French.

The clerk pointed toward the rear of the store. He hadn't said a single word during the entire transaction.

Before changing, Reid examined himself for the first time in a clean mirror. Jesus, he looked awful. His right eye was swelling fiercely and blood was staining the bandages. He'd have to find a drug store and buy some decent first-aid supplies. He slid his now-filthy and somewhat bloody jeans down over his wounded thigh, wincing as he did. Something clattered to the floor, startling him. The Beretta. He'd nearly forgotten he had it.

The pistol was heavier than he would have imagined. *Nine hundred forty-five grams, unloaded,* he knew. Holding it was like embracing a former lover, familiar and foreign at the same time. He set it down and finished changing, stuffed his old clothes in the shopping bag, and tucked the pistol into the waistband of his new jeans, at the small of his back.

Out on the boulevard, Reid kept his head low and walked briskly, staring down at the sidewalk. He didn't need more visions distracting him right now. He tossed the bag of old clothes in a trash can on a corner without missing a step.

"Oh! *Excusez-moi,*" he apologized as his shoulder bumped roughly into a passing woman in a business suit. She glared at him. "So sorry." She huffed and stalked off. He stuffed his hands in his jacket pockets—along with the cell phone he had swiped from her purse.

It was easy. Too easy.

Two blocks away, he ducked under a department store awning and took out the phone. He breathed a sigh of relief—he'd targeted the businesswoman for a reason, and his instinct paid off. She had Skype installed on her phone and an account linked to an American number.

He opened the phone's Internet browser, looked up the number to Pap's Deli in the Bronx, and called.

A young male voice answered quickly. "Pap's, how can I help you?"

"Ronnie?" One of his students from the year prior worked part time at Reid's favorite deli. "It's Professor Lawson."

"Hey, Professor!" the young man said brightly. "How's it going? You want to put in a takeout order?"

"No. Yes…sort of. Listen, I need a really big favor, Ronnie." Pap's Deli was only six blocks from his house. On pleasant days, he would often walk the distance to pick up sandwiches. "Do you have Skype on your phone?"

"Yeah?" said Ronnie, a confused lilt in his voice.

"Good. Here's what I need you to do. Write down this number…" He instructed the kid to make a quick run down to his house, see who, if anyone, was there, and call back the American number on the phone.

"Professor, are you in some kind of trouble?"

"No, Ronnie, I'm fine," he lied. "I lost my phone and a nice woman is letting me use hers to let my kids know I'm okay. But I only have a few minutes. So if you could, please…"

"Say no more, Professor. Happy to help. I'll hit you back in a few." Ronnie hung up.

While he waited, Reid paced the short span of the awning, checking the phone every few seconds in case he missed the call. It felt like an hour passed before it rang again, though it had only been six minutes.

"Hello?" He answered the Skype call on the first ring. "Ronnie?"

"Reid, is that you?" A frantic female voice.

"Linda!" Reid said breathlessly. "I'm glad you're there. Listen, I need to know—"

"Reid, what happened? Where are you?" she demanded.

"The girls, are they at the—"

"What's happened?" Linda interrupted. "The girls woke up this morning, freaking out because you were gone, so they called me and I came right over…"

"Linda, please," he tried to interject, "where are they?"

She talked over him, clearly distraught. Linda was a lot of things, but good in a crisis wasn't one of them. "Maya said that sometimes you go for walks in the morning, but both the front and back doors were open, and she wanted to call the police because she said you never leave your phone at home, and now this boy shows up from the deli and hands me a phone—?"

"Linda!" Reid hissed sharply. Two elderly men passing by looked up at his outburst. "Where are the girls?"

"They're here," she panted. "They're both here, at the house with me."

"They're safe?"

"Yes, of course. Reid, what's going on?"

"Did you call the police?"

"Not yet, no … on TV they always say you have to wait twenty-four hours to report someone missing … Are you in some sort of trouble? Where are you calling me from? Whose account is this?"

"I can't tell you that. Just listen to me. Have the girls pack a bag and take them to a hotel. Not anywhere close; go outside the city. Maybe to Jersey …"

"Reid, *what?*"

"My wallet is on my desk in the office. Don't use the credit card directly. Get a cash advance on whatever cards are in there and use it to pay for the stay. Keep it open-ended."

"Reid! I'm not going to do a thing until you tell me what's … hang on a sec." Linda's voice became muffled and distant. "Yes, it's him. He's okay. I think. Wait, Maya!"

"Dad? Dad, is that you?" A new voice on the line. "What happened? Where are you?"

"Maya! I, uh, had something come up, extremely last minute. I didn't want to wake you …"

"Are you kidding me?" Her voice was shrill, agitated and worried at the same time. "I'm not stupid, Dad. Tell me the truth."

He sighed. "You're right. I'm sorry. I can't tell you where I am, Maya. And I shouldn't be on the phone long. Just do what your aunt says, okay? You're going to leave the house for a little while. Don't go to school. Don't wander anywhere. Don't talk about me on the phone or computer. Understand?"

"No, I don't understand! Are you in some kind of trouble? Should we call the police?"

"No, don't do that," he said. "Not yet. Just … give me some time to sort something out."

She was silent for a long moment. Then she said, "Promise me that you're okay."

He winced.

"Dad?"

"Yeah," he said a bit too forcefully. "I'm okay. Please, just do what I ask and go with your Aunt Linda. I love you both. Tell Sara I said so, and hug her for me. I'll contact you as soon as I can—"

"Wait, wait!" Maya said. "How will you contact us if you don't know where we are?"

He thought for a moment. He couldn't ask Ronnie to get any further involved in this. He couldn't call the girls directly. And he couldn't risk knowing where they were, because that could be leverage against him…

"I'll set up a fake account," said Maya, "under another name. You'll know it. I'll only check it from the hotel computers. If you need to contact us, send a message."

Reid understood immediately. He felt a swell of pride; she was so smart, and so much cooler under pressure than he could hope to be.

"Dad?"

"Yeah," he said. "That's good. Take care of your sister. I have to go…"

"I love you too," said Maya.

He ended the call. Then he sniffed. Again it came, the stinging instinct to run home to them, to keep them safe, to pack up whatever they could and leave, go somewhere…

He couldn't do that. Whatever this was, whoever was after him, had found him once. He had been supremely fortunate that they weren't after his girls. Maybe they didn't know about the kids. Next time, if there was a next time, maybe he wouldn't be so lucky.

Reid opened the phone, pulled out the SIM card, and snapped it in half. He dropped the pieces into a sewer grate. As he walked down the street, he deposited the battery in one trash bin, and the two halves of the phone in others.

He knew he was walking in the general direction of Rue de Stalingrad, though he had no idea what he would do when he arrived there. His brain screamed at him to change direction, to go anywhere else. But that sangfroid in his subconscious compelled him to keep going.

His captors had asked him what he knew of their "plans." The locations they had asked about, Zagreb and Madrid and Tehran, they had to be connected, and they were clearly linked to the men who had taken him. Whatever these visions were—he still refused to acknowledge them as anything but—there was knowledge in them about something that had either occurred or was going to occur. Knowledge he didn't know. The more he thought about it, the more he felt that sense of urgency nag at his mind.

No, it was more than that. It felt like an obligation.

His captors had seemed willing to kill him slowly for what he knew. And he had the sensation that if he didn't discover what this was and what he was supposed to know, more people would die.

"Monsieur." Reid was startled from his musing by a matronly woman in a shawl gently touching his arm. "You are bleeding," she said in English, and pointed to her own brow.

"Oh. *Merci.*" He touched two fingers to his right brow. A small cut there had soaked the bandage and a bead of blood was making its way down his face. "I need to find a pharmacy," he murmured aloud.

Then he sucked in a breath as a thought struck him: there was a pharmacy two blocks down and one up. He had never been inside it—not to his own untrustworthy knowledge, anyway—but he simply knew it, as easily as he knew the route to Pap's Deli.

A chill ran from the base of his spine up to the nape of his neck. The other visions had been visceral, and had all manifested from some external stimulus, sights and sounds and even scents. This time there was no accompanying vision. It was plain knowledge recall, the same way he knew where to turn at each street sign. The same way he knew how to load the Beretta.

He made a decision before the light turned green. He would go to this meeting and get whatever information he could. Then he would decide what to do with it—report it to the authorities perhaps, and clear his name regarding the four men in the basement. Let them make the arrests while he went home to his children.

At the drug store, he bought a thin tube of super glue, a box of butterfly bandages, cotton swabs, and a foundation that nearly matched his skin tone. He took his purchases into the restroom and locked the door.

He peeled off the bandages that he had haphazardly stuck to his face back in the apartment and washed the crusted blood from his wounds. To the smaller cuts he applied the butterfly bandages. For the deeper wounds, ones that would ordinarily require stitches, he pinched the edges of the skin together and squeezed a bead of super glue, hissing through his teeth all the while. Then he held his breath for about thirty seconds. The glue burned fiercely but it subsided as it dried. Finally, he smoothed the foundation over the contours of his face, particularly the new ones created by his sadistic former captors. There was no way to completely mask his swollen eye and bruised jaw, but at least this way there would be fewer people staring at him on the street.

The entire process took about half an hour, and twice in that span customers banged on the door to the restroom (the second time, a woman shouting in French that her child was nearly to bursting). Both times Reid just shouted back, "*Occupé!*"

Finally, when he was finished, he examined himself again in the mirror. It was far from perfect, but at least it didn't look like he had been beaten in a subterranean torture chamber. He wondered if he should have gone with a darker foundation, something to make him appear more foreign. Did the caller know who he was supposed to be meeting? Would they recognize who he was—or who they thought he was? The three men who had come to his home didn't seem so sure; they had checked against a photograph.

"What am I doing?" he asked himself. *You're preparing for a meeting with a dangerous criminal that is likely a known terrorist,* said the voice in his head—not this new intrusive voice, but his own, Reid Lawson's voice. It was his own common sense, mocking him.

Then that poised, assertive personality, the one just beneath the surface, spoke up. *You'll be fine,* it told him. *Nothing you haven't done before.* His hand reached instinctively for the grip of the Beretta tucked into the back of his pants, concealed by his new jacket. *You know all this.*

Before leaving the drug store, he picked up a few more items: a cheap watch, a bottle of water, and two candy bars. Outside on the sidewalk, he devoured both chocolate bars. He wasn't sure how much blood he had lost and he wanted to keep his sugar level up. He drained the entire bottle of water, and then asked a passerby for the time. He set the watch and slipped it around his wrist.

It was half past six. He had plenty of time to get to the rendezvous place early and prepare.

It was nearly nightfall before he reached the address he'd been given over the phone. The sunset over Paris cast long shadows down the boulevard. 187 Rue de Stalingrad was a bar in the 10th arrondissement called Féline, a dive of a joint with painted-over windows and a cracked façade. It was situated on a street otherwise populated by art studios, Indian restaurants, and bohemian cafes.

Reid paused with his hand on the door. If he entered, there would be no turning back. He could still walk away. No, he decided, he couldn't. Where would he go? Back home, so they could find him all over again? And living with these strange visions in his head?

He went inside.

The bar's walls were painted black and red and covered with fifties-era posters of grim-faced women and cigarette holders and silhouettes. It was too early, or perhaps too late, for the place to be busy. The few patrons that milled about spoke in hushed tones, hunched protectively over their drinks. Melancholy blues music played softly from a stereo behind the bar.

Reid scanned the place left to right and back again. No one looked his way, and certainly no one there looked like the types that had taken him hostage. He took a small table near the rear and sat facing the door. He ordered a coffee, though it mostly sat in front of him steaming.

A hunched old man slid from a stool and limped across the bar toward the restrooms. Reid found his gaze quickly drawn to the movement, scanning the man. *Late sixties. Hip dysplasia. Yellowish fingers, labored breathing—a cigar smoker.* His eyes flitted to the other side of the bar without moving his head, where two rough-looking men in overalls were having a hushed but fervent conversation about sports. *Factory workers. The one on the left isn't getting enough sleep, likely a father to young children. Man on the right was in a fight recently, or at least threw a punch; his knuckles are bruised.* Without thinking, he found himself examining the cuffs of their pants, their sleeves, and the way they held their elbows on the table. *Someone with a gun will protect it, try to conceal it, even unconsciously.*

Reid shook his head. He was getting paranoid, and these persistent foreign thoughts weren't helping. But then he remembered the strange occurrence with the pharmacy, the recollection of its location just by mere mention of needing to find one. The academic in him spoke up. *Maybe there's something to be learned from this. Maybe instead of fighting it, you should try opening up to it.*

The waitress was a young, tired-looking woman with a knotty brunette mane. "*Stylo?*" he asked as she passed him by. "*Ou crayon?*" Pen or pencil? She reached into the tangle of hair and found a pen. "*Merci.*"

He smoothed a cocktail napkin and set the tip of the pen to it. This wasn't some new skill he'd never learned; this was a Professor Lawson tactic, one he had used many times in the past to recall and strengthen memory.

He thought back to his conversation, if he could call it that, with the three Arabic captors. He tried not to think of their dead eyes, the blood on the floor, or the tray of sharp implements intended to cut whatever truth they thought he had out of him. Instead he focused on the verbal details and wrote the first name that came to mind.

Then he muttered it aloud. "Sheikh Mustafar."

A Moroccan black site. A man who spent his entire life in wealth and power, treading on those less fortunate than him, crushing them beneath his shoe—now scared shitless because he knows you can bury him to his neck in the sand and no one would ever find his bones.

"I've told you all I know!" he insists.

Tut-tut. "My intel says otherwise. Says you might know a hell of a lot more, but you may be afraid of the wrong people. Tell you what, Sheikh… my friend in the next room? He's getting antsy. See, he's got this hammer—it's just a little thing, a rock hammer, like a geologist would use? But it does wonders on small bones, knuckles…"

"I swear it!" The sheikh wrings his hands nervously. You recognize it as a tell. "There were other conversations about the plans, but they were in German, Russian… I didn't understand!"

"You know, Sheikh… a bullet sounds the same in every language."

Reid snapped back to the dive bar. His throat felt dry. The memory had been intense, as vivid and lucid as any he knew he had actually experienced. And it had been *his* voice in his head, threatening casually, saying things he would never dream of saying to another person.

Plans. The sheikh had definitely said something about plans. Whatever terrible thing was nagging at his subconscious, he had the distinct feeling it had not yet happened.

He took a sip of the now-lukewarm coffee to calm his nerves. "Okay," he told himself. "Okay." During his interrogation in the basement, they had asked about fellow agents in the field, and three names had flashed across his mind. He wrote one, and then read it out loud. "Morris."

A face immediately came to him, a man in his early thirties, handsome and knowing it. A cocky half-smirk with only one side of his mouth. Dark hair, styled to make him look young.

A private airstrip in Zagreb. Morris sprints alongside you. You both have your guns drawn, barrels pointed downward. You can't let the two Iranians reach the plane. Morris aims between strides and pops off two shots. One clips a calf and the first man falls. You gain on the other, tackling him brutally to the ground...

Another name. "Reidigger."

A boyish smile, neatly combed hair. A bit of a paunch. He'd wear the weight better if he was a few inches taller. The butt of a lot of ribbing, but takes it good-naturedly.

The Ritz in Madrid. Reidigger covers the hall as you kick in the door and catch the bomber off guard. The man goes for the gun on the bureau, but you're faster. You snap his wrist... Later Reidigger tells you he heard the sound from out in the corridor. Turned his stomach. Everyone laughs.

The coffee was cold now, but Reid barely noticed. His fingers were trembling. There was no doubt about it; whatever was happening to him, these were memories—*his* memories. Or someone's. The captors, they had cut something out of his neck and called it a memory suppressor. That couldn't be true; this wasn't him. This was someone else. He had someone else's memories mingling with his own.

Reid set the pen to the napkin again and wrote the final name. He said it aloud: "Johansson." A shape swam into his mind. Long blonde hair, conditioned to a sheen. Smooth, shapely cheekbones. Full lips. Gray eyes, the color of slate. A vision flashed...

Milan. Night. A hotel. Wine. Maria sits on the bed with her legs folded under her. The top three buttons of her shirt are open. Her hair is tousled. You've never noticed how long her eyelashes are before. Two hours ago you watched her kill two men in a gunfight, and now it's Sangiovese and Pecorino Toscano. Your knees almost touch. Her gaze meets yours. Neither of you speak. You can see it in her eyes, but she knows you can't. She asks about Kate...

Reid winced as a headache came on, spreading through his cranium like a storm cloud. At the same time, the vision blurred and faded. He squeezed his eyes shut and gripped his temples for a full minute until the headache receded.

What the hell was that?

For some reason, it seemed that the memory of this woman, Johansson, had triggered the brief migraine. Even more unsettling, however, was the bizarre sensation that gripped him in the wake of the headache. It felt like … desire. No, it was more than that—it felt like passion, reinforced by excitement and even a bit of danger.

He couldn't help but wonder who the woman was, but he shook it off. He didn't want to incite another headache. Instead he set the pen to the napkin again, about to write the final name—Zero. That's what the Iranian interrogator had called him. But before he could write it or recite it, he felt a bizarre sensation. The hairs on the nape of his neck stood on end.

He was being watched.

When he glanced up again, he saw a man standing in Féline's dark doorway, his gaze locked on Reid like a hawk eyeing a mouse. Reid's blood ran cold. He was being watched.

This was the man he was here to meet, he was certain of it. Did he recognize him? The Arabic men hadn't seemed to. Was this man expecting someone else?

He set the pen down. Slowly and surreptitiously, he crumpled the napkin and dropped it into his half-empty cold coffee.

The man nodded once. Reid nodded back.

Then the stranger reached behind him, for something tucked in the back of his pants.

CHAPTER FIVE

Reid stood with such force that his chair nearly toppled. His hand immediately wrapped around the textured grip of the Beretta, warm from his lower back. His mind screamed at him frantically. *This is a public place. There are people here. I've never fired a gun before.*

Before Reid drew his pistol, the stranger pulled a billfold from his back pocket. He grinned at Reid, apparently amused by his jumpy nature. No one else in the bar seemed to have noticed, except the waitress with the rat's nest of hair, who simply raised an eyebrow.

The stranger approached the bar, slid a bill across the table, and muttered something to the bartender. Then he made his way to Reid's table. He stood behind the empty chair for a long moment, a thin smirk on his lips.

He was young, thirty at best, with close-cropped hair and a five o'clock shadow. He was quite lanky and his face was gaunt, making his sharp cheekbones and jutting chin look almost caricature-ish. Most disarming was the black horn-rimmed glasses he wore, looking for all the world as if Buddy Holly had grown up in the eighties and discovered cocaine.

He was right-handed, Reid could tell; he held his left elbow close to his body, which likely meant he had a pistol hanging from a shoulder holster in his armpit so he could draw with his right, if need be. His left arm pinned his black suede jacket closed to hide the gun.

"*Mogu sjediti?*" the man asked finally.

Mogu...? Reid didn't immediately understand the way he had with Arabic and French. It wasn't Russian, but it was close enough for him to derive the meaning from context. The man was asking if he could sit down.

Reid gestured to the empty chair across from him, and the man sat, keeping his left elbow tucked all the while.

As soon as he was seated, the waitress brought a glass of dark amber beer and set it before him. "*Merci,*" he said. He grinned at Reid. "Your Serbian is not so good?"

Reid shook his head. "No." Serbian? He had assumed the man he would be meeting would be Arabic, like his captors and the interrogator.

"In English, then? *Ou francais?*"

"Dealer's choice." Reid was surprised at how calm and even his voice sounded. His heart was nearly bursting out of his chest from fear and... and if he was being honest, at least a shred of anxious excitement.

The Serbian man's grin widened. "I enjoy this place. It is dark. It is quiet. It is the only bar that I know of in this arrondissement that serves Franziskaner. It is my favorite." He took a long swig from his glass, his eyes closed, and a grunt of pleasure escaped his throat. "*Que delicioso.*" He opened his eyes and added, "You are not what I expected."

A surge of panic rose in Reid's gut. *He knows,* his mind screamed at him. *He knows you're not who he's supposed to meet, and he has a gun.*

Relax, said the other side, the new part. *You can handle this.*

Reid gulped, but somehow managed to maintain his icy demeanor. "Nor are you," he replied.

The Serbian chuckled. "That is fair. But we are many, yes? And you—you are American?"

"Expat," Reid answered.

"Are not we all?" Another chuckle. "Before you I met only one other American in our, um... what is the word... conglomerate? Yes. So for me, it is not so strange." The man winked.

Reid tensed. He couldn't tell if it was a joke or not. What if he knew that Reid was a fake and was leading him on or buying time? He placed his hands in his lap to hide his trembling fingers.

"You may call me Yuri. What may I call you?"

"Ben." It was the first name that came to mind, the name of a mentor from his days as an assistant professor.

"Ben. How did you come to work for the Iranians?"

"With," Reid corrected. He narrowed his eyes for effect. "I work *with* them."

The man, this Yuri, took another sip of his beer. "Sure. With. How did that come to be? Despite our mutual interests, they tend to be a, uh … closed group."

"I'm trustworthy," Reid said without blinking. He had no idea where these words were coming from, nor the conviction with which they were coming. He said them as easily as if he'd rehearsed it.

"And where is Amad?" Yuri asked casually.

"Couldn't make it," Reid replied evenly. "Sends his regards."

"All right, Ben. You say the deed is done."

"Yes."

Yuri leaned forward, his eyes narrowed. Reid could smell the malt on his breath. "I need to hear you say it, Ben. Tell me, is CIA man dead?"

Reid froze for a moment. CIA? As in, *the* CIA? Suddenly all the talk of agents in the field and visions of detaining terrorists on airfields and in hotels made more sense, even if the entirety of the matter didn't. Then he remembered the gravity of his situation and hoped that he hadn't given any cues to betray his charade.

He too leaned forward and said slowly, "Yes, Yuri. CIA man is dead."

Yuri leaned back casually and grinned again. "Good." He plucked up his glass. "And the information? You have it?"

"He gave us everything he knew," Reid told him. He couldn't help but notice that his fingers were no longer trembling beneath the table. It was as if someone else was in control now, as if Reid

Lawson was taking a backseat in his own brain. He decided not to fight it.

"The location of Mustafar?" Yuri asked. "And all he told them?"

Reid nodded.

Yuri blinked a few times expectantly. "I am waiting."

A realization struck Reid like a heavy weight as his mind put the little knowledge he had together. The CIA was involved. There was some sort of plan that would get a lot of people killed. The sheikh knew about it, and told them—told *him*—everything. These men, they needed to know what the sheikh knew. That's what Yuri wanted to know. Whatever this was, it felt big, and Reid had stumbled into its midst ... though he certainly felt as if this was not the first time.

He did not speak for a long time, long enough for the smile to evaporate from Yuri's lips into an expectant thin-lipped stare. "I don't know you," Reid said. "I don't know who you represent. You expect me to give you everything I know, and walk away, and trust that it gets to the right place?"

"Yes," said Yuri, "that is exactly what I expect, and precisely the reason for this meeting."

Reid shook his head. "No. See, Yuri, it occurs to me that this information is too important to play whisper-down-the-alley and hope it gets to the right ears in the right order. What's more is that as far as you're concerned, there's only one place it exists—right here." He tapped his own left temple. It was true; the information they were looking for was, presumably, somewhere in the recesses of his mind, waiting to be unlocked. "It also occurs to me," he continued, "that now that they have this information, our plans will have to change. I'm done being the messenger. I want in. I want a real role."

Yuri just stared. Then he let out a sharp, braying laugh and at the same time slapped the table so hard it jarred several nearby patrons. "You!" he exclaimed, wagging a finger. "You may be an expat, but you still have that American ambition!" He laughed again, sounding very much like a donkey. "What is it you want to know, Ben?"

"Let's start with who you represent in this."

"How do you know I represent anyone? For what you know, I could be the boss. The brains behind the master plan!" He held both hands up in a grand gesture and laughed again.

Reid smirked. "I don't think so. I think you're in the same position I am, ferrying information, swapping secrets, having meetings in shitty bars." *Interrogation tactic—relate to them on their level.* Yuri was clearly a polyglot, and seemed to lack the same hardened demeanor as his captors. But even if he was low-level, he still knew more than Reid did. "How about a deal? You tell me what you know, and I'll tell you what I know." He lowered his voice to nearly a whisper. "And trust me. You want to know what I know."

Yuri stroked his chin stubble thoughtfully. "I like you, Ben. Which is, how do you say, um … conflicting, because Americans usually make me ill." He grinned. "Sadly for you, I cannot tell you what I do not know."

"Then point me to who can." The words flowed out of him as if they bypassed his brain and went straight to his throat. The logical part of him (or more appropriately, the Lawson part of him) screamed a protest. *What are you doing?! Get what you can and get out of here!*

"Would you care to go for a ride with me?" Yuri's eyes flashed. "I will take you to see my boss. There, you can tell him what you know."

Reid hesitated. He knew he shouldn't. He knew he didn't want to. But there was that bizarre sense of obligation, and there was that steely reserve in the back of his mind that told him again, *Relax.* He had a gun. He had some sort of skill set. He had come this far, and judging by what he now knew, this went way beyond a few Iranian men in a Parisian basement. There was a plan, and the involvement of the CIA, and somehow he knew that the endgame was a lot of people being hurt or worse.

He nodded once, his jaw clenched tightly.

"Great." Yuri drained his glass and stood, still keeping his left elbow tucked in. "*Au revoir.*" He waved to the bartender. Then the

Serbian led the way toward the rear of Féline, through a small dingy kitchen, and out through a steel door facing a cobblestone alley.

Reid followed him into the night, surprised to see that it had grown so dark so quickly while he was in the bar. At the mouth of the alley was a black SUV, idling gently, with windows tinted nearly as dark as the paint job. The rear door opened before Yuri reached it, and two goons climbed out. Reid didn't know how else to think of them; each was broad-shouldered, imposing, and doing nothing to try to hide the TEC-9 automatic pistols swinging from harnesses at their armpit.

"Relax, my friends," said Yuri. "This is Ben. We take him to see *Otets.*"

Otets. Phonetic Russian for "father." Or, on the most technical level, "maker."

"Come," Yuri said pleasantly. He clapped a hand on Reid's shoulder. "It is a very nice ride. We will drink champagne on the way. Come."

Reid's legs did not want to work. It was risky—too risky. If he got in this car with these men and they discovered who he was, or even that he wasn't who he said he was, he might very well be a dead man. His girls would be orphans, and they would likely never know what became of him.

But what choice did he have? He couldn't very well act like he'd changed his mind suddenly; that would be far too suspicious. It was likely he had already taken two steps past the point of no return simply by following Yuri out here. And if he could keep up the charade long enough, he could find the source—and discover what was going on in his own head.

He took a step forward toward the SUV.

"Ah! *Un momento, por favor.*" Yuri wagged a finger at his brawny escorts. One of them forced Reid's arms up at his sides, while the other patted him down. First he found the Beretta, tucked into the back of his jeans. Then he dug into Reid's pockets with two fingers and pulled out the wad of euros and the burner phone, and handed all three to Yuri.

"This you can keep." The Serbian gave him back the cash. "These, however, we will hang onto. Security. You understand." Yuri tucked the phone and the gun into the inside pocket of his suede jacket, and for the briefest of moments, Reid saw the brown hilt of a pistol.

"I understand," Reid said. Now he was unarmed and without any way to call for help if he needed to. *I should run*, he thought. *Just start sprinting and don't look back...*

One of the goons forced his head low and pushed him forward, into the back of the SUV. Both of them climbed in after him and Yuri followed, pulling the door behind him. He sat beside Reid, while the hunched goons, nearly shoulder to shoulder, sat in a custom rear-facing seat opposite them, right behind the driver. A dark-tinted partition separated them from the front seat of the car.

One of the pair knocked on the driver's partition with two knuckles. "*Otets*," he said gruffly.

A heavy, telltale click locked the rear doors, and with it came a stark comprehension of what Reid had done. He had gotten into a car with three armed men with no idea where he was going and very little idea of who he was supposed to be. Fooling Yuri hadn't been all that difficult, but now he was being taken to some boss... would they know that he wasn't who he said he was? He fought down the urge to jump forward, yank open the door, and leap out of the car. There was no escape from this, at least not at the moment; he would have to wait until they arrived at their destination and hope that he could get out in one piece.

The SUV rolled forward through the streets of Paris.

Chapter Six

Yuri, who had been so talkative and animated in the French bar, was uncharacteristically silent during the car ride. He opened a compartment alongside his seat and took out a well-worn book with a torn cover—Machiavelli's *The Prince*. The professor in Reid wanted to scoff out loud.

The two goons across from him sat silently, eyes directed straight ahead as if they were trying to stare holes through Reid. He quickly memorized their features: the man on the left was bald, white, with a dark handlebar mustache and beady eyes. He had a TEC-9 beneath his shoulder and a Glock 27 tucked in an ankle holster. A jagged pale scar over his left eyebrow suggested a shoddy patch job (not all that dissimilar from what Reid was likely due for once his super-glue intervention healed). He couldn't tell the man's nationality.

The second goon was a few shades darker, with a full, unkempt beard and a sizable paunch. His left shoulder appeared to be sagging slightly, as if he was favoring his opposite hip. He too had an automatic pistol tucked under one arm, but no other weapons that Reid could discern.

He could, however, see the mark on his neck. The skin there was puckered and pink, raised slightly from being burned. It was the same brand he had seen on the Arabic brute in the Paris basement. A glyph of some sort, he was certain, but not one that he recognized. The mustached man did not appear to have one, though much of his neck was hidden by his shirt.

Yuri did not have a brand either—at least not one that Reid could see. The collar of the Serbian's suede jacket rode high. *Could be a status symbol,* he thought. *Something that had to be earned.*

The driver directed the vehicle onto A4, leaving Paris behind and heading northeast toward Reims. The tinted windows made the night all the darker; once they left the City of Lights, it was difficult for Reid to make out landmarks. He had to rely on the route markers and signs to know where they were heading. The landscape slowly shifted from the bright urban locale to an idle, bucolic topography, the highway gently sloping with the lay of the land and farms stretching on either side.

After an hour of driving in utter silence, Reid cleared his throat. "Is it much further?" he asked.

Yuri put a finger to his lips and then grinned. *"Oui."*

Reid's nostrils flared, but he said nothing more. He should have asked just how far they would be taking him; for all he knew, they were going clear to Belgium.

Route A4 became A34, which in turn became A304 as they climbed ever further north. The trees that dotted the pastoral countryside grew thicker and closer, wide umbrella-like spruces that swallowed the open farmland and became indistinguishable forests. The gradient of the road increased as the sloping hills turned to small mountains.

He knew this place. Rather, he knew the region, and not because of any flashing vision or implanted memory. He had never been here, but he knew from his studies that they had reached the Ardennes, a mountainous stretch of forest shared between northeastern France, southern Belgium, and northern Luxembourg. It was in the Ardennes that the German army, in 1944, attempted to launch their armored divisions through the densely forested region in an attempt to capture the city of Antwerp. They were thwarted by American and British forces near the river Meuse. The ensuing conflict was dubbed the Battle of the Bulge, and it was the last major offensive of the Germans in World War II.

For some reason, despite how dire his situation was or might soon become, he found some small measure of comfort in thinking about history, his former life, and his students. But then his thoughts again transitioned to his girls being alone and scared and not having any idea where he was or what he had gotten himself into.

Sure enough, Reid soon saw a sign that warned of an approach to the border. *Belgique*, the sign read, and below that, *Belgien, België, Belgium*. Less than two miles later, the SUV slowed to a stop at a single small booth with a concrete awning overhead. A man in a thick coat and wool-knit cap peered out at the vehicle. Border security between France and Belgium was a far cry from what most Americans were used to. The driver rolled down the window and spoke to the man, but the words were muted by the closed partition and windows. Reid squinted through the tint and saw the driver's arm reach out, passing something to the border officer—a bill. A bribe.

The man in the cap waved them through.

Only a few miles down N5, the SUV pulled off of the highway and onto a narrow road that cut parallel to the main thoroughfare. There was no exit sign and the road itself was barely paved; it was an access road, likely one that was created for logging vehicles. The car jostled over the deep ruts in the dirt. The two goons bumped against one another opposite Reid, but still they continued to stare straight forward at him.

He checked the cheap watch he had bought at the pharmacy. Two hours and forty-six minutes they had been traveling. Last night he had been in the US, and then woken up in Paris, and now he was in Belgium. *Relax*, his subconscious coaxed. *Nowhere you haven't been before. Just pay attention and keep your mouth shut.*

Both sides of the road appeared to be nothing but thick trees. The SUV continued on, climbing up the side of a curving mountain and down again. All the while Reid peered out the window, pretending to be idle but looking for any sort of landmark or sign that would tell him where they were—ideally something he could recount later to the authorities, if need be.

There were lights ahead, though at his angle he could not see the source. The SUV slowed again and rolled to a gentle stop. Reid saw a black wrought-iron fence, each post topped in a dangerous spike, stretching to either side and vanishing into the darkness. Alongside their vehicle was a small guard house made of glass and dark brick, a fluorescent light illuminating the inside. A man emerged. He wore slacks and a pea coat, the collar flipped up around his neck and a gray scarf knotted at his throat. He made no attempt to hide the silenced MP7 hanging from a strap over his right shoulder. In fact, as he stepped toward the car, he gripped the automatic pistol, though he did not raise it.

Heckler & Koch, production variant MP7A1, said the voice in Reid's head. *Seven-point-one-inch suppressor. Elcan reflex sight. Thirty-round magazine.*

The driver rolled down his window and spoke with the man for just a few seconds. Then the guard rounded the SUV and pulled open the door on Yuri's side. He bent and peered into the cab. Reid caught the scent of rye whiskey and felt the sting of the frigid rush of air that came with it. The man glanced at each of them in turn, his gaze lingering on Reid.

"Kommunikator," said Yuri. *"Chtoby uvidet' nachal'nika."* Russian. *Messenger, to see the boss.*

The guard said nothing. He closed the door again and returned to his post, pressing a button on a small console. The black-iron gate hummed as it rolled aside, and the SUV pulled through.

Reid's throat tightened as the full gravity of his situation pressed in on him. He had gone to the meeting with the intention of getting information about whatever was happening—not just to him, but with all the talk of plans and sheikhs and foreign cities. He had gotten into the car with Yuri and the two goons in the heat of finding a source. He had let them take him out of the country and into the middle of a dense forested region, and now they were behind a tall, guarded, spiked gate. He had no idea how he might get out of this if something went awry.

Relax. You've done this before.

No I haven't! he thought desperately. *I'm a college professor from New York. I don't know what I'm doing. Why did I do this? My girls ...*

Just give in to it. You'll know what to do.

Reid took a deep breath, but it did little to calm his nerves. He peered out the window. In the darkness, he could just barely make out their surroundings. There were no trees behind the gate, but rather rows upon rows of stout vines, climbing and weaving through waist-high latticework ... It was a vineyard. Whether it was actually a vineyard or merely a front, he wasn't sure, but it was at least something recognizable, something that could be seen by helicopter or a drone flyover.

Good. That'll come in handy later.

If there is a later.

The SUV drove slowly over the gravel road for another mile or so before the vineyard ended. Before them was a palatial estate, practically a castle, built in gray stone with arching windows and ivy climbing up the southern façade. For the briefest of moments, Reid appreciated the beautiful architecture; it was likely two hundred years old, maybe more. But they did not stop there; instead, the car circled around the grand home and behind it. After another half mile, they pulled into a small lot and the driver cut the engine.

They had arrived. But where they had arrived to, he had no idea.

The goons exited first, and then Reid climbed out, followed by Yuri. The bitter cold took his breath away. He clenched his jaw to keep his teeth from chattering. Their two large escorts seemed to not be bothered by it at all.

About forty yards from them was a large, squat structure, two stories tall and several times as wide; windowless and made of corrugated steel painted beige. Some sort of facility, Reid reasoned—perhaps for winemaking. But he doubted it.

Yuri groaned as he stretched his limbs. Then he grinned at Reid. "Ben, I understand we are now very good friends, but still..." He pulled from his jacket pocket a narrow length of black fabric. "I must insist."

Reid nodded once, tightly. What choice did he have? He turned so that Yuri could tie the blindfold over his eyes. A strong, meaty hand gripped his upper arm—one of the goons, no doubt.

"Now then," Yuri said. "Onwards to Otets." The strong hand pulled him forward and guided him as they walked in the direction of the steel structure. He felt another shoulder brush against his own on the opposite side; the two large goons had him flanked.

Reid breathed evenly through his nose, trying his best to remain calm. *Listen,* his mind told him.

I am listening.

No, listen. *Listen, and give in.* Someone banged three times on a door. The sound of it was dull and hollow as a bass drum. Though he couldn't see, Reid imagined in his mind's eye Yuri banging with the flat of his fist against the heavy steel door.

Ca-chunk. A deadbolt sliding aside. A *whoosh*, a rush of warm air as the door opened. Suddenly, a mélange of noises—glass clinking, liquid sloshing, belts whirring. Vintner's equipment, by the sound of it. Strange; he hadn't heard anything from outside. *The building's exterior walls are soundproofed.*

The heavy hand guided him inside. The door closed again and the deadbolt was slid back into place. The floor beneath him felt like smooth concrete. His shoes slapped against a small puddle. The acetous odor of fermentation was strongest, and just under that, the sweeter familiar scent of grape juice. *They really are making wine here.*

Reid counted his paces across the floor of the facility. They passed through another set of doors, and with it came an assortment of new sounds. *Machinery—hydraulic press. Pneumatic drill. The clinking chain of a conveyor.* The fermentation scent gave way to grease, motor oil, and ... *Powder. They're manufacturing something here; most likely munitions.* There was something else, something familiar, past the oil and powder. It was somewhat sweet, like almonds ... *Dinitrotoluene. They're making explosives.*

"Stairs," said Yuri's voice, close to his ear, as Reid's shin bumped against the bottommost step. The heavy hand continued to guide him as four sets of footfalls climbed the steel stairs. *Thirteen steps. Whoever built this place must not be superstitious.*

At the top was yet another steel door. Once it was closed behind them, the sounds of machinery were drowned out—another soundproofed room. Classical piano music played from nearby. *Brahms. Variations on a Theme of Paganini.* The melody was not rich enough to be coming from an actual piano; a stereo of some kind.

"Yuri." The new voice was a stern baritone, slightly rasped from either shouting often or too many cigars. Judging by the scent of the room, it was the latter. Possibly both.

"Otets," said Yuri obsequiously. He spoke rapidly in Russian. Reid did his best to follow along with Yuri's accent. "I bring you good news from France ..."

"Who is this man?" the baritone demanded. With the way he spoke, Russian seemed to be his native tongue. Reid couldn't help but wonder what the connection might be between the Iranians and this Russian man—or the goons in the SUV, for that matter, and even the Serbian Yuri. *An arms deal, maybe,* said the voice in his head. *Or something worse.*

"This is the Iranians' messenger," Yuri replied. "He has the information we seek for—"

"You brought him here?" the man interjected. His deep voice rose to a roar. "You were supposed to go to France and meet with the Iranians, not drag men back to me! You would compromise everything with your stupidity!" There was a sharp crack—a solid backhand across a face—and a gasp from Yuri. "Must I write your job description on a bullet to get it through your thick skull?!"

"Otets, please ..." Yuri stammered.

"Do not call me that!" the man shouted fiercely. A gun cocked—a heavy pistol, by the sound of it. "Do not call me by any name in the presence of this stranger!"

"He is no stranger!" Yuri yelped. "He is Agent Zero! I have brought you Kent Steele!"

CHAPTER SEVEN

Kent Steele.

Silence reigned for several seconds that felt like minutes. A hundred visions flashed quickly through Reid's mind as if they were being machine-fed. *The CIA. National Clandestine Service, Special Activities Division, Special Operations Group. Psych ops.*

Agent Zero.

If you're exposed, you're dead.

We don't talk. Ever.

Impossible.

His fingers were trembling again.

It was simply impossible. Things like memory wipes or implants or suppressors were the stuff of conspiracy theories and Hollywood films.

It didn't matter now anyway. They knew who he was the whole time—from the bar to the car ride and all the way to Belgium, Yuri had known that Reid was not who he said he was. Now he was blindfolded and trapped behind a steel door with at least four armed men. No one else knew where he was or who he was. A heavy knot of dread formed deep in his stomach and threatened to make him nauseous.

"No," said the baritone voice slowly. "No, you are mistaken. Stupid Yuri. This is not the CIA man. If it was, you would not be standing here!"

"Unless he came here to find you!" Yuri countered.

Fingers grabbed at the blindfold and yanked it off. Reid squinted in the sudden harshness of the overhead fluorescent lights. He blinked in the face of a man in his fifties, with salt-and-pepper hair, a full beard shorn close to the cheek, and sharp, discerning eyes. The man, presumably Otets, wore a charcoal gray suit, the top two buttons of his shirt undone and curling gray chest hairs peeking out from beneath it. They stood in an office, the walls painted dark red and adorned with gaudy paintings.

"You," the man said in accented English. "Who are you?"

Reid took a jagged breath and fought the urge to tell the man that he simply didn't know anymore. Instead, in a tremulous voice, he said, "My name is Ben. I'm a messenger. I work with the Iranians."

Yuri, who was on his knees behind Otets, leapt to his feet. "He lies!" the Serbian screeched. "I know he lies! He says that the Iranians sent him, but they would never trust an American!" Yuri leered. A thin rivulet of blood eked from the corner of his mouth where Otets had struck him. "But I know more. See, I asked you about Amad." He shook his head as he bared his teeth. "There is no Amad among them."

It seemed odd to Reid that these men seemed to know the Iranians, but not who they worked with or who they might send. They were certainly connected somehow, but what that connection might be, he had no idea.

Otets muttered curses under his breath in Russian. Then in English he said, "You tell Yuri you are messenger. Yuri tells me you are the CIA man. What am I to believe? You certainly do not look like I imagined Zero to be. Yet my idiot errand boy speaks one truth: the Iranians despise Americans. This does not look good for you. You tell me the truth, or I will shoot you in your kneecap." He hefted the heavy pistol—a TIG Series Desert Eagle.

Reid lost his breath for a moment. It was a very large gun.

Give in, his mind prodded.

He wasn't sure how to do that. He wasn't sure what would happen if he did. The last time these new instincts took over, four men ended up dead, and he, quite literally, had blood on his hands. But there was no way out of this for him—that is, for Professor Reid Lawson. But Kent Steele, whoever that might be, might find a way. Maybe he didn't know who he was, but it wouldn't matter much if he didn't survive long enough to find out.

Reid closed his eyes. He nodded once, a silent acquiescence to the voice in his head. His shoulders went slack and his fingers stopped trembling.

"I am waiting," said Otets flatly.

"You wouldn't want to shoot me," Reid said. He was surprised to hear his own voice so calm and even. "A point-blank shot from that gun wouldn't blow out my knee. It would sever my leg, and I'd bleed out on the floor of this office in seconds."

Otets shrugged one shoulder. "What is it you Americans like to say? You cannot make omelet without—"

"I have the information you need," Reid cut him off. "The sheikh's location. What he gave me. Who I gave it to. I know all about your plot, and I'm not the only one."

The corners of Otets's mouth curled into a smirk. "Agent Zero."

"I told you!" said Yuri. "I did well, yes?"

"Shut up," Otets barked. Yuri shrank like a beaten dog. "Take him downstairs and get all of what he knows. Start by removing fingers. I don't want to waste time."

On any ordinary day, the threat of having his fingers cut off would have sent a shock of fear through Reid. His muscles tensed for a moment, the small hairs on the nape of his neck standing on end—but his new instinct fought against it and forced him to relax. *Wait*, it told him. *Wait for an opportunity*...

The bald goon nodded curtly and grabbed onto Reid's arm again.

"Idiot!" Otets snapped. "Bind him first! Yuri, go to file cabinet. There should be something there."

Yuri hurried to the three-drawer oak cabinet in the corner and rifled through it until he found a bundled length of coarse twine. "Here," he said, and he tossed it to the bald brute.

All eyes instinctively moved skyward toward the bundle of twine spinning in the air—both goons, Yuri, and Otets.

But not Reid's. He had a shot, and he took it.

He cupped his left hand and arced it upward at a sharp angle, striking the bald man's windpipe with the meaty side of his palm. He felt the throat give beneath his hand.

As the first blow landed, he kicked out his left boot heel behind him and struck the bearded thug in the hip—the same hip the man had been favoring on the ride to Belgium.

A wet choking gasp escaped the bald man's lips as his hands flew to his throat. The bearded brute grunted as his large body spun and collapsed.

Down!

The twine slapped the floor. So did Reid. In one motion he fell into a crouch and yanked the Glock from the bald man's ankle holster. Without looking up, he leapt forward and tucked into a roll.

As soon as he jumped, a thunderous report tore across the small office, impossibly loud. The shot from the Desert Eagle left an impressive dent in the office's steel door.

Reid came out of the roll only a few feet from Otets and propelled himself forward, toward him. Before Otets could pivot to aim, Reid grabbed his gun hand from underneath—*never grab the top slide, that's a good way to lose a finger*—and pushed it up and away. The gun went off again, a piercing boom only a couple of feet from Reid's head. His ears rang, but he ignored it. He twisted the gun down and to the side, keeping the barrel pointed away from him as he brought it to his hip—and Otets's hand with it.

The older man threw back his head and screamed as his trigger finger snapped. The sound nauseated Reid as the Desert Eagle clattered to the floor.

He spun and wrapped one arm around Otets's neck, using him as a shield as he aimed at the two goons. The bald man was out of commission, gasping for breath in vain against a crushed windpipe, but the bearded man had loosened his TEC-9. Without hesitating, Reid fired three shots in quick succession, two in the chest and one in the forehead. A fourth shot put the bald man out of his misery.

Reid's conscience screamed at him from the back of his mind. *You just killed two men. Two more men.* But this new consciousness was stronger, pushing his nausea and sense of preservation back.

You can panic later. You're not finished here.

Reid spun fully around, with Otets in front of him as if they were dancing, and leveled the Glock at Yuri. The hapless messenger was struggling to free a Sig Sauer from his shoulder harness.

"Stop," Reid commanded. Yuri froze. "Hands up." The Serbian messenger slowly put his hands up, palms out. He grinned wide.

"Kent," he said in English, "we are very good friends, are we not?"

"Take my Beretta out of your left jacket pocket and set it on the floor," Reid instructed.

Yuri licked the blood from the corner of his mouth and wiggled the fingers of his left hand. Slowly, he reached into the pocket and pulled out the small black pistol. But he didn't set it on the floor. Instead he held it, barrel pointed downward.

"You know," he said, "it occurs to me that if you want information, you need at least one of us alive. Yes?"

"Yuri!" Otets growled. "Do as he asks!"

"On the floor," Reid repeated. He didn't take his gaze off of Yuri, but he was concerned that others in the facility might have heard the roar of the Desert Eagle. He had no idea how many people were downstairs, but the office was soundproofed and there was machinery running elsewhere. It was possible no one had heard it—or perhaps they were used to the sound and thought little of it.

"Maybe," said Yuri, "I take this gun and I shoot Otets. Then you need *me*."

"Yuri, *nyet*!" Otets cried, this time more stunned than angry.

"See, Kent," said Yuri, "this is not *La Cosa Nostra*. This is more like, uh ... disgruntled employee. You see how he treats me. So maybe I shoot him, and you and I, we work something out ..."

Otets clenched his teeth and hissed a flurry of curses at Yuri, but the messenger only grinned wider.

Reid was growing impatient. "Yuri, if you don't put the gun down now, I'll be forced to—"

Yuri's arm moved, just the slightest bit of an indication of rising. Reid's instinct kicked in like an engine shifting gears. Without thinking he aimed and fired, just once. It happened so quickly that the report of the pistol startled him.

For a half-second, Reid thought he might have missed. Then dark blood erupted from a hole in Yuri's neck. He fell first to his knees, one hand weakly trying to stanch the flow, but it was far too late for that.

It can take up to two minutes to bleed out from a severed carotid artery. He didn't want to know how he knew that. *But it takes only seven to ten seconds to pass out from blood loss.*

Yuri slumped forward. Reid immediately spun toward the steel door with the Glock aimed at center mass. He waited. His own breath was stable and smooth. He hadn't even broken a sweat. Otets took sharp, gasping breaths, cradling his fractured finger with his good hand.

No one else came.

I just shot three men.

No time for that now. Get the hell out of here.

"Stay," Reid growled at Otets as he released his hold on him. He kicked the Desert Eagle into the far corner. It skittered under the file cabinet. He had no use for a cannon like that. He also left the TEC-9 automatic pistols that the thugs had; they were largely inaccurate, good for little more than spraying bullets over a wide area. Instead, he shoved Yuri's body aside with his foot and grabbed up the Beretta. He kept the Glock, tucking a pistol, and his hands, into each of his jacket pockets.

"We're getting out of here," Reid told Otets, "you and me. You'll go first, and you'll pretend that nothing is wrong. You're going to walk me outside and to a decent car. Because these?" He gestured to his hands, each stuffed into a pocket and wrapped around a pistol. "These will both be aimed at your spine. Make one single misstep, or say a word out of line, and I'll bury a bullet between your L2 and L3 vertebrae. If you're lucky enough to live, you'll be paralyzed for the rest of your life. Understand?"

Otets glared at him, but he was smart enough to nod.

"Good. Then lead the way."

The Russian man paused at the steel door of the office. "You won't get out of here alive," he said in English.

"You'd better hope I do," Reid growled. "Because I'll make sure you don't either."

Otets pulled the door open and stepped out onto the landing. The sounds of machinery instantly came roaring back. Reid followed him out of the office and onto the small steel platform. He glanced downward over the railing, looking out over the shop floor below. His thoughts—*Kent's thoughts?*—were correct; there were two men working a hydraulic press. One at a pneumatic drill. One more stood at a short conveyor, inspecting electronic components as they slowly rolled toward a steel surface at the end. Two others wearing goggles and latex gloves sat at a melamine table, carefully measuring some sort of chemicals. Oddly, he noticed they were an assortment of nationalities—three were dark-haired and white, likely Russian, but two were definitely Middle Eastern. The man at the drill was African.

The almond-like scent of the dinitrotoluene floated up to him. They were making explosives, as he had discerned earlier from the odor and sounds.

Six in all. Likely armed. None of them so much as looked up toward the office. *They won't shoot in here—not with Otets in the open and volatile chemicals around.*

But neither can I, Reid thought.

"Impressive, no?" said Otets with a smirk. He'd noticed Reid inspecting the floor.

"Move," he commanded.

Otets stepped down, his shoe clanking against the first metal stair. "You know," he said casually, "Yuri was right."

Get outside. Get to the SUV. Crash the gate. Drive it like you stole it.

"You do need one of us."

Get back on the highway. Find a police station. Get Interpol involved.

"And poor Yuri is dead ..."

Give them Otets. Force him to talk. Clear your name in the murders of seven men.

"So it occurs to me that you cannot kill me."

I've murdered seven men.

But it was self-defense.

Otets reached the bottom step, Reid right behind him with both hands stuffed in the pockets of his jacket. His palms were sweaty, each gripping a pistol. The Russian stopped and glanced slightly over his shoulder, not quite looking at Reid. "The Iranians. They are dead?"

"Four of them," Reid said. The din of the machinery nearly drowned out his voice.

Otets clucked his tongue. "Shame. But then again ... it means I am not wrong. You have no leads, no one else to go to. You need me."

He was calling Reid's bluff. Panic rose in his chest. The other side, the Kent side, fought it back down, like dry-swallowing a pill. "I have everything the sheikh gave us—"

Otets chuckled softly. "The sheikh, yes. But you already know that Mustafar knew so little. He was a bank account, Agent. He was soft. Did you think we would trust him with our plan? If so, then why did you come here?"

Sweat prickled on Reid's brow. He had come here in the hopes of finding answers, not only about this supposed plan but about who he was. He had found much more than he bargained for. "Move," he demanded again. "Toward the door, slowly."

Otets stepped off the staircase, moving slowly, but he did not walk toward the door. Instead, he took a step toward the shop floor, toward his men.

"What are you doing?" Reid demanded.

"Calling your bluff, Agent Zero. If I am wrong, you will shoot me." He grinned and took another step.

Two of the workers glanced up. From their perspective, it looked like Otets was simply chatting with some unknown man, perhaps a business associate or representative from another faction. No reason for alarm.

The panic rose again in Reid's chest. He didn't want to let go of the guns. Otets was only two paces away, but Reid couldn't very well grab him and force him to the door—not without alerting the six men. He couldn't risk shooting in a room full of explosives.

"*Do svidaniya*, Agent." Otets grinned. Without taking his eyes off of Reid he shouted in English, "Shoot this man!"

Two more of the workers looked up, glancing between each other and Otets in confusion. Reid got the impression that these men were laborers, not foot soldiers or bodyguards like the pair of dead goons upstairs.

"Idiots!" Otets roared over the machinery. "This man is CIA! Shoot him!"

That got their attention. The pair of men at the melamine table rose quickly and reached for shoulder holsters. The African man at the pneumatic drill reached down near his feet and lifted an AK-47 to his shoulder.

As soon as they moved, Reid sprang forward, at the same time yanking both hands—and both pistols—out of his pockets. He spun Otets by the shoulder and held the Beretta to the Russian's left temple, and then leveled the Beretta at the man with the AK, his arm resting on Otets's shoulder.

"That wouldn't be very wise," he said loudly. "You know what might happen if we start shooting in here."

The sight of a gun to their boss's head prompted the rest of the men into action. He was right; they were all armed, and now he had six guns on him with only Otets between them. The man holding the AK glanced nervously at his compatriots. A thin bead of sweat ran down the side of his forehead.

Reid took a small step backward, coaxing Otets along with him with a nudge from the Beretta. "Nice and easy," he said quietly. "If they start shooting in here, this whole place could go up. And I don't think you want to die today."

Otets clenched his teeth and murmured a curse in Russian.

Little by little they backed away, tiny steps at a time, toward the doors of the facility. Reid's heart threatened to pound out of his chest. His muscles tightened nervously, and then went slack as the other side of him forced him to relax. *Keep the tension out of your limbs. Tight muscles will slow your reactions.*

For each tiny step that he and Otets took back, the six men took one forward, maintaining a short distance between them. They were waiting for an opportunity, and the farther they stepped from the machines, the less likely setting off an inadvertent explosion would be. Reid knew it was only the threat of accidentally killing Otets that kept them from shooting. No one spoke, but the machines droned on behind them. The tension in the air was palpable, electric; he knew that any moment someone might get antsy and start firing.

Then his back touched the double doors. Another step and he pushed them open, nudging Otets along with him with a shove from the Beretta's barrel.

Before the doors swung shut again, Otets growled at his men. "He does not leave here alive!"

Then they closed, and the pair of them were in the next room, the wine-making room, with bottles clinking and the sweet smell of grapes. As soon as they were through, Reid whipped around, the Glock aimed at chest level—still keeping the Beretta trained on Otets.

A bottling and corking machine was running, but it was mostly automated. The only person in the entire wide room was a single tired-looking Russian woman wearing a green headscarf. At the sight of the gun, and Reid, and Otets, her weary eyes went wide in terror and she threw both hands up.

"Turn those off," Reid said in Russian. "Do you understand?"

She nodded vigorously and threw two levers on the control panel. The machines whirred down, slowing to a halt.

"Go," he told her. She gulped and backed away slowly toward the exit door. "Quickly!" he shouted harshly. "Get out!"

"*Da*," she murmured. The woman scurried to the heavy steel exit, threw it open, and dashed out into the night. The door slammed shut again with a resonant boom.

"Now what, Agent?" Otets grunted in English. "What is your plan of escape?"

"Shut up." Reid leveled the gun at the double doors to the next room. Why hadn't they come through yet? He couldn't very well keep going without knowing where they were. If there was a back door to the facility, they might be outside waiting for him. If they followed, there was no way he could get Otets into the SUV and drive away without getting shot. In here there was no threat of explosives; they could take a shot if they had it. Would they risk killing Otets to get to him? Jangled nerves and a gun were not an ideal combination for anyone, even their boss.

Before he could decide on his next move, the powerful fluorescent lights overhead went out. In an instant they were plunged into darkness.

CHAPTER EIGHT

Reid couldn't see a thing. There were no windows in the facility. The workers in the other room must have thrown some breakers, because even the sounds of the machinery in the next room faded and fell silent.

He quickly reached out for the place he knew Otets to be and grabbed onto the Russian's collar before he could make a run for it. Otets made a small choking sound as Reid yanked him backward. In the same moment, a red emergency light came on, just a bare bulb jutting from the wall just over the door. It bathed the room in a soft, eerie glow.

"These men are not fools," Otets said quietly. "You will not make it out of this alive."

His mind raced. He needed to know where they were—or better yet, he needed them to come to him.

But how?

It's simple. You know what to do. Stop fighting it.

Reid took a deep breath through his nose, and then he did the only thing that made sense in the moment.

He shot Otets.

The sharp report of the Beretta echoed in the otherwise silent room. Otets screamed in pain. Both hands flew to hold his left thigh—the bullet had only grazed him, but it bled liberally. He spat a long, angry slur of Russian curses.

Reid grabbed onto Otets's collar again and yanked him backward, nearly off his feet, and forced him down behind the bottling conveyor. He waited. If the men were still inside, they would have definitely heard the shot and would come running. If no one came, they were outside somewhere, lying in wait.

He got his answer a few seconds later. The swinging double doors were kicked open from the other side hard enough to smack against the wall behind them. The first through was the man with the AK, tracking the barrel left and right quickly in a wide sweep. Two others were right behind him, both armed with pistols.

Otets groaned in pain and gripped his leg tightly. His people heard it; they came around the corner of the bottling machine with their weapons raised to find Otets sitting on the floor, hissing through his teeth with his wounded leg prostrate.

Reid, however, was not there.

He stole quickly around the other side of the machine, staying in a crouch. He pocketed the Beretta and grabbed an empty bottle from the conveyor. Before they could even turn, he smashed the bottle over the head of the nearest worker, a Middle Eastern man, and then jammed the jagged bottleneck into the throat of the second. Warm blood ran over his hand as the man sputtered and fell.

One.

The African with the AK-47 spun, but not fast enough. Reid used his forearm to shove the barrel aside, even as a fusillade of bullets ripped through the air. He stepped forward with the Glock, pressed it beneath the man's chin, and pulled the trigger.

Two.

One more shot finished off the first terrorist—since clearly that's what he was dealing with, he decided—still lying unconscious on the floor.

Three.

Reid breathed hard, trying to will his heart into slowing down. He didn't have time to be horrified by what he had just done, nor did he really want to think about it. It was as if Professor Lawson had gone into shock, and the other part had taken over completely.

Movement. To the right.

Otets crawled from behind the machine and made a grab for the AK. Reid turned quickly and kicked him in the stomach. The force of it sent the Russian rolling over, holding his side and groaning.

Reid took up the AK. *How many rounds were fired? Five? Six.* It was a thirty-two-round magazine. If the clip was full, he still had twenty-six rounds.

"Stay put," he told Otets. Then, much to the Russian's surprise, Reid left him there and went back through the double doors to the other side of the facility.

The bomb-making room was bathed in a similar red glow from an emergency light. Reid kicked open the door and immediately dropped to one knee—in case anyone had a gun trained on the entrance—and swept left and right. There was no one there, which meant there had to be a back door. He found it quickly, a steel security door between the stairs and the southern-facing wall. Likely it only opened from the inside.

The other three were out there somewhere. It was a gamble—he had no way to tell if they were waiting for him right on the other side of the door, or if they had tried to circle around to the front of the building. He needed a way to hedge his bet.

This is, after all, a bomb-making facility...

In the far corner on the opposite side, past the conveyor, he found a long wooden crate roughly the size of a coffin and filled with packing peanuts. He sifted through them until he felt something solid and hauled it out. It was a black matte plastic case, and he already knew what was inside it.

He set it on the melamine table carefully and opened it. More to his chagrin than surprise, he recognized it immediately as a suitcase bomb, set with a timer but able to be bypassed by a dead man's switch as a fail-safe.

Sweat beaded on his forehead. *Am I really going to do this?*

New visions flashed across his mind—Afghani bomb-makers missing fingers and entire limbs from poorly built incendiaries.

Buildings going up in smoke from one wrong move, a single mis-connected wire.

What choice do you have? It's either this, or get shot.

The dead man's switch was a small green rectangle about the size of a pocketknife with a lever on one side. He picked it up in his left hand and held his breath.

Then he squeezed it.

Nothing happened. That was a good sign.

He made sure to hold the lever closed in his fist (releasing it would immediately detonate the bomb) and he set the suitcase's timer for twenty minutes—he wouldn't need that long anyway. Then he plucked up the AK in his right hand and got the hell out of there.

He winced; the rear security door squealed on its hinges as he shoved it open. He leapt out into the darkness with the AK leveled. There was no one there, not behind the building, but they had certainly heard the telltale squeak of the door.

His throat was dry and his heart was still pounding like a kettle-drum, but he kept his back to the steel façade and carefully eased his way to the corner of the building. His hand was sweating, gripping the dead man's switch in a death grip. If he released it now, he would most certainly be dead in an instant. The amount of C4 packed into that bomb would blow the walls of the building out and flatten him, if he wasn't incinerated first.

Yesterday my biggest problem was keeping my students' attention for ninety minutes. Today he was white-knuckling a lever to a bomb while trying to elude Russian terrorists.

Focus. He reached the corner of the building and peered around its edge, sticking to the shadows as best he could. There was a silhouette of a man, a pistol in his grip, standing sentry on the eastern façade.

Reid made sure he had a solid grip on the switch. *You can do this.* Then he stepped out into plain sight. The man spun quickly and began to raise his pistol.

"Hey," Reid said. He lifted his own hand—not the one holding the gun, but the other. "Do you know what this is?"

The man paused and cocked his head slightly. Then his eyes went so wide with fear that Reid could see the whites of them by the moonlight. "Switch," the man muttered. His gaze fluttered from the switch to the building and back again, seeming to come to the same conclusion that Reid already had—if he released that lever, they'd both be dead in a heartbeat.

The bomb-maker abandoned his plan of shooting Reid, and instead sprinted away toward the front of the building. Reid followed hastily. He heard shouts in Arabic—"Switch! He has the switch!"

He rounded the corner to the front of the facility with the AK aimed forward, the stock rested in the crook of his elbow, and his other hand holding the dead man's switch high over his head. The sprinting bomb-maker hadn't stopped; he kept running, up the gravel road that led away from the building and screaming himself hoarse. The other two bomb-makers were gathered near the front door, apparently ready to go in and finish Reid off. They stared in bewilderment as he came around the corner.

Reid quickly surveyed the scene. The other two men held pistols—*Sig Sauer P365, thirteen-round capacity with fully extended grips*—but neither pointed them. As he had presumed, Otets had made his escape through the front door and was, at the moment, halfway to the SUV, limping along while holding his hurt leg and supported under one shoulder by a short, portly man in a black cap—the driver, Reid assumed.

"Guns down," Reid commanded, "or I'll blow it."

The bomb-makers carefully set their weapons in the dirt. Reid could hear shouts in the distance, more voices. There were others coming from the direction of the old estate house. Likely the Russian woman had tipped them off.

"Run," he told them. "Go tell them what's about to happen."

The two men didn't have to be told twice. They broke into a brisk run in the same direction their cohort had just gone.

Reid turned his attention to the driver, helping along the lamed Otets. "Stop!" he roared.

"Do not!" Otets screamed in Russian.

The driver hesitated. Reid dropped the AK and pulled the Glock from his jacket pocket. They had gotten a little more than halfway to the car—*about twenty-five yards. Easy.*

He took a few steps closer and called out, "Before today, I didn't think I had ever fired a gun before. Turns out I'm a really good shot."

The driver was a sensible man—or perhaps a coward, or even both. He released Otets, unceremoniously dropping his boss to the gravel.

"Keys," Reid demanded. "Drop them."

The driver's hands shook as he fetched the keys to the SUV from his inner jacket pocket. He tossed them at his own feet.

Reid motioned with the barrel of his pistol. "Go."

The driver ran. The black cap flew off his head but he paid it no mind.

"Coward!" Otets spat in Russian.

Reid retrieved the keys first, and then stood over Otets. The voices in the distance were getting closer. The estate house was a half mile away; it would have taken the Russian woman about four minutes to reach it on foot, and then another few minutes for the men to get down here. He figured he had less than two minutes.

"Get up."

Otets spat on his shoes in response.

"Have it your way." Reid pocketed the Glock, grabbed Otets by the back of his suit jacket, and hauled him toward the SUV. The Russian cried out in pain as his gunshot leg dragged across the gravel.

"Get in," Reid ordered, "or I'll shoot your other leg."

Otets grumbled under his breath, hissing through the pain, but he climbed into the car. Reid slammed the door, circled around quickly, and got behind the wheel. His left hand still held the dead man's switch.

He slammed the SUV into drive and stomped the gas. The tires spun, kicking up gravel and dirt behind it, and then the vehicle lurched forward with a jolt. As soon as he pulled back onto the narrow access road, shots rang out. Bullets smacked the passenger side with a series of heavy thuds. The window—just to the right of Otets's head—splintered in a spider web of cracked glass, but held.

"Idiots!" Otets screamed. "Stop shooting!"

Bullet-resistant, Reid thought. *Of course it is.* But he knew that wouldn't last long. He pressed the accelerator to the floor and the SUV lurched again, roaring past the three men on the side of the road as they fired on the car. Reid rolled down his window as they rolled by the two bomb-makers, still running for their lives.

Then he tossed the switch out the window.

The explosion rocked the SUV, even at their distance. He didn't hear the detonation so much as he felt it, deep in his core, shaking his innards. A glance in the rearview mirror showed nothing but intense yellow light, like staring directly into the sun. Spots swam in his vision for a moment and he forced himself to look ahead at the road. An orange fireball rolled into the sky, sending up an immense plume of black smoke with it.

Otets let out a jagged, groaning sigh. "You have no idea what you've just done," he said quietly. "You are a dead man, Agent."

Reid said nothing. He did realize what he had just done—he had destroyed a significant amount of evidence in whatever case might be built against Otets once he was brought to the authorities. But Otets was wrong; he was not a dead man, not yet anyway, and the bomb had helped him get away.

This far, anyhow.

Up ahead, the estate house loomed into view, but there was no pausing to appreciate its architecture this time around. Reid kept his eyes straight ahead and zoomed past it as the SUV bounced over the ruts in the road.

A glimmer in the mirror caught his attention. Two pairs of headlights swung into view, pulling out from the driveway of the house. They were low to the ground and he could hear the high-pitched whine of the engines over the roar of his own. Sports cars. He hit the gas again. They would be faster, but the SUV was better equipped to handle the uneven road.

More shots cracked the air as bullets pounded the rear fender. Reid gripped the steering wheel with both hands, the veins standing out stark with the tension in his muscles. He had control. He could do this. The iron gate couldn't be far. He was doing fifty-five through the vineyard; if he could maintain his speed, it might be enough to crash the gate.

The SUV rocked violently as a bullet struck the rear driver's side tire and exploded. The front end veered wildly. Reid instinctively counter-steered, his teeth gritted. The back end skidded out, but the SUV didn't roll.

"God save me," Otets moaned. "This lunatic will be the death of me…"

Reid wrenched the wheel again and righted the vehicle, but the steady, pounding *thum-thum-thum* of the tire told him they were riding on the rim and shreds of rubber. His speed dropped to forty. He tried to give it gas again but the SUV quaked, threatening to veer again.

He knew they couldn't maintain enough speed to break the gate. They would bounce right off it.

It's an electronic gate, he thought suddenly. It was controlled by the guard outside—who would no doubt at this point be aware of his escape attempt and be ready with the dangerous MP7—but that meant there *had* to be another exit to this compound.

Bullets continued to pound against the fender as his two pursuers fired on them. He flicked on the high beams and saw the iron gate coming up fast.

"Hang onto something," Reid warned. Otets grabbed the handle over his window and muttered a prayer under his breath as Reid yanked the wheel hard to the right. The SUV skidded sideways in the gravel. He felt the two passenger-side tires come off the ground and, for a moment, his heart leapt into his throat with the notion that they might roll right over.

But he held control, and the tires set down again. He stomped the accelerator and drove right into the vineyard, crashing through the thin wooden trellises as if they were toothpicks and rolling grapevines flat.

"What the hell are you doing?!" Otets screeched in Russian. He bounced heavily in his seat as they drove over the planted rows. Behind him, the pair of sports cars squealed to a halt. They couldn't follow, not through the field—but they were probably aware of what he was looking for, and they knew where to find it.

"Where's the other exit?" Reid demanded.

"What exit?"

He yanked the Beretta from his jacket pocket (no easy feat, with the violent bouncing of the car) and pressed it against Otets's already-shot leg. The Russian screamed in pain. "That way!" he cried, pointing a crooked finger to the northwestern edge of the compound.

Reid held his breath. *Please hold together*, he thought desperately. The SUV was sturdy, but so far they had been lucky they hadn't broken an axle.

Then, mercifully, the vineyard ended abruptly and they were back on a gravel road. The headlights shined on a second gate—made of the same wrought iron, but on wheels and held together by a single link of chain.

This is it. Reid clenched his jaw and slammed the gas once more. The SUV lurched. Otets howled some indistinguishable curse. The front end collided with the iron gate and smashed it open, knocking one side right off its hinges.

Reid breathed an intense sigh of relief. Then the headlights flashed again in his rearview—the cars were back. They had doubled back and taken the other road, likely branching from the opposite side of the estate house.

"Dammit," Reid muttered. He couldn't keep going like this forever, and if they shot out the other rear tire he'd be dead in the water. The road here was straight, and seemed to be inclining upward. It was also better paved than behind the gate, which only meant that the sports cars would catch up that much faster.

The trees were thinning on the right side of the road. Reid's gaze flitted from the road to the passenger window. He could have sworn, through the cracked glass, he saw a shimmer, like…like water.

A rush of memory came to him, but not the flashing visions of his new mind. These were actual memories, Professor Lawson's memories. *We're in the Ardennes. The Battle of the Bulge took place here. American and British forces held the bridges against German panzer divisions on the river…*

"Meuse," he murmured aloud. "We're on the river Meuse."

"What?" Otets exclaimed. "What are you babbling about?" Then he ducked instinctively as bullets splintered their rear windshield.

Reid ignored him, and the bullets. His mind raced. What was it he recalled reading about the Meuse? It sliced through the mountains, yes. And they were on an incline, heading upward. There were quarries here. Red marble quarries. Sheer cliffs and steep drops.

The SUV shuddered in protest. A heavy and very disconcerting clunking sound rumbled from its underbelly.

"What is that?" Otets shouted.

"That's our axle breaking," Reid answered. He focused on the road ahead. They had very little time…

Another bang rocked the SUV and threatened to tear it from the road. *Not a bullet*, Reid thought. That was their other rear tire blowing out. He was out of time and running out of road. He scanned for a break in the trees wide enough.

The sports car immediately behind him must have noticed the blowout. It crept up on his rear end and bumped their fender. The SUV veered slightly. For a brief moment, Reid thought about slamming the brakes, letting the car crash into them. With the momentary distraction, he could gain the element of surprise. He still had two guns. But no; there was a good chance that the two pursuing cars had the same bullet-resistant plating as the SUV.

There was only one way he could think of to get out of this.

But that's impossible, he thought. *That's lunacy.*

No. It's not. You still don't understand? You've been trained for every situation. You've been in every situation. Look at what you've done so far. Don't you get it yet? You are Kent Steele.

"I am," he murmured. "I am." He didn't know how it was possible, and his brain was still an utter mess, but he knew it was true. And the voice in his head was right. There was a way.

He yanked the wheel to the right. The SUV screeched and groaned as it skidded sideways. Reid piloted it between two narrow trees, directly toward the river. "You're going to want to jump out of the car when I say jump."

"What are you doing?!" Otets screamed. "Are you insane?"

"I might be." The car jolted with a teeth-rattling quake as the axle broke, but by that time their momentum was too much to stop it. Reid grabbed onto the door handle with one hand and steered with the other. "But if you don't want to die, you'll jump."

Otets whimpered another prayer under his breath, his eyes squeezed shut.

Reid clenched his jaw tightly. *Here we go.* The sports cars behind him squealed to a stop, the drivers watching in disbelief as the SUV careened over the edge of the red marble quarry and plummeted sixty feet down into the darkness of the Meuse.

CHAPTER NINE

The fall felt impossibly long.

As the SUV's front tires lost the ground beneath them and rolled out over nothing, Reid threw open the driver's side door and, with a burst of adrenaline, leapt out of the car. A half second before that he shouted "Jump!" He heard Otets's high-pitched moan of fear as he too threw open his door.

And then they fell through darkness toward the rushing water below. Reid thought it strange, in that moment, that there was no hypnic jerk, no falling sensation as they dropped quickly toward the Meuse—and then thought it was stranger still that his mind could be so cognizant and lucid while plummeting over a cliff.

They hit the river's surface a half second before the SUV and several feet away. An electric shock scorched Reid's entire body as they struck the frigid water. Every muscle went as taut as rubber bands stretched to their limit. The air rushed from his lungs so quickly he nearly passed out. The heavy vehicle bobbed for a moment and then sank; the suction of it sent them both tumbling over and over in the blackness until he didn't know which way was up.

Finally, his head broke through the surface. He sucked in a ragged breath, his body already threatening to give out in the freezing water. He looked around for Otets but saw nothing but bubbles. It would be too dark for him to see beneath the surface. If Otets had sunk with the car, if he hadn't gotten out in time, there would be nothing that Reid could do. He'd be dead already...

Something broke through the water a few feet from him. He reached for it and grabbed soggy clothing. The Russian's body was limp. He had lost consciousness—at least, hopefully that was all it was. He hauled Otets toward him and made sure his head was out of the water. It would be difficult to get anywhere with an unconscious man.

Don't panic. Move your limbs.

Reid positioned himself into a backwards butterfly stroke and wrapped his legs around Otets's torso. He moved his arms in wide circles, slowly and methodically—he didn't want to splash around too much and potentially give his position away to anyone looking down from above. He doubted the sports cars and Otets's men would simply give up and go home.

The current was strong, but he let it carry them southeast as they made their way to shore. It took several minutes, but soon it was shallow enough that he could stand. He took Otets's body over his shoulders in a fireman's carry and hauled him onto a narrow span of rocky beach.

The cold was worse out of the water. The subzero wind blew right through him and stiffened his wet clothes. He dropped Otets and checked to make sure he was still breathing by holding one finger just below his nostrils. He felt shallow, uneven breaths—Otets was alive, but had likely swallowed a good amount of water.

Reid huddled down, rubbing his chest rhythmically with both arms. He would need to find some shelter for them, and fast, before they both succumbed to hypothermia. He estimated he had between five and ten minutes before they'd both be dead. He gritted his teeth to keep them from chattering and hefted Otets up once again. To distract his mind from the raw, biting cold and the suspicion that he could be frozen in minutes, he tried to think of something else, anything else. Warm beaches. Hot showers. A cozy fireplace. His mind went to his girls, sitting in a hotel somewhere and worried sick over where their father might be and what was happening. He thought of Kate, his deceased wife and mother to his kids, and what she would do in this situation. He almost laughed bitterly—Kate would never have gotten into a situation like this. He barely knew how *he* had gotten into a situation like this.

Kent knew. Somewhere in the recesses of his mind was that knowledge, Kent's knowledge, of what had happened and why, for a while, he was no longer Kent Steele. It was clearer to him now; there was no denying it. They were memories, and they weren't false implanted memories like some top-secret CIA mind-control project or other such urban myth nonsense. The CIA, these flashing visions... they were his. They were his instincts, his voice, his training. No implanted memories could simulate the intuition, compulsion, and situational awareness he'd exhibited back in the facility or in the basement with the Iranians.

He didn't know how, but he *was* Kent Steele. Agent Zero. He didn't know why, but he—or someone else, perhaps—had taken all of that away from him. Suddenly Professor Reid Lawson felt like the lie. That other life, the quiet life in the Bronx and walks to the deli and lectures about pirates, all felt implanted and false.

No, he told himself. *That was your life, too. The girls are your children. Kate was your wife. It was all yours.*

But so was this.

Reid didn't even realize he had reached a road until headlights were blaring in his vision. He squinted, panicking, caught like a half-frozen deer in headlights. Otets's men had found him. There must have been a bridge or some quick way across the river, and he had carelessly stumbled right into the road in front of them. He couldn't run—even if he dropped Otets, he had so little strength left in his freezing limbs.

The car came to an abrupt halt and idled there for a few seconds. Then the driver's side door swung open. Reid couldn't see anyone, not even a silhouette, beyond the headlights.

"*Hallo?*" A woman's voice, pinched with nervousness. "*Heb je hulp nodig?*"

No recognition of her words sparked in Reid's mind. "Um, D-*deutsche?*" he stammered. "E-English? *Francais?*"

"*Francais, oui,*" she said back. "*As-tu besoin d-aide?*" Do you need help?

"*Oui, si'l vous plait,*" he said breathlessly. Yes, please. He took a couple of small steps toward her car. He heard her gasp in surprise—he must have looked awful. Frost had sprouted on his collar and in his hair, and it was likely his lips were a rich shade of blue. He told her in French, "We fell into the river..."

"Quickly!" she said urgently. "Into the car! Come along, get in." Her French-speaking accent registered something inside him—not the Kent Steele side, but the Reid Lawson side. She was Flemish, and her first attempt to talk to him must have been Dutch.

She opened the back door and helped him lay Otets across the seat. Warm air rushed out at Reid like a welcome breeze. The woman retrieved a thin blanket from the trunk. Instead of laying it over the Russian, Reid balled it up and used it to prop Otets's feet, to help the blood circulate to his heart and avoid shock. Then he climbed into the front seat and held his hands to the air vents.

The Flemish woman got back into the car and reached to turn the heater up. "Wait," Reid said in French. "Slow is better." He knew that if they tried to warm up too quickly after even the slightest onset of hypothermia, they could both go into shock—especially Otets, if he hadn't already.

"I should take you to the hospital," the woman said as she buckled her seatbelt. "It is not far—"

"No hospitals, please." He had a feeling that Otets's men might check the hospitals. Besides, he didn't want to be questioned—in fact, he planned to do the questioning, as soon as he was in a position to do so.

"But what about your friend?" she protested. "He could die!"

"No hospitals," Reid said firmly.

She glanced at him and her gaze met his. He could see the uncertainty flickering behind her green eyes, a conflict between wanting to do the right thing and potentially putting herself in some kind of danger.

He quickly looked her over; she was around forty, plain-featured, with calluses on her fingers and light etches crisscrossing the backs of her hands. *A farmer. Mostly likely barley, considering the area.*

The rest of their conversation was in French. It felt strange for Reid to speak it, to suddenly know the words as they came to his mind in English, but it was stranger still to hear a foreign language and instantly understand it as it was spoken.

"We were drinking," he explained. "We weren't watching where we were going, and we ran our car into the river…" "Your car is in the river?!" she exclaimed. "You're lucky to be alive!"

Reid rubbed his chest. His limbs were warming already, though his clothes were still stiff from the freezing night air. As he shrugged out of his wet jacket, he said, "Yes, but we're not hurt. Not badly, anyway. If we go to the hospital, they will ask questions. And if they find the truth, they will have to call the police."

She shook her head. "That was extremely stupid of you."

"I know. But please, no hospitals. Is there any place we can stay the night? An inn or a hostel, perhaps."

"But your friend," she said again, "he looks like he needs help…"

"He'll be okay. He's just very drunk." Reid hoped she hadn't noticed the gash across Otets's leg where the bullet had grazed him.

The woman sighed and shook her head. She murmured something in Dutch, and then in French she said, "I have a farm not far from here. There is a cabin. You can stay the night there." Her hesitant gaze met his again as she added, "It would be very good if I did not later regret this."

"You won't. I promise. Thank you."

They drove in silence for several minutes. Otets occasionally let out a soft moan, and at one point he vomited a small amount of river water onto the floor of the car.

At length, the woman asked him, "You are American?"

"Yes."

"And your friend?"

"Also American." Reid didn't want the woman to be in anyone's line of fire if the men from Otets's facility went canvassing the area for an American with a Russian man.

The digital clock on her car radio told him it was nearly one in the morning. "May I ask what you were doing out this late at night?" he ventured.

"My mother is ill in Brussels," she told him. "I was just returning from a visit."

"I'm sorry to hear that."

"Doctors say she'll live."

The rest of their drive was quiet. Reid had the distinct impression that the woman knew he was lying but didn't want to ask. That was a good idea on her part—plausible deniability—and besides, he wasn't going to share the truth, regardless of how hospitable she was being.

After about fifteen minutes they came to a dirt road that wound through a field of short-stalked winter barley. At the end of the narrow road was a small cabin, a single story made of stone and wood with a high peaked roof. She parked the car in front of it.

"Do you need help carrying him inside?" she asked.

"No, no. I'll get him. You've done more than enough." Reid did not want to leave the warmth of the car, but he forced his legs to move again. Nerve pain prickled up his thighs like needles, but he managed to sling Otets over his shoulders once more and carry him into the cabin.

The Flemish woman led the way, opening the door for them. She flicked on a switch and a single bare bulb glowed overhead. Reid set Otets down on a small green sofa that might have been older than he was. The cabin smelled musty and looked like it hadn't been used in some time; there was a fine coat of dust on every surface, and when she turned on the electric stove in the corner it was accompanied by a mild burning scent.

"That odor will fade," she told him. "There is a bed in the back room, some towels in the bathroom. There may be some food in the cupboards—help yourselves to whatever you'd like." She bit her lip, as if considering whether or not to ask. "Are you certain you'll be all right? It's not every day one finds two frozen men on the side of the road..." "We'll be fine," he assured her. "I can't thank you enough." *I could at least try*, he thought. He still had the bundle of euros in his pocket. They were soggy and wet, but he peeled off two bills, a hundred each, and held them out to her. "For your trouble."

She shook her head. "No trouble. I'm happy to help those in need."

"You didn't have to." He pushed the bills into her hand. "Please."

She took them and nodded graciously. Then she gestured toward the window. "See that light across the field? That is my house." She quickly added, "I'm not alone there."

"We won't be trouble. I gave you my word. We'll be gone in the morning."

The woman nodded once and then hurried out of the cabin. A moment later Reid heard her car's engine as it pulled away down the dirt road.

As soon as she was gone he pulled the curtains shut and stripped out of his wet shoes and clothes. It was not easy, stiff with frost and clinging to his skin as they were. He realized how exhausted his muscles felt—how generally exhausted he was. When was the last time he slept that he wasn't drugged or knocked unconscious? He could barely remember.

He draped his clothes on the mantel over the electric stove and then stood in front of it for several minutes, wearing just his boxer shorts and slowly warming his body and working his limbs to get the blood flowing fully again.

Then he turned his attention to Otets.

First he got the Russian out of his charcoal-gray suit. He pulled off his wingtip shoes, his cold wet socks, his jacket, trousers, and finally his white shirt. When he rolled Otets over to pull the shirt out from under him, Reid noticed that his back was covered in pale pink vertical scars, each about four to six inches long. They were either shallow swipes from a knife, or lashes from a whip; he couldn't tell which, but they looked like they were decades old, acquired in youth.

Otets occasionally mumbled unintelligibly under his breath. Reid couldn't understand if he was speaking Russian or English, but judging by the snarl of his lip, whatever he was saying wasn't pleasant. He unceremoniously dumped the soggy clothes into a pile, and then rolled Otets off the sofa and dragged him over to the electric stove, laying him on the threadbare carpet in front of it.

The kitchen of the cabin was little more than a short corridor with a steel sink, a hot plate, a cutting block, and two drawers. Reid filled a glass with water from the tap. When he brought it back, Otets had managed to pull himself up slightly, propped on his elbows.

"You," he said weakly in English. "You are madman. You know this?"

"I'm starting to figure that out," Reid said. "Drink."

Otets did not argue; he drank the entire glass, and when he was finished he took several small gasping breaths. He glanced down at himself as if only just now noticing that he was stripped to his briefs. "What is this you are doing?" he asked.

"I need you coherent." Back in Otets's facility, Reid's plan had been to get the Russian out of there and turn him over to the authorities. But he needed to know what was happening—to him, and possibly to many others, if his cogent hunch about a threat was right. He'd heard mention more than once now about a plan of some sort. And he was, after all, Kent Steele, CIA agent. He had figured this out before, or at least some of it. He would find out what he could, and then turn Otets over to the powers-that-be and get his life back.

"I will not tell you anything." Otets's head lolled slightly. His eyes were half-closed and bleary. He was in no position to fight back, let alone escape.

"We'll see." Reid retrieved the Glock from his jacket pocket. The Beretta was gone; he had lost it in the river, most likely. He returned to the kitchenette, set the glass in the sink, and disassembled the pistol. He knew it would still fire just fine despite the plunge in the river, but water in the chamber could corrode the barrel. He set the pieces on a dish towel and then opened each of the two drawers.

All right, he asked himself, *what can we use?*

The contents of the drawers were sparse, but among them he found a serrated steak knife—old, yet sturdy and sharp. He held it aloft and looked at his reflection in the blade. His stomach turned at the very thought of using it on a person.

He decided it was time to amend his acronym. With his girls, he used to ask himself, "What would Kate do?" The letters were the same—WWKD?—but the name was different.

What would Kent do?

The reply came instantly: *You already know the answer.*

He shuddered a little. It was strange having another voice in his head—no, not another voice, since Kent's voice was his own. It was another personality in his head, one that was so vastly different from the Reid Lawson that he thought he was that it was nearly nauseating.

Kent killed people.

In self-defense.

Kent went undercover in known terrorist cells.

Necessary for the security of our nation.

Kent drove cars over cliffs.

Out of necessity. Also, it was fun.

Reid leaned over the steel sink with both hands until the mild feeling of nausea passed. It was from swallowing river water and nothing else—definitely not insanity slowing creeping in, he told himself.

He desperately wanted the information that Otets knew, or even the information that Kent knew, but he couldn't shake the awful feeling that maybe he had done this to himself. It didn't seem to make sense, not based on what he currently knew, but still he couldn't get the thought out of his head. What if he had stumbled upon something so dangerous and potentially damaging that he needed to forget it? What if he, as Kent Steele, had the memory suppressor implanted for his own safety—or for the safety of his family?

"Why?" he asked himself quietly. "Why did this happen?" No memories sparked. No visions flashed.

He sighed, and then he gathered his supplies. From the drawers he took the steak knife and an old brown two-pronged extension cord. He found a tea kettle in the cupboard and filled it with water, and then retrieved a towel from the tiny bathroom in the rear of the cabin. Then he brought them all back to Otets.

The Russian looked like he was regaining some of his strength, or at the very least, some of his sense. He stared at Reid evenly as he set out all four objects on the floor between them.

"You intend to torture me," he said in English. It wasn't a question.

"I intend to get answers."

Otets shrugged with one shoulder. "Do what you will."

Reid was quiet for a long moment. Was getting information really worth what he was thinking about doing?

If it means keeping people alive—especially my girls—then yes.

"I'm going to be honest with you," said Reid. Otets glanced up in surprise, but his eyes remained narrow and suspicious. "You know who I am. Kent Steele, Agent Zero of the CIA, right? The problem is... I don't know that. I don't know what it means. Or at least I didn't, until very recently." He gestured to the butterfly bandage on his neck, where the Iranian interrogator had cut out the memory suppressor. "It seems I had my memory altered. I don't know why. I know some things—they come back in flashes—but not enough."

Why am I telling him all this?

You know why. Because he can't leave this room alive.

I won't kill an injured, unarmed man.

You'll have to.

"I don't believe you," said Otets firmly. "This is a... um, how do you say... ploy. This is a trick."

"It's not," Reid said simply. "And I don't need you to believe me. I need to work this out for myself, really. I was on to something— rather, Kent was on to something. The men we apprehended at Zagreb, Tehran, Madrid... I've had this feeling that they were connected, and now I have the distinct impression that they were connected to you. The sheikh, Mustafar, he knew things. He gave us those things, but he didn't know enough. I was building a case against some plan, an attack maybe, but I don't know enough to know what it is."

Otets smirked with half his mouth. "The sheikh knew nothing."

"The sheikh gave us things," Reid replied. He had seen it in his flashback. "Names, dates, locations…"

The smirk blossomed into a vicious grin. "The sheikh knew only enough to keep him involved. That is the beauty of our operation. Each of us is merely a piece in the puzzle, none more important than the next. Torture me if you wish, Agent, but I cannot tell you what I do not know—and I know only enough to keep myself involved as well."

"The Iranians who captured me," said Reid. "And Yuri, the Serbian, and the American he mentioned, and the Middle Eastern men in your facility…you're all working together. What's the connection?"

Otets said nothing. He merely stared in defiance, his mouth a straight line.

Reid casually picked up the extension cord and measured it out in spans, an arm's width each. "Do you know what these things are for?" He picked up the steak knife and cut the extension cord into two pieces.

"Gulag," said Otets. "You know this word, 'gulag'?"

"Russian prison camp," said Reid.

"Yes. Your government believes gulags were all closed when the Soviet Union dissolved. But no." Otets jerked a thumb over his shoulder, gesturing toward the crosshatched scars on his back. "There is nothing you can do to me worse than what has already been done."

"We'll see." Reid's arm shot out and grabbed Otets's wrist. The Russian tried to pull away, to struggle against him, but he was still too weak. Reid stuck out his opposite elbow and swiftly jabbed at Otets's forehead. The blow stunned him just enough for Reid to bind both wrists together tightly with the severed extension cord. The other piece he tied around both ankles.

He forced Otets to lie on his back, and then Reid straddled him across his chest, sitting atop him with his full weight pinning down his upper arms.

Imagine if that woman walked in here right now, said the Kent side of him. *What would she think was going on?*

Shut up. I don't want to do this. Even as he thought it, his hands were reaching for the towel.

It's the only way. Other than the knife. Or the gun. Would you prefer one of those?

Nausea rose up in his gut again, but he took a deep breath through his nose and forced it back down.

Otets stared up at him passively. He knew he didn't have the strength to fight. "Do what you will," he said. "I will tell you nothing."

Reid wrapped the towel around Otets's face, bunching up the ends behind his head and pulling it taut. He gripped it tightly in one fist under the Russian's head.

"Last chance," he said. "What is the plot? What's the connection between you, the Iranians, and the sheikh?"

Otets said nothing. His breaths came fast and anxious.

"Fine." Reid grabbed the tea kettle and poured water over the towel.

Some would call waterboarding an interrogation technique. Most would simply call it torture. It came to public prominence in 2004 when leaked CIA reports detailed its use on suspected terrorist cells. Reid knew all of this, but he knew more, and it came flooding back to him as he liberally poured water over Otets's face.

Waterboarding simulates the effects of drowning. The porous surface—in this case, a towel—becomes saturated and impermeable. The captive cannot breathe; water fills their passageways.

The average adult male can hold their breath for less than a minute.

After a few minutes, hypoxia will set in—lack of oxygen to the brain—and the captive will pass out. Of course, you want to try to stay within that threshold.

Potential side effects are damage to lungs. Brain damage. Extreme pain. Long-term psychological consequences. And, sometimes, death.

The muscles in Otets's neck went taut, standing stark against his white skin. He tried to jerk his head, but Reid held him fast. There was nowhere for him to go anyway, nowhere to escape the water. He grunted and choked beneath the towel. His bound limbs writhed beneath Reid.

He counted to sixty, and then pulled the towel off.

Otets sucked in a ragged gasp. His sclerae were bulging and red—he'd popped a few small blood vessels in his eyes. His shoulders heaved.

"What is the plot?" Reid asked again. "What is the connection?"

Otets glared up at him, his teeth clenched and breaths hissing. Still he said nothing.

"Have it your way." Reid held the towel over his face again, pulling it tight. Otets grunted and tried to thrash, but he couldn't move. Reid poured the water. Otets gagged and choked beneath the towel.

Reid counted again, staring at the wall. He didn't want the memory of what he was doing burned into his mind—but the vision came anyway.

A CIA black site. A captive, bound to a table on a slight incline. A hood over his head. Water, pouring. Not stopping. The captive thrashes so hard he breaks his own arm…

He shuddered and pulled the towel off again. Otets sucked in a deep, rattling breath. Small flecks of blood came with his exhalation; he'd bitten his tongue.

"We both know," Otets sputtered, "I will not leave this cabin alive."

"Maybe not," said Reid. "But we have *hours* until morning. We can do this over and over and over. And this can get far, far worse. You will tell me what I want to know. It's up to you how long that takes."

Otets gulped and winced. He gazed at the ceiling. He was thinking—and Reid knew that even if he was a killer, even if he was a terrorist, there was still a logical man in there. He knew Reid was right.

"Yuri used the word 'conglomerate,'" Reid said calmly. "What did he mean by that?"

Otets said nothing. Reid motioned with the towel again.

"Wait!" he cried out hoarsely. "Wait." Otets took a few panting breaths. "We are…many," he said at last. He did not meet Reid's gaze, but continued staring at the ceiling. "Once we were independent of one another, working within our own regions and countries. We called ourselves liberators and activists. You call us extremists, zealots, and terrorists."

"What does that mean, many?" Reid asked. "You're talking about different factions, cells, working together?" Suddenly the sheikh's words flashed through his mind again: *There were other conversations about the plans, but they were in German, Russian…I didn't understand!*"

"Unified," said Otets, "under Amun."

"Amun?" Reid repeated. "Who is Amun?"

Otets scoffed. "Amun is not a who. Amun is a what. As I told you, we each know only enough to keep us involved. Amun promises a new world. Niches for all. Amun has brought us together."

Reid shook his head. That name, Amun, sparked something in his memory—but not his new memories as Kent Steele. It was in his academic mind, the Professor Lawson side of him. "Are you talking about Amun-Ra? The Egyptian god?"

Otets grinned maliciously. "You know nothing of Amun."

"That's where you're wrong." He did know of Amun, or Amun-Ra, as the ancient Egyptian god was called after the New Kingdom was established. But the god had a storied history well before that. Reid had no idea whether this god Amun had anything to do with what Otets was describing, but his brain was churning.

"Amun started out as a small-time deity in the city of Thebes," Reid said. "As the city grew, so did Amun's influence. Eventually Thebes became the empire's capital and Amun, over centuries, became hailed as the 'king of gods,' a creator, much like the Greeks' Zeus. As Egypt grew, Amun's deification absorbed other gods, like the Tibetan god of war, Monthu, and the sun-god Ra…hence his rechristened namesake in the New Kingdom as Amun-Ra.

"Egypt's eighteenth dynasty brought some changes to Amun's regime. The pharaoh Amenhotep IV moved the capital from Thebes, and promoted a cult-like monotheistic worship of a god called Aten, along with many strict governmental changes that took power away from Amun's high priests. It didn't last long; immediately following Amenhotep's death, the priests struck the pharaoh's name from most records, reversed his bureaucratic amendments, and restored worship of Amun.

"They even convinced the new pharaoh, Amenhotep's son, to change his name to Tutankhamun—which literally meant 'the living image of Amun.'

"For more than two thousand years Amun was the high deity of Egypt, but slowly his influence declined as Christianity, and the Byzantine Empire, spread. That is, until about the sixth century when the last of the 'cult of Amun,' as they had come to be known by then, died out."

Reid smirked slightly, having proverbially taken Otets to school. The brief lecture had actually made him feel a little more like Reid Lawson again—and oddly, it felt almost foreign to him. He made a mental note to remain wary of that.

Otets, however, simply raised an eyebrow dubiously. "You know facts," he said. "But not truth."

"And what is the truth?" Reid asked.

"Amun brings us together, but we are each only a cog. We know only the other cogs we turn—we never see the clock."

Reid scoffed. "You're telling me that you, and others, are working toward some imminent end, but you don't know what it is?"

Otets tried to laugh, but it came out as a sputtering cough. "It is brilliant, is it not? My people, we have one job—make explosives and give to Iranians. They, in turn, work with others, who work with others. No one knows the full plan. We do not know names or who else is involved." His voice croaked. "We know only voices and numbers. Therein lies the difference—in a clock, remove a cog and the whole machine stops working. In Amun, no cog is so important it can take us apart."

"So Amun is a group?"

"Amun is much more. Amun is a force. And soon, this world will know it."

"No," said Reid. Organizing dissenters from around the world under a single banner? What Otets was describing would be impossible. There would be too much dissension among them, too many differing ideologies. But... if it was true that he knew very few of the people involved... "The sheikh said—"

"I told you, the sheikh knew almost nothing," Otets spat. "The information he gave you would already be changed by now. He was weak; he was a bank account to us, nothing more. A local faction had a bounty on Mustafar's head. We agreed to protection, destroyed them, in return for his funding."

A new thought sent a fresh chill through Reid—*What if that was what I discovered? Did Kent realize he had been fooled by false information, that he'd painted a target on his back? Was that the reason for the memory suppressor?* Ever since he had escaped the Parisian basement he had felt that powerful sense of obligation to keep going, to do something about this and discover what he had already discovered—but if Kent had done this to himself, maybe it was because he knew he would never back down otherwise.

"You called me Zero," said Reid. "And so did the Iranians. How do you know that name? What does it mean to you?"

"Agent Zero," said Otets slowly. "Many of us know you as Kent Steele, but *all* know of Agent Zero. Like a legend—an urban myth. A name that inspires fear in the most stalwart."

"Why?"

"Because of what you did."

Reid was growing frustrated with the short answers. "What did I do?"

"You truly do not remember, do you?" The Russian grinned. Blood stained his teeth. "That is for you to discover. Go ahead and kill me. I am no one of consequence, in the grand scheme."

"We'll see," said Reid. He dropped the dripping wet towel to the floor. "I'm not going to kill you. I'm going to call Interpol, and get the CIA involved. I'm going to turn you in. I'm going to tell them everything you've told me. But first, I want to know how the Iranians found me, back in New York. You knew they were coming to find me. You sent Yuri to that meeting to make sure I was dead, and to see if I had information on you. Isn't that right?"

"Of course," said Otets plainly. "I had to make sure my facility was not compromised."

"But how did they know who I was, and where to find me?"

Otets finally met Reid's gaze as he grinned maliciously. "Think about it, Agent. You already know the answer. The only people who would know where to find you were *your* people."

"My people?" Reid shook his head. "You mean someone in the CIA, working with you? With Amun?"

"Some*one*?" Otets chuckled hoarsely. "No. As I said—we are many."

Reid's mind flashed back to the meeting with Yuri. *"Before you I met only one other American in our, um… what is the word… conglomerate?"*

Reid grabbed the sopping towel and held it between both fists, mere inches from Otets's face. The Russian jerked his head back instinctively. "Names," Reid demanded. "I want names, or we're going again."

"In my jacket pocket," said Otets. His eyes were wide in fear, staring at the towel.

Reid tossed it aside and rose. He rifled through the wet charcoal-gray suit jacket. There was nothing in his pockets but a cell phone, and it had been thoroughly submerged in the river. But the SIM card would likely be salvageable, if he could find a…

There was movement in his periphery. He dropped the phone and spun just in time to see Otets lunging at him with the steak knife.

CHAPTER TEN

Reid leapt to the right to avoid the rushing blade. The knife's tip missed him by inches, but he overcompensated and tripped over the green sofa.

Otets's legs were free; while Reid was straddling him, he hadn't noticed that the binding around his ankles had come loose. The Russian held the knife in both hands, still bound at the wrists. His eyes were wide and bloodshot—standing there in just his briefs, he looked like a maniac.

Reid scrambled to his feet and put up both hands, palms out. "Don't," he said. "You're still weak from the river. Just drop the knife. No one needs to get hurt."

Otets shook his head vigorously, spraying water from his wet hair. "You still do not get it. I told you, I cannot leave here alive. If Amun finds out I gave you information, I am a dead man anyway."

"The police will put you in custody, somewhere safe, where no one can get to you—"

Otets laughed wildly. "Do not be stupid! Do you really believe we cared what Mustafar might have told you? Of course not! We only wanted to know his location ... so we could find him and kill him for his betrayal."

"Wait—"

Otets lunged forward, stabbing straight toward Reid's sternum. He twisted his torso to the left and, before he even knew what he was doing, forced Otets's elbows straight down. His wrists, straight up. In a motion quicker than Reid's own shocked thoughts, he

103

drove the knife into Otets's throat, guided by the Russian's own two hands.

A gurgle escaped his lips. A thin fountain of blood arced across the cabin, spattering the wall and floor. Otets collapsed in a heap, leaking liberally on the thin carpet.

Reid heaved a ragged, breathy sigh. It had happened so fast, and his body simply reacted without thinking. Once again he had someone else's blood on his hands. He sat heavily on the sofa, holding both hands out in front of him. His fingers did not tremble this time.

He had no captive to turn over to the authorities now, no one to corroborate his claims. Otets's bomb-making facility was destroyed, and he doubted the Russian was foolhardy enough to leave evidence or a paper trail. He had four dead bodies in a basement in Paris, a huge hole in the earth in Belgium, and now the possibility that someone—or more than one someone—was actively working against him in the CIA.

I didn't do this to myself, he decided. *This was done to me. To make me forget what I had learned ... so I wouldn't get in the way.*

He was certain of it. Kent had found something he wasn't supposed to find—possibly in Sheikh Mustafar—and his own people suppressed his memory. This organization, Amun, must have discovered that he was still alive from the mole (or moles) in the CIA. They found his location and gave it to the Iranians.

He had never felt so alone as he did in that moment, sitting in a tiny cabin in Belgium with the dead body of a Russian terrorist at his feet. Where would it be safe for him? Could he trust any authorities—or anyone at all, for that matter?

He had no idea what he was going to do, at least in the long term, but he knew what he had to do next. First, he put his clothes back on, now dried and warmed by the electric stove. He pulled on the sturdy brown boots and his bomber jacket. In the kitchen, he reassembled the Glock and put that in a pocket. He took apart Otets's phone, saved the SIM card, and crushed the rest of it thoroughly beneath a heel. The broken pieces he flushed down the toilet.

He put the knife, the extension cord, and the tea kettle back where he found them. He checked the pockets of Otets's slacks, but found nothing more than the phone. There was no wallet, no identification, no nothing.

Reid used the wet towel to clean as much of the blood as he could off of the walls and floor. Then he rolled Otets's body in the threadbare carpet, along with his still-wet clothes.

In a nightstand drawer of the rear bedroom was a Bible, and he found a pen in one of the kitchen drawers. On the inside front cover of the Bible he scribbled a note—he couldn't find any paper in the cabin.

Finally, he took the wool blanket from the cabin's bedroom. He turned off the lights and the electric stove and left the Bible on the front porch, just outside the door. In the morning, the Belgian woman would come to check on them, and hopefully she would question the book's placement and at least open the front cover, where she would find several more hundred-euro bills and Reid's note, written in French:

I'm sorry.

I gave you my word that we wouldn't cause you any trouble, but I was forced to break that. Please do not go into the cabin. The man that came here with me is dead inside. You should call the police. Ask them to get Interpol involved. Tell them that this man goes by a codename of "Otets." He ran a vineyard across the Meuse. His facility exploded last night. If they dig a little deeper, they'll find more.

I'm sorry this happened. I never meant to involve you.

The very first rays of dawn peeked over the horizon as Reid arrived in Brussels. He had started out by walking from the barley farm to the road, the wool blanket draped over his shoulders and around him. It was a bit scratchy, but at least it kept him warm against the freezing night. The occasional car passed by, and Reid stopped and stuck out a thumb—he wasn't sure if that was a universal hitchhiking gesture or not, and apparently neither did Kent, since no memory flashed. Eventually a pickup truck stopped for him. The driver spoke Dutch and only a little German, but he understood two things: *Brüssel*, and the fistful of euros Reid offered him.

The language barrier made for a quiet two-hour ride to the city. Reid had a lot of time to think. He felt awful about the position he had put the Flemish woman in, but he had little choice; he couldn't very well hide Otets's body. He couldn't have buried it, not with the ground frozen, and even if he could, if it had ever been discovered, the woman would take the blame. The decision to ask her to involve Interpol was a logical one, based on Otets's dealings. It was likely that the explosion at the facility had been seen or heard by someone and reported. He couldn't be sure that the local police would be able to separate the bomb components from the factory equipment and machinery.

He had thought briefly about leaving his name—or rather, Kent's name. The notion wasn't for the sake of some haughty claim or taunt, but rather in the hopes that it might reach CIA ears and rattle some cages. Assuming that Otets had told the truth, the mole, or moles, in the organization would likely get nervous and do something brash. Make a misstep. Furthermore, he didn't want the Belgian woman to take any sort of fall for what he had done. Ultimately, though, he decided against it. He needed to remain incognito for as long as he could.

He did not mention the name Amun in his note either, simply because he wasn't fully sure yet what it meant or what it was. If the wrong people thought that he knew, it might cause panic—and he needed answers more than he needed to be evading more bullets.

He asked the driver to drop him off somewhere downtown. He got out on Hallenstraat and paid the man. As he looked around, no visions flashed in his head. No memories sparked. Apparently Kent had never been to Brussels, or at least not this part of it.

The city's downtown took his breath away. The architecture was stunning; the amount of history on every block was simply awe-inspiring. He had once thought similarly of New York, when he had first moved there, but few structures in the US were more than two hundred years old. Here, in Belgium, he was standing in the center of more than a thousand years of Western civilization. The Professor Lawson side of him would have been downright giddy to explore such a historically rich city.

With that thought came a tinge of mild panic. He hadn't even realized it, but the further he delved into this plot, the less he still felt like Professor Reid Lawson. With each new development, with every life-threatening situation, and with all the new memories that returned, he was feeling more and more like Kent Steele.

He shook the thought from his head. He had two goals here in Brussels, both of which could be accomplished at one place. He paused at a street vendor and asked her in French where he might find the nearest Internet café, and then he followed her directions the six-block distance to a place called Cyber Voyageurs.

The café was just opening for the day when he arrived. The clerk, a young man wearing round, silver glasses, yawned at him and asked something in Dutch.

"English?" Reid asked.

"Yes, English. Can I help you?"

Reid ordered a coffee and pulled the SIM card out of his pocket. "I dropped my phone in the road and a car ran it over. But I managed to save the SIM. Can you get the information off of this?"

"That should not be a problem, as long as it is not damaged. Give me a few minutes." The young man took the card into a back room.

While Reid waited, he sipped his coffee and sat down at a computer to accomplish his second goal. First he created a new email account with an innocuous address, and then he logged into Skype.

"*I'll set up a fake account,*" Maya had told him yesterday, "*under another name. You'll know it.*"

He set up his own fake account, using the new email address and the name Alan Moon. It was the first name that popped into his head—the name on the side of the board game he had last played with his daughters before being taken hostage. Then he searched.

"You'll know it," he muttered to himself, stroking his chin stubble. "Let's try..." He searched for the name Kate Lawson. It seemed like the most likely choice in fake names for Maya to use. Several Kate Lawsons came up, but he was certain that Maya would include some identifying detail that would tell him it was her. "Too obvious," he scolded himself. "She's smarter than that." He tried Kate's maiden name, Schoeninger. Still nothing. He tried Katherine Lawson and Katherine Schoeninger, to no avail.

Then he almost smacked himself in the forehead. It should have been apparent right away. Kate's middle name was Joanne—and so was Maya's. He typed in "Katherine Joanne," and then almost laughed out loud. One of the results had the avatar of a tiny red plastic man, holding a rifle. It was a game piece, a soldier from Risk.

He clicked on the profile to send a message, but the words didn't come easily.

Am I being paranoid?

He closed his eyes.

No. You're being safe. Let's think this through.

If I'm right, and the CIA did this to me, then they know about my girls. And if Otets wasn't lying, and there are moles in the agency, it wouldn't be that hard for them to find a hotel reservation under the name Lawson.

He typed a message: *I need you to leave there. No questions asked. Don't tell me where you're going. Don't tell Aunt Linda. Don't tell anyone. Don't use your real names.*

Reid swallowed the lump in his throat as he fully realized what he was asking of Maya. He was asking his sixteen-year-old daughter to take her younger sister and simply leave, to go somewhere without telling anyone at all. But they needed to be safe. If something happened to them, he would never forgive himself.

Remember, he typed, *no phones. No police. Get on a bus and go somewhere you've never been before.* If they had done as he had asked and taken the cash advances on his credit cards, they should have enough money to last a little while. *Check in here with a message at least every twelve hours so I know you're okay. I'll check it as often as I'm able.*

He wanted to say more. He wanted to tell Maya that he was fine, and that he would be home soon. But he couldn't bring himself to type the words, knowing that they weren't at all true. He was far from fine. He had no idea if he would ever see them again.

I love you both.

Reid didn't wait for a reply. Maya told him she would check the account occasionally from the hotel computers, and he didn't expect her to be sitting in front of one, waiting for him to reach out (at least he certainly hoped she wasn't). He logged out and then cleared the computer's browsing history.

The young man came out of the back room, frowning and pinching the SIM card between two fingers as if it were an offensive insect. "I am sorry," he told Reid, "but there seems to be a problem."

Reid's heart sank. "You couldn't get anything off of it?"

The clerk shook his head. "Almost nothing. No contact, no photos…just a single text message. It could be that the card was damaged—"

"The text message," Reid interrupted. "What did it say?"

"It is an address," the man said. "But that is all."

"That's fine," Reid said quickly. "Can you write it down?" It was possible that the SIM card was damaged in the river, but he thought it was more likely that Otets was clever enough not to store contacts and sensitive information in a phone. He probably had an address book somewhere under lock and key (though now it was certainly incinerated). Reid felt a crushing pang of disappointment in his gut. The amount of hard evidence he had destroyed in that explosion might have put a lid on this whole thing, or at the very least given him a better lead than a single address sent by text message. "I don't suppose you got the phone number that sent it?" he asked.

The clerk shook his head. "It was blocked." He scribbled the address onto the back of a receipt, folded it, and handed it to Reid, who in turn slid a fifty-euro bill across the counter.

"You never saw me," he said. "And you certainly didn't write down an address."

The clerk nodded solemnly and pocketed the note. "I've already forgotten it."

Reid took a seat at a table in the far corner to finish his coffee, though it mostly sat there growing cold as he weighed his options. He could barely process everything that had happened in the last ten hours.

Try to chunk it, his academic brain told him. *Take these individual pieces and make them into a coherent concept. Then come to the logical conclusion.*

First and foremost, he decided, was that if everything he thought he knew was correct, then his girls were not safe. Hopefully he had taken care of that with his message, but that also meant that he could no longer simply give up and go home.

With Otets dead, he had no one to turn over to the authorities. He had no solid evidence; only the locations of bodies, burnt or shot or stabbed, and all at his hand. How would that look? And then, of course, was the bigger problem that he wasn't sure he could even trust the authorities.

Finally, there was himself—not the him that he knew, but this new aspect that was slowly spilling into his consciousness like a capsized oil tanker. His sense of urgency, of obligation, was growing stronger. The Kent Steele side of his brain was pushing him to keep going.

And at this point, he didn't see any other choice.

Reid unfolded the receipt paper the clerk had given him and checked the address, hoping it was close by. He deflated with a deep sigh when he saw it was in Zurich.

How the hell am I supposed to get to Switzerland?

A flight would take barely an hour, but he didn't have a passport or any identification at all; even if he could pay the airfare in cash, they wouldn't let him on a plane. The same would apply with a train. He didn't have a car—though a sudden flashing memory zipped through his brain to tell him that he knew how to disable an alarm and hotwire a vehicle. Even so, not every border would be as lax as France/Belgium was, and if the car was reported stolen, he'd have bigger problems on his hands.

He left the café and paced down the block, pausing to buy a scone so he would have something in his stomach. He took a seat on a bench and ate slowly, thinking. A truck rumbled past him, emblazoned with a yellow delivery company logo ... and it gave him an idea.

He stepped back into the bakery and asked where the closest supermarket was. The woman behind the counter told him there was a Carrefour Market about a twelve-minute walk from there. He thanked her and headed southeast on Rue Grétry. He found the market easily—it took up nearly half a city block—but instead of going inside, he went around to the rear, to the loading bays.

It took about forty-five minutes of milling about, but a truck finally pulled into the loading bay and slowly backed its trailer up to the rolling steel door at the back of the market. A portly driver in a derby cap climbed out and went inside for a few minutes, and then came out with his paperwork and lit a cigarette while the employees inside unloaded his cargo.

Reid approached and smiled. "*Deutsche?*" he asked.

"*Ja,*" said the man, somewhat suspiciously.

"I'm looking for a ride," Reid said in German. He flashed a few bills. "Heading south."

The truck driver took a long drag on his cigarette. "You are American?"

"Yes. I lost my passport, and I have no other way back."

The man smirked. "Drink a bit too much, eh? Ended up in Brussels?"

What is wrong with Americans that everyone assumes that? Reid thought. Still, it was a decent enough alibi. "Yes," he said, trying to look sheepish. "My family is waiting for me in Zurich."

The driver blew a plume of smoke through his nostrils. "I could lose my job for that."

"And I could be stuck in Belgium for weeks waiting for the embassy to help me," Reid countered. "Please."

The driver grunted and kicked at a small stone, sending it skittering across the lot. "I'm heading south," he said, "but not far enough for where you want to go. There's a truck depot on the way. We can stop in and I'll help get you another ride."

"Thank you." Reid handed him the bills.

The man pointed down the block. "Behind that building is a parking lot. Wait for me there."

Reid did as he was asked, hurrying down to the smaller lot adjacent to a business complex and waiting for the driver to pick him up. The truck rumbled into the lot about ten minutes later. The driver lifted the rear trailer gate just enough for Reid to scoot inside.

The trailer was refrigerated to protect the load of foodstuffs it was hauling, but Reid didn't mind. He still had the wool blanket, and he draped it over himself and hugged his knees to his chest. He'd dealt with worse cold mere hours ago. Besides—it was much better than being stopped at a border with no passport or identification.

As the truck rumbled southbound down E411, he pulled the blanket over his head to create a pocket of heat. He realized how exhausted he was and tried to doze off, but every time the truck hit a rut in the road he jolted alert. He wasn't yet accustomed to these new instincts; his muscles went taut as steel cables and his eyes scanned for threats. He had to constantly remind himself that he was in the back of a truck, alone, heading down a highway.

He thought about what he might find at the address in Zurich. If everything he had been through so far was any indication, he was certain it would be nothing good. In fact, he couldn't shake the feeling that there might have been a reason that it was the only piece of data in Otets's phone.

He couldn't help but feel that he might be walking into another trap.

CHAPTER ELEVEN

Reid took no time to appreciate the beauty of the wondrous city. Funny, he thought, that it used to be the tax-collecting hub of Roman provinces nearly two thousand years earlier, and now one of the world's financial capitals. *If we live through today, maybe we can come back and see it again sometime.* Kent's voice—it was his own inner voice, but the Kent side—teasing him.

The drive to Zurich had taken about seven hours, with only one short break at a rest stop in Luxembourg where the truck driver, as promised, organized a ride for Reid into Switzerland. The second truck was (thankfully) not refrigerated, but the trailer was still chilly with the winter weather. He left his wool blanket behind in the trailer when they arrived in the city.

He checked the address again, and paused to ask for directions to the street. It was a twenty-minute walk from where the truck had dropped him off. The weather was brisk, so he stuffed his hands in the pockets of his bomber jacket, his right fist wrapped around the Glock, as he tried to formulate a plan. He had no idea what he would find there, but he assumed the worst. Another violent faction hiding in plain sight, like the Iranians in Paris? Perhaps a bomb-making depot like Otets's facility? He couldn't very well just burst in with a gun drawn. Pretending to be a member hadn't worked out very well for him last time. No, he would have to scope it out first. He couldn't go in blind.

The address was an apartment on the southern end of the city, overlooking the Limmat, on the third floor of a white building that looked like it might have been an inn at one point. The year etched into a cornerstone told him that it was about three hundred and fifty years old, but the steel stairs winding up the northern side of the structure were certainly newer. From the street level he could see the entrance to the apartment on the third-story landing, the white paint on the door faded with age.

Reid meandered toward the riverbank and sat on a bench. In his periphery he could see the building and the apartment. From there he would be able to take note if anyone came or went. He admired the view of the river. Across the way was a tall stone cathedral with a sharp, rust-colored spire jabbing heavenward. A handful of geese landed on the water. All the while he kept the apartment in his field of vision, but there was no movement. No one came or went. The door never opened.

After twenty minutes he turned up the fleece collar of his jacket. It was cold; the temperature was in the twenties, maybe less. The few people he saw out and about hurried along toward their destination. A light snow began to fall.

An hour passed before he couldn't stand it any longer. The waiting and the frigid air were both getting to him and there had been no signs of life.

Reid took the steel stairs up to the third floor with one hand around the gun in his pocket. *I'll have the element of surprise,* he told himself. Not like at Otets's facility. And even then, they thought they had the drop on him and he'd escaped, hadn't he?

Despite the chill in the air, he felt tiny beads of sweat prickle on his brow, and...

And he realized something. He wasn't scared. He was nervous, and anxious, and even a little excited, but he wasn't afraid of what he might find. It was a very strange epiphany—because while *that* notion scared him, the concept of entering the apartment with unknown factors inside didn't.

The thought of not being scared was frightening.

He paused outside the door and put his ear to it. He couldn't hear anything coming from inside. The nearest window was a few feet from the entrance, but too far to reach from the landing.

There were only two ways to go from there: inside, or back down the stairs.

He stood outside the door for what felt like several moments too long.

You already know the answer, said the voice in his head. *There's no going back now. There's nothing to find behind you. Here, there might be something.*

Reid reached out and very carefully tried the knob. It was locked. He reared back, lifted his right foot, and kicked hard, planting his boot heel just above the lock. The jamb splintered and the door flew open. He had the Glock up instantly, trained at center mass and pivoting left and right and left again mechanically.

He was staring into a small but cozy kitchen, with an iron-grilled stovetop, cherry cabinets, a white single-basin sink, and a body on the floor.

The smell of death hit him immediately. His stomach turned at both the sight of the body and the fact that he recognized the scent as blood and early decay. It was lying halfway in the kitchen, its lower half over the threshold at an angle in such a way that the torso and upper body were obscured behind the doorway to the next room.

Reid choked down his impulse to gag and kept the gun aloft. *Murderers don't normally stick around,* he told himself, but even so, he ignored the body for now and stepped over it as he cleared the rest of the apartment—which, it turned out, was only one other room. Beyond the kitchen was a decently large parlor, with a small round dining table in one corner and a Murphy bed in the wall. Off to the right was a clean white bathroom with a claw-footed tub.

The apartment was empty. Well, mostly.

Reid pocketed the Glock and knelt beside the body. It was a man, face-down in a white collared shirt, black slacks, and black socks. He wasn't wearing shoes. And he was lying in a wide, liberal pool of dark, sticky blood.

The smell of death was strong; this wasn't a recent murder. Reid didn't want to touch the body, so he got down on his hands and knees, careful to avoid any blood, and peered into the puffy, bloated face. This man had been dead at least twenty-four hours, maybe a little more.

And then—a memory flashed through his head like a bolt of lightning. He saw the same face, but alive … a boyish smile, neatly combed hair, carrying a bit of extra weight in his chin and neck.

The Ritz in Madrid. Reidigger covers the hall as you kick in the door and catch the bomber off guard. The man goes for the gun on the bureau, but you're faster. You snap his wrist … Later Reidigger tells you he heard the sound from out in the corridor. Turned his stomach. Everyone laughs.

"Jesus," Reid whispered. He knew this man—he used to know this man. No, it was even more than that …

A hotel room in Abu Dhabi. Two a.m. Reidigger looks exhausted as he idly eats a slice of cold pizza. He offers you one. You're busy cleaning your gun.

"No thanks."

"Kent," he says, "I know this is hard, but—"

"No," you tell him. "You don't know."

"We're worried about you—"

"I'm going to find him, Alan. And I'm going to kill him. If you're not going to help me, then stay out of the way."

Reid sniffed once. His emotions were confusing and overwhelming. Tears were stinging in his eyes and he barely knew why. This man had been a friend, but he could hardly recall more than a few memories.

Your wedding. You stand next to Kate and hold both her hands. She's never looked more beautiful. You both say "I do." You head down the aisle, holding hands and smiling. Scanning the crowd as they applaud.

Near the back, you spot him. He wasn't supposed to come—could have blown your cover—but he snuck in anyway. He had to see. He gives you a grin and nods subtly before slipping out the back door …

Reid covered his face with both hands and sighed, trying to get a grip on himself. This man's name was Alan Reidigger, he knew. He was a friend. And he was an agent of the CIA.

You need to look around. Check his pockets. Find something. Or else this is a dead end.

"I don't want to touch the body." He was barely aware that he was talking to himself.

Reidigger hated getting his hands dirty—literally. Check the sink.

In the kitchen cupboard beneath the single-basin sink, Reid found a pair of yellow rubber gloves. He pulled them on up to his elbows, and then, after a moment of hesitation, he carefully lifted Reidigger's shoulder.

"Good god," he whispered. The front of the agent's shirt was completely soaked in blood. He had been stabbed—and not just once. There were small puncture wounds up his thighs, his abdomen, in both arms...

This was not a quick death. Someone wanted information from him.

Reid stood quickly and paced the parlor, taking deep breaths to calm himself. Once he'd worked up the nerve, he checked Reidigger's pockets. They were empty. He looked around the rest of the small apartment, but he didn't find a wallet, keys, a cell phone, or a service gun. They had taken it all.

Reid groaned in frustration. He had come this far, from France to Belgium to Switzerland, and for what? To find an old friend that he could barely remember, dead on a kitchen floor with no identification?

A phone rang. It startled Reid so much in the otherwise silent apartment that he spun and crouched into a defensive stance. It rang again. He followed the sound to a gray chaise in the corner. He lifted a pillow and found a black cordless phone beneath it.

A landline? The phone continued to ring in his hand as he decided whether or not he should answer it. The small display on the phone said that it was an unknown caller. He knew he shouldn't, but he had no other leads. Nowhere to go from here.

He pressed the green button on the phone and held it to his ear, but said nothing.

Someone breathed on the other end of the line for a moment. Then a male voice said, "It must be cold up there."

But you can't beat the view. The words spun through his head instantly, as instinctively as he might say "bless you" when he heard a sneeze.

It was a code. This was a call from the CIA—or rather, someone in the CIA. It was a code, and he knew it. But he said nothing.

"Did you hear me?" The voice seemed familiar somehow, but it didn't trigger any new memories. "I said, 'It must be cold up there…' Alan, are you there?"

"Alan's dead." He said it quietly, but didn't try to mask his voice. He had already answered the phone. Now he wanted to see if they recognized him. Besides, he wanted them to know what had happened.

"What? Who is this?" the voice demanded.

"You should send someone." Reidigger deserved to be brought home and buried.

There was a very pregnant pause. "Jesus," the voice breathed. "You sound almost like…" And then: "Kent?"

Reid stayed silent.

"I don't believe this," said the voice. "You were KIA… is it really you? That's incredible. Listen, stay there, okay? We'll send a team to get Reidigger and extract you—"

"Can't stay here," said Reid. "And I can't trust you."

"Kent, wait, just listen to me a second. Don't hang up. We'll come—" Reid ended the call. He muted the phone's ringer and tossed it back on the chaise.

Whether the mystery caller knew it or not, he had just given Reid three crucial pieces of information. First: he recognized Kent's voice, which corroborated a lot of what he had learned so far. Second: the man on the line hadn't seemed nearly as concerned with Reidigger's death as he was about hearing that Kent Steele was still alive, which raised Reid's suspicions that things were not on the up-and-up on the agency's side of things.

Third, and most importantly: they thought he was dead. The voice said he was KIA, killed in action. Did they genuinely think that, or was it deception? If the agency believed him dead, it would mean they weren't the ones that had put the memory suppressor in his head.

I couldn't have done this to myself. I wouldn't have. Even the Kent side of him agreed with that. *Someone must have done it.* A vision flashed across his mind—the hotel room in Abu Dhabi. Cold pizza. *"We're worried about you."*

Maybe it wasn't malevolent.

His gaze slowly swept over the room, toward the body lying on the floor.

Maybe it was an act of mercy.

Reid's heartbeat doubled its pace. One hand covered his mouth as he came to the realization. Someone else, someone besides Kent, must have known about the memory suppressor. The list of people that Kent would have known were on his side must have been a short one.

Reidigger was a friend. He was trustworthy. He would have been on that list.

The Iranians had gotten their information from a different source. They had tortured it out of this man, Reidigger. They had tortured and killed him to get Kent's location in New York.

Alan Reidigger had died because of him.

He felt something ignite in his chest, a feeling he'd never had before, or maybe just couldn't remember. It was heat, rising like a steadily fed fire. Anger...no. It was more than that. It was anger, and it was desire, and its kindling was the knowledge and accountability that he could do something about this. It was not the cold, mechanical instinct with which he had killed the Iranians and tortured Otets. It was the opposite—this was a savage ferocity blended with a passion to wrap his hands around the neck of the people that did this and watch the light die slowly in their eyes.

You have to get out of here, and soon. This time it was the Reid Lawson part of his mind urging him. Now that the CIA knew he was there they would undoubtedly send someone, maybe even a team, to the apartment. But despite his few new discoveries, he had no leads; nowhere to go from here.

He quickly tossed the place for any clues of what Reidigger might have been after, what op he was on in Zurich. He rifled through every cabinet and drawer. He checked the call history on the cordless phone, and even lifted the lid of the toilet tank. There was nothing, not even a suitcase—the killers had taken everything but the bloody clothes on Reidigger's back. It seemed they didn't want to make it easy on anyone who might have found him to identify the body and alert the proper authorities.

But he was an agent. And a smart one, at that. There's something here. If it was me, where would I hide it?

Reid ran his hands along the solid plaster walls, looking for any place where they might have been opened and patched over. He inspected the popcorn stucco ceiling. He looked for air vents or crawlspaces and found nothing.

Down, he thought. *Under.*

He walked the length of the floor, starting at one end and shifting his weight carefully from foot to foot on the hardwood. Occasionally a board would creak, and he knelt, working his fingertips into the edges to check for loose floorboards.

There were none.

He was starting to get frustrated. Maybe there was nothing to find but a cordless phone.

Or maybe the phone was where it was for a reason.

He had found it under a pillow on the chaise lounge. He couldn't tell if he was getting paranoid or if he was being thorough, but either way, he shoved the heavy chaise out of the corner and checked the floor beneath it.

Maybe your paranoia is making you thorough, he thought with a grim chuckle as he pried up a loose floorboard. Sure enough, in the space between two thick parallel joists was a small black backpack. He recognized it immediately.

A GOOD bag.

On any long-term op, an agent would have a GOOD bag prepped—a "Get out of Dodge" bag, or as some people called it, a bug-out bag. In the event one had to grab their stuff and run. A

GOOD bag would contain all the necessities for up to seventy-hours off the grid, and (in an agent's case) the means to get to another location or safe house quickly.

He pulled out the bag and unzipped it. Reidigger's bag was methodical and complete. Inside he found two bottles of water, two MREs, a first-aid kit, a thermal sweater, a change of socks and boxer shorts, a flashlight, duct tape, a Swiss army knife, a length of nylon rope, two road flares, and a trash bag. In the single front pocket were two American passports, an ample fold of cash in both euros and American dollars (for which Reid was most thankful, since his own stack was getting quite low), and a snub-nosed Walther PPK.

He took out the small silver and black pistol. It was a tiny gun in his hand, less than four inches high and one inch wide. *Six round magazine, .380 ACP caliber, non-slip slide surfacing.* Also in the front pouch was a spare clip.

Reid put the pistol back in the bag and took out the two passports. He was certain they would both bear some fake name and Reidigger's photo. The first one featured the former agent with a patchy beard and the alias Carl Fredericks, from Arkansas. He opened the second passport.

He fell back on his rear and thudded against the floorboards, staring in shock.

His own picture was staring back at him.

His face—Reid Lawson's face—gazed placidly from the ID page of the passport. He was at least five years younger, maybe more, in the picture, but there was no denying it. It was him. The name on the passport was Benjamin Cosgrove.

Ben. The same alias he had given Yuri, the first one that had popped into Reid's head when he needed a fake name, was here on this passport.

How?

He flipped through the pages to see if there were country stamps, and a small folded slip of paper fluttered out. He snatched it up and opened it—it was a handwritten note, and as soon as he saw it he immediately knew that it was Reidigger's handwriting.

Hey Zero, the note began.

If you're reading this, it's because what we did came back to bite us in the ass. I always thought it might, which is why I've been carrying this around ever since. And if I'm not reading this over your shoulder right now, well... I hope it was quick. Take the bag and GOOD. Do what you have to do. I should have let you finish it then. I hope you haven't had to pay for that now. —Alan

Reid read the note a second and then a third time. What did that mean, "what we did"? What was it that he had to do? Obviously he—as Kent Steele—was onto something. He had arrested the sheikh. He'd learned of the plot, and maybe even about Amun. But what did he know then that he didn't know now? He desperately wished that Reidigger was still alive to tell him something more, give him some sort of clue as to what he was supposed to do next.

Maybe he had. Reidigger was smart.

If Alan had thought for a second that something would happen to him and Kent would come back to find this, he would have known that a vague note wouldn't suffice. He had to have given Reid something more to go on.

He stuck the note and the passport back into the bag, and for good measure, he shook out Reidigger's fake passport as well. Sure enough, something fell out of his, too. It was a photograph, a folded four-by-six, the edges worn and the center crease white from being folded and unfolded dozens of times. It was a picture of the two of them, him and Reidigger, smiling and standing in front of an ornate fountain.

Why did Reidigger have this? He always was the sentimental type—the kind of guy that would break protocol for a picture. Or risk blowing his own cover to sneak into a friend's wedding.

No, he decided, it was more than that. There had to be a stronger motive for Alan to have kept this particular picture and left that particular note. He scrutinized it, looking past the faces...

I know this place. The Fontana delle Tartarughe—the Turtle Fountain, in the Piazza Mattei. The Sant'Angelo district of Rome, Italy.

He knew it—he knew it as Professor Reid Lawson, since it was a famous Renaissance-era fountain built by architect Giacomo della Porta—but it was more than that. He knew it as Kent Steele. He had been there, which was obvious from the photograph, but the place held a greater significance.

This was a meeting place. If anyone had to go dark, we would reconvene here. A vision flashed through his mind of four people—himself, Reidigger, a younger man with a cocky smile, and the mysterious woman, the gray-eyed Johansson. They had reconned the area. Determined it was a good place for a safe house. *There was an apartment building just off the plaza. It's quiet there, not much foot traffic. A good place to lay low.*

He folded the picture again, stuck it in the passport, and tucked it back into the bug-out bag. He replaced the floorboard and pulled the chaise back into position, and then slung one strap of the bag over a shoulder.

"I'm sorry," he murmured to Reidigger's body. "I don't know what we did, but I'm certain you didn't deserve this. I'm going to find out. And I'm going to make it right."

He pulled the broken door closed as best he could, and then hurried down the steel stairs to the street level. Zurich Hauptbahnhof, the city's central train station, was a short walk away. And then he'd be on his way to Rome.

The photograph had to be more than just nostalgia, Reid decided. It was a compass. He didn't know what he might find there, but Reidigger wanted him to follow it.

CHAPTER TWELVE

Deputy Director Shawn Cartwright took a deep breath before knocking twice on the oak office door. The message he had received only moments earlier had been explicit: *Come straight to the director's office. ASAFP.*

He hadn't even finished his coffee yet.

He pushed the door open a few inches. "Director Mullen? You wanted to see me, sir?"

"Cartwright, yes! Come in. Have a seat." Mullen sat behind his desk and smiled, but his nostrils flared. That was never a good sign—the pleasantry was likely a ruse.

Cartwright entered the office and closed the door behind him. At forty-four, he was considered relatively young in the hierarchy of the Central Intelligence Agency—at least he still had all his hair, though he did take to dyeing it black last year to hide the oncoming gray. He had spent five years heading up the Special Operations Group, which (as he liked to joke) was a fancy way of saying that he wasn't allowed to tell his wife how his day was. Eighteen months ago, he had been promoted to Deputy Director, overseeing the Special Activities Division in all international affairs. He was a man who built his reputation on efficiency, though his predecessor had mucked up so poorly with leaked documents and exposed field agents that it made it easy for him to look good.

Despite his advancement and general success, Cartwright had some trepidation in dealing with CIA Director Mullen. His superior was an expert at subterfuge and pretense, concealing his emotions while reading others'. Mullen's days in the field were long past him, but he still kept himself sharp with his daily interactions. Cartwright had to resort to the tiniest idiosyncrasies and mannerisms to detect the director's current mood—hence the flared nostrils, and the sinking feeling in his gut as he took a seat opposite Mullen.

"Good morning," said Mullen. He somehow managed to make the greeting sound spirited and joyless at the same time. He tented his fingers. He was a discerning man, fifty-six, his bald pate shining and waxed and ringed by a ridge of gray hair from ear to ear. "Did you happen to hear any whispers this morning, Cartwright?"

"Whispers, sir?" He had indeed heard whispers, in the elevator, and there was no use in trying to hide it from Mullen. "I might have heard some…rumblings. Something about an explosion in Belgium—a possible munitions factory?"

"Incendiaries," Mullen corrected. "At least that's what Interpol is saying at the moment. Hell of a blast; people saw it from miles away, on the highway. The facility was fronting as a vintner—"

"Vintner, sir?"

"Winemaker."

"Ah."

"And that's all you've heard?" Mullen asked casually.

"Yes, sir, that's all I've heard."

Mullen pursed his lips and nodded. "Then I suppose I get to be the one to tell you about the dead Russian found at a farmhouse about twelve miles away. Stabbed in the throat with a steak knife."

"Jesus," said Cartwright. "Connected?"

"Undoubtedly," Mullen replied. Cartwright was struggling to see why this meeting was between just the two of them, rather than a team briefing, when Mullen added, "There's more. Alan Reidigger is dead."

Cartwright stared in stunned shock. "Reidigger? Christ." When Cartwright was head of Special Ops Group, Reidigger had been one of his field agents. Alan hadn't been the most physically fit guy, or even the most cunning, but he was likeable, able-bodied, and very good at blending in. "How?"

"I'm glad you asked," said Director Mullen. He touched the screen on a tablet in front of him and opened an audio application. "This came from Steve Bolton, current head of Spec Ops, about eight minutes ago. Reidigger hadn't checked in for more than twenty-four hours, so he took a chance and called him. Here, give it a listen."

Mullen pressed the play button. "Alan's dead," said a male voice, tinny and distant. "Can't stay here. And I can't trust you."

Cartwright shook his head in confusion. "Sir, I'm not sure I follow."

"No?" said Mullen. "Try again." He pressed play on the audio clip.

"Alan's dead."

"Can't stay here. And I can't trust you."

The voice sounded familiar, but Cartwright was struggling to place it. Mullen played the clip again, watching the deputy director carefully. He played it again.

On the fourth time, Cartwright's eyes widened with both realization and sheer dread.

"No …" he said quietly. "No, there's no way." He avoided Mullen's discerning gaze. "He's dead. Zero is dead."

"He is certainly supposed to be," Mullen agreed. "It was *your* job to oversee that."

"And I did," Cartwright insisted. "This must be someone else, someone that knew him, or maybe wants us to think he's alive …"

"We're running a full voice analysis on this," said Mullen. "But I don't think we need to." The director folded his hands and leaned forward in his chair. "Cartwright, do you know how many bodies they've pulled out of that fire so far in Belgium? Six. And forensics is saying that every single one of them was already dead. Then we have tracks that led to an SUV at the bottom of a river—a goddamn sixty-foot drop! And last but not least, a dead Russian with his throat cut. That sound like anyone in particular to you, Deputy Director?"

Cartwright could do little more than shake his head and stare blankly at a coffee ring on Mullen's desk. It certainly sounded like someone they knew—someone they had known. Near the end, Zero had gotten reckless, unpredictable, wild even. One of the higher-ups had referred to him as "feral."

"But he's dead," was all Cartwright could say.

"Well, this whole thing is just tits-up." Mullen sighed. "So why don't you run through it with me quick? Because this need-to-know just became very need-to-know." At the time, Mullen hadn't wanted any details. He just wanted it done. And the thought of recounting the ordeal turned Cartwright's stomach.

"All right. I put Morris and, uh…" He sighed. "I put Morris and Reidigger on it…"

Mullen scoffed in disbelief. "His own guys? Christ, Cartwright."

"They volunteered!" he said defensively. "They knew how he was getting. They both came to me, separately, with their concerns. He was going to get himself shot or killed or both, and his reckless-ness could have compromised them, too. And then, after…well, you know what happened…and Zero got worse, they came back to me. They knew we were going to do it anyway, so the two of them offered to be the ones to carry it out. They were his friends. They wanted it done quick and clean."

"And they did it," Mullen said.

"Yes, sir."

"And now one of them is dead."

"…Yes, sir."

"And we have pretty good reason to believe that Zero was there."

Cartwright gulped. "It would appear so, sir."

"Your agents, did they have proof that they eliminated him?" Mullen asked prudently.

The deputy director looked up sharply. "Proof, sir?" Good lord, what was the director suggesting—that he should have asked his agents to bring him an ear? "Since when does Special Ops get proof? No, they buried it, and they sent him to the bottom of the river."

"At least that's what they told you," Mullen said.

"I trusted my guys." Director or not, Cartwright was starting to get irritated.

"The other one, Morris. He still works under you, yes? Where is he now?"

Cartwright thought for a moment. "Um... Morris is UC somewhere near Barcelona. He should be checking in sometime in the next six hours. What do you want me to do? Call him in?"

"No." Mullen stroked his chin. "But pull him off his op. I want him ready to fly on a moment's notice. Someone has murdered an agent, and as soon as this guy crops up again—whether it's Zero or not—you get Morris there. Clear?"

"Clear, sir."

"Take care of it this time. I'm not putting Bolton on this, or anyone else. This is up to you. We can't have this getting out. We can't have Internal Affairs sniffing around here. And we certainly can't risk a story leaking to the general public."

"Understood, sir."

"Good. Go."

Cartwright stood and buttoned his suit jacket. His legs felt weak. If Steele was still alive... well, he didn't want to think about what could happen.

With his hand on the doorknob, Mullen called out once more. "And Cartwright? It's shoot to kill. You understand? I won't have him rampaging across Europe again. That would be very bad for me... and for you."

"Yes, sir."

Cartwright hurried back to his office, nodding to colleagues as he passed and forcing a smile. As soon as he was inside with the door closed and locked, he heaved a sigh and made a call to Morris on the secure line.

He didn't bother with greetings or small talk. "We have reason to believe that Agent Zero might still be alive," he said sternly. "I need you to make it not so."

CHAPTER THIRTEEN

Reid noticed that the businesswoman across the aisle from him on the train had a tote bag with the corner of a laptop computer sticking out. "Excuse me," he leaned over and said quietly, "do you speak English?"

She raised an eyebrow suspiciously, but nodded once. "Yes."

"I know this may be forward, but may I borrow your computer for a moment? I just want to check in on my children."

At the mention of children, the woman softened visibly. "By all means." She pulled the computer from her bag and handed it to him.

"Thank you. I'll just be a few minutes."

The train ride from Zurich to Rome took nearly ten hours. A flight would have only taken about an hour and a half, and now that Reid had a passport, he could have hopped on a plane—but that would have meant dumping both the Glock and the Walther, and he wasn't in favor of the idea of going forward unarmed. So instead he had gotten on a train at Zurich Hauptbahnhof and took the overnight trip to Italy.

The seats were comfortable enough to sleep, but all he could manage was catnapping for twenty or thirty minutes at a time. He was having trouble quieting his mind. Would there be anything to find at the fountain? He would have to check the apartment, the former safe house for his team, but he doubted it was even still in use. He was very much aware that it could be another dead end—and then what would he do? Give up? Turn himself in to the CIA?

Absolutely not. Not while they think you're supposed to be dead. Not while they suspect you might have killed Reidigger. The last thing you want is to end up in a black site prison cell, like the sheikh. Death would be preferable.

He had to believe that there would be something at the fountain. He had to keep telling himself that Reidigger was a friend, and that there was a reason he had kept the photograph.

Reid powered the computer on and logged into Skype's website. He had a message waiting from Katherine Joanne's account.

It was just four simple words: *Are we in danger??*

His heart nearly broke, thinking of his girls holed up in a hotel with barely a clue of why they were there or what was happening, just the vague instructions that they should leave there, go somewhere they've never been before, avoid use of their phones, and not tell anyone where they were going. Even worse was that he couldn't answer Maya's question because he had no idea if the girls were in any real danger or not. The only thing he could do was assume that the same people who knew about him also knew about them—and that was enough for him to question their safety.

He decided that honesty was the best policy. Maya may have only been sixteen, but she was smart and capable, and he was asking a lot of her. Too much. She deserved something more to go on.

He typed: *It's possible. I don't know for sure. I'm sorry that I can't tell you more. I just want you both to be safe. Please, take care of your sister. I love you both.*

As he moved the cursor to log out, an icon appeared to show Katherine Joanne as online. A new message appeared: *You keep saying that. Like you're not coming back.*

He waited a moment for more, his throat tight, but nothing else came. He typed back, *I will. I promise.* And then he quickly logged out before the urge to tell her more grew too strong. He certainly wanted to—they were both so smart, and maybe even old enough to handle the truth, especially Maya—yet he simply couldn't risk endangering them any further. He wondered if Amun knew about the girls at all, or if they had simply decided to leave the children out of it. If it was the latter, how long would that last until they tried to use the girls against him? He hoped the kids had found some-where safe, outside the city, like he'd asked. He hoped their Aunt Linda was resisting the urge to get the police involved. He hoped the girls were staying off their phones. Most of all, he hoped that Reidigger hadn't said anything about them, despite the obvious tor-ture he had been through.

Reid stared blankly at the log-out screen as unthinkably hor-rible thoughts swam in his imagination—the very notion of the same kind of men that had come for him getting to his girls made him shiver.

I would kill every single one of them if they touched a hair on their heads.

He couldn't tell if that was Kent's thought or Reid's thought— the willingness to kill, to do unspeakable things to defend his family. It didn't matter, he realized; they were both a father. Besides, they were both the same person. Kent's thoughts, Reid's thoughts … they were both a part of him. The further he got, the more he grew to know Kent, and the less distinguishable the two personalities became. They were *him*, plain and simple. He knew that much now. One was just more vague and fuzzy than the other.

There was something else, some small nagging notion gently tugging at the edge of his subconscious like a child pulling on their mother's skirt. He'd felt this before; it almost felt like déjà vu, but he wasn't getting the feeling he'd been on a train from Zurich to Rome before. It was as if his mind wanted him to relive some memory that it knew was there, even if he didn't.

He saw Kate. He saw her in her white wedding dress on the day they said their vows. He saw her on a beach in Mexico on their hon-eymoon. He saw her smiling as she leaned over Maya's crib.

He saw her petrified, too far for him to reach in time, her mouth opened in the silent yawn of a scream …

And then the mental image of Kate blurred, turning amor-phous and indistinguishable. His forehead throbbed as a headache came on, swiftly and painfully. He held his temples and took even breaths.

The woman across the aisle leaned over. "Are you okay?"

"Yeah," he murmured. "Migraines."

The headache slowly receded over the course of a minute. *Strange*, he thought. He shook it off.

He was about to close the computer and give it back to the woman when he got another idea. He opened a new browser tab and did an Internet search for "Amun." Not surprisingly, the first several pages of results all had to do with the same subject, the ancient Egyptian god.

Reid had no idea what correlation, if any, there might be between the Egyptian god and the terrorist organization. But still he perused pages and read everything he could about Amun's rise and eventual decline. He already knew most of it. He tried to narrow his search to the sixth century's "cult of Amun," the last surviving group that worshiped the ancient god before Christianity stifled and extinguished the old deity's following. Yet he found little information about them, and even less that was new to him. He scanned several websites, looking for some detail, some sort of connection or possible explanation.

Then he saw it, and his blood ran cold.

On a website dedicated to Egyptian heritage and culture, he saw a symbol—a hieroglyph, somewhat crude but based on those found in archaeological digs. It appeared to be a feather, and next to it a rectangle, and below that a zigzagging line, the way a child would draw mountains.

He had seen that glyph before, a few times now, seared into the necks of three of the men he had killed. It was the hieroglyph of Amun.

What does it mean? Fanatics? Remnants of the cult? But why?

He rubbed his face. He was too tired to think straight without jumping to wild conjecture. Besides, he needed real leads, not stories about ancient gods and long-dead pharaohs. He closed the computer and gave it back to the woman, settled into his seat, and napped intermittently for the rest of the train trip.

They arrived in Rome as the sun was coming up once again. Reid was far from well rested, but at least he had managed to get some sleep. He bought an espresso at the train station, and while he waited, he struggled to remember what day it was, how long it had been since he was kidnapped from his home. Had it only been two days? It felt like a lot longer, as if it could have been weeks ago.

Much like in Paris, Kent's memories guided him along the streets of Rome. He knew it well, it seemed; street signs and sights ignited his limbic system like a lively pinball machine. He didn't even have to break his brisk stride to find the Piazza Mattei, and with it, the Fontana delle Tartarughe.

The fountain was not particularly large, or even all that grand in comparison to many others that Rome had to offer, but it was quite beautiful. In it, four bronze men held up a vasque, each with a hand upraised as if reaching for the very realistic turtles around the edge of the marble basin.

He stood there for a long moment, admiring it, fighting the urge to chuckle sardonically. How many times had Reid Lawson told himself that he would make this same trip? How often had he promised that one day he and the girls would visit Italy, Spain, France, Greece? And now here he stood, not for leisure but out of necessity, because his life quite literally depended on it.

A vision flashed—in his mind he saw four people, standing around the fountain, admiring it as if they were tourists. He was among them. Reidigger was there. A younger man, with dark hair and a cocky smile. *Morris.* And the blonde woman from his memories, the one with the slate-gray eyes. *Johansson.*

The four of us planned an op here, in the hotel across from the piazza. We reconned the area and established our safe house here. We stood in front of this fountain and asked an Asian tourist to take our picture. It was Reidigger's idea. Morris pretended not to like it. We knew we shouldn't. But we did it anyway.

He looked past the fountain, at the tall, white-bricked building behind it. It was the former manor house of the Mattei family, long since renovated into luxury apartments. He knew right away that the safe house was through the stone archway, into the courtyard, and up the stairs, the smallest unit on the second floor at the end of the hall. It had a window facing the fountain.

Reid glanced upward at the window. He couldn't see anything in the morning sunlight other than white curtains tied back with sashes from the inside.

He thought about whether or not he should go up. Would he find anything there? Was it even a safe house anymore, or would he be breaking in to find a family eating breakfast?

Why did I even come here? This was stupid of me, following an old photo for no good reason. I should have thought this through. I should have…

He felt a familiar yet distinct sensation, just like he had in the dive bar in Paris—he was being watched. He was certain of it; Kent's instincts were screaming at him. He acted casual, pretending to admire the fountain while circling around it and checking his periphery. As far as he could tell, he was alone in the piazza, but he was also surrounded on every side by several stories of windows.

I need to move.

He stuck his hand in his jacket pocket and wrapped it around the Glock. There was only one way for him to go; he wasn't about to leave, to give up after traveling so far. So he crossed the piazza and walked under the domed stone archway of the apartment building and into the courtyard, eager to get out from the view of all those windows.

The courtyard's gardens were well cared for—a new memory flashed of springtime in Rome, vibrant flowers growing in impeccable rows—though it was too cold for that now.

He followed the paved walkway to a set of stone stairs that led up and into the building. Just inside the foyer, to his left, was another set of stairs, which emptied into a corridor with two doors on each side. Reid ran his left hand along the wall as he quietly made his way down the hall. The plaster felt rough and old and uneven, yet there was a rich history in these walls. He had once been a small, almost negligible part of it, whether he remembered it or not.

He paused at the last door on the left. Behind it would be the safe house, the apartment that his team had established as a meeting place.

Reid adjusted the bug-out bag on his shoulder and clicked the safety off the Glock 27. He didn't take the pistol out, but leveled the barrel toward any potential threat he might find on the other side of the door.

He wanted to trust that Reidigger had sent him there for a reason. He wanted to believe that Alan had been on his side. He wanted to assume that the photograph was a clue that would point him to a safe place, another lead, the next step on this bizarre journey.

He tried the knob, gripping it with only two fingers and turning it slowly, very slowly.

It turned in his grasp.

He pushed the door open a few inches and carefully glanced into the apartment.

He was looking into a small living room. Almost everything about it looked old, right down to the plumbing and the worn exposed beams overhead. Someone had spruced the place up a bit from the image he had in his mind; there were fresh flowers on the coffee table and a few colorful throw pillows on the sofa, but otherwise every wall and piece of furniture was white or gray. It was a bizarre dichotomy, as if some vivid life form was trying to break through a neutral, bland existence.

Reid chanced pushing the door a bit further. He took a cautious step across the threshold, turning his body sideways and slipping inside. It didn't appear anyone was there.

Then—the telltale clink of a glass cup. A sink running. Someone yawned.

Reid froze. He could see only the edge of the kitchen, around the corner from the living room. But someone was there, moving around. He held his breath and took another step, moving his body entirely into the apartment. He slowly, slowly pushed the door closed behind him.

The hinges squealed.

"Hello?" A woman's voice. She came around the corner.

She had light, creamy skin and blonde, tousled hair pulled back into a loose ponytail. It was still early; she was in pajama pants and a tank top, as if she had just woken up.

But her face told a different story. Her slate-gray eyes were wide in shock and her mouth agape as she stared directly at Reid.

A teacup slipped from her grasp and shattered on the floor.

It was her. The woman from his memories.

Johansson.

CHAPTER FOURTEEN

"**K**ent Steele is alive."

The words ran through his head like a mantra, over and over. *Kent Steele is alive. Kent Steele is alive.* How strange it was that four seemingly simple words could raise such incredible ire, could make his blood boil and his lips curl involuntarily into a furious snarl.

Rais stood in front of the mirror in the dingy bathroom, his shirt off and draped over the shower rod. Two of the four light bulbs were burnt out in the vanity over the sink as he mixed bleach powder and peroxide in a small stainless steel bowl with a plastic spoon.

Amun had put the defector agent in direct contact with him. Rais did not know the agent's name; within Amun they referred to him only as Agent One, a flippant codename based on his former teammate, the infamous Agent Zero. Rais refused to refer to Kent Steele by anything but his real name. Agent Zero was a boogeyman, a monstrous bugbear that could become shadow and be anywhere. The name was whispered in fear and trepidation, even among members of Amun. But Rais knew all too well that Kent Steele was just a man, of flesh and blood.

Before today, Agent One's intel had always been sound. It had helped Amun stay one step ahead of the CIA in the past, to feed them false information and dead-ends, to throw other agents off their scent. But now—Kent Steele was alive.

With two fingers, Rais gently touched the dark, jagged scar that ran diagonally from just below his left nipple, down over his sternum, almost all the way to his belly button. Nearly two years ago, he had been personally assigned to kill Steele. But it had not gone well for him, not that time. His brethren had found him half-dead and holding in his own innards. Amun's doctors struggled for hours to keep him alive. Five months it had taken Rais to recover.

He began applying the bleach mixture to sections of his short, dark hair with a brush.

Agent One's intel had always been sound, except for a single instance: when he told Amun that Steele was dead. He promised he had taken care of it himself.

Yet Kent Steele was alive.

If it was anyone else, even Rais, Amun would act swiftly and mercilessly. Agent One would be dead within the hour for his transgression. But they needed him, and the agent knew it.

The call had come less than an hour earlier.

"Kent Steele is alive," Agent One told him over the phone, by way of greeting.

Rais prided himself on control over his emotion, but he found himself wavering as shock and fury washed over him. How strange that four seemingly simple words could inspire such bloodlust. His hand absentmindedly touched the scar on his chest.

Rais had been silent for a long moment. "That would be impossible," he said at last, evenly, keeping his voice from betraying his scorn. "Because you killed him."

"Thought I did," the agent said simply, as if merely thinking one had done something was to will it into existence. "Seemed he had some help from another, someone I thought was on my side. That guy's dead now, though, thanks to your people."

"Are you certain?" Rais asked. He chuckled so lightly it came out as barely a hiss of breath. "You seem to have some trouble telling the difference between dead and alive."

Agent One scoffed through the phone. "Look, your people told me you're the guy that gets things like this done, right? And I hear that you've got something of a personal, uh, *rapport* with Steele."

"Do you know where he is?" Rais asked.

"No, but I think I know where he'll be," the agent said. "There's only one place for him to go, and I'm going to catch him there. But if he's smart enough not to go there, that's where you come in."

"How will I know where to find him?" Rais asked.

"There's a way to flush him out. I don't like it much, but it might be necessary."

"Which is?"

"Hell no," Agent One snapped. "It's only a last resort. If I fail to get him, I'll tell you. I'm just putting you on alert." Then he hung up.

Rais let the color set for twenty minutes, sitting on the closed toilet lid and thinking. The bleach mixture made his scalp itch, but he ignored it. After the agent's call, Rais had immediately set to changing his appearance so that he might not be recognizable to Kent Steele. Back when they had last encountered each other, Rais had a thin beard, which he had shaved off. He bleached his dark hair, and while he waited for the color to set he put blue contacts in his eyes to hide his emerald-hued irises.

What the snarky Agent One did not know was that Amun had already put Rais on alert. Four of the Iranians were found dead in a Parisian basement after failing to check in at the appointed time. The explosion at the Russian's facility was all over the news—though according to the media, a gas pipeline had been responsible for destroying the vineyard. There was no mention of bomb-making or connections to any radical extremist groups.

Rais switched phones, flipping open an ancient Nokia, and made a call. On any given day he used up to five different phones and changed them out regularly. He fully realized that some might call him paranoid. He thought of himself as thorough.

The man on the other end of the call answered but did not speak.

"We are tracking Agent One's movement?" Rais asked quietly.

"Yes," came a hoarse whisper.

"I want to know where he goes." Rais snapped the phone shut. He was sure the agent would fail again, and when he did, Rais would find Steele and make absolutely certain that he was dead.

He touched the glyph on his right bicep. It was rectangular, no larger than a quarter, the skin there raised and pink where the symbol had been seared into his flesh. It was an incredible honor to be marked with the glyph of Amun. The physical and mental trials one had to perform to become a member of the inner circle would, and often did, send most men to madness or suicide.

The mark on Rais's arm, however, was not as visibly apparent as so many others. It was common to have the glyph branded on the neck, to wear and display it proudly, but Rais's position required an amount of subterfuge, the ability to blend into a crowd and not be easily identifiable. His superiors understood that and had allowed the brand on his arm, rather than his neck.

Some of his peers, on the other hand, did not understand and a few had even gone so far as to mock him and question his devotion to the cause. Rais had an elementary solution to the chastisement: he had put both his thumbs into the eye sockets of the last man who had questioned his loyalty.

Once the bleach had set, Rais washed his hair in the dirty, ringed tub. He wondered where Steele might go next. It would be impossible to track his whereabouts without the annoying agent first making a move. Rais had no choice but to wait. He was a patient man—a trait not often shared by many of his background. Others who had denounced the culture and heritage of their birthplace might have been inclined to forget it, to push it from memory and focus on the present, but not Rais. It was important for him to remember where he came from. It reminded him of his motivations and strengthened his resolve.

Rais had earned his mark, though his position within Amun compelled him to hide it when necessary. His formative years of military training and subsequent time spent stealing on the streets of Egypt served him equally well as an assassin. He had gained prominence among his brothers. He had found purpose.

And then Kent Steele entered the picture.

It had been an epic confrontation. Just thinking about it raised the hairs on Rais's arms. He had very nearly bested the agent—had him on his back with a gun to his head. But it misfired. A faulty trigger pin, just a tiny oblong of metal, had made the decision between life and death for him. Steele had a knife in his boot, and he opened Rais from navel to pectoral, and then he left him to die slowly, holding his own insides.

Five months it took him to fully recover. Five torturous, grueling months of negative-pressure wound therapy and vacuum-assisted closure, of medical corsets and necrotic tissue.

Rais checked himself in the mirror, content with his clean-shaven cheeks, bleach job, and blue eyes. To him, he still looked like himself, like Rais, but he hoped it would be enough to dupe Steele, at least temporarily—enough for him to get close, and to plunge a knife between the agent's ribs. He would not fail this time.

He pulled on a black T-shirt and left the bathroom. The living room smelled like smoke again; the other three were sitting at the small round table, sharing cigarettes and playing dominos. Rais scowled. These men, this trio of Serbians, they were not Amun. They were a faction of some liberation movement that Amun had gathered into the fold in order to assist with their grand scheme. Rais had been assigned to this place, this rural, ramshackle house in eastern Spain, to keep tabs on these three. They were responsible for tracking and noting flight paths going to and from Sion, but Amun thought them to be somewhat unreliable—and based on what Rais had seen so far, they were right to be concerned.

These fools, they thought they were Amun. That was the promise: join us, become us, and enjoy the fruits of the new world alongside us. Gain your own foothold in the earth. A piece for everyone, and everyone is a piece.

These men had no idea.

The largest of the three, a bearded, imposing man named Nikola, glanced up and immediately let out a snort at Rais's altered appearance—his clean cheeks, blond hair, and blue eyes.

"What is this you are doing?" he asked in accented English. "You look like, eh, movie star." His two cohorts laughed.

Rais smirked. "I am going to kill someone. So I must reestablish my Western credentials."

Nikola frowned. "What does this mean?"

Rais strode over to their small, round table and plucked up the silenced Sig Sauer that sat in its center. Without a moment's hesitation, he fired three quick shots, each a sharp *thwip* of compressed air, into the foreheads of the three Serbians.

"Useless," he muttered. He rubbed his prints from the gun and set it in the center of the table. He took the SIM cards from each of their phones and crushed them. Then he set about wiping the place clean of any indication he had been there.

He made a call to alert Amun to the unfortunate demise of the three Serbians. Then he grabbed his bag and left the house, headed toward Barcelona. Amun was tracking the agent, and the agent was tracking Steele. The irritating turncoat Agent One feeding them information—he would fail. It would be Rais who struck the final blow.

CHAPTER FIFTEEN

"**K**ent?"

The shattered remains of the teacup lay between them—Reid, just inside the door to the apartment, and the woman, the gray-eyed Johansson from his memory, just beyond the small adjacent kitchen. Her face drained of color. Her bottom lip trembled.

"You..." She shook her head, and her blonde hair shook with it. "You're dead."

People keep telling me that, he thought, but he didn't say anything. He didn't know this woman. Maybe he had, once, but he didn't now.

"I don't...I just..." she stammered, at a loss for words. "Is it really you?"

He didn't know what to say. He decided on the only thing that made sense to him in the moment: "Yeah. It's me."

"God. You look like hell." She let out a short laugh. "Kent, I just can't believe this!" She moved to take a step forward, but Reid held up both hands. She froze, an eyebrow raised.

He pointed down at the floor. "Glass." Her feet were bare on the tiled floor.

She looked down quizzically, as if only now noticing that a cup had broken, and then she leapt deftly over the shards toward him. Before he could even get his hand out of his pocket, she flung her arms around him and pulled him close, burying her head in his neck.

"God, I can't believe it! You're alive! Why didn't you reach out, try to contact me? Jesus, you're alive!"

Reid let her hug him, but he didn't hug her back. Still, there was something about her, just the sight and feel of her, that stirred something inside him. Before, it had been passion and excitement. This time it was warmth, a feeling bordering on joy, like seeing an old friend come through the gate of an airport—maybe more than that. He could smell her hair, a fruity shampoo, lavender skin lotion, and...

The two of you sit at the bar in a dive joint in Malta. The place is packed, but no one else matters. The light of the neon sign in the window dances in her gray eyes. Your fingers touch, just barely. You lean toward her. She does too...

He grunted as a headache came on again. It felt like an intense pressure in his head, as if something was in his skull and trying to escape.

Johansson pulled away. "Are you okay?" she asked in alarm. "What's wrong?"

"It's... kind of a long story," he groaned.

"Are you in some kind of trouble?"

"Yeah," he said simply.

"Were you followed here? Have you seen any of the other—"

"Wait." The pain subsided and he shrugged away from her grasp. "Just wait a second. How do I know I can trust you?"

She took a step back and furrowed her brow. "What are you talking about? It's me. Maria. Of course you can trust me. You know me."

"No. I don't." He shook his head. "I'm sorry."

"I don't understand."

"Like I said. It's a long story."

"Well, I want to hear it," she insisted.

He scrutinized her. She seemed sincere, in both her concern about him and her desire to help. Reid Lawson might not have been all that great at reading people, but he trusted that Kent Steele was, and there were no alarm bells going off in his head.

Even so, he had questions. "You say I can trust you, but you're holed up in a safe house?"

"It's not what you think," she said. "I'm... well, I'm squatting, on the US government's dime." She frowned. "You don't remember?"

"No." Reid looked her up and down. There was nowhere on her slight figure she could have been hiding a gun. At the same time, he couldn't help but notice that her skin was flawless, not a discernible scar anywhere. Her hair fell in glossy waves around her shoulders, so bright and perfectly blonde it seemed nearly luminescent. The feeling stirred inside him again—one of longing, of desire.

Snap out of it, he scolded himself.

"You," he said. "You're CIA."

"I was. Not anymore. I haven't been for a little while now. Shortly after you … well, after you died, I was disavowed."

Disavowed. She went rogue. The agency denied all responsibility or even knowledge of her as an agent.

"Why?"

She pushed the door fully closed behind him, stepped over the glass remains of the teacup, and waved him inside. "I went looking for what you were looking for," she said vaguely. "Then I refused to come back when they called me. So I was disavowed."

Johansson disappeared for a moment into the kitchen and emerged again with a thin broom and a plastic dustpan. She knelt to clean up the broken cup.

Reid decided to trust her, at least until she gave him a reason not to. He slowly took his hand out of his pocket as he stepped into the living room. "And you're sure we're safe here?" he asked, looking around.

"No one else knows about it besides the four of us."

"The others, Reidigger and Morris … they didn't come looking?"

Johansson snorted. "No, Kent. Disavowed means that active agents forget your face. Yeah, they were friends, but they're still on the job, far as I know. If the agency caught wind they had found me, they'd be up shit's creek, too."

Reid shook his head. He wanted very much to tell her about Reidigger, but he didn't feel it was the right time. He wanted answers first.

But so did she. As she stood again, she said, "Christ, Kent, where have you been? And what is going on with your head? Why are you acting like you don't remember any of this?"

"Because I don't." He dropped Reidigger's bug-out bag on the sofa, and then carefully peeled the butterfly bandage from his neck and turned slightly to show her the wound where the Iranian interrogator had sliced the small, grain-like device out of him.

"Oh my god," she breathed. "That looks like it's getting infected. Come with me." She grabbed his hand and led him into a small bathroom off the kitchen with frosted glass windows and white fixtures. "Sit." He did so, sitting on the toilet lid while she rummaged in a cabinet for first-aid supplies. "I'll clean this up," she said, "but you're going to have to tell me everything."

"I will," he promised.

He started at the most logical place, the beginning. Reid told her about sitting in his study in New York, close to midnight, when the three Iranians came for him. He told her how they drugged him and put him on a cargo plane to Paris. He told her about the basement, and the interrogator, and cutting the tiny rice-like device out of his neck.

"He called it a memory suppressor." He winced as Johansson pressed a warm, damp washcloth to the wound.

"Jesus," she murmured. "How did you even get your hands on one of those?"

He looked up sharply. "You know about it?"

"I know a little. I've heard things." She rubbed the dried blood from the edges of the wound, and then squeezed pink water from the washcloth into the sink. "The agency's been obsessed with memory control as far back as anyone can remember. Suppressing memories, altering memories, accessing memories... I'm sure there's some really bizarre stuff going down in some underground clean-room somewhere."

"But this is real," he said, "obviously. I didn't remember anything at all about being Kent."

"And the memories didn't come back when they cut it out?" she asked.

"No. I mean, a little. They were fuzzy at first, strange and disjointed. They've been coming back a bit at a time, especially when I see something or hear certain words, it triggers a vision in my head. It's like flipping through channels on a TV, and just getting a brief glimpse of what's on." He looked her in the eye. She didn't. "What have you heard about it?"

She sighed. "I know it was highly experimental, potentially dangerous. It supposedly works based on cognitive therapy—"

"What does that mean?"

"It means that after they put it in you, someone's there to tell your brain what to forget," she explained. "Sort of like hypnosis—power of suggestion and that kind of stuff." She squeezed some ointment onto a cotton ball and dabbed at his neck.

"So you're saying I couldn't have done this to myself."

"No," she replied. "That would have been impossible."

"This whole situation is impossible," he muttered. "Three days ago I thought I was a European history professor living in the Bronx with my kids. Now I'm a CIA agent who was killed in action for trying to uncover a terrorist plot. How can that be?"

Johansson shrugged. "We all have our cover, Kent. According to most of the world, I'm a CPA from Baltimore. I can even do your taxes. We're well trained. We lead two lives. That's the way it's always been."

He shook his head. "But I would have gaps in my memory. If I was here before, as Kent, where would I have thought I was as Reid?"

"Your mind fills it in," she said simply. "Our brains are pretty amazing. We think in terms of reality. You must have been somewhere, so your brain makes up the details for you." She tore open the paper packaging on a fresh bandage. "It's like this study that was done a few years ago, on insurance claims. This company interviewed a dozen witnesses of a car accident, and they asked, 'What color was the driver's hat?' Only a couple of people actually remembered, but not a single person said, 'I don't know.' Their brains filled in the detail, and they were all sure of themselves. The insurance company got five different answers."

"So you're saying that not only do I have Kent's memories, but some of my memories as Reid might not even be real?" *Jesus*, he thought, *that's the last thing I need, to start doubting what I thought was certain.*

"I don't have all the answers. I'm just telling you what I've heard." She pressed the bandage over the wound on his neck and smoothed the edges with her fingertips. Her hands felt warm. Something stirred again, deep inside him. He definitely noticed that she was leaning over his shoulder, the low neck of her tank top forming shadows between her breasts. He could feel her soft breath near his ear.

"These visions … have you had any about me?" she asked, trying to sound casual.

"Not really," he said candidly. "I know you were a part of my team. Maybe even … a friend."

"That's it?"

"That's it. I'm sorry. I don't know why, but every time you cross my mind, the memory fades and I get this intense headache, like a migraine that only lasts for a minute or so."

"Hmm." She straightened and chewed her lower lip, thinking. "Could be a side effect of the way they cut it out of you. I can't imagine that was good for your limbic system. I hope it's not permanent." Then, quietly, she added, "I'd like you to remember me."

They were silent for several seconds, both staring at the white tiled floor. Then Johansson cleared her throat and said, "Take off your pants."

"What?"

"Take off your pants." She pointed. A small amount of blood had soaked through his jeans. Apparently the super glue he'd used to close the knife wound on his thigh hadn't held.

"Oh. Yeah. Okay." He slid out of his bomber jacket and then took off his jeans, draping both over the tub. He sat again on the toilet and Johansson knelt on the floor in front of him, poking at the wound.

"Super glue, Kent?" She scoffed. "Anyway, back to Paris. The Iranians in the basement. What happened with them? How'd you get out?"

"I killed them." He scanned her for any physical response to his statement, but there was none. She was impassive.

"I'm going to need tweezers for this," she muttered. "And then...?"

"Then I went to a bar." He told her about the meeting with Yuri, the car ride to Belgium, and escaping Otets's compound.

She chuckled lightly. "You know, when I heard about that, my first thought was of you. It had 'Kent Steele' written all over it."

He raised an eyebrow. "And how did you hear about it?"

"I read about it in the news, online," she said simply.

She read about an explosion at a vineyard and thought of me? Strange.

"I didn't see a computer when I came in," he countered.

Johansson rolled her eyes. "On my phone. Jeez, you're being paranoid."

Don't tell her about Reidigger, his mind whispered to him. Only Amun and the CIA knew about that. If she brought it up, he would know she was still on the inside.

"So how did you know to come here?" she asked.

He winced as she tugged dried super glue from his cut with a pair of tweezers. "I saw a fountain in Belgium," he lied. "It triggered a memory."

"Odd," she said. "You wouldn't have known I was here."

"But I knew the safe house was. Speaking of, why are you here?"

"Like I said, I'm squatting." She flashed a smirk. "You and Reidigger set this up a while back," she explained. "We were on an op that was going to take us to Milan. The two of you signed a five-year lease on the place under the alias of a wealthy entrepreneur from California. You hid it in the expense report as an armored transport and ammunition."

Okay," he said slowly, "but what I meant was, how did you end up here? You said you went looking for what I was looking for."

"I'm guessing you don't remember that part," she said softly. "You were looking for someone, a member of the Fraternity—"

"The Fraternity?"

"That's what we called them. The terrorist collective."

Should I tell her about Amun?

No. Not yet. Wait and see what she knows first.

"Did you find him?" he asked.

"No," she said, not hiding the disappointment in her voice. "Guy's a ghost."

"What's so important about him?" Reid pressed.

"To you? He was a lead. To me?" She was quiet for a moment. "He's the one they said killed you."

"Well, obviously not, if I'm here—ow!" He hissed as Johansson pulled the last bit of glue from the cut. "How long have I been dead?"

"Um..." She bit her lip again and looked upward. "It'll be nineteen months next week."

"Nineteen months," he repeated wistfully. That was certainly odd, that she knew the anniversary of his death down to the week. He had the distinct feeling, and the inkling of memory, that the two of them had been more than just teammates or friends. "I was on to something—*we* were on to something," he said. "A plot, by this 'Fraternity,' that's been in the works for a while...a couple years, maybe more. What do you know about that?"

She shrugged as she cleaned the wound on his thigh. "Only what we found out together."

"Remind me."

Johansson sighed. "All right." She took another bandage from the cabinet and unwrapped it. "A little more than two years ago, the NSA intercepted some suspicious emails. They were to an Iranian-born engineer living in Virginia. The guy was clean, but the emails weren't—the engineer was trying to talk his brother out of doing something, begging him to go home, and the replies were chock-full of threats and 'death in the name of Allah' kind of stuff. We got involved, and traced the IP to Spain..."

"The Ritz, in Madrid," Reid said knowingly. "The suitcase bomber." The vision flashed through his head again. *You kick in the door and catch the bomber off guard. The man goes for the gun on the bureau, but you're faster. You snap his wrist... Later Reidigger tells you he heard the sound from out in the corridor. Turned his stomach.*

"Exactly," said Johansson as she carefully pressed the bandage over his thigh. "You were the one that nabbed him. Guy was young, and scared out of his mind. He was a sleeper for an Islamic radical group that had just been inducted into the Fraternity, but we didn't know that yet. He could only give us two names, a couple of his associates. It took us a while, but we tracked them to an airstrip in Zagreb..."

"Trying to board a plane." Reid had had that vision too, of him and Morris chasing down the two Iranians on the tarmac.

"...Right," said Johansson slowly. "Are you sure you lost your memory? You seem to know a lot of this."

"In the basement, in Paris, they asked about all of these places," Reid explained. "Some of it came back to me. But like I said, it was all disjointed and muddled." *But it's starting to come together now.*

"Anyway," she continued, "those two were tougher nuts to crack. Believe me, we tried."

Another familiar vision flashed through Reid's mind, the same one that had come to him when he was waterboarding Otets—*A CIA black site. A captive, bound to a table on a slight incline. A hood over his head. Water, pouring. Not stopping. The captive thrashes so hard he breaks his own arm...* He shook the awful sight out of his head.

"Ultimately it was the plane itself that gave us the next lead," Johansson told him. With his wound clean, she sat on the floor in front of him, her knees drawn up near her chest. "It was owned by a holdings company out of Tehran. After a little digging we found out it was a shell corporation used for money laundering. The owner was a wealthy sheikh—"

"Mustafar." *You know, Sheikh... a bullet sounds the same in every language.* He had said that, at the CIA black site in Morocco.

"Right. He was bankrolling the Iranians, who were funneling the money to the Fraternity—that's the first time we heard about them, and that's where they made their mistake. The sheikh had everything to lose, and he spilled his guts. He gave us names, locations, dates..."

"But they turned out to be false leads, right?" Reid interjected. "The sheikh didn't actually have anything valuable."

"The few things he did know were dead ends, literally. The Fraternity knew we'd gotten to the sheikh and they tied their loose ends quickly," said Johansson. "It was a trail of cold bodies with no evidence. Then it got worse. That first guy, the suitcase bomber from Madrid? Someone got to him. A member of the Fraternity managed to infiltrate a secure black site just to kill him." She shook her head. "I mean, the guy had already given us the little info he had. But they still wanted him dead. To risk that much just to silence one man... it's lunacy."

"And the other two?" Reid asked. "The would-be pilots from Zagreb?"

"Same. By the time we discovered the first guy dead and put in the alert, they'd already been done. And you had a hunch about that."

"I did?"

She nodded. "All three were killed in the same method—two to the chest, one to the head, from a silenced Sig Sauer. We thought it was a general MO for Fraternity assassins, but you had the bullets analyzed. It turned out they came from the same gun. Same guy did all three, in the span of six hours."

Reid had another hunch now, though he didn't share it with Johansson. Based on what he now knew, it seemed to him that Amun had used the Iranians as scapegoats to throw the CIA off their own trail. It made some sense, considering America's track record with the Middle East. It could have been that the sheikh himself was little more than a red herring for them to follow.

Instead he asked, "So that was the lead I chased? The assassin?"

"Yeah. You went alone, without telling us. You must have found him... because last I heard was that he killed you."

"Why would I have gone without you? I mean, without the team."
He thought he might already know the answer—*because I didn't think
I could trust you*—but he wanted to hear her take.

"I don't know," she said simply. "By that point, you were, uh,
personally invested."

"What does that mean?"

She shrugged. "If I'm being honest? You got obsessed. You got
reckless. You were leaving bodies behind with no explanation and
no probable cause. The agency was an inch away from disavowing
you, but then word came down that you were KIA."

Reid rubbed his face and sighed into both hands. "But I wasn't.
And like you said, I couldn't have done this to myself—someone put
that suppression chip into my head."

"You think it was them." It didn't sound so much like a question
as a statement. "The agency, you think they did this to you? It would
have been much easier to just kill you."

He blinked in shock. "Jesus. Do we—do they do that?"

"It's not unheard of."

He shook his head. He had no idea if he should believe her or
not; after all, Reidigger had obviously known that Kent was still
alive, had even planned for it, and he was still CIA, right up until
his untimely death. Johansson could have been lying to him. Yet
every physical indicator, every response she gave, seemed sincere.
She had appeared genuinely shocked to see him alive, and genuinely intending to help.

But she had been well trained. Deception was undoubtedly part
of that.

"After my death," he said, fully aware of how strange that phrase
sounded, "you said you went looking for what I was looking for. The
assassin?"

"Yeah. But I never found him."

"Any leads come out of that?" he asked.

"Nothing substantial enough to follow."

Her eyes, her large gray irises, they flitted to the right for just
a split-second, almost imperceptibly. Almost. She was lying, Reid

knew. Unless—*unless she's giving you an obvious tell so that you believe everything else.*

Dammit.

That complicated things. Either she was being completely honest about her story up to the point of finding a lead, or she was extremely cunning and intentionally misleading him. He really hoped it was the former; she already had a leg up on him simply by virtue of having her memory. She knew him far better than he knew her, which was barely at all.

Johansson climbed to her feet and soaked a cotton ball in hydrogen peroxide. "Let me take a look at that cut over your eye." She dabbed it gently. He winced at the sharp sting of chemicals. "You've been on the run for days," she said softly. "You should really get some sleep."

"I can't stay here." *I'm not even sure I can trust you.*

"Yes you can. You trusted me before. Even if you can't remember, I know you can feel it. Trust me again." She touched his rough cheek, lifting his stubbled chin and looking him in the eyes.

"Johansson, I—"

"Maria," she said. "My name is Maria." She leaned in and kissed him. Her lips were soft, moist, and … and familiar. A yearning rumbled inside him, but it wasn't new or unknown. He remembered the feel of her lips on his. His hands had explored the curve of her hips, her soft thighs, the scent of her hair …

He pulled away. "I don't know you," he said quietly.

"But I know you." She ran her fingers through his hair, down the back of his head, her fingernails gently trailing down his neck. A pleasant tingle ran down his spine. It had been a long time since anyone had touched him intimately—at least that he could remember. "Just stay a while. Let's figure this out together."

She kissed him again, more passionately this time.

He didn't pull away.

CHAPTER SIXTEEN

Morris peered through the scope of the rifle. There was still no movement.

He yawned, absently stroking the smooth butt stock of the modified HTR 2000. It was a truly beautiful machine, as stunning to him as the loveliest woman. Bolt-action, American-made, twenty-eight-inch barrel with 0.8 minute of arc and an effective firing range of 800 feet—not that he needed that kind of distance on this job, but he certainly wasn't going to use a Barrett or an Armalite to shoot through a window.

He'd acquired the rifle from an ex-Israeli Special Forces member and modded it himself with a suppressor and tripod rig. He named it Betsy, after his first high school girlfriend, a leggy cheerleader who had taken his virginity in the bed of a Ford F-150.

He wondered how Betsy was doing these days.

Then he realized how incredibly bored he was.

Morris had arrived hours earlier, while it was still dark out. When he had gotten the call from Deputy Director Cartwright that Kent Steele was somehow believed to be alive, he had immediately hopped on a plane from Barcelona to Rome. No, that wasn't quite true; first he trashed his hotel room in a fit of blind rage, shouting obscenities and cursing his own stupidity and breaking anything he could break. *Then* he'd gotten on a plane to Rome. No, that wasn't quite true either; after his fit, he'd made the call and put Amun's wild dog on alert.

Then he'd gotten on a plane.

He stationed himself in a room on the fourth floor of the Hotel Mattei and insisted to the front desk that he required a room with a view of the Fontana delle Tartarughe. His first course of action was a drink from the mini bar, and his second was setting up the tripod and sighting in Betsy on the second-floor window of the apartment directly across the piazza.

Of course he knew that Johansson was there. He'd known for a few months, but by the time he'd discovered that she was crashing at their former safe house, she was no longer a threat. She had called off her hunt. Morris had, admittedly, always been fond of her. She was tough, an expert at subterfuge, and probably smarter than any of them. More importantly, she didn't let any of that on until she needed to. He respected that.

When morning came, he peered through the scope and saw that Johansson was awake. He watched as she passed by the window in his sights. She was making herself some tea.

Then, mere moments later, there he was. The man of the hour. Agent Zero himself.

Kent Steele had done exactly what Morris thought he would do and stupidly returned to the safe house.

Morris had a clear line of sight on Steele as he entered the piazza and roamed around it, trying his best to appear casual. But Morris knew better. Kent could feel the barrel on him. The man always had a great sense about him, an instinct that seemed to border on precognition.

Morris could have put a bullet in Kent's skull right then and there. He could have reloaded, adjusted aim to the kitchen window, and popped off Johansson before she ever even knew that Kent was just outside her apartment.

But he refrained.

He had another opportunity just a few minutes later, through the window, when Kent entered the apartment. Johansson turned the corner and froze in shock. She dropped her teacup. Her back was to Morris, and over her shoulder, in the doorway, was Kent—a clear center mass bead from Betsy to his somehow-still-beating heart.

But still, Morris refrained.

Then the two of them vanished into the rear of the apartment, where Morris knew the bathroom and small bedroom were, and hadn't come out since. Possibly catching up on some sleep, Morris assumed. Or catching up on each other.

Morris had wanted very much to take the shot, but the deputy director's instructions had been crystal clear: wait. Observe and report. Call back when there's activity and you can confirm it's really Steele. On the phone, before the sun had risen, Morris had pretended to be surprised to find Johansson in the apartment. He suspected that was the reason Cartwright had told him to hold off. If Steele had been alone, he'd be dead by now.

That call had been hours ago now, and Morris was bored out of his mind.

He'd been on plenty of long, tedious ops before—days and nights spent watching, waiting, listening in on tapped phone lines and intercepting messengers, but he'd always had at least one other person to shoot the shit with, someone to make the time more bearable. Given his scruples, he'd be out there every day chasing hot leads and detaining criminals, terrorists, dissidents. That was what he enjoyed most. That was the secret-agent lifestyle he'd dreamed about ever since he was a kid, the dream he had promised himself he would never give up on. He had carried that into adulthood. All of those naysayers who told him he was being unrealistic, including his own family, they got to eat major crow the day he was hired by the CIA.

The reality, of course, was that the job was a far cry from Bond movies or impossible missions. But sometimes it was close enough.

Agent Clint Morris had been the youngest person ever admitted to Spec Ops Group. At twenty-nine he had been assigned to Kent Steele's team, almost four years past now. How excited he had been to work with the legendary Agent Zero. He had liked Steele back then. What others perceived as cockiness and arrogance in Morris, Steele saw as self-assuredness and competence. He treated Morris like an equal.

But then Morris had to kill him.

After his wife's death, Kent was getting impulsive, heedless. He threw himself into the investigation fully, sacrificing his own physical and mental health in pursuit of Amun (or "the Fraternity," as the CIA was calling it). He was killing criminals indiscriminately, not listening to orders, and refusing his team's help.

When the orders came down from Langley that Kent was to be stopped by whatever means necessary, it was Reidigger who volunteered. Morris had always had a soft spot for his round-faced, jovial teammate—but he didn't actually think for a second that Alan could pull the trigger on Kent, so he volunteered as well, to back him up. Cartwright agreed.

And then came that night on the Hohenzollern Bridge in Cologne, Germany. Morris and Reidigger had spent three weeks trying to catch up to Steele, and when they finally had, it was not the standoff that either of them expected.

They spotted him on the pedestrian footpath of the bridge, overlooking the Rhine pensively. To Morris, it looked like he was thinking about jumping.

And he, cocky and conceited as he was capable of being, he fell for Reidigger's ploy.

"I'll do it," Reidigger had said. "He's my best friend. I feel responsible. You hang back; we don't want to spook him or he'll run again."

And Morris had agreed. Alan had seemed so sincere, so brokenhearted about what he had to do that Morris held his position, about fifty yards downwind from Kent. Reidigger walked slowly toward him with his hands out, as if he were approaching a wild stallion. Kent didn't try to run. He and Alan spoke quietly for a few minutes. Just as Morris was getting impatient, Alan drew on him.

Reidigger always was a slow draw. Kent could have defended himself. He could have snatched the gun out of Alan's hand and taken him apart.

But he didn't. He didn't move at all.

A single shot rang out. Morris sprinted ahead, unholstering his Glock 27 as he ran. He wasn't even halfway there when Kent's body teetered over the railing and plummeted to the darkness of the river below.

When Morris reached Alan, he was leaning against the rail with both hands, staring down at the Rhine.

He sniffed once. "It's done," he said.

The official word from the CIA was that Amun's assassin, the one Kent was tracking, had killed him.

There was no team after that. Johansson went rogue, trying in vain to chase down the assassin that had killed their captives (and that she believed had killed Kent). Reidigger requested reassignment and was sent to Switzerland to aid in the investigation of a human trafficking ring moving through Zurich. But Morris stayed on the Fraternity case, even going undercover with Special Activities Division to try to infiltrate their ranks.

It had been about a year and a half since Kent Steele had fallen off Hohenzollern Bridge. And now he was alive. Morris had no idea how they had managed it, he and Reidigger. There was no doubt that Alan had been in on it, especially since Amun had gotten Kent's location from him. Now he was dead, too. Morris did feel awful about that; Alan had always been a good person. But he was no stranger to death, and such things were a means to an end.

Morris peered through the scope again. Still no movement through the window. He could clearly see the white curtains, tied back with sashes, the stainless steel sink of the kitchen, a marble countertop, and a corner of a small dining table. That was his view, his opportunity to take a shot—if Cartwright would allow it. He hoped he would. Morris really didn't want Amun's dog on this.

The assassin had not been very pleased to hear the news that Kent was alive. Morris didn't know him, had never met him—he didn't even know his name, nor the assassin his. He hated having to speak to the assassin; he knew that he was the one that killed their captives at the black sites. He was the one that Amun called in to do the dirtiest of dirty work, to take care of traitors, turncoats, and anyone who failed to do their job.

Morris sincerely regretted even mentioning, over the phone, having another way to lure Kent Steele out of hiding. He had momentarily forgotten who he was talking to—not an agent, who lives by rules and protocol, but a man who kills because someone whispered a name in his ear. There was no way that he would ever tell Amun about Kent's kids. It was definitely a way to get to him, but Morris was absolutely not going to allow that. He had already said too much just by mentioning another way.

But soon he wouldn't have to worry about that. Once Cartwright gave the word, he and Betsy would take care of Kent, and Johansson too, if need be, and the whole mess would be over. Morris would go back to his UC op—as far as the CIA was concerned, anyway.

He had been supplying Amun with intel for about seven months. His undercover attempts to infiltrate a lesser faction of the organization had gone fruitless for a year; none of them would let an American anywhere near them. With superiors breathing down his neck and threatening to pull him back to Langley, Morris got desperate, and he got himself captured.

His captors did not kill him, as he suspected they might. They didn't even torture him. Instead, when they discovered he was CIA, they brought him before a man with a strange mark burned into his neck. The man called himself Amun, and he gave Morris a choice.

One option was to provide their group with information and feed the CIA false leads. In return, he would be rewarded handsomely.

The other option was to die very slowly.

Morris chose door number one. It was a win-win in his book. To the CIA, it appeared that his UC op was suddenly successful; he gave them leads in the form of scapegoats, lesser factions of dissidents that looked like a trail of bread crumbs that might lead to the top. They never would, of course. Amun, as promised, funneled money into his offshore account. When he spoke to them, they referred to him only as Agent One.

But Morris was no Judas. He had agreed only so he could stay alive, and he had a plan. He was close to surmising Amun's endgame. It was happening soon, that much he knew, and once he had the full picture, he would organize a massive strike against the terrorist organization and take them out in one fell swoop. He would stop them and become a true American hero.

Once they were gone, he'd continue on with the CIA for another two or three years, to avoid scrutiny, and then retire in his midthirties to a tropical paradise and live on the two point five million he had accrued in his Swiss bank. Maybe he would buy himself a villa on the beach.

He considered it to be a very good plan. There was only one hitch, one stick in his spokes, one thorn in his side—Kent Steele was still alive.

It would be dark again soon. Morris stretched and yawned. He had been up half the night and the whole day. He peered through Betsy's scope, adjusting his view with the changing daylight... and he saw them. Kent. Johansson. There they were, standing in the small kitchen, talking while she poured a drink.

He quickly made the call, reaching for his phone and pressing the button without taking his eye from the scope.

"Cartwright."

"Sir," said Morris, "I've got Steele and Johansson in my crosshairs. Say the word and they'll both be stains faster than you can ask me what she's wearing."

"What are they doing?" Cartwright asked.

Morris was thrown by the question. "Doing? Uh... they're in a kitchen, talking."

"Stand down."

"Sir?" Morris asked.

"Stand *down*," Cartwright said firmly. "Kent may have intel on the Fraternity. If he does, Johansson will get it out of him. Give them time."

What? Morris thought. *Johansson was disavowed. Wasn't she? Unless...* He almost scoffed. He wouldn't put it past anyone in the agency to make such a claim just to keep tabs on field agents. *I really need to stop taking people at their word,* he thought.

But he didn't say any of that. Instead he just asked, "Orders, sir?"

"Hold your position. Observe and report. If Steele tries to leave, use whatever force necessary. At first light, infiltrate and take him out."

Morris smirked. "Yes, sir."

"*Quietly,* Morris. No shooting out of hotel windows. You got that?"

He frowned. "Yes, sir."

"And Morris—take *him* out. Only him." Cartwright ended the call.

Morris groaned. "Looks like it's going to be a long night, Betsy." He stroked the gun's butt stock. Then he snapped to attention with a sudden realization. If Kent *did* have info on Amun, and he gave it to Johansson, and if Johansson really was still an agent... that could spell a lot of trouble for him, with all his false leads and misinformation.

He shook his head. He didn't like it, and Cartwright *definitely* wouldn't like it, but he would have to take them both out. And he'd have to do it in such a way that made it look like Johansson was caught in the crossfire.

But he had all night to plan. And though he was already tired, he was certain the thought of killing Kent Steele in the morning would sustain him.

CHAPTER SEVENTEEN

You hold her in your arms. You breathe in her scent. You feel her skin on yours. It's so familiar, like a part of you. Like slipping into your favorite sweater.

She smiles. She tells you she loves you.

Kate.

You've never been this happy. But when you look into her eyes, they grow wide, fearful. Her mouth stretches into a gaping, silent scream.

She slips from your grasp. She's falling away. You try to catch her, to get to her, but the darkness around you is thick, viscous. You claw at the air but you're barely moving.

Desperate, you push and you strain and you reach… and your fingers find hers. You grab tightly. Pull her close. Tell her she's safe. Nothing can hurt her.

But the scent, it's different now. The feeling isn't as familiar. You look into her eyes—they're gray, the color of slate.

Maria holds you firmly. "Stay," she says softly. "Just stay awhile…"

Reid woke. For a moment, he forgot where he was. Slanted daylight streamed in through the apartment windows as the sun rose on the piazza outside. Right—Rome. The safe house. The remnants of the dream still echoed through his head. *Just a dream*, he thought. *It doesn't mean anything.* He sat up and rubbed his eyes. He had opted to sleep on the beige sofa. It was a bit cramped, but still some of the best rest he'd ever gotten. He'd slept all through the night and half the day before.

A spoon clinked against a ceramic mug. Maria was in the kitchen, stirring a cup. "Morning, Zero." She smiled. "You still take your coffee the same? Two sugars, no milk?"

"Mm-hmm." He didn't like that she knew so much about him while he knew so little, almost nothing, about her. "Zero," he murmured. "Why do they call me that?"

"It's a call sign. A codename. At least that's how it started." She set the steaming mug down on the coffee table. "You led our team, and you had a knack for going after the worst of the worst. We often had to go dark. So we had codes, and names, to avoid any scrutiny. Yours was Zero. And Zero has gained quite a bit of infamy with the criminal underground."

He sipped the coffee. It was exactly how he liked it. "What was yours?"

She smiled. "Marigold."

He couldn't help but notice that she was already dressed, in jeans and a white V-neck shirt and sneakers. She wore small silver hoops in her ears and a thin watch around her right wrist.

"Are you going somewhere?" he asked.

"There's a market nearby," she said. "I was going to pop down there, grab a few things, something to eat…or if you'd prefer, there's a lovely little café down the street—"

"I'm not here to play house with you," he said. She frowned. He hadn't meant it to sound as irritable as it had come off. He was still a bit disoriented; the bizarre dream had his head jumbled. "I mean, I need to stay focused on the task at hand."

"Sure," she said simply. "Even so, you should eat something…"

"What were we?" he asked point-blank.

She blinked. "What?"

Reid reached for his T-shirt and pulled it on. "I know we were colleagues. Teammates. Friends. But was there more?" It certainly felt like there was more. The day before, she had kissed him. He had kissed her. He'd stayed the night, but slept on the sofa. He didn't know her. And yet he had the distinct impression that the two of them had indeed been more.

She drew a long sigh. "You could say there's always been a sort of, uh, tension between us. We both wanted there to be more."

He nodded slightly. It seemed that each time she was close—close enough to smell her scent, to look in her gray eyes—a brief vision would flash. The two of them on a beach. In a bar, laughing and going shot for shot. Racing Vespas along Italian avenues.

But each time a vision flashed, it would blur quickly and spur a headache in his forehead. He found himself forcing his mind to avoid thinking about her, to actively try not to recall memories.

Even so, he needed to ask the one question on his mind. "So we never…?" He very nearly said "hooked up," a phrase he'd picked up from his students, but it didn't seem at all appropriate for the situation.

She smiled thinly. "I didn't say that."

"Oh." It was a vague response, and he didn't like it much. At least that would explain why Maria had felt so familiar to him. "When?"

She shrugged coyly with one shoulder. "Is that really what you want to talk about?"

Reid wasn't sure. He had other questions—if it had happened, where did it happen? Was Kate still alive at the time? If not, how long did they wait after her death to act on their impulses? Was it accidental, fueled by passion or alcohol, or was it a mutual acknowledgment of a long time coming? As trivial as those things might ordinarily seem, it was suddenly important to him to know the details of an intimate encounter—because it would give him some sort of insight into what sort of person Kent Steele was. What sort of person he had once been.

But at the same time, without the details or the memory of them, it might as well have never happened. He didn't ask anything further, partly because he was afraid of recalling a memory that he wouldn't like—and partly because he wasn't sure he could recall the memory, and he'd have to take Maria at her word. He wasn't sure he'd like the answers.

His internal scuffle must have been etched on his face, because Maria gently offered, "You were always loyal to her, if that's what you're asking."

Reid said nothing. He was fully aware that Maria could have just been telling him what he wanted to hear, but still, he felt a little better for it. Kate had been the love of his life. He couldn't bear the thought of having wronged her.

She took a seat on the sofa beside him. Their thighs nearly touched. "Do you ... You remember her, right?"

"Of course I do."

"And, the ... uh ... the end?"

"Yes. Of course," he said. He had been afraid to say it aloud, to talk about it, for so long. But now it felt necessary to face it. "Kate died of an embolism in her brain that caused a massive stroke. Yes, I remember all of that."

"Right," Maria murmured. "A stroke."

The sudden discomfort in the air was palpable. The room felt several degrees too warm. Reid stood and pulled on his jeans, his socks, and his boots. "You're right," he said a little too loudly. "We should eat. But first, I want you to tell me what leads you found when you were tracking the assassin."

Maria furrowed her brow. "What are you talking about?"

"Yesterday, when we talked, you said that you were tracking the Fraternity assassin, but didn't find anything substantial. You were lying." He didn't actually know that for sure, but he had decided to call her bluff. He couldn't keep staying there with her and sharing what he knew unless he believed he could trust her—and at the moment, he didn't. Not fully.

Maria chewed her bottom lip for a moment. "I was lying," she admitted. "But only because I don't want you to follow it. There's a reason I gave up the chase."

Reid waited for her to continue, but she remained quiet. "Are you going to tell me what that was?" he asked impatiently.

"I thought you were dead," she murmured. "We all did. Now you're here. But I'm afraid that if you keep going like this, you will die."

Just stay awhile. Her voice, from his dream, echoed in his head.

"Tell me," he demanded.

Still she said nothing. Her gray eyes refused to meet his. A vision of the dream flashed through his mind again—Kate, distraught and terrified, dissolving into Maria, holding him, begging him to stay...

Reid felt heat rise in his face. "Tell me!" His arm lashed out, seemingly on its own, and swatted the mug off the table. Maria winced as it shattered against the wall, the dark coffee leaving streaks down the white plaster.

"There you are," she said quietly. "There's the Kent I know." Her gaze lifted slowly to meet his. "I bet you're feeling more like him every day."

Reid turned away quickly—not out of anger as much as embarrassment. He had never lashed out like that before, at least not as Reid Lawson. She was right. This new personality—or old personality, as it were—was eking back into him, little by little. He had no idea how to stop himself from becoming Kent again, or if he even wanted to.

He stared out the kitchen window. In the piazza below, water bubbled from the turtle fountain. Across the way, the sun peeked from behind the Hotel Mattei.

"I'm sorry," he said. "That's not like me."

She rose from the sofa and stood beside him, staring out the window as well. "Yes, it is. You just don't know it yet. You're becoming obsessed again."

"I can't help how I feel. I just...I *need* to do this, to see this through. It's coming. It's going to happen soon, I can feel it. And right now, I don't even know what it is, let alone how to stop it."

"You can't."

Reid looked up at her sharply. "What do you mean?"

Maria bit her bottom lip pensively. "You want to know what I found out? I'll tell you. This thing, this Fraternity...It's big, Kent. Too big to take on alone. I spent months chasing down leads. Half of them were fake. The other half, I'd get a name. Just a name, or sometimes a location. And if that wasn't a dead end, it would just lead to another name—another link in a very, very long chain. They have spent *years* collecting factions from all over the world. It's not just Europe. It's not just the Middle East. It's liberation movements in Africa. It's guerrilla fighters in South America. It's even at home ..."

"Our own people," he finished. "Yeah. I heard that too."

"That was when I stopped, when I learned that. I got in too deep and the Fraternity caught wind of it. They tried hard to get to me. I was sure they were going to kill me. I was disavowed—I was one person with no one at my back and no one I could trust, not even the agency."

"So you just gave up? Hid out here?" Once again his words came out harsher than intended.

She turned on him, her gaze angry and hard. "I did *not* just give up!" she said firmly. "I saved my own life! I came to realize what you were too goddamn stubborn to understand! You were obsessed with chasing down one man, your next lead. But what you failed to realize—the thing that we all thought got you killed—was that even if you found him, it would be nothing but disappointment. The only thing he would give you, if anything, was one more name. One more link in the chain. Much as it pains me to admit it, the Fraternity set it up brilliantly. No one knows who's at the top; all they know is who they work with directly. It's just like it was before, two years ago ... we can chase down every lead and at the end of the day we'll still have nothing but another name."

"Eventually that chain has to end," he countered. "There's someone at the top. There always is. Sooner or later, we'd find it."

"Ever the optimist." Maria shook her head and smiled sadly. "You're right. But it would be a lot later than sooner. It would be too late. That's what they've done." She scoffed. "Do you remember that thing in the eighties, that publicity stunt called Hands Across America? It was something like six million people, all holding hands, forming a human chain across the country. Imagine you're standing in New York, and you've got a person to your left, and a person to your right. That's all you know. That's all that matters to you. You're doing your part. You're linking the chain. You have no idea who the links are in Illinois, or Arkansas, or California. It doesn't matter what their name is, or what your differences might be, what kind of person they are—but you know they're there, doing the same thing you are. Linking the chain. All of you, united in a single cause. It's like that. That's what they've done. And that's what I realized, Kent. They won't ever let you get to the top. You'll be dead long before that."

Reid sighed and rubbed his forehead. "Then what would you have me do?" Her words from the dream came to him again. *Just stay awhile.* "We can't just let this happen. People will die, Maria. I'm going to keep following, with or without your help. And it's not because of Kent's obsession or sense of duty. It's because I have two girls at home that are scared out of their wits right now, in hiding, with no idea if they'll ever see me again or not. No one should live that way, ever. And if Amun had their way—"

Maria looked up sharply. "Amun?"

Dammit! he scolded himself. His tongue had slipped and in his haste to convince her to give him the lead, he'd shown his hand.

"How do you know that name?" she demanded.

"I..." He had already let it slip; he might as well be honest. "I heard it from the Russian in Belgium. It's what they call themselves, the Fraternity. I think it's sort of the nucleus of the group, like the glue holding them all together—"

Maria smacked him in the arm, hard enough for him to wince. "Christ, Kent, why didn't you say that earlier?!"

"Because I didn't think I could trust you!" he blurted out.

She threw her hands up in frustration as she marched to the back bedroom.

"Where are you going?"

She emerged again a moment later, a cell phone in hand. "My last lead, before I quit," she explained as she scrolled the screen, "came from a low-level thug in Jordan. He thought he was tough, but after I pulled off a few fingernails—"

"Jesus, Maria..."

"—he gave me an address, and the name 'Amun.' He said I'd know it was him by a scar, a burn mark, on his neck..."

169

"A brand," Reid confirmed. "I've seen it a few times now. It's a hieroglyph of an ancient Egyptian god."

She looked up briefly enough to shoot him an irritated glance at just how much he'd kept from her, and then continued scrolling. "Anyway, the guy's place must have been tapped, because I was intercepted en route. That's when they told me about moles in the agency. Their network. I gave up, I came here. But if this guy is Amun, then ... god, I might have been a lot closer than I thought!"

"From what I gathered," Reid told her, "Amun isn't one person. It's a group. Saying that he's Amun might be the equivalent of someone saying they're American or Catholic or Republican. What's with the phone?"

"I saved all the addresses in my contacts under fake names," she explained. "This one was in Eastern Europe. Slovenia, if I recall ..."

She didn't get the chance to find it.

A jarring crash startled them both as the door to the apartment splintered and flew open.

CHAPTER EIGHTEEN

Reid's instincts kicked into gear instantly. He didn't have time to get a look at his assailant; as soon as he saw the black suppressed barrel of a pistol, he leapt to the right. Maria leapt to the left, toward the kitchen.

The gun barked sharply twice, both shots striking the window overlooking the Fontana. Reid tucked into a roll, almost hitting the wall by overshooting in the tiny living room. He came up in a crouch and scooped up the largest shard of the shattered coffee mug, its pieces still strewn over the carpet.

Two more shots rang out. Reid threw himself back to the floor just in time and the bullets smacked against plaster, sending chips of it flying in his face. He grabbed the edge of the coffee table, hurled it upright, and took cover behind it. *He's using nine-millimeter rounds. This is two and a half inches of wood. It should hold.* As soon as he thought it, a shot splintered the wood right in front of him, center mass.

Thankfully, the table held.

The assailant fired off two more shots, but not at Reid. Maria gasped in pain. Reid winced; she was hit.

"Good to see you again, Zero," said a taunting yet familiar male voice. "Come on out of there, and I won't kill her."

Reid hazarded a peek around the edge of the coffee table. The assailant had his gun trained on Maria, but he was staring at Reid. He was in his early thirties, square jawed, five o'clock shadow and a cocky half-smirk on his face. *Morris,* his brain told him. *Your former teammate.*

171

Maria held her right bicep with her left hand, blood between her fingers. It looked like the bullet had only grazed her.

"Don't," she told him.

Reid gripped the ceramic shard tightly, obscuring it in his palm as he stepped out from behind the upturned coffee table.

"There he is." Morris's smirk widened. "You're looking well for a dead guy."

"Why?" Reid demanded. He already knew the answer—or at the least the possibilities. Either Morris was an Amun mole in the CIA, or the agency had sent him to take Kent out. He just didn't know which.

Morris rolled his eyes. "Come on, Kent. We're not going to stand here and do the big monologue thing. I just wanted to get a good look at you." He shook his head, and for a moment his gaze softened, as if he was genuinely disappointed. "Alan was such a fool. None of this had to happen."

He aimed the pistol at Reid.

As soon as the gun was off of her, Maria reached for her back pocket. In the same moment, she lunged forward, bringing up a slender, curved blade—a black-handled fillet knife.

Before Morris could squeeze off a shot, Maria swung the blade upward and sliced through the muscle of his forearm, about five inches above the wrist.

"Ah! Bitch!" Morris screamed in agony as the gun slipped from his grip. Maria kicked the pistol—but not toward Reid. It skittered across the tile and under the kitchen table.

Morris lashed out with his good arm and struck a solid blow across Maria's cheek. Reid surged forward and swung his elbow upward, into the younger man's solar plexus. A blow like that should have stunned him, knocked the wind right out of him, but Morris was trained. He caved his torso inward, moving with the strike so that it barely glanced against his ribs, and responded in kind with a vicious right hook.

Reid took the hit on the chin. His head jerked back. Stars swam in his vision. For a moment, he was barely cognizant of Morris's good arm, coming back around for a second strike aimed at his windpipe.

He barely got his arm up in time to feebly block the attack. He staggered backward. Morris reached behind him for something on his belt—presumably he had another gun on him.

Get it together! the voice in his head demanded. *This isn't how you go out.*

Reid gritted his teeth and surged again. This time he grabbed onto Morris's arm—his right arm, the one Maria had wounded—and squeezed it tight.

Morris threw back his head and howled in pain.

Reid's other hand still gripped the ceramic shard. He swung it in an arc and sliced superficially across Morris's forehead. The wound bled amply and quickly, blood running into Morris's eyes before he could wipe it away.

Reid grabbed the younger man by the collar and belt and dropped to one knee, at the same time using his leverage to pull down on one arm and push up with the other. Morris flipped ass-over-teakettle; for the briefest of moments his body was completely off the ground, and in that half-second of weightlessness Reid twisted his body, shoving Morris in a judo-throw.

The body struck the kitchen window. Glass shattered into a thousand pieces as Morris flew out over nothing. A hand lurched out and, somehow, impossibly, grabbed the window frame.

Morris howled again. He had caught himself, but a small shard of glass pierced his hand. His other arm flailed wildly, still reaching for the spare pistol at the small of his back.

A woman screamed. Down in the piazza, a middle-aged tourist couple had witnessed the ordeal—the shattered window, Morris catching himself. The man quickly pulled out a cell phone, presumably to call the police. Reid deliberated for a moment—he could force Morris off the window frame and drop him down to the pavement with a single blow. The drop couldn't have been more than sixteen feet or so—likely not enough to kill him, but probably enough to shatter his legs. But he wanted answers. He wanted to know who had sent him.

Maria climbed to her feet from where she'd fallen on the kitchen floor. Her cheek was already swollen and her bicep bled amply, but it looked like the cut was superficial. "Do it!" she said urgently. "Drop him. He won't stop otherwise."

Reid shook his head. "I need to know why he came, what he knows—"

Maria groaned in exasperation. "Then what's your plan B?"

Lead him away from here. Away from Maria. Into a more public place where he can't just shoot openly.

"I have to go." Reid grabbed the bug-out bag and his bomber jacket from the sofa. "Don't follow me. It's me he's after. I'll divert his attention, lead him elsewhere…"

A gunshot cracked the air. They both ducked instinctively. Morris had loosed his other gun and fired indiscriminately into the apartment. He couldn't see where he was shooting. Down in the piazza, the two tourists screamed and scurried for their lives.

Maria shoved Reid hard, through the open door and into the hall. He stumbled back and hit the opposite wall. "I'll come with you," she said. "We can go together, track the next lead…"

He shook his head. "No. I'd be better off on my own—"

Another shot clapped like thunder. Maria took cover around the corner and flattened herself against the wall. Reid hazarded a peek into the apartment, just as Morris's head appeared in the window frame. He looked demonic, like a man possessed, his teeth clenched and eyes furious, blood running down his face.

"Steele!" he howled. He took aim, but the barrel was shaky. Reid ducked. The bullet struck plaster. Maria's arm snaked around the corner of the door frame and yanked him back out into the hall with her.

"Take this." She shoved her cell phone into his hands. Her blood smeared across the screen. "The address is in there. Slovenia. Find it."

"I will," he promised. He quickly opened the bug-out bag and pulled out Reidigger's Walther PPK. He gave it to Maria. "Here, just in case. How will I find you again?"

She gestured to the blood-smeared cell phone. "I'll find *you*. Now go!"

He ran. Down the hall and taking the stairs two at a time, he pulled the bomber jacket over his shoulders and gripped the black nylon backpack in his fist. More shots rang out above him. If the tourists hadn't called the police, someone else in the building certainly would have by now.

He reached the courtyard but didn't slow. As he entered the piazza, his boots pounding the pavement, he hazarded a glance over his shoulder.

Morris did too, still hanging by one hand from the window frame. Blood ran over his knuckles and soaked his sleeve. His right hand would be ruined, the forearm sliced and the palm pierced. His other gripped a silver pistol—a Ruger LC9, by the look of it.

He scowled at Reid with an avarice so deep he felt it in his core. Reid expected him to take aim, try to fire across the piazza, but he didn't.

Instead, Morris let go.

A vision flashed suddenly and swiftly across Reid's mind—*a bridge. Night. The air rushes in your ears as you plunge toward the water below...*

Morris bent his legs as he struck the concrete and tucked into a roll. He came up on one knee and took aim with his left hand. The barrel was shaky, his grip tremulous, but he had a clear line of sight.

Reid darted to the right as the thunderclap of the shot boomed in his ears. He was nearly out of the piazza, zigzagging left and right in a serpentine pattern. Another shot rang out. A marble turtle atop the Fontana exploded.

He had to get out of the piazza, get to somewhere public where he could lose himself in the crowd. Somewhere that Morris couldn't open fire.

Reid glanced over his shoulder once more before he rounded the corner to the street. Morris climbed to his feet and gave chase.

CHAPTER NINETEEN

Reid exited Piazza Mattei and ran a short distance down Via dei Funari. Despite the cold February weather, there were quite a few people out—and many of them had either paused, puzzled by the sound of nearby gunshots, or hurried along to get to shelter. There were cell phones in hands everywhere he looked. Too many.

He had no idea how Morris could even be walking after dropping from the window like that, let alone running after him. He had to remind himself that this was not a foot soldier or terrorist lackey, but rather a well-trained field agent—perhaps as well-trained as himself.

Reid slowed to a brisk walk, trying to appear inconspicuous. But his heart rate did not slow. He felt as if it might pound out of his chest. Morris was an active agent, and he had tried to kill them. Or at least he had tried to kill Kent—he wasn't sure if Maria had also been a target.

I probably led that maniac right to her, he thought glumly. He found himself hoping that she was all right. Whether he could fully trust her or not, she had fought back and helped him escape. She had given him her phone, which had the address, the lead to Amun in Slovenia.

But…

But she had kicked the gun underneath the kitchen table, instead of kicking it to him.

It was the heat of the moment. She wasn't thinking straight.

And she didn't reappear when Morris started shooting in the piazza.

She might have been hit.

The Kent side of him wanted to trust her. They had a history. But Reid did not. There were still more questions than answers.

He stuffed his hands in the pockets of his jacket…and then he broke his stride in bewilderment. He turned both pockets inside out. The Glock—it was gone.

"Son of a bitch!" he shouted in anger. She had taken it; there was no doubt in his mind. He had given her the Walther, and she took the Glock. He was unarmed.

He yanked open the bug-out bag to make sure everything else was still there: the money, the passports, the clothing, the spare clip for the PPK. It was all accounted for, even the Swiss Army knife, which he took out of the bag and put in his pocket. Not that it would do much good against a gun.

Reid fumed. How could he have been so stupid? He'd let his guard down and she had taken the gun while he slept.

And she could have killed you with it, easily, in your sleep. But she didn't.

Maybe she didn't trust him any more than he trusted her.

Somewhere in the distance, sirens wailed as police and emergency personnel were dispatched to the piazza. He snapped out of his reverie, slung the bag over his shoulder, and hurried on his way.

Morris, he assumed, would not be on the street. He was bleeding badly; he would leave a trail and no doubt draw attention to himself. The younger agent would hide somewhere, treat his wounds, and strike at Kent another day.

Even so, Reid wanted to be off the street. He decided to take a right at Via di Ambrogio, head south toward the library, where he could hide out for a few hours. Let the heat die down a bit before he tried to move again. He stepped off the sidewalk to cross the street—

A crack nearly split his eardrums, impossibly loud and devastatingly close. The bullet smacked the street sign behind him. Reid jumped into a crouch; if he hadn't made a right turn at that precise moment, his skull would be open.

The avenue broke out into chaos as passersby screamed and ran every which way toward cover. The crowd parted like the Red Sea as Reid scanned left and right.

"I don't believe it," he murmured.

Morris strode toward him briskly. His square jaw was set in a hard scowl and he was limping slightly on his left leg. His right hand dangled uselessly at his side, dripping blood onto the sidewalk. With his left, he raised the gun again.

Reid dashed into the street. The light was green; cars came to a screeching halt. A red Fiat nearly struck him, skidding sideways mere inches away. Reid leapt and vaulted over the small car. He couldn't believe Morris was still on the hunt, out in the open. *This is a desperate man. This is a man who has something to lose. And that makes him even more dangerous.*

A Ruger LC9 has a seven-round clip. How many shots did he fire? Five? Six? He couldn't remember how many times Morris had fired into the apartment while he was hanging on the windowsill.

Reid sprinted down the next block, skirting around panicked people rushing to get off the street. There had to be somewhere he could go, somewhere he could vanish quickly.

Subway. Make a left.

Once again he ran across an intersection with oncoming cars. Drivers honked as they slammed their brakes and swore loudly in Italian. He glanced over his shoulder. Morris looked like the villain out of an eighties slasher flick, striding briskly, not running, but not stopping either. Reid had put some distance between them. The agent wasn't firing at him, but not because he couldn't make the shot.

Maybe he's out of rounds.

Or maybe he knows he only has one left.

He reached the entrance to the Rome Metro tunnel and hurried down the stairs. He vaulted the turnstile, ignoring the wide-eyed Italians who shouted scornfully about metro cards. There was no train at the platform, and he couldn't very well stand there and wait for one.

Restroom, he thought. He hurried a little further down the platform, found a men's room, and shouldered the door open. There was no one inside, but there was no lock on the door either.

I've cornered myself, he thought dismally.

No. You've led him into a trap. Close quarters.

"Okay," Reid murmured to himself. "Okay, calm down." He struggled to control his breathing. Morris was well trained, perhaps nearly as well trained as Kent was, but he was injured. He was either out of rounds or had only one left. Those were good enough odds to take.

Reid pulled out the Swiss Army knife and flicked the blade open. It was tiny, only three inches long, but in the right place it could still be lethal.

Disarm him first. Then go for the jugular, in the throat. Or the femoral, in the thigh.

He flattened himself against the wall behind the door and waited, the knife held at his hip, ready to thrust it forward.

Someone pushed slowly on the door. It opened wide and nearly hit Reid. He tightened his grip on the knife, waiting to see the barrel of the gun leading in. But no gun came.

"Oh!" said the startled man as the door swung closed to reveal Reid behind it. "Sorry, didn't see you there."

Reid quickly palmed the knife to hide it from view. The man had no accent—or rather, he had an American accent. His hair was implausibly blond, the result of an obvious and recent bleach job. His eyes were a cold blue. On any other day, Reid might have laughed. The guy couldn't have looked more American if he was holding a hot dog and draped in the stars and stripes.

He glanced quizzically again at Reid and then headed to a urinal. There was something about his face, something vaguely familiar, like seeing someone out in public that you'd swear was your friend or your cousin, but upon a second look you realize it's just a stranger, a near doppelganger.

Reid didn't want to draw suspicion, so he pocketed the knife again—keeping the blade open—and went to the sink. He twisted the cold water knob on one of the three faucets and inspected his face in the smudged mirror. His face was still a bit swollen in a couple of places from where the Iranians had beaten him. At least Maria had applied fresh bandages. He still looked like hell. There was two days' worth of stubble on his chin, and he could swear that it had a grayish tint. It must just be the poor fluorescent lighting, he decided.

He kept an eye on the door in his periphery. Maybe Morris wouldn't think to look in the bathroom. *Of course he would. He's a highly trained agent. He may be desperate, but he's not an idiot. He must have seen come down here.*

"Hey, buddy," said the blond American at the urinal. "You got the time?"

"Hmm?" Reid had barely heard him.

"The time?" the guy repeated as he zipped up.

"Oh, uh … yeah." He glanced down at the cheap watch he had bought back in Paris. He had nearly forgotten he was even wearing it. The face was cracked, and the clock had stopped—probably after his and Otets's dip in the chilly river. "Sorry, I—"

If he hadn't been standing in front of a mirror and watching his periphery, he wouldn't have seen it. But he did—he saw the movement of an elbow as it reached into a jacket pocket.

In the same instant, the mirror shattered with the impact of two suppressed shots.

CHAPTER TWENTY

Move! Kent's instincts kicked in so fast it was as if he'd been shoved by an unseen force. He propelled his body backward and hit the white wall of the bathroom as the mirror exploded. Shards of silvery glass rained down on the sink and tiled floor.

The blond man's reaction time seemed just as fast as Reid's. He had a gun leveled at him again in an instant, finger on the trigger.

Reid froze. The stranger had him dead to rights.

In that moment, the image of his girls flashed in his mind. As newborns, asleep on his chest while he lay on the sofa. As children, playing tag with Kate in the backyard. As teens, growing up so fast he could hardly keep up.

In a half second, they would be orphans. They would never know that their father died in a subway bathroom in Italy, his brains dashed across white tile.

The door to the bathroom swung open.

The would-be assassin's gaze flitted to the doorway, just for an instant. But that was all Reid needed. He kicked at the partially open stall door to his left. It swung wide and the steel edge nailed the blond man full-on in the face. His head jerked back and blood spouted from his nose.

The newcomer was a portly Italian man in an ill-fitting suit with a newspaper under one arm. He stood in the doorway with his mouth agape as Reid leapt forward and grabbed the blond stranger by the throat and right wrist, forcing the barrel of the gun down toward the floor.

"Get out!" Reid barked at the Italian. The chubby man did not have to be told twice; he dropped his newspaper and scurried out of the bathroom.

Reid shoved the blond man against the wall, pinning him between two urinals and pinching his airway partially closed. The stranger did not cry out or even show any sign of distress; he merely stared at Reid, his gaze stoic and flat.

That face, Reid thought. *It seems so familiar.* Yet nothing sparked in his memory.

"Who are you?" he demanded. "CIA? Amun?"

The blond man's lips curled into a sneering smirk. "You know me," he rasped.

"I don't." Reid slammed the man's wrist against the top edge of the urinal. "Drop the gun."

"No."

He pinched harder, blocking off the trachea. "I will collapse your windpipe, and you will die," he warned.

"Do it," the man choked. His gaze remained stoic. His face was turning an impressive shade of crimson.

"Just drop the ..." Reid trailed off as his gaze momentarily fell on the gun. He recognized it immediately—and then a memory flashed through his mind. It wasn't a new vision, but rather a recollection of the conversation with Maria just the day before, when she told him about their black-site captives.

"*All three were killed in the same method,*" she had said. "*Two to the chest, one to the head, from a silenced Sig Sauer.*"

"You're Amun," Reid said quietly. "You... you're the assassin I was chasing. The one that supposedly killed me."

The man tried to choke out a few words. Reid relaxed his grip just for a moment. The blond assassin sucked in a breath and then rasped, "Is that what they told your people? That I did it?"

The door to the bathroom creaked on its hinges as it swung open again, but Reid did not take his gaze off the blond stranger.

"Let him go, Zero," said Morris behind him. "And you, Blondie— drop the gun."

"You're empty," Reid chanced.

"You want to find that out for sure?" Morris threatened. "Let him go and step away slowly, or I swear to Christ I will blast you in half."

"You're going to shoot me anyway," Reid countered.

"True," Morris agreed, "but I'd rather it not be in the back. Come on now. Off him."

The blond man smirked. Reid's nostrils flared. He slowly loosened his grip on the man's windpipe and then released his wrist.

"Hands up, both of you," Morris ordered.

Reid put his hands up, near his ears. The assassin did not—nor did he drop his gun.

"Are you deaf?" Morris shouted at him. "Drop the gun, or I will end you!"

The assassin chuckled so lightly it was barely a hiss of breath through his teeth. "You must be Agent One. What a pleasure to meet you in person."

Panic flashed across Morris's eyes. "How did you find me?" he murmured.

The assassin shot him a flat look. "We are many," he said simply.

Morris kept his shaky barrel trained on the assassin. Reid knew he could do something, jump in and take him out, but he decided that Morris was the lesser of two evils here. The agent had lost a lot of blood. His grip was tremulous. He most certainly had one or fewer rounds in the clip, and his dilemma was obvious—should he shoot the assassin, or use his last bullet on Kent Steele? As it stood, his attention was on the Amun assassin, so Reid simply took a small step backward and did nothing.

The blond assassin realized it too. "What should you do, Agent?" he said slowly. "You and I, we are both here for the same reason. We both want Kent Steele dead. We are, as they say, playing for the same team."

Morris is working with Amun. That much seemed evident. However, it was equally clear that Morris didn't trust the assassin, and certainly didn't want to face him with an empty clip.

"Morris," said Reid, "it doesn't matter, all right? What you do right now, that's what is going to define you. I know you—or I did. You wouldn't have been on my team if you weren't a good person. If you didn't want to do the right thing."

For the briefest of moments, Morris's gaze became vacant, as if he were remembering something long forgotten. His finger tightened ever so slightly on the trigger.

But the assassin chuckled softly again. "Morris," he said thoughtfully. "Agent Morris. Good to know."

Morris deflated visibly. *The assassin didn't know his name.* Reid had just made the decision for him.

The agent pulled the trigger.

The assassin was fast. He saw it coming. He bladed his body sideways to avoid the bullet that would have certainly hit his heart. At the same time he lifted the Sig Sauer and fired three times in less than two seconds.

Two to the chest. One to the head.

Blood and brain matter spattered what remained of the broken mirror behind him. For a brief moment, it appeared as though Morris was being held up by invisible strings—his arms aloft but his wrists hanging limply, his head cocked at an odd angle.

Reid jumped forward as if he was going to catch his former friend, his old teammate. And he did, in a way. He grabbed onto Morris as he fell backward and used the agent's body as a shield. The momentum of Morris's fall pushed them both closer to the door.

The assassin grunted and fired off four more shots. Three hit Morris; the fourth hit the solid wood door as Reid yanked it open. He heard the stranger roar in fury as he dashed out onto the platform.

There was a train there.

The doors were closing.

CHAPTER TWENTY ONE

Reid sprinted as fast as he could, closing the short distance in only six wide strides, and quite literally leapt through the narrow opening of the doors as they whooshed closed. He nearly ran right into a young couple gripping the steel handles overhead.

But the doors did not close. He had tripped the sensor at the top of the door, and they slid open again. Reid looked up, his eyes wide with desperation as he saw the assassin emerge from the bathroom, blood running from his nostrils and holding his Sig Sauer at waist level and slightly behind him to obscure it from passersby.

His gaze was locked tightly on Reid. He could tell that the assassin was weighing his options—board the train and pursue him, or simply shoot through the open doors.

The blond man started to raise the gun. Reid jumped aside, out of the doorway, but he knew that wouldn't help much. *He could penetrate the glass of the windows*, Reid thought, *and possibly hit innocent people.*

Then there was a shout, and two police officers came running down the platform. The portly businessman, the one who had barged into the bathroom, pointed and shouted in Italian. "There! That's him!"

The blond assassin gave Reid one more sneering, hateful glance as he tucked the pistol into his jacket. The last thing Reid saw as the train pulled away from the platform was the back of his blond head as he sprinted away from the police.

Reid slung the bug-out bag off his shoulders and set it in his lap as he dropped into an empty seat. He heaved a huge sigh of relief—three times in the last few minutes he had been certain he was about to die. He couldn't help but wonder if that was what Kent Steele's life was like all the time. If that was just a part of being Agent Zero.

As his heart rate finally and mercifully slowed, Reid noticed that the other passengers on the train seemed to be avoiding him; the people to his left and right had abandoned their seats, and no one even wanted to stand close by. At first he thought that it was simply to steer clear of the lunatic who had leapt onto a train.

But then he noticed that there was blood on his coat, on the sleeves and the lapel. Not his own; it was Morris's blood.

Morris was dead. Reidigger was dead. Maria might be dead. It seemed that anyone connected to him—connected to Kent Steele, that is—was dropping fast. It was almost a small blessing that he barely remembered them as friends. At least it made it a little easier to cope with all the wanton violence that seemed to surround him as Zero.

Morris and the blond assassin had known each other; that part was clear. There was no doubt in Reid's mind after what he had just witnessed that Morris had been the mole in the CIA. But there was no trust there; the young agent had shot at the Amun member, had made an attempt to take him out. *Maybe it was against his will,* Reid thought. Or maybe it was simply greed. He might never know now.

He took the cell phone out of his pocket, the one Maria had given him. Despite the questions he had about their relationship, both past and present, he found himself hoping that she was all right. Luckily the phone was still intact after that whole ordeal. He scrolled idly through the contacts. There were more than a hundred programmed in there, but it wouldn't take him long to find the lead.

Suddenly the phone vibrated in his hands. He nearly dropped it, startled by the sudden sensation.

The caller was unknown.

Maria, he thought. *She's alive. She's safe. She's reaching out.*

He pressed the green button to answer it, but said nothing.

Someone breathed on the other line. Then a male voice said, "It must be cold up there."

A chill ran down his spine. It was the code, same as in Reidigger's apartment in Zurich. This was a call from the CIA.

Why would they call her? How would they have this number?

She was disavowed.

Wasn't she?

"But you can't beat the view," Reid answered quietly.

The male voice hissed a long sigh. "Hello, Zero," he said. Then: "Is she alive?"

"I don't know."

"Morris?"

"…No."

Another sigh. "Damn. Will you at least tell us where?"

"Floor of a bathroom in the Rome Metro, just off Via di Ambrogio." By the time they got to Morris's body, Reid would be long gone.

"Jesus, if that's not an ignoble end—"

"He was working with them," Reid interrupted. "Morris was working with Amun."

"There's no way," said the man. "Morris was undercover for more than a year tracking them down. His job was to make them *think* he was working for them. He must have been convincing enough—"

"The assassin they sent after me knew that he was an agent," Reid cut in again. "He called him 'Agent One.'"

"And how do we know you're clean?" asked the voice. "You pop up suddenly after a year and a half, and now your whole former team is either dead or MIA? How do we know you're on the right side?"

"You don't." He ended the call and silenced the phone.

Maria was still with them, he decided. She was still with the agency, or they wouldn't have had her number. They wouldn't have used the code. She wouldn't have acted so strangely and spared Morris's life twice when she had the opportunity to take him out. She had never been disavowed. She had lied about her lack of leads.

She had taken his gun. What else had she lied about? Had they ever really been together? Or worse, had their tryst been more than she implied?

He did not want to care if Maria was alive or dead. But he couldn't stop the other side of him, the familiarity of her and the strange longing to be near her. Much like the inexplicable wave of overwhelming sadness that had struck him upon seeing Reidigger's body, he simply couldn't help how he felt.

He decided that he hoped she was alive—not just because of the unremembered history between them, but so that he could get answers.

He rode the subway for three more stations before disembarking. Along the way he opened Maria's phone, took out the battery and the SIM card. Once back on the street level, he tossed the two halves and the battery in separate corner trash bins, and then asked a passerby for directions to the nearest wireless store. He kept his eyes open and his senses alert to any potential threats. The blond assassin was still out there somewhere, and Morris might not have been the only one sent after Agent Zero.

Reid's first order of business, he decided, was to get the contact information off of Maria's SIM card. Once he had the address, he would find a way to get to Slovenia. Find the next lead, this Amun member in hiding. Force him to talk. Get some real answers. No more false leads and deceit.

By whatever means necessary.

And if Maria is alive—if she finds us and she's not who she claims to be—you might have to kill her, before she kills you.

CHAPTER TWENTY TWO

Deputy Director Cartwright pocketed his phone. The line had gone dead. Steele had hung up on him. At least there was no doubt now—Zero was alive. And he had taken out Morris. Probably Reidigger. The two men that Cartwright himself had sent after him. And maybe even Johansson too, seemingly for good measure.

Cartwright rubbed his temples. The very last thing he wanted to do at the moment was the long walk to Director Mullen's office to tell him that Morris was dead. He could already anticipate what Mullen would say, what he would order.

Though … maybe he didn't have to tell Mullen himself.

He called out through the partially open door of his office to his assistant. "Lindsay, get Steve Bolton down here ASAP, would you?"

"Right away, sir."

It took Bolton four minutes to get there. The chief of the Special Ops Group was a tall man, with sharp features and a sharp haircut. He had a way of standing that made most people uncomfortable, folding his arms and puffing out his chest as if he wanted to make himself larger or more imposing than he was. Cartwright always thought that Bolton looked more like a high school gym teacher than a CIA supervisor; like he should have a whistle hanging around his neck instead of a gun at his hip.

"Sir?" Bolton said by way of greeting, folding his meaty arms as he stood in the doorway.

"Bolton, come in. Need a favor. Close the door." Cartwright didn't bother mincing words. As soon as the door was closed he said, "Clint Morris is dead."

Bolton's features went slack, as did the taut muscles in his forearms. "Christ," he murmured. "Zero?"

Cartwright nodded. "And I need *you* to report it to Director Mullen."

"Me? Morris was your man."

"True," said Cartwright, "but I don't have time for political bickering. I already know what he'll say. I'm getting on the first available plane to Zurich. If this is going to be handled properly, I need to be there, not here."

Bolton clearly wasn't happy with the prospect, but Cartwright was his superior, so he didn't argue. Instead he sighed unhappily and asked, "What do you want me to tell him? Besides Morris being dead."

"That's it," said Cartwright as he slipped into his black jacket.

Bolton scoffed. "We must have something more to go on. What's Zero's angle? Who's he working with?"

"Working with?" Cartwright snorted. Bolton hadn't gotten to spend much time around Kent; he was promoted to Spec Ops Group to replace Cartwright when he was sent up to deputy director. "I'd bet my whole salary he's not working with anyone."

"But…" Bolton's brain seemed to be working overtime. "No," he said. "He's just one guy."

"Yeah," Cartwright muttered as he clasped his briefcase. "That's the problem. He's just one guy." On his way out of the office, he patted Bolton twice on the shoulder. "If Mullen asks, I'll be in Zurich, trying to find out who's still alive and why the dead ones are dead."

Premio Insurance was a small shop, located in an old, narrow building on Via da Vinci in Rome. It consisted of a cramped reception area and two equally tiny back offices. The walls were wood panel and the carpets used to be white.

The woman at the front desk, her name was Anne. She was thirty-three and from Omaha. It was a great job—she got paid a respectable wage to live in Rome and spend eight hours of her day sitting at a desk, turning people away.

She didn't know a single thing about selling insurance.

The bell over the door chimed and Anne put on her best smile. "Good morning," she said. "I'm afraid we're not taking on new clients at the ... oh, my."

The woman who entered the shop was tall and blonde, quite pretty, with intense slate-gray eyes. At the moment, her mouth was little more than a thin line in her face. She wore a white V-neck shirt that was fairly saturated in blood, particularly down the right side. Black, dried blood had crusted over a wound on her arm, but she barely seemed to notice.

She also made no attempt to hide the small silver pistol, a Walther PPK, tucked in the waistband of her jeans.

"I want to talk to Cartwright," the woman said flatly.

Anne blinked several times rapidly. "I'm so sorry, ma'am, but I don't know who—"

"Listen, lady," the woman snapped. "I've had a *really* bad morning. I'm extremely pissed off. I've got four more shots in this clip. And I want to talk to Cartwright. Now."

Anne licked her lips slowly, deliberating. When people came into the shop—not for insurance, of course—they were supposed to deliver a line: "Excuse me, miss, but my car broke down and I need to use the telephone." She was supposed to politely nod and direct them to the back offices. That was the entirety of her job.

She'd also never been threatened with a gun before.

"... One moment," Anne said slowly. She picked up the phone on her desk. It looked like an old rotary-style telephone, but she didn't have to turn the dial; it connected automatically to an operator in Langley. Anne whispered quickly about the strange, bloody woman who had appeared in the office.

Then she cradled the receiver against her shoulder and asked, "Who should I say is asking?"

The blonde woman leaned over the desk. "Tell them it's Maria Johansson. And that Cartwright wants to take this call."

❧ ❧ ❧

The receptionist directed Maria to one of the two back offices and then returned to her desk. Maria closed the door behind her and wrinkled her nose distastefully at the tacky décor. It looked more like something one would find in the American Midwest than in Rome—wood-paneled walls, fake certificates for excellence in customer service, even a cheesy motivational poster featuring a cat clinging to a clothesline by its claws, with the caption, "Hang in there!"

There was no one in the office. There would be no one in the other office, either; the receptionist was the only person who worked here, usually the only inhabitant of the place ever, save for the infrequent occurrence that a field agent required assistance and had no other recourse. "Coming in from the cold," they called it. Sometimes an agent would have to go dark for a while, if an op went south or someone was tailing them. It could be a few days or even weeks, but eventually they would show up at one of the appointed stations—like the insurance office in Rome—and report in.

There was a code, a metaphor, for everything. And it was not at all lost on Maria how most of those codes involved terms like cold, dark, shadows, and silence.

In the center of the office was a simple oak desk, papers and pens and random office supplies arranged atop it as if someone had simply stepped away for lunch mid-task. On one side was an armless swivel chair, and on the other were two green-cushioned guest seats. But Maria did not sit. Instead, she paced the twelve-foot room, waiting anxiously.

Ordinarily, she never would have come here. Before today, she would have thought it dangerous, foolhardy even. If there were moles in the agency, as she suspected, they could have eyes on this place. But she needed to know what had happened and why. And if Kent was still alive.

The corded phone on the desk rang. She snatched it up quickly, halfway through the first ring.

The person on the other end breathed evenly for a long moment. Then he said, "The shadows are getting long."

Maria winced, squeezing her eyes shut. She had grown to hate the codes, the metaphors, the deceit. But she knew them all and remembered them well. "It'll be dark soon," she said softly.

"Hello, Agent Johansson." Deputy Director Cartwright did not sound pleased.

"Just Johansson, remember?" she corrected flatly. "Cartwright, what the *hell* was that about?"

"Sorry?"

"Don't," she warned. "Don't play that game. Not with me." *Deny. Disclaim. Disavow.* It was their way, the superiors—they knew everything until the shit hit the fan, and then suddenly they knew nothing. "Kent is alive. Or he was. You sent Morris after us."

Cartwright was silent for a long moment. "We have reason to believe that Agent Morris may have been working with the Fraternity…"

"Bullshit," she hissed. "I don't believe that for a second. You sent him to kill…wait. What did you just say? He 'may have been'? Is Morris dead?"

"Yes," Cartwright sighed.

"And Kent?"

"Alive and well. In fact, I just spoke to him not too long ago, on the phone. *Your* phone."

Johansson shook her head. Morris was dead, and Kent was alive—which could only mean one thing. Kent had killed an active CIA agent. That could spell a lot of trouble for him.

"And what about before?" she asked. "When Kent was claimed KIA? Was that really the Fraternity, or did you lie to me about that too?"

"Maria," Cartwright said gently. "We both know why you're standing where you are, why you're talking to me. Personally, I don't give a damn about your feelings. I care about facts. And the fact is that Kent Steele is a danger to himself and others. He's a danger to us—"

"He's going after the Fraternity," Maria argued. "He's doing his job, or what his job was supposed to be—"

"And falling right back into old habits," Cartwright interrupted. "Did he tell you about the bomb-making facility that he blew up? The four Iranians left dead in a Paris basement? No questioning, no debriefing…just carnage. He's not on a mission. He's on a warpath. He doesn't care who gets in his way. Now I've got two dead agents on my hands…"

"Two?"

Cartwright scoffed. "He didn't tell you? No, of course not. Why would he?" He sighed. "Maria, Alan Reidigger is dead."

"No." She shook her head, as if denying it would simply make it not so.

"He is. He was killed in Zurich, multiple stab wounds—and by multiple, I mean *dozens*…"

"Stop," she breathed. She didn't want to think of that, not about Alan. "Even if that's true, it wasn't at Kent's hands. They were friends…" She trailed off. Her throat tightened.

He didn't know her. He had lost his memory. Maybe he hadn't remembered Reidigger either. Maybe he thought Alan had information. Maybe. She didn't want to believe it. She wanted desperately to trust him.

But you don't, she thought. *Not completely. Or else you wouldn't have taken his gun while he was sleeping.*

"He's dangerous, Maria. You know he is. Help us to help him. We can bring him in."

"No. You sent Morris. You'll kill him if you get the chance."

"I won't," Cartwright insisted. "I told Morris to use non-lethal force. He must have gone rogue. Listen, I'm on a plane right now. I'll be at HQ in Zurich in a few hours. Meet me there, debrief, on the record, and I'll give you a team. You can get him yourself. Bring him in safely." He paused before adding, "Isn't that what you want?"

"I don't know where he's going," Maria lied. She knew the address in Slovenia by heart. "When Morris came at us, we got separated. He could be anywhere."

"You know him better than anyone," Cartwright countered. "I need you. You're the best I've got in the field."

"I'm not in the field," she said quickly.

Cartwright chuckled. "Right. Of course not. This is a secure line, Maria. We can talk freely. You and I are the only ones that know. Not even Morris knew about you."

Of course Morris hadn't known. Neither did Reidigger. The entire agency, beyond Cartwright, thought she had been disavowed. It was true that the ordeal with Kent and the Fraternity had shaken her, but she had never been a quitter.

"Well?" Cartwright said. "Are you in or not?"

Johansson chewed her lower lip. Her options weren't ideal. Either she could go on her own, try to find Kent, and let the agency send others to track him. Or she could take Cartwright's offer, head the team, and personally make sure things didn't get messy.

She knew that if she chose the former, they would take the first shot they got at Kent. And if she was with him, it would spell trouble for her, just like it had with Morris.

"I'm not coming to Zurich," she told him. "There's no time for all that. Send two agents to Ljubljana."

"What's in Ljubljana?" Cartwright asked.

"An airport. I'll meet them in terminal four. I want guys I know... give me Watson and Carver."

"Carver's on an op—"

"Then pull him," Maria snapped.

"Should I remind you who you're speaking to—"

"Otherwise there's no deal," she said firmly. "Watson and Carver. Plainclothes and dark."

Cartwright scoffed. "Be reasonable. There's no way I'm sending two agents in dark—"

"No phones, no tracking, or there's no deal," she said. "I can get him, and you can't afford another mess on your hands like last time."

Cartwright grunted. "Fine. They'll be in Ljubljana by thirteen hundred hours. Be there." He hung up.

Johansson replaced the receiver on the cradle. She didn't trust him, not for a second—but it came with the territory. She didn't trust anyone in the agency at this point. And she knew that the feeling was mutual. Cartwright wouldn't trust her; he would send his guys with different orders, she was certain. But at least she would be there. She'd know where they were. As much as she didn't want to admit it, Cartwright was right about one thing—Kent was dangerous, but especially to himself. She didn't want the deputy director knowing about his memory loss; they would only use it to their advantage.

She knew where Kent was going. The address was a warehouse in Maribor, Slovenia. She would have to get there quickly; Kent was undoubtedly already on his way, and if she didn't act fast, she'd be following a trail of bodies to find him.

CHAPTER TWENTY THREE

"**H**ey, buddy." A lanky kid in his early twenties with a flat-brimmed cap leaned over the aisle conspiratorially. "You American?"

"Yeah," Reid murmured. "Why?"

"We just took gold in snowboarding. Saw it online." The kid grinned.

"What?" Reid had been scanning through papers at the time and had no idea what the kid was talking about.

"The Olympics?" the kid said. "We just took gold."

"Oh. Uh, great." Reid forced a smile. He'd forgotten that the games were even going on. He wished he could get excited about something like a sporting event at the moment. In fact, in his normal life, he might be following it with his girls, watching and chanting "USA!" He wasn't big on sports—he followed basketball, though he rarely watched games—but there was something about the Olympics that inspired ubiquitous patriotism, however brief it might be.

After getting off the subway in Rome, Reid had found a nearby wireless shop and had them pull the information off of Maria's SIM card for him. They emailed a copy to the address he had established and he printed out a hard copy, several sheets' worth of names and addresses. While he was there he used one of their display phones to log into his Skype account. There was a single message from Maya, checking in as he had asked.

Safe, it said. *Away from NY. Told no one.*

His heart skipped a beat when he saw that the message was time-stamped nearly fourteen hours earlier. He quickly did the math in his head, accounting for the time difference; that would have been around four in the afternoon the day before. He had asked her to check in every twelve hours.

Panic rose in his chest. Had something happened to them? If it had, how would he ever know? How could he find them?

Calm down. It's early yet over there.

They could just be sleeping.

He typed out a quick message—*It's been more than 12 hours. Check in, please.* He waited for ten minutes. Then twenty. The clerk at the wireless store finished pulling the contacts from Maria's phone and printed them for him, but still there was no reply from Maya. Reid was desperate, but he knew he couldn't stay there. Not while the blond Amun assassin was still at large. He had to get out of Rome as soon as possible.

Though it broke his heart to think that any harm might have befallen his girls, he forced himself to leave the café and wandered into a travel agency a few blocks over, where he paid a hundred and fifty euros for a ticket on a tourist bus line that was heading to Ljubljana, Slovenia's capital, with a transfer in Venice.

The other passengers were a blend of American, Canadian, English, a few French, and a middle-aged couple from Australia. They chatted excitedly to each other about their travels through Europe, what they had seen and had yet to see, and how their countries were faring in the winter games.

Reid kept to himself—aside from the lanky kid across the aisle who updated him on snowboarding—as he pored over the printed contacts he had gotten from Maria's phone. He did not recognize any of the names. None of them incited any visions or memories. He knew she was smart; it was possible they were all fake, or mostly fake, to throw anyone off the trail who might have gotten their hands on the phone. There was not a single address in the phone listed under Slovenia, but on his second pass over the documents he finally found it—a street and a block number followed by the letters "MBX."

The airport code for Maribor, a city in eastern Slovenia.

The contact name attributed to the address was Elene Stekt. *What sort of name is that?* he wondered. *Hungarian? Dutch?* Something seemed simultaneously strange and familiar about the name. He stared at it for several minutes before he realized.

It was an anagram of his own name—rather, one of his names. It couldn't be a coincidence that Elene Stekt also spelled Kent Steele.

But Maria thought I was dead. Why would she hide my name on this particular contact?

He came to two possible conclusions. Either she had lied to him about that as well, and knew that he was still alive before he'd ever shown up... or she had done it after he arrived in Rome, which meant that she had intended to give him the phone well before Morris ever came for him.

His thoughts were interrupted by a loud woman two rows behind him on the bus, wishing other passengers a happy Valentine's Day. Reid hadn't been keeping track of the days. His thoughts went again to his girls, especially Maya—she had a date in the city with some boy today. That seemed like ages ago, that night she cooked dinner and admitted she needed to buy a dress. His heart broke anew for his girls, but he forced himself to think of something else.

His mind drifted back to the Amun assassin in the subway bathroom in Rome. The experience had rattled him; the blond stranger was fast, well trained, and unafraid. But what bothered Reid most was that he had the odd feeling that he wasn't a stranger at all. His face had seemed just on the edge of familiarity.

"*You know me,*" the assassin had sneered.

Reid closed his eyes and tried to conjure the image of the assassin's face. He pictured blond hair, blue eyes, sharp features, shorn cheeks. Blood eking from his nose where Reid had hit him with a stall door. The snarl on his lips as he tried to kill him. It had all seemed so personal, like this man had a vendetta. But the image did not trigger any memories. Instead, it blurred and faded, and spurred a fresh headache that pounded at his temples.

Reid groaned in frustration and rubbed his forehead. If Maria was right and these headaches and faded memories were side effects of the implant being torn out, did he have to worry about long-term damage? How useful would he be to himself, or anyone, if he couldn't remember details that might prove crucial?

Try as he might to stay focused on the task at hand, he found himself vacillating between thoughts of his girls, of the sneering assassin, of Morris, and of Maria.

The bus arrived in Ljubljana by dusk, pulling into a station adjacent to the Jože Pu nik Airport. A time and temperature display just outside the bus station told him that it was only nine degrees outside. Reid ducked into a restroom and put on the thermal sweater from Reidigger's bug-out bag under his jacket. Then he walked over to the airport, to a rental agency, and signed out a motorbike using his alias, Benjamin Cosgrove. The clerk there spoke decent English and insisted that Reid needed a valid credit card to rent a vehicle— until he slid a fifty-euro note across the counter. He signed Ben's name to a contract stating that he wouldn't leave the city limits with it.

Then he drove the hour and a half to Maribor.

He had never driven a motorcycle before—at least Reid Lawson hadn't—but Kent Steele handled the bike expertly. The February wind was cold and biting, but his fleece-lined bomber jacket and the thermal sweater kept him warm enough. A car might have been better for the weather, but the bike would be much easier to conceal and stash somewhere.

He entered the city from the southwest. Maribor was a simply stunning city; its Old Town section was rustic and charming, comprised of well-lit orange-roofed villas appointed along the Drava River, colorful and bright even at night. It was a major cultural hub, not only of Slovenia but of the whole of Europe. Its downtown contained tall gray spires, centuries-old cathedrals, and a landscape of rich and storied architecture.

But that's not where Reid was going.

Before leaving Maribor proper, he parked the bike at a public park and took a seat on the bench. He was starving; he hadn't eaten anything all day, so he removed one of the MREs from Reidigger's

GOOD bag and tore it open. A "meal, ready to eat" was a light-weight, self-contained ration used by the US military when a facility wasn't readily available. In this particular case, it was a pouched meal that claimed to be beef brisket, but turned out to be barely palatable. Still, he needed something in his stomach. He ate quickly with the plastic spoon included in the kit, and then tossed the remnants in the trash.

While he ate, he planned.

He was keenly aware that save for the three-inch Swiss Army knife, he was wholly unarmed. He would have to play this very carefully. After considering his options and conferring with Kent's knowledge of makeshift weapons, he got back on the bike and drove to a retail district, where he stopped into a hardware store and bought two cans of aerosol lubricant spray, a European knock-off brand of WD-40.

The white-haired hardware store clerk was a native Slovenian, but had taken enough German in school for simple conversation. Reid pretended to be a tourist motorbiking across the country. He showed the clerk the address and asked the easiest way to get there.

The old man frowned. "Why do you want to go there?" he asked.

"To see a friend," Reid replied.

The clerk shrugged and issued a vague warning. "Keep tight hold on your backpack." He didn't know the precise address, but he was able to give Reid directions to the street he was seeking.

He got back on the bike and traveled east, nearly to the city's limits. The grandeur of Maribor proper melted away as Reid found himself in an area that anyone would describe as the slums—cracked concrete and crumbling foundations, graffiti-strewn facades and tireless coupes on cinder blocks. It was as if a veil had been lifted; as if the splendor of Maribor's Old Town was a front to hide the poor neighborhoods, the ghettos, the leaning buildings that looked like they had been haphazardly stacked atop one another. There were few people out at this time of night, and those who were had somber expressions and stared at the ground sullenly. Even so, he felt as if there were eyes on him from somewhere nearby—possibly noticing he was American, marking him as a potential target for theft.

The address from Maria's phone led him to a flat, wide, two-story industrial building with large, rolling steel garage bay doors lining the street-facing side. The foundation was, unsurprisingly, crumbling and Reid could have sworn the eastern face of the brown-bricked building was visibly sagging. He stowed the bike behind a rusted dumpster a block away and used the cover of darkness to edge his way along the drooping façade of the warehouse, down an alley.

The adjacent gray building looked like it might have been low-income apartments at some point, but now seemed to be abandoned. He took a chance and entered a broken door at the ground level facing the alley.

The interior smelled strongly of mold and urine. There were holes in the wooden floor, gaping openings with jagged edges yawning into darkness below. He stepped carefully and made his way to a thoroughly untrustworthy-looking staircase. After testing his weight on the bottommost few stairs, he took a chance and started up.

On the second floor he found a position near a broken window and watched the warehouse across the narrow alley. His vantage point was little more than ten feet away; he could clearly see a single lit window, the only light on in the whole building, it seemed. There was no window covering. Reid moved to a closer window and adjusted his position to account for parallax. Inside the opposite building he could see a trio of men playing cards—poker, by the looks of it—and a fourth man watching over their shoulder. They were in a former office that had apparently been haphazardly arranged into some sort of living quarters; behind them was a kitchenette, and he could see the edge of a ratty sofa from his view.

Three of the men were white, two were bearded, one was bald, and the fourth was Arabic. There must not have been much heat in the building; all four wore jackets, no doubt hiding guns beneath them. Reid couldn't tell which, if any, or if all, were Amun. Even if he had binoculars to sight in on their necks, the high collars of their coats would have obscured the brand.

They seemed to be at ease. He would at least have the element of surprise on his side.

Reid unzipped the bug-out bag and took out the roll of duct tape and the two road flares that Reidigger had packed, and then the two cans of aerosol oil he'd purchased in Ljubljana. He uncapped the cans and duct-taped a flare to the side of each. Then he put them back in the bag and carefully headed down the stairs again to the ground level. From there, he stole quickly down the alley and around to a steel security door on the western side.

He paused with his fingers on the handle and took a breath. No matter what happened, he promised himself, he would have to do whatever was necessary to get information. Like Maria had said back in Rome—he was one person with no one at his back and no one he could trust, not even the agency.

By whatever means necessary.

I will. I have to.

He pulled the door open. It squealed shrilly on its hinges.

Just inside was a small landing, a steel staircase leading up, and a single man sitting in a folding lawn chair and reading a newspaper. As soon as Reid took a single step inside, the thug tossed the paper aside and leapt up, scowling deeply. He was large, more fat than muscle, with long, dark hair pulled into a tight ponytail.

"Who are you?" he barked in Russian as his hand moved to the revolver holstered at his hip.

Reid did not answer—at least, not with words. As soon as he yanked the door open, he took two brisk strides and jabbed quickly with his right fist. He caught the man just behind the chin, on the part of the jaw commonly referred to by fighters as "the knockout button" or "the off-switch." The leverage behind the strike rattled the thug's head hard enough to jar his brain. His large body went limp and he collapsed to the floor.

Reid first relieved him of his revolver—a break-action MP-412 REX, Russian model, .357 Magnum. The gun felt heavy and unwieldy in his hand, but he was in a pinch. It would have to do. He snapped open the chamber. It was fully loaded.

Reid bent again to check the thug's neck when he moaned and stirred. His eyes opened and he rolled over onto his forearms, attempting to rise. Reid quickly snaked his arm around the Russian's neck and squeezed him into a sleeper hold. The thug struggled. He was regaining his strength—and he was strong.

Reid shifted his arm slightly, just enough to see the man's neck. There was no brand there. But while his gaze was averted, the thug loosed a lockback knife from his pocket and whipped it open.

Reid twisted both arms in opposite directions and snapped the thug's neck. The large man slumped back to the floor, his eyes wide, mouth frozen in a wide grimace.

It takes only seven pounds of pressure to break the hyoid bone.

Reid took a calming breath.

Whatever it takes, he reminded himself.

He headed up the stairs.

On the landing outside their door, he opened the bug-out bag as quietly as possible and took out one of his makeshift flash-bangs, the aerosol lubricant with a flare taped to the side. He put his ear to the door; he could hear the voices inside, chatting with each other in both Russian and what he assumed was Slovenian (he didn't recognize it). There was the occasional shout of a curse and laughter from the others as someone won or lost a poker hand.

They were at ease. They heard nothing. They suspected nothing.

He made sure the Swiss Army knife was in his jacket pocket, blade open and at the ready.

Then he kicked in the door.

At the same time he splintered the jamb, he popped the flare. The four men at the table leapt up, shouting in Slovenian and Russian, overlapping one another. Reid threw his small bomb through the doorway. It arced in the air. The men squinted in the sudden, blasting light of the phosphorous tip of the flare as it ignited in sheer, blinding white. Reid ducked around the corner, his hands over both ears and eyes squeezed shut.

The aerosol can bounced once on the table and exploded.

Chapter Twenty Four

The blast was instant and impressive, louder than the chug of a shotgun. The orange fireball lasted only a half second but sent a wave of scorching heat throughout the office-turned-living space. The four men either leapt to the floor or were forced to it, sent reeling by the improvised flash-bang.

Reid rounded the corner and entered the makeshift apartment. A haze of smoke filled the room. The explosion had cracked the thin card table in half. There were several small fires burning, scattered playing cards smoldering into ash. One of the men stood, wobbling on his legs—the bald man he had seen through the window. A thin trail of blood fell from each ear. He barely even seemed to notice that anyone had entered the apartment before Reid drove an elbow into his solar plexus, doubling him over. A swift knee to the forehead rendered him unconscious.

Reid spun with the stolen revolver raised and scanned the room. The Arabic man was on the floor, unmoving. A third man was making a feeble attempt to draw a gun from a shoulder holster, but he was disoriented. His eyes were bloodshot. His face was a shiny red and his eyebrows were gone. The rapid fireball must have gotten him right in the face.

He pulled out the pistol, but it clattered to the floor in his shaky hand. He staggered. Reid kicked at his hip and the man fell, spinning to the floor. He checked the man's neck. No brand. He inspected the two unconscious men. No brands there, either.

There were four. He had definitely seen four men through the window. He hurried toward the rear of the apartment, leading with the pistol as he entered a dingy space with walls of bare drywall. There were two mattresses on the floor and a lamp without a shade, but no person. He heard a clatter from behind a closed door to his left. He kicked it open. It was a bathroom, filthy and smelling strongly of mildew and burnt hair.

The fourth man had forced a window open and was trying to wriggle out of it, but the opening was barely more than a foot wide. He was about a third of the way out, his head and arms through but his midsection hanging over the tub and his legs kicking at the air.

Reid grabbed him by the back of his belt and yanked him back into the bathroom. The man fell into the yellow-ringed tub in a heap. He had an impressive burn down the left side of his face, and most of his beard was scorched off.

The man glared up at Reid with a mask of hatred. In that moment, he could clearly see the brand, the glyph of Amun, standing in sharp relief against the bright red skin of the man's neck.

"Amun," Reid said.

For a moment, a glimmer of fear registered in the man's eyes. This stranger knew who he was. "Zero," the man murmured.

Then Reid flipped the pistol around in his hand and smacked the man sharply on the temple. He slumped into the tub, unconscious.

Reid hurried out to the living room. The single still-conscious man was crawling on his hands and knees toward the door. Reid grabbed him by an ankle and dragged him back in as he yelped and protested in Russian. He took the duct tape out of the bug-out bag and bound the man by his wrists and ankles, and then tore off a short strip and covered the man's mouth.

He quickly did the same with the two unconscious men. They would likely be awake soon, and they wouldn't stay disoriented forever.

Back in the bathroom, he twisted a long strip of duct tape around the Amun man's wrists. He hauled him upright and slapped his cheek a few times. The man grunted and groaned as he came to.

"English?" Reid asked. "Hmm?"

"To hell with you," the man muttered. His accent was difficult to place; Romanian, it seemed, or possibly Bulgarian. "I tell you nothing. You may as well shoot me." His voice was weak and his words slurred slightly.

Reid shook his head and set the REX revolver down on the back of the toilet. "I'm not going to shoot you," he said. He took the Swiss Army knife out of his pocket. "See this? You know what this is? It's a handy little tool. I was a Boy Scout, decades ago—had one just like it. Let's see... it's got a screwdriver. A can opener. A knife, of course." He opened each implement, showed it off, and then snapped it shut again. "Tweezers. Little saw blade here... actually, I think that's for scaling fish." Reid opened the corkscrew and scoffed lightly. "Corkscrew. Isn't that funny? Like anyone is using a Swiss Army knife to open a bottle of cabernet."

These were Kent Steele's words. Kent's tactics. Kent's by-any-means-necessary mentality.

The terrorist's nostrils flared as his lips curled into a snarl. "Do your worst," he sneered. "I am Amun. We are trained. Prepared for anything."

"Anything," Reid repeated softly. "No. Not for me." He grabbed the man's bound wrists and pulled them straight, forcing his forearms across the edge of the tub. He pressed the tip of the corkscrew to the man's left forearm. The man tried to pull back, but he was weakened and Reid held him fast. "What is it you're doing here?"

"To hell with you," the man spat again.

Reid sighed disappointedly. He twisted the corkscrew as he pressed. The tip of it pierced the skin. Blood pooled around it and ran down the side of the yellow tub. The man hissed through his teeth, spraying spittle across the cracked tile floor.

"Amun prepares you for things. For people like me. The other agents. Our black sites. What we might do to you." Kent had taken over, and this time the Reid Lawson side of him did not protest. It was necessary, Reid knew. As much as the idea of tormenting another human being might ordinarily turn his stomach, this was his only lead. It was this, or people would die. "But you see, all those preparations just force me to get more creative."

He twisted again, applying downward pressure as the corkscrew penetrated muscle. The man gritted his teeth again, hissing quick breaths, his eyes squeezed shut.

"Please, just tell me what I want to know." He twisted again. The man yelped. "I've got nothing but time. Nowhere else to go from here."

"Then…" the man panted. "Then that makes you…my prisoner." The corners of his blistering mouth curled into a grin, lips twitching with the pain.

Reid shook his head. "That's where you're wrong, friend. Because I'm going to get to the bone soon." He twisted again. The man made a choking sound, trying desperately not to cry out. "It takes a lot of pressure to penetrate bone—trust me, I know. Bones are strong; one of the strongest substances found in nature."

He wrenched down on the corkscrew again. This time the man screamed.

"But it's just a matter of physics. Pressure and leverage. This will penetrate bone. That's going to hurt a lot more. When it gets to the marrow, this pain is going to be ten times worse. If it gets all the way through, it'll split the bone in the center. Even if you somehow regain use of this arm, it'll never be the same again."

The tip of the corkscrew scraped against the radius in his forearm. The man howled in agony.

Reid was bluffing; a corkscrew and downward pressure was not strong enough to penetrate bone, but he knew that the combination of pain and fear with the right threat could be more powerful than force.

"To hell…" the man grunted. Reid twisted a little further and the words caught in his throat, escaping as a pained whimper.

"You've got two arms," Reid said. "Two legs. And a whole lot of vertebrae…you know that word, 'vertebrae'? Your spine. There are thirty-one pairs of spinal nerves. You think this is bad? It gets so much worse."

"I heard … stories," the man wheezed. "But I did not … think them true."

"Stories? Of what?"

"You." The man's eyes met Reid's. His pupils were almost fully dilated. He was afraid. "You are the devil."

"No," Reid said quietly. "I'm not the devil. I'm just a man in a corner. And your people put me there. Now … let's begin." He stood and put one foot against the tub, as if preparing himself for the necessary leverage to push the corkscrew into bone. He sucked in a deep breath—

"Trucks!" the man grunted. "Trucks!"

Reid paused. "What about trucks?"

"Trucks come." His voice wavered, his breaths coming fast and uneven. Blood ran liberally over the edge of the tub. "They come. We unload the cargo. Put it on another truck."

"That's it? You unload one truck and load another?" Reid shook his head. "What's on the trucks?"

"I don't know," the man hissed.

Reid shook his head. He put his foot up again, preparing to wrench down.

"I don't know!" the man screamed. "I don't know! I don't know!"

Reid believed him. He knew all too well by now that Amun's MO was keeping people in the dark as often as possible. "Some of those men out there spoke Russian. Have you ever heard the name Otets before?"

The man nodded weakly. "Yes."

"The drivers of these trucks, who were they?"

The man shook his head. His chin drooped. "I don't know … Middle Eastern …"

The bombs, Reid thought as he pieced it together in his mind. *Otets made bombs. Gave them to the Iranians. They drove them here. Changed trucks. Why? To avoid being followed or tracked? No … that would be too simple.* Maria had told him that Amun's trail was thorough, and they worked hard to keep their members from knowing too much. *They change trucks so that no single person knows where they came from and where they're going.* He wouldn't have been surprised to learn that there were multiple depots like this one on whatever route they took.

"That's all I know," the man said breathlessly. "I swear it."

"No," Reid countered. "You're Amun. You must know something more. Where are the others in your organization? Where are they headquartered?"

The man said nothing. He stared at the floor and shook his head feebly.

Reid knew there was only so far he could get with threats. He turned the man's arm slightly and twisted the corkscrew again. It bit further into the muscle as it slipped between the radius and ulna of his forearm.

The man threw back his head and howled in agony.

"Where?"

"There is…no…one place…" he said raggedly. "We are…everywhere…"

"Give me something," Reid threatened. "We've got hours to do this." That wasn't true either; the three men in the other room were only bound with duct tape. They would work their way out of it eventually.

He twisted again. The man tried to scream but it came out as a hoarse hiss of air.

"You must know something," Reid said.

"The…the…the…" the man stammered.

"The what?"

"The…sheikh…"

"Sheikh?" Reid frowned. "Mustafar? What about him?"

"He knows…he knows…" The man was panting again. Half of his face was shiny-red from the explosion; the other had completely drained of color. "He knows."

You know, Sheikh…a bullet sounds the same in every language.

"No, we have the sheikh. We've already interrogated him," said Reid. "He doesn't know anything. He was a patsy. A scapegoat."

"The sheikh," the man said again. His voice was barely above a whisper. "He's not... he's not..." His eyes rolled up and he slumped forward. His forehead bounced lightly against the rim of the tub before Reid could catch it. Unconscious from either shock or blood loss, Reid assumed.

He groaned in frustration. *The sheikh's not what?* Not telling the truth? The sheikh didn't know anything; he had learned that already from a triggered memory. He was a false lead, a trail gone cold. This man was a member of Amun—it made sense for him to try to throw Reid off, feed him bad intel.

But what if that's not what this was? he thought. *What if he was trying to tell me something about Mustafar?* The man had been under significant duress. Even so, the sheikh was being held at a CIA black site in Morocco. There was no chance that Reid could get to him, not without being discovered.

He rose slowly and washed the blood from his hands in the dirty sink. He left the corkscrew in the man's arm as he searched his pockets. There was a cell phone, and much like Otets's previously, there was no information saved, no call history, no contacts.

Reid dialed 112 on the phone—the number for emergency services, the 911 of the European Union. A woman answered flatly in Slovenian.

"English?" Reid asked.

"Yes, what is your emergency?" she said.

"There's a fire." He gave her the address to the warehouse. Then he ended the call abruptly and tossed the phone into the tub. He retrieved the revolver from atop the toilet and slung his bag over one shoulder.

Out in the living room, one of the men had worked his way out of the bonds around his wrists and was frantically tugging at the duct tape around his ankles. When he saw Reid emerge, he rolled over and reached for his gun. Reid already had his in hand. He fired once. The kick of the .357 was significant, almost exhilarating. The shot struck the man in the forehead and left an impressive hole.

He tucked the revolver into the back of his pants. Then, with a grunt of effort, he pulled the stove away from the wall, reached behind it, and yanked out the gas line.

The other two men were conscious on the floor, duct tape still over their mouths, watching him with wide eyes.

He knew he couldn't let them live—especially not the Amun member. They would report it immediately. They would know the trail that Agent Zero was following.

Reid stood in the doorway as he took the second aerosol can, with the road flare duct-taped to it, out of his bag. He popped the flare, tossed it across the floor, and then leapt down the stairs.

Three seconds later the first explosion, the blast of the aerosol can, came barely an instant before the second, much larger blast. The entire apartment was incinerated in the blink of an eye. Windows exploded outward; walls caved. A fireball whooshed out through the open door and filled the stairwell, but by that time Reid was already on the ground floor, pushing his way through the steel security door and hurrying out into the cold night.

He strode briskly down the block, keeping alert of his periphery for anyone who might have seen him leave the building. There didn't seem to be anyone around. When he arrived at the dumpster he was not at all astonished to find the motorbike missing. He scoffed. Likely some unseen pair of eyes from a surrounding building had watched him hide it, and had stolen it the moment he went into the warehouse.

Reid doubled back and slipped down the narrow alley as the apartment burned. A flaming playing card fluttered down and landed nearby. Sirens wailed in the distance as emergency vehicles raced to the blaze before it spread to the building's ramshackle neighbors.

At the mouth of the alley, Reid turned left. He slowed his pace and stuck his hands in the pockets of his bomber jacket to appear casual. Just out for an evening stroll—*no, Officers, I didn't hear any gunshot or explosion.*

The hairs on the back of his neck stood up.

He was being watched.

There were no streetlamps in this part of the city. The boulevard was dark; he would be little more than a silhouette to an assailant. He slowly reached for the gun at his back as he heard footfalls getting closer behind him.

His first thought was of the Amun assassin from the subway—that somehow the man had tracked him here, or assumed he would come. Reid drew the revolver as he spun, leveling it at shoulder height, ready to fire the veritable cannon into whatever threat was in his path...

"Kent!" She froze when she saw the size of the gun in his hand.

"Maria." He blinked in surprise—not in surprise that she was there, but by his own reaction to seeing her alive. It was a sensation of relief, of solace.

Still, he didn't lower his gun. He had the distinct feeling that she hadn't come alone.

CHAPTER TWENTY FIVE

Rais was furious.

He had him. He *had* Kent Steele on the business end of his Sig Sauer, and again he had managed to slip from his grasp.

Damn that fat Italian for barging in at the most inopportune moment.

Damn that Agent One—Agent Morris, as it turned out—for getting in the way.

It was no small relief that at least this time it hadn't ended with Rais's sternum open, but the mere fact that Agent Zero still drew breath caused him such fury that it manifested as a swirling tempest of a tension migraine, making it difficult for him to think straight.

If that insipid Agent Morris hadn't gotten in the way... if the police hadn't shown up... if that train hadn't been there at that precise moment... if only.

Worst of all—worse than Steele getting away, worse than Amun losing their CIA asset—was the fact that Steele had not even seemed to recognize him. Despite dyeing his hair blond and wearing blue contacts, Rais was up close, face to face. Given their history, there was no reason that Steele should not have fully realized who he was. But he simply didn't.

It was not an act. Rais could tell that there was not a glimmer of recognition behind Steele's eyes.

He had never felt more insignificant.

After eluding the police in the subway station, Rais had ducked into a department store and quickly purchased a green jacket and a baseball cap to hide his blond hair. He took out the blue contacts and tossed them in a trash can, along with his brown coat. Then he scoured the city for Kent Steele, checking every metro station he could find on the route. He knew it was no use; Steele was a professional. He was long gone, possibly even already out of Rome by then.

Rais knew he had no other recourse. He had no way to track the agent until Steele acted again. In the meantime, he would have to report to Amun and tell them that they had lost Agent One. Being Amun meant that he had taken an oath to never lie to or deceive his brothers. He would have to tell them that it was by his own hand, and he would have to accept the consequences.

He took out a phone and called an Amun contact who could quickly organize flight plans. The nameless man on the other end—he was just a number to Rais—directed him to a private airstrip just north of Rome. Less than an hour later, he was the only passenger on a four-seat Cessna 210, flying from Rome to Bern, the capital of Switzerland.

Upon arriving, Rais took a taxi to the Hotel Palais. It was so called because it was a literal palatial estate, overlooking meticulously appointed gardens and a forest beyond. Palais was a Swiss institution, a venue for diplomats and politicians, the self-proclaimed "guest house" of the Swiss government.

Fools, Rais thought as he entered the hotel and crossed the marble-floored lobby. *You have no idea who is among you.* Overhead the vaulted ceiling was entirely glass, affording a view of the clear blue sky. The whole thing made Rais sick. The opulence of it. The haughtiness. The wastefulness. But that was Amun's way—hiding in plain sight, blending in with the elite and the libertines and the disenfranchised alike.

He took the elevator to the third floor and followed the rich scarlet carpet to a corner suite, where he knew several of Amun were posing as a branch of a nonprofit group of traveling pediatricians. He knocked sharply on the door twice, waited three full seconds, and then knocked three more times in quick succession. That was his personal code, his identifier to his brothers. A moment later the door opened slightly, and a sharp-featured German man who slightly resembled a rat answered.

He let Rais in wordlessly. The hotel suite opened on a wide parlor with huge windows and white furniture. *Gaudy*, Rais thought distastefully. *Ostentatious.*

Three men sat on the white furniture, two on a sofa and one in an armchair so that they formed a triangle around a glass coffee table laden with a sweet-smelling tea. They wore suits, each with a high collar to hide the brand of Amun on their necks. The suite, the suits, even the tea was all a ruse, of course, in case they were interrupted by housekeeping or hotel management or the police. Each of the three could provide full documentation of their medical credentials. They could provide phone numbers to references that could substantiate their claims. They could even answer complex medical questions, if need be.

One of the three was, in fact, a surgeon and had been one of the team that had saved Rais's life after Steele opened his belly. Rais did not know his name; only that he was German, and so in his mind he referred to him simply as the German doctor. The rat-faced sycophant that had opened the door was his attendant. The second man in the room was Rais's immediate superior, the man that he called Amun. Rais knew that he was not *the* Amun, but he did not know his real name.

The third man in the room was instantly recognizable, despite the western suit and tie. Rais had only ever seen the sheikh in Muslim garb before; it was somewhat odd to see him wearing lapels and spectacles, but appearances needed to be maintained.

Rais nodded to each in turn. "Doctor. Amun. Sheikh Mustafar."

None of them said anything to him. The only one to even look his way was Amun, who rose slowly from the armchair. He was Egyptian; his skin was light brown and his beard black but thin. He couldn't have been more than a year or two older than Rais.

"Zero?" he asked simply.

Rais' gaze fell to the lush carpet. He shook his head slightly.

Amun backhanded him swiftly. The garnet in his pinky ring cut deeply into Rais's lip as his head jerked to the side.

Rais did nothing in return.

"Do you have any idea what it cost us to put you back together?" Amun's voice was barely a whisper. "Remind me why we wasted our efforts."

Rais had no valid answer. Instead he said, "Agent One is dead."

"Disappointment!" Amun hissed. " Failure. *American.*" He spat out the last word as if it was a horrible curse. "Go. Wait for me. I will decide what to do with you."

Rais swallowed blood as he retreated to the rear bedroom of the suite and shut the door behind him. He felt deeply shamed. He had failed—twice now. And he knew the way of Amun all too well, having carried it out himself many times. He was certain this meeting would end with a bullet in his skull.

He was American, once. But no longer; he had killed that part of him. He was Amun now. He held no emotional connection to his heritage. He had nothing to look back fondly on in the first twenty years of his sordid life.

Rais had been born and raised in a suburb outside Albany, New York, to a complacent, timid mother and an alcoholic, hardly employed father. His childhood had not been a pleasant one. His father was a bitter man convinced that this world was united solely against him, especially in those instances when his addiction caused him the loss of yet another job, which occurred every few months. The cycle was vicious: employment; fleeting, faux happiness; decline; dismissal; all spiraling into binging, violence, and blackouts. In those latter weeks-long bleak times, his father would lash out at his wife and young son with belt, switch, hands, whatever he had available. Once it had been a leather shaving strop.

At eighteen, Rais had enlisted in the US Army. He spent the next two years mostly at Fort Drum near Watertown, New York, a mere stone's throw from the Canadian border. Ironically, it had been an extremely liberating experience; while most young men had some trouble acclimating to the strict, regimented lifestyle of an army grunt, Rais reveled in it. Compared to his home life, the army was a cakewalk. He learned to fight, to shoot, and to run; as a forward observer, he learned about ordnance and rapid intervention and radio calls. He did not need to learn to follow orders. That had been ingrained in him since birth.

He spent brief stints in Japan, Germany, and South Korea, and then it happened. Two years into his six-year contract, the events of September 11, 2001, unfolded three hundred miles south of his base. A few months after, his unit was deployed to Afghanistan. Rais's three-man team scouted a section of Kandahar considered to be the last-known whereabouts of a prominent Al Qaeda bomb-maker. Rais was ordered to call in a strike on a building believed to be their headquarters. He could clearly see that it was full of women, children, and families that had nothing to do with the conflict.

Rais refused.

The bombs fell anyway.

One hundred and twelve people died that day. The Afghani bomb-maker was not among them. As far as Rais knew, none of those that perished in the conflagration had any ties to terrorism.

He fled. At twenty-one years old, he deserted the army and stowed away on an oil vessel that traveled through the Persian Gulf and into the Red Sea, docking in Egypt. He hid out, lived on the streets for months, surviving on scraps and the infrequent charity of others. After a little more than a year he fell in with a group of youths that called themselves activists, though political dissidents was a more appropriate term. He learned to pick pockets, to go unnoticed in a crowd, how to mix homemade incendiaries, and to evade authorities.

Eight months later, in a Cairo dive bar, he met a man who called himself Amun. It was a serendipitous encounter; the man was looking for someone willing to steal dynamite from a nearby tantalite mine. Rais was looking for purpose.

They talked at length; rather, Rais talked, and the man called Amun asked questions and listened. Rais spoke of his experiences, his opinions about the United States, his motivations for deserting. He found himself being more honest with the man that he had ever been before, with anyone. Amun spoke very little of his own experiences. He seemed fascinated with Rais's story.

Rais saw the man again the next week, and the week after that. Each time they met, this man that called himself Amun spoke a little more. He gave Rais books to read. He asked him opinions on world powers, politics, and the so-called "war on terror." Then, finally, after two months of intermittent visits, he asked Rais to come with him. He drove him to a compound in the desert. He introduced him to others.

Rais noticed immediately that they all had a scar on their necks—some sort of strange symbol. A glyph.

After speaking at length with several higher-ups in the organization, Rais was invited to live at the compound. He underwent severe trials to prove himself. They trained him, indoctrinated him, taught him … but they never ordered him. He always had a choice. At least that's what they told him, that he could leave anytime he wished. To this day he doubted that was true, but it didn't matter. He didn't want to leave.

By then he had already denounced his former homeland, at least mentally, but when it came time to do so officially and be welcomed into the sanctum of Amun, he chose a new name for himself—Rais, after the infamous Murat Rais. The name had a long and storied history shared by several men, though most prominent to him was the eighteenth-century Scotsman Peter Lisle, who converted to Islam and became an Ottoman corsair, adopting the name Murat Rais from another. Lisle eventually gained the position of Grand Admiral of Tripoli's navy.

Rais earned his mark, though his position within Amun required that it be hidden whenever possible. His years of stealing on the streets of Egypt and the marksmanship training from the US Army served him equally well as an assassin, and he quickly gained prominence among his brothers. Those few that knew his name knew that he carried out his duties with the utmost solemnity—his duties to eliminate, to cleanse for Amun's new world.

And now, it seemed, it was his turn to be cleansed.

❧ ❧ ❧

Rais waited in the bedroom of the suite for the meeting to finish and his fate to be decided. He did not try to eavesdrop but could still hear pieces of the hushed conversation taking place between the German doctor, the sheikh, and Amun.

"The serpents have already begun to arrive," he heard Amun say. The serpents, Rais knew, was a codename for heads of state and other undesirables to their cause.

The sheikh said something inaudible, and the German doctor responded.

"Nearly everything is in place. There is only one final piece." He switched to German, likely for the sake of his assistant, and said, "Go now. You know your duty."

"We do not wait. We do not waver," said Mustafar. "As Amun, we endure."

Rais did not know the full extent of the plot; he knew only pieces, though admittedly more than most other Amun members. He knew the plan involved striking once in a centralized location where not only dozens of heads of state would be present, but people from nearly every developed nation on the planet. He knew the second phase involved sowing dissension in the ranks of prominent government organizations, via well-placed agents of Amun.

The American CIA was one such entity.

There were other phases, he was aware, but he did not know their details. The plan had been meticulously crafted over the course of years. Finally it would be enacted—though Rais would not be alive to see it.

At long last the meeting adjourned. Through the door Rais heard Amun bid farewell to his guests with the parting phrase, "As Amun, we endure."

While he waited, he sank to his knees and murmured a prayer, one he had learned on his first day at the compound in the Western Desert of Egypt.

"Amun, who hears the prayer, who answers the cry of the poor and distressed...Repeat him to son and to daughter, to great and to small."

Rais closed his eyes. "Relate him to generations of generations who have not yet come into being; relate him to him who does not know him and to him who knows him."

He heard the door to the bedroom open, but still he kept his eyes closed as he murmured, "Though it may be that the servant is justified in doing wrong, yet Amun is justified in being merciful. As for his anger—in the completion of a moment there is no remnant. As Amun we endure."

Silence reigned. The door had opened, but Rais did not know if he was alone or not. He expected the bullet to tear into his forehead at any moment. He wondered if he would even hear it, or if the world would simply fall away.

"Rise," said Amun gently.

Rais opened his eyes. The Egyptian was standing before him, arms slack at his sides—and surprisingly, neither hand held a pistol.

"I have failed," Rais said. He looked up and met Amun's gaze. "I know better than most the penalty for failure. I am prepared."

Amun sighed. He reached out and wiped blood from the corner of Rais's mouth with the pad of his thumb. "Your life is not mine to take," he said. "It belongs to Amun."

Rais frowned in confusion.

"Yes, you failed," said Amun. "Agent Zero still draws breath—but so do you. Amun has chosen your destiny. What is seen as failure today may become little more than an impediment on a longer road. You have but one task, Rais, and that is to eliminate Zero from this world." Amun leaned close, close enough for Rais to smell the tea on his breath. "Only then are you permitted to die."

Rais nodded slowly. He had prepared himself mentally for the darkness that would assuredly follow the end of his life, but now he saw only light and possibility.

"The world will change in two days' time," Amun continued. "Zero cannot be allowed to interfere. A CIA task force has being sent to collect him and bring him here, to Switzerland."

"How do you—" Rais stopped himself. He wanted desperately to know how Amun could have that information, but he already knew he would not be permitted to know. He realized, however, that there was only one possible answer: Agent One had not been their only mole inside the American CIA.

"I will find him," Rais promised as he rose to his feet. "I will kill him."

Amun opened a drawer in the bureau, took out a burner phone, and gave it to Rais. "We will update you as we gain information. Now go."

Rais took the phone and left the bedroom without another word. He exited the suite, took the elevator to the ground floor, and hurried out of the Hotel Palais. He had been given a second chance, new life—and this time nothing would keep him from killing Kent Steele.

Chapter Twenty Six

"**M**aria."

She stood only a few arms' lengths from him on the dark street in Maribor as sirens grew louder a few blocks away, roaring toward the burning warehouse. Her features became evident as his eyes adjusted to the darkness—blonde hair, porcelain skin, her scent on the slight breeze.

Kent kept the revolver trained on her.

He wanted to ask her how she had found him, but he already knew.

"You knew the address," he said. "You had it memorized. You only gave me your phone so they could track me."

"No," she said. "I gave you the phone in case *I* needed to track you."

"I ditched it."

"I thought you might." She smirked and gestured toward the MP-412 REX in his hand. "That is a very large gun. Can you lower it, please?"

"I don't think so." He kept his aim on her. "You took my gun—"

"You were supposed to be dead. I wasn't sure I could trust you—"

"I'm still not sure I can trust *you*," he countered. "You lied to me. You're with them."

"It's more complicated than that," she said.

"Then explain it to me."

She sighed. "I told you the truth—most of it. I really was on Amun's trail, and they caught wind of it. They did put a hit out on me. Three times I dealt with their assassins. They always seemed to know where I was, or where I was going to be. But…I was never disavowed. I suspected moles in the agency. So I went dark and hid out at the safe house. Cartwright organized it. He spread the intel that I was disavowed. I didn't know they stopped looking for me. Every day I expected someone to come—one of theirs." She paused for a long moment. "But they didn't. You came."

"It was Morris," said Reid. "He was working with them."

"Cartwright said the same." Maria shook her head. "I don't want to believe that."

"It's true. In Rome, after I got away, there was an assassin. They knew each other, he and Morris."

"This assassin, did he…? Or did you…?"

"He did," Reid confirmed. "He killed Morris. Not me."

Her gaze fell to the street. "And what about Alan?"

Reid blew a soft sigh. Of course she would know about that. It didn't look good for him that he'd kept it from her. "That wasn't me. I found him dead in Zurich. I think Amun tortured and killed him to get to me."

"Why?"

"Because he…" Reid trailed off. He was fairly certain that Reidigger had helped him put the implant in his head, but he wasn't going to tip his hand to her again; not until he was certain he could trust her. He lowered his pistol to hip level, but he didn't take his finger off the trigger. That distinct feeling, the hairs on the back of his neck, hadn't gone away. "You didn't come alone."

"There are two others with me," she said plainly. "Watson and Carver. You know them. Or you did."

"And they're here for what? Waiting in the shadows for their chance to strike?"

"No," said Maria. "I took their guns." Very slowly, she reached behind her and pulled out two pistols—each a standard-issue Glock 27. She held them up for Reid to see, and then cautiously put them down on the pavement. "They're watching to make sure you don't hurt me." Then louder she said, "And they would be very stupid to try anything. They know you. They know what you're capable of."

Reid noticed the shadows shift in his periphery. He turned slightly to see a tall African-American man in a long coat reveal himself from the mouth of an alley. *Watson*, he knew. Across the street, in the dark doorway of an apartment building, was a second man in a baseball cap—Carver, presumably. Both showed themselves, but neither moved further.

"The lead," said Maria. "What did you find?"

"Nothing," Reid lied. "Dead end."

She raised an eyebrow suspiciously. "So you blew it up?"

"They did. There was a bomb. I barely got out in time."

"Hmm." Clearly she didn't believe him, but she didn't prod further.

"Is that really what you're doing here, Maria? Following a lead?" he asked. "Or did you come here for me?"

"I came here to help you," she said vaguely.

"Help me." He scoffed. "Help me how? Are we going to be a team again? You and me and these two?"

"No, Kent. I want to help you…and as strange as this might sound, I think the best way for me to do that is if you come with me. Come in from the cold."

He almost laughed. "You think that the best way for me to stay out of the hands of people I don't trust is to walk right into the den of people I can't trust?"

"Yes, I do." She took a small step toward him. "Because right now I know you better than you know yourself. I know that you may never trust them again, not fully." She took another step closer. His grip tightened around the revolver. "But we have resources. You can be reinstated. We can help you." She took one more step, until she was close enough that he could reach out and touch her.

From this close, he could see the intensity in her slate-gray eyes. She seemed sincere; he had to remind himself again that she was very well trained. Deceit was second nature.

But he had to be able to get to the sheikh if he was going to follow the potential lead that the Amun member had given him. It was possible, maybe even likely, to be a dead end, but he had nothing else to follow, nowhere else to go from there. And since Mustafar was being held in a CIA black site, he wouldn't get within a half mile of the sheikh before being gunned down.

But he didn't tell her any of that. Instead he said, "I need more than that. You're right that I can't trust them. I need you to give me one good reason to trust *you*."

She thought for a long moment. "You don't remember me. But I remember you. I care about you, Kent…more than you might think. I don't want to see you hurt."

He shook his head. "Without the memories, those are just words to me."

"Okay then." She spoke quietly so that Watson, standing about twelve feet from Reid's right, couldn't hear. "How about this: you have two girls back home. I know you're smart enough to have sent them somewhere, but that can't last forever. The agency knows about them, which means that Amun might know as well. We can put a security detail on them. I don't know who might be bad, but I know a few that are definitely good. People I know we can trust."

Reid frowned. "What does that mean, you don't know who might be bad?"

In almost a whisper she told him, "I don't think Morris was the only one. I never had reason to suspect him; neither did Cartwright. And Morris wouldn't have known where I was before the safe house. He didn't have access to that information. But somehow Amun did. There's someone else—maybe more than one, and higher up. Come in, and help me find them. We can't do that from the outside."

"If you're right, and it's someone higher up in the agency, they may have been the ones that tried to have me killed before," Reid reasoned. "What's to stop them from trying again?"

"We go on official record," she said. "We can go over Cartwright's head. I have a contact, someone I can call. You tell your story— the attempted murder, the memory implant, Paris, Belgium,

Rome…and we send it up the chain, past even Director Mullen. Make sure everyone knows that Kent Steele is not just alive, but back from the dead. Get the National Security Council involved. Hell, if they try anything stupid, we send it to the press. Make it public. We protect your girls. We take down Amun. We find the moles."

Reid thought for a long moment. Coming in from the cold seemed like a monumentally foolish idea at face value, but Maria's arguments were valid. It could help to flush out moles in the agency. His girls could be protected.

And most importantly, he could get to the sheikh. Otherwise, what would he do? It would either be a wild goose chase or he would have to make his whereabouts known to try to coax Amun out of hiding. Even so…

"It's risky," he said.

"You can handle it." Maria grinned. "You've handled worse things than bureaucracy."

Reid glanced over his shoulder. Agent Watson hadn't moved. Neither had Carver. If the agency truly wanted him dead, they would have supplied these two with a better method than just a pair of service pistols. He was out in the open on a dark street in the slums of Slovenia; they would have tried something by now.

The girls will be safe.

You can get to the sheikh.

"Fine," he said at last. "You say you care about me. You say I can trust you. This is your chance to prove it." He thumbed the hammer of the revolver into safety position and tucked it into the back of his pants. "I'll come with you. But I'm not giving up the gun."

"I wouldn't ask you to." She stooped and picked up the two Glocks from the street. Then she motioned with her head and the two agents, Carver and Watson, emerged from their shadowy positions. Neither said a word as the four of them headed toward a black SUV parked on the next block.

"Where are we going?" Reid asked as they walked.

"Zurich," she replied, "to the CIA's European headquarters." She chuckled softly.

"What's funny?"

"Oh, nothing really," Maria said. "I was just thinking about the look on Cartwright's face when he sees you. He is not going to believe his eyes."

CHAPTER TWENTY SEVEN

Deputy Director Cartwright peered through the two-way glass into an interrogation room, in absolute shock. Agent Zero, back from the dead.

Johansson sat beside him in a hard plastic chair, the two of them chatting quietly to each other.

This was troublesome. He hadn't expected Johansson to actually bring Zero in. He had given Watson and Carver explicit instructions—don't try anything unless Zero tries to run. Cartwright had fully expected Zero to run. Johansson had her claws in him, that much was certain.

Deputy Director Shawn Cartwright hadn't even been in Zurich for six hours when he got the call that Johansson had convinced Kent Steele to come in from the cold, and without a single shot fired (much to his chagrin, as she had relieved Agents Watson and Carver of their service pistols). At the time, Cartwright was asleep in a Hilton near the airport. Upon receiving the call he had leapt out of bed to dress and demanded that a car be sent to fetch him immediately.

CIA headquarters in Europe was on the fifth floor of the American consulate in Zurich, in a contemporary-designed gray and white building that looked more like a small hotel than a government building. A large American flag flew in the courtyard. A sturdy steel fence surrounded the perimeter, accessible only by an electronic gate with a guard house and twenty-four-hour security detail.

Cartwright flashed his badge at the security guard and the gate slid aside for him. It was nearly two a.m.; Johansson and Steele had gotten on a plane in Slovenia and flew straight to Zurich, where a waiting car picked them up and brought them to the consulate. They had arrived at the consulate before him. Cartwright didn't much care for that part—Johansson had waited until the plane was nearly wheels-down before she made the call that she was bringing Steele in. Cartwright had been asleep for less than an hour when his cell phone rang, mere inches from his head, startling him twice—first when waking him, and then again with the news.

He showed his identification three more times before he was granted admission to the fifth floor—once at the building's entrance, again at the elevators, and a third time to the seated guard who greeted him when the doors opened.

They knew his face, but it was protocol. It was also irritating.

An executive assistant led him to the debriefing room, where he glimpsed in on Johansson and Steele through the two-way glass. He told the assistant to turn on the camera and record everything.

Then he took a breath, put on his best smile, and went into the room. The two agents abruptly stopped talking and looked up at him. At first, Zero didn't seem to recognize him, but after a few moments he narrowed his eyes and nodded once.

"Deputy Director," he said.

Cartwright's smile widened. Zero's face was bruised and swollen. There were bandages on his neck and forehead. He looked like hell. "Good to see you, Zero."

Kent shook his head. "Don't call me that."

"Fine." Cartwright lowered himself into a chair opposite Kent and folded his hands atop the table. "Hello, Kent." He turned to Johansson. "Leave us, please."

She glanced over at Kent as if waiting for his approval—*has she forgotten who the boss is here?*—but he nodded again and she left the room.

Once the door was closed, Cartwright cleared his throat and began. "Ordinarily you would know how this sort of thing works— you tell us everything, start to finish, and we corroborate it with whatever evidence we have available. But I have questions first, so let's start with those." He pointed to a camera in the upper corner opposite his seat. "Everything said in here is on the record. We're not going to hook you up to a polygraph because, frankly, we know you can beat that. We ask that you be completely honest. Treat this room like any court of law. The penalty for perjury is imprisonment—and you know all too well where we send agents that turn their back on us."

Kent nodded again, saying nothing. Cartwright was having trouble reading him. Did Steele know that he had been the one to send Reidigger and Morris after him? If he did, he wasn't showing it.

"All right then," said Cartwright, a little too loudly. "I think it's been well established that contrary to what we believed, you're not dead. So where have you been these last nineteen months?"

"Riverdale, in the Bronx," Kent said simply. "I've been teaching European history."

Cartwright stared blankly. "Is that a joke?"

"No."

"Under what alias?"

"Reid Lawson."

"Really." Cartwright almost scoffed. In the follow-up report after Zero was announced KIA, they ran checks on every one of his aliases—but they hadn't bothered to check his birth name. Even Cartwright himself never would have thought that he'd be so obvious. Yet there he had been, hiding in plain sight the entire time. "And your girls? How are they?"

Kent's eyes narrowed. "Not in New York, if that's what you're asking."

"Good," Cartwright said gently. "I'd hate to see anything happen to them." He had never met Steele's girls, but he was aware of them. It was hard for him to imagine the cold, seemingly indifferent Agent Zero as a loving father.

"I want answers too." Kent leaned forward, his steely gaze unblinking. "Did you send Agent Morris after me?"

Cartwright frowned deeply. "No. No, of course not. In fact, upon further investigation, it seems you were correct—Agent Morris was working with the Fraternity. We did a little digging and discovered a bank account in the Cayman Islands with more than two million dollars in it. It was under the name of a fake holdings company. The CEO was listed as Morris's grandmother—except she's been dead for seven years." Cartwright had been shocked to discover Morris's involvement with the Fraternity, but it was fortuitous for him, since it took the scrutiny off of Morris's failed attempt on Zero's life. "My turn. Did you kill Clint Morris?"

"No," said Kent. "But I witnessed it. He was killed by an Amun assassin—"

"Amun?"

"That's what the Fraternity calls themselves."

Cartwright's brow furrowed. "What does it mean?"

"Amun was an ancient Egyptian god," Kent explained. "I don't have all the details yet, but I believe this group is based on a fanatical cult that died out in the sixth century."

"What are they after?"

"I'm not entirely sure. Some vague notion of 'a return to old ways.'"

Cartwright smirked. "What, like pharaohs and pyramids?"

"Don't be pedantic," Kent said. Cartwright's smirk vanished. "I'm not certain what they aim to achieve, but I do know that at the height of their influence, Amun's priests were powerful. They controlled regimes. They whispered in the pharaoh's ear and he listened. I believe they want to do something similar again—to control. But just like they did with the eighteenth dynasty of Egypt, if they want to regain control, they'd first have to destroy the established hierarchy."

Cartwright would never admit it out loud, but he was a little impressed. This Agent Zero sitting across from him was a far cry from the self-assured, borderline-haughty Kent Steele that he knew before. "When do they plan to do this? Do we have a timetable?"

Kent shrugged one shoulder. "That's what I'm trying to figure out. That's why I'm here—I need help to get to them."

"And we'll give it to you," Cartwright said. It was an outright lie. His intention was to take Steele's debrief, pin the murders of Reidigger and Morris on him, and then throw him in a black-site cell for the rest of his life—which would be rather short, once they organized an unfortunate accident to befall him. "But first, a few more questions. Did you kill Alan Reidigger?"

"No. He was dead when I found him in the apartment here in Zurich."

"And why did you go to the apartment in Zurich?"

"A Russian bomb-maker had Reidigger's address in his phone. I believe that someone gave the address to the Russian, who in turn gave it to the Iranians—the same men that took me from my home in New York four days ago."

"And who is this someone? Morris wouldn't have had access to that information." Cartwright's eyes narrowed as he realized Kent's insinuation. "Are you suggesting that someone within the CIA—?"

Before he could finish his question, someone rapped twice on the door and then pushed it open without waiting for a reply. It was the executive assistant, a woman in a gray business suit with her hair pulled up in a tight bun.

"Excuse me, sir," she said politely. "There's a—"

"Excuse *me*," Cartwright said sharply, "this is a closed meeting, and we are not finished here."

The woman held out a cell phone. "But you have a call, sir. It's Director Mullen. He said it's urgent."

Cartwright's throat ran dry.

Kent Steele sat back in his chair and folded his arms. "You're going to want to take that," Kent said.

Cartwright took the phone. "Thank you," he said curtly. He waited until the woman left and then put the phone to his ear. Kent raised an eyebrow, but otherwise showed no emotion.

"Director," said Cartwright.

"Cartwright," Mullen barked through the phone. "Do you enjoy your position?"

"Most of the time, sir." *Though this was not one of those times*, he thought bitterly.

"Then you'd better have one hell of a good explanation for why the goddamn DNI just called me directly!" Mullen shouted.

The color drained from Cartwright's face. *The DNI? How?*

Mullen may have been the director of the CIA, but *his* boss was the Director of National Intelligence—and the only person the DNI answered to was the president himself.

Cartwright was at a loss for words. "Sir, I ... I don't know ..."

"Save it," Mullen snapped. "The director just called for an emergency conference ..." Mullen continued, but Cartwright barely heard it because at the same time, Kent Steele rose from his seat and headed toward the door.

Cartwright lowered the phone and hissed, "Where do you think you're going? We're not finished here! Sit down!"

"Are you sure?" Kent asked. "Seems like we're finished here."

"Cartwright? Cartwright! Are you listening to me?" Mullen's voice sounded small and distant.

Cartwright put the phone back to his ear as Steele left the room. "Sir, yes. Sorry. Emergency conference. When?"

"Right now." Mullen hung up.

Cartwright gulped.

He hastily left the room to find Steele gone. But someone was waiting outside in the hall—Maria Johansson leaned against the smooth wall with her arms folded and a satisfied smirk on her face. "Seems there's an emergency conference," she said casually. "I'll walk with you."

Cartwright fumed. He balled his fists angrily at his sides, but maintained a calm expression on his face as they walked side by side down the hall.

"How?" he asked quietly. "How in the hell did you contact the DNI directly?"

Johansson shrugged. "You haven't been keeping up on your political appointments, have you, Deputy Director?"

"What does that have to do with anything?"

"My father," said Johansson, "was appointed to the National Security Council six months ago. I heard the recommendation came from John Hillis himself."

Cartwright was aghast. "Your father ...?" She was right; he hadn't been paying close enough attention. His eyes widened with sudden realization. Her father was a former senator who had previously sat on the Homeland Security Council. And in the time it had taken Cartwright to get from his hotel to the consulate, she had managed to contact the DNI. Which meant...

Which meant that Steele's debrief was little more than a bid to buy some time while the conference was arranged. They had played him, plain and simple.

"I don't believe this," he murmured.

"You should get used to that." Johansson smirked again. "I think the next hour or so is going to be quite eye-opening."

The lights were dimmed in Conference Room C, the smallest in the facility. There were six people present—Cartwright, Steele, Johansson, two other deputy directors, and the Director of Operations in Zurich, who oversaw the daily activity of the European headquarters. There were two wide LCD screens hastily installed at either end of the conference table. On one was CIA Director Mullen, his bald head shining more than usual in the bright light of his home office.

On the other screen was an older man, in his mid-sixties. The skin beneath his chin hung in jowls but his eyes were as sharp and observant as a bird of prey. Director of National Intelligence John Hillis did not look pleased.

A young male technician plugged two cables into the back of Hillis's monitor. "Sir?" he said. "Can you hear us?"

"Yes. Thank you, son."

"I'll be right outside if you need me." The technician left in a hurry.

Hillis's gaze floated around the table before he spoke. "I have called this emergency conference in order to attempt to substantiate claims that have very recently come to my attention," he said sternly. "These claims involve potential terrorism within the Central Intelligence Agency. I find this to be gravely sobering, and it is of

the utmost importance that we get to the bottom of this immediately." His discerning eye fell on Kent. "Agent Steele."

"Yes, sir."

"You have the floor. I will remind you that everything you say
is on record, is being recorded, and will be shared with both the
National Security Council and the Homeland Security Council."

"Understood, sir. Thank you." Kent Steele rose from his seat.
"We didn't have time for a complete debrief before this conference
was called, so I would like to do that now, on the record. Some
parts of what I'm about to tell you may sound beyond belief. All I
ask is that you keep an open mind. Given our choice in careers and
what we've all seen, I think you'll agree that the events of the last
four days are not implausible." He took a deep breath. Cartwright
noticed Johansson nod assuredly his way. "Nineteen months ago,
Kent Steele, also known as Agent Zero, was announced killed in
action. Yet here I am. For the past year and a half, I've been living
in New York with my two daughters, teaching European history at
Columbia University. Up until four days ago, I had no memory of
ever being an agent in the CIA."

No memory? Cartwright blinked in surprise. *What's his angle here?*

Steele told them everything. He began with his kidnapping
from his home in the Bronx by a trio of Iranian men. Waking up in
a basement in Paris. Having a memory suppression chip torn from
his skull. At that, Cartwright was in utter shock. A memory suppressor… he knew that such things existed. If it was true, it was a
brilliant ploy, and he had no doubt whatsoever that Alan Reidigger
had a hand in it. Alan had double-crossed Cartwright, from the
very moment he had volunteered to kill his best friend right up to
his untimely murder.

Kent told them about the bomb-making facility in Belgium. He
told them about finding Reidigger's body in Zurich, along with a
photograph that led him to Rome. He explained how he recon-
nected with Johansson and about Morris's subsequent attack.

Cartwright's mind was reeling a mile a minute as Steele spoke.
If he's being honest, and his memory really was gone, perhaps he doesn't

remember who came for him nineteen months ago. If Zero did recall, he wasn't saying. But that would make sense too; he would be stupid to call Cartwright out right then and there. If he remembered, he had a trump card. Even if he truly didn't, the deputy director would still have to tread extremely carefully from that moment on.

"Agent Johansson came for me in Maribor," Steele said as he came to his conclusion. "She convinced me that the best course of action was for me to come in, despite my distrust. Together we have deduced that this organization, Amun, could not have gotten all of their information from Agent Morris. He would not have known Agent Reidigger's or Johansson's whereabouts, and he certainly would not have known that Reidigger knew *my* location. Therefore, we have strong reason to believe that someone higher than the field-agent level in the CIA is supplying Amun with intel."

Steele fell quiet. The conference room was devastatingly silent. Cartwright could tell by their expressions that the other directors were equally stunned. Even Mullen, who ordinarily had complete control over the subtleties of his reactions, was clearly astonished.

"One final thing, Directors," said Kent. "I understand that my actions of late were in no way sanctioned by the CIA or the US government. I've probably broken a dozen laws in the last twenty-four hours alone. I am fully aware of this, and I will accept whatever punitive measures you deem necessary." He murmured, "Thank you," and took his seat once again.

Director Hillis cleared his throat. "Forgive me, Agent Steele, but I believe we all need a moment to process what you've just told us." He tented his fingers in front of his mouth and sighed into them. "If this is all true, it is an extremely bizarre set of circumstances—but as you said, not entirely implausible. These are very serious allegations, and we have to consider them carefully."

The DNI's gaze fell on Mullen's screen at the far end of the conference table. "Director Mullen, effective immediately, I will be enlisting the aid of the NSA to monitor all communication by every member of the CIA in a supervisory role. That will include personal email and cell phones."

"Sir," Mullen said carefully, "I'm not sure it's wise to…"

Hillis shot him a dangerous glare, and Mullen fell silent. Cartwright could tell that the CIA director wanted to contest further, but he didn't dare.

"Yes, sir," Mullen said tightly.

"And you, Agent Steele," said Hillis. "You mentioned that you believe this terrorist attack is happening soon. How soon, and on what basis do you believe this?"

"I'm afraid I don't have an answer for either of those questions, sir." Steele shook his head. "It's primarily a feeling—as if I discovered something before the memory suppressor that I haven't yet remembered."

A feeling. Cartwright almost scoffed out loud.

"Well then, Agent," said Hillis, "you had better get back out there and find out."

Cartwright snapped to attention. He was on his feet before he even realized he had stood. "Sir, if I may…"

Hillis glowered. Cartwright felt himself withering under the fierce stare. "Um, sorry, sir. Deputy Director Cartwright, Special Activities Division. Agent Steele was a field agent under my supervision when I was heading the Special Operations Group, at the time of his alleged death. I knew him well—rather, I know him well. I believe that given his memory loss and, uh, personal attachment to this case that he should be considered compromised."

"Cartwright, was it?" Director Hillis regarded Cartwright evenly for a long moment. "Special Activities Division. Hmm. From everything this man just told me, he made more progress in four days than your entire division has in two years. Why in the world would we pull him?"

Because he might find out about me. About us. What we tried to do to him. "Well, sir… uh, I believe he could pose a danger to the, uh…"

"You're blabbering, Cartwright. Sit down."

"Yes, sir." Cartwright sat meekly.

"Director Mullen, I want Agent Steele reinstated immediately and given access to the full resources of the CIA. Whatever he needs, he gets."

"Sir, if I may, I'd like to partner with Agent Johansson," Steele spoke up. He glanced over at her across the table from him. "She's the only one I believe I can trust at the moment."

"Done," said Hillis. "And while you're doing what needs to be done, you can rest assured that we will be doing everything we can to find whoever might be supplying these extremists with information. Let's get to work. Dismissed." As the deputy directors and two agents rose from their seats, the DNI added, "Except you, Mullen. And Cartwright. I want to speak to you two."

Cartwright felt a tinge of panic as he slowly lowered himself back into the chair. Mullen's face went ashen as the other four people filed out of the conference room.

Hillis pinched the bridge of his nose irritably. "Memory suppressors? Rogue agents? Moles? And we knew *none* of this?" He shook his head. "This is your opportunity, right now, to tell me anything you might know about all this that hasn't been said."

Neither man spoke. Cartwright stared at the wood-grain tabletop.

"All right then," said Hillis. "Lucky for you, we have to fix these leaks and put an end to this plot first. But you can bet that as soon as that's done, we'll be launching a full investigation into what happened to that man nineteen months ago. If I discover that you two had anything to do with it, it'll be much more than just your jobs on the line. Am I clear?"

"Yes, sir," they murmured.

"Good. Go." Director Hillis clicked his camera off and the screen went black.

Mullen glanced over at Cartwright and shook his head disdainfully. Without another word, he too leaned forward and turned off his camera, leaving Cartwright alone in the conference room.

He had majorly screwed the pooch. Not only was Steele alive, but now he had the CIA over a barrel. He had the Director of National Intelligence looking over his shoulder. Cartwright's calls and emails and even text messages would be monitored closely.

He had no choice but to work with Agent Zero, give him whatever he asked for, and hope he never discovered that Cartwright and Mullen had ordered the hit on him by two CIA agents.

At length he rose from his chair and left the conference room. Of course, Steele and Johansson were waiting for him in the hall. There were a thousand things that Cartwright wanted to say to them, wished he could say, but ultimately he just forced a smile. "Excellent work, Agents. Simply stellar. I want you to know that no matter what happens, I'll be recommending you both for Valor Awards—"

"I want a security detail assigned to my girls," Kent interrupted. "Right away."

"Watson and Carver," Johansson added. "They can take the kids to a safe house."

"We have resources stateside that we can use—" Cartwright began.

"Strange, I'm pretty sure I just heard the Director of National Intelligence say that whatever Kent needs, he gets." Johansson raised an eyebrow.

Cartwright smiled, his teeth clenched tightly behind it. "Of course. Where are your girls?"

"No," said Kent. "You get the agents on a plane, and I'll tell you where to send them after I arrange it on my end."

"Sure thing." Cartwright's jaw was aching from his forced smile. "Watson and Carver will be on the next plane out." He made a mental note to have Steve Bolton in Langley arrange the agents' transportation and pickup.

"And we'll need a jet," Steele added. "A fast one. We need to get to Morocco tonight."

Cartwright frowned. Even Johansson looked up sharply. "What's in Morocco?" she asked.

"Sheikh Mustafar."

"We already interrogated the sheikh," she said. "He's been sitting in a black-site hole for more than a year and a half. You told me you remembered that."

"I remember what he told us," said Kent. "I want to know what he *didn't* tell us."

CHAPTER TWENTY EIGHT

"Funny," said Maria, "I recall you telling me you didn't find any leads in Slovenia." She sat across from Reid in a plush, cream-colored seat. They were the only two passengers on a Gulfstream G650, a sixty-five-million-dollar aircraft traveling at Mach 0.86 toward Morocco.

I wasn't sure I could trust you, he thought. He still wasn't sure—though after what she had done for him, contacting the DNI and allowing his statement to be made, he believed he was getting closer.

"I'm sorry I kept it from you," he said simply. "Really though, I should thank you. I couldn't have handled any of that without your help."

"Your kids will be safe," she promised. "Watson and Carver are trustworthy. You have my word on that." She laughed lightly. "You have to admit it's a little ironic that we're taking a luxury jet to travel to one of the worst places on Earth."

"Hmm. I'm not sure that qualifies as irony; a reversal of expectations would have to occur. Like if we got there and find that the black site has been razed and a five-star hotel was built in its place."

"Oh, my apologies, Professor." Johansson smiled. Reid glanced over to find her staring at him.

"What is it?"

"You're different now. You know that?"

"No. I don't know. How am I different?"

"It's hard to define." She thought for a moment. "Kent was always so confident—even arrogant sometimes. He was fiercely intelligent, just like you. He was bold. Fearless. Had a hell of a temper."

Again she laughed slightly. "I shouldn't be saying it like that. You're still him. Or, he's you. I shouldn't be talking like he was someone else…but in some ways it feels like it."

"So…different is good, right?"

"Yeah. Different is good. I mean, less arrogant is good." She laughed softly. "You just seem like you're on more of an even keel now. Before, on a case, Kent would get…obsessed. He would focus like a laser. The work was the only thing that mattered. That's a good thing, usually, but there's a lot more to life than that. It feels like you understand that better now."

He nodded, but said nothing. She spoke about Kent, the old Kent, with a sort of quiet reverence, but at the same time there was a mild strain in her voice that suggested there was plenty about who he used to be that left something to be desired.

The intercom crackled and the pilot's voice came through. "Agents, we've reached cruising altitude."

Reid immediately powered on a laptop. He was eager to reach out to his girls.

Less than a half hour ago they had been standing in the Zurich consulate talking with Cartwright. They had been given a change of clothes, though Reid had opted to keep his boots and the bomber jacket; he'd grown fond of them. He'd ditched the bulky REX revolver in favor of the familiarity of a Glock 27, with an LC9 strapped to his ankle. He left the bug-out bag behind as well, in a locker, along with the revolver and his old clothes. The Swiss Army knife he stuck in his jacket pocket. He didn't keep it for its utility or because he thought he'd need it, but rather because it had become something of a memento to him from the old friend that he could barely remember.

Then he and Johansson were escorted quickly to an airstrip where they boarded the Gulfstream, en route to Morocco.

He logged into his Skype account to see a message waiting from Katherine Joanne's account. *We're safe,* it said. *I'm sorry, I couldn't get to the computer sooner.*

Reid breathed a sigh of relief. Maya had missed her last check-in, but the message put his mind at ease. He set his fingers to the keyboard, but he wasn't sure what to say. He wanted to be honest without being specific. Finally he typed:

Listen carefully. You deserve some answers, but I can't give them all to you. I can say this: I'm not in the country. I'm helping some important people do a very vital job, and I have to see it through. It's much bigger than me. But knowing that the two of you are safe is my foremost concern. I'm sending two men to protect you. They're going to take you somewhere and keep you safe. We can trust them.

He paused and glanced over at Maria, who was reading over a transcription of their last interrogation of the sheikh. She had faith in the two agents that Cartwright was sending for his girls—and at the moment, that had to be good enough for him. Reid decided he would too. It was better than the girls being alone somewhere and him having no idea what might be happening.

He typed: *I don't want you to tell me where you are. I want you to give me a landmark, somewhere public, where these two can meet you. It doesn't have to be nearby. It just has to be somewhere you can get to without any trouble.*

Before he had even pressed the enter key on his lengthy message, a green icon appeared to tell him that Maya had logged in. He waited a few moments for her to read over the message, and then received one in turn.

Maya typed: *Tell me something so that I know it's you.*

A thin smile curved his lips. She was as cautious as she was smart. Reid was incredibly proud—and at the same time he desperately hoped that she never got any ideas in her head to join the CIA.

I'm sorry you missed your Valentine's date in the city, he typed.

Two full minutes passed before her next message came. *Wonderland Pier,* it said. *Near the monkeys. Remember it?*

Reid almost laughed out loud. Wonderland Pier was a tiny amusement park on the Jersey shore, near Ocean City. He had taken the girls there when they were younger. At the entrance to the park, just off the pier, there was a display of animatronic monkeys playing instruments. Sara, who was only ten at the time, had been so terrified of them that she had promptly burst into tears.

He immediately called Cartwright. "I've got a location—Wonderland Pier, Ocean City, New Jersey, at the entrance to the park."

"Got it," Cartwright confirmed. "Watson and Carver's ETA is about eleven hours. It would be, what, almost ten p.m. EST right now? So have the kids be there by nine in the morning. Tell them not to panic if they don't show right away, but not to wait for more than an hour."

"All right," said Reid. Then, although it felt strange to say it to Cartwright, he added, "Thank you."

"Sure. Specs?"

"Specs, right. Sara is fourteen, about four-foot-nine, blonde hair, shoulder-length. Maya is sixteen, five-three, brunette, long hair. Tell the agents to approach using the name Katherine Joanne, so they know it's the right guys."

At the mention of Kate, Maria glanced up, but she said nothing.

"Great. Don't worry, we'll get them," Cartwright said. "I'll confirm with you personally when it's done." The deputy director hung up.

Reid relayed Cartwright's message to Maya: *Be there by 9 am. Don't wait for more than an hour. Don't look for them. They'll look for you. Their names are Watson and Carver. They'll ask for your Skype ID. If anyone approaches you by any other name, you run and get help.*

Okay, Maya confirmed.

I love you both.

We love you too.

Reid logged out and closed the computer. He stared into space for a while, his thoughts drifting to fond memories with his girls and Kate at the shore. Walking the pier. Playing miniature golf and riding the carousel.

He hadn't even realized that he'd drifted until he felt Maria's hand on his.

"They'll be okay," she said reassuringly. "If they're anything like you, they can handle more than you think."

"Yeah," he said distantly. He snapped out of his fog. "Let's focus. I want to review that transcript after you. Then we'll see what our friend the sheikh isn't telling us."

Maria was right about two things: a Gulfstream jet landing at a black site in the Moroccan desert was indeed ironic. And it really was one of the worst places on Earth.

It was eight in the morning local time when they arrived at the black site. It had been organized to look like a US Army FOB, or forward operating base. The perimeter was surrounded in an uneven, hastily erected chain-link fence topped with barbed wire. The grounds were comprised of rows of semi-permanent canvas tents interrupted by squat, domed steel structures. Everything, it seemed, from the trucks to the tents to the steel domes, was in drab colors that matched the sand around it.

They were greeted on the makeshift airstrip just outside the site by a Special Forces member in Oakley sunglasses and an olive drab bandana wrapped around his head. He had a thick black beard and carried an AR-15 on a strap over his shoulder.

"Agents, I'm SFO Sergeant Jack Flagg. Welcome to Hell Six." He shook both their hands briefly. To Reid he added, "Looks like you've been through the wringer, sir."

Reid ignored the comment—he was well aware that his face had seen better days. "Why do you call it Hell Six?" he asked instead.

"This site is Designation H-6," Maria replied.

"But I think you'll see why we call it what we do," said Flagg. He had a slight Texas drawl to his voice. "They already told me why you're here. This way."

A blustery wind blew as Flagg led them through the camp. Reid pulled his jacket tighter around him. He had always associated this sort of desolate place with a hot, arid climate; he couldn't believe it could get so cold in the desert.

The sergeant pulled open the steel door of one of the many nondescript, depressingly dull steel domes and led them inside. There were no windows and no other point of egress, and it was illuminated by only a single bare forty-watt bulb in the peak of the ten-foot ceiling. The floor was packed clay, the sand having been dug out for the placement of the structure.

There were no other people inside, but there was a square iron grate in the center of the floor, and chain manacles hanging on the far eastern wall, secured firmly into the steel façade by thick iron spikes.

"Just a sec," said Flagg. With a grunt of effort, he pulled open the hinged iron grate; it was a trapdoor set in the ground. It opened on a small subterranean room of dirt walls about eight feet below with a slanted wooden ladder leading downward. He took off his AR and handed it to Reid by the strap. "Hang onto this a moment, would you?" The sergeant unholstered a sidearm, a desert-brown Sig Sauer XM17, and descended the wooden ladder.

"Come on," they heard him say. "Up and at 'em. You got visitors."

It took nearly a full minute until Flagg's head showed again. He held his pistol aloft with one hand, the other hanging at his side as he dragged something up—or someone.

The sheikh was a far cry from what Reid's vision had shown him from twenty months earlier. Back then, the sheikh had been terrified, but he at least appeared healthy—color in his cheeks, a slight paunch, muscle tone in his arms and legs.

The dismal figure that Flagg pulled up from the hole was like a completely different creature. His arms and legs were bone thin and knobby at the joints, reminiscent of gnarled tree branches. His cheeks were sunken, the cheekbones jutting prominently and making his eyes look too large for his face. They had shaved his head bald, but his beard was long, gray, and scraggly. He wore a sleeveless brown tunic, belted at the waist with a length of rope, and brown shorts that were almost comically oversized on his thin legs.

At the top of the ladder, the sergeant released his grip on the sheikh and he dropped to the dirt at their feet. His eyes,

Reid noticed, were glazed over and stoic, staring at nothing in particular.

"What's wrong with him?" Maria asked. "He looks catatonic."

"Oh, don't let him fool you," said Flagg. "He's in there. He's often like this; doesn't move much. Barely eats. Most days he just sleeps or sits around with that vacant look in his eye. But we hear him, mumbling to himself, near every day."

"What does he say?" Reid asked.

"Most times we can't even understand him," Flagg admitted. "But there were a few times, early on when he was more coherent, I heard him good and clear. He'd say the same thing, over and over. I can't remember it all, but it sounded like some kind of prayer. Not like any prayer I ever heard before, but that's how it seemed."

"Do you recall any of it?" Kent asked.

"Just one part," Flagg admitted. "It went, 'For his anger, in the moment there are no remains,' or something like that. Does that make any sense to you?"

Reid shook his head. "No, sorry." He had never heard any prayer like that either, not in the Christian or Muslim ideologies. "Will you give us a few minutes with him?"

"Sure thing." Flagg gestured toward the AR-15 in Reid's hands. "You want to hang onto that? You look like you'd know what to do with it."

He'd almost forgotten he was holding it. The rifle felt so familiar in his hands. When he looked down he noticed he was holding the butt end up, barrel pointed down at a forty-five degree angle, his index finger flat against the trigger guard.

"Uh, no thanks. We'll be fine." He handed it back to Flagg. He didn't think Mustafar would give them any trouble. The sheikh couldn't have been more than ninety pounds soaking wet.

"All right then. I'll be right outside if y'all need me."

As soon as Flagg exited, Reid knelt beside the sheikh. Mustafar was on his hands and knees in the dirt, a thousand-yard stare in his eyes.

"Sheikh Mustafar," he said loudly. "Do you know me?"

"A bullet..." The sheikh's voice was hoarse and rasping. He coughed violently and then took a few recovering breaths. "A bullet sounds the same in every language."

"Yes. I said that. You remember me then?"

Slowly, very slowly, the sheikh's glazed glance turned upward until it met Reid's. "Agent Zero," he said quietly.

"That's right. I'm here to ask you some questions."

"You asked questions before," said the sheikh in his gravelly voice. He settled back on his haunches. Then he raised his left hand, palm out. "You asked questions, and you took." Slowly he turned the hand so that its back was facing Reid and Maria.

There were no fingernails on his hand. Just dry, cracked skin.

"You asked questions I did not have answers to. Then you took. What have you come to take this time, Agent?" Mustafar grinned wide. He was missing more than half his teeth.

Reid glanced away. If he had done that as well, he had no memory of it.

Whatever it takes. Remember?

He forced himself to look back at the sheikh and his jack-o'-lantern smile. "You still have a lot I can take. Trust me when I say you're going to want to be honest." Reid stood and paced around the sheikh. "Recently I interrogated a man who suggested that you might know something. He didn't get the chance to tell me what you might know, on account of his death. He called himself Amun."

Reid watched carefully for some reaction, some glimmer of recognition from Mustafar. But there was none.

"What did he think you know?"

The sheikh said nothing.

Reid recounted the conversation in his mind. *He knows.* That's what the Amun man in Slovenia had said. *He knows.* Then before he lost consciousness he had muttered two more vague phrases: *The sheikh... he's not...*

"I'll ask you again," Reid said. "What did he think you know?"

Maria shook her head. "How do we know the guy in Slovenia wasn't just trying to throw us off the trail by wasting time?"

"We don't know," Reid replied. "But we're here, and I'm going to find out."

Still the sheikh said nothing. He stared into the dirt and muttered something under his breath.

"What is that? What are you saying?" Reid demanded. "Speak up."

The sheikh grinned up at him again, but he fell silent.

"Pliers?" Maria suggested.

Reid nodded without taking his eyes off Mustafar. "Pliers. And something sharp."

As Maria headed toward the door to fetch implements, Reid ran the scene through his head once more, his interrogation of the Amun member in the warehouse. *He knows*, the man had said.

He knows.

The sheikh...

He's not...

The sheikh...

He's not...

"Son of a bitch," Reid said breathlessly. "Maria, wait." She paused at the door. "I have a hunch." He reached out for a handful of the sheikh's beard.

Suddenly Mustafar moved, and far quicker than either of them would have assumed he was able, in his state. He jerked his head back, out of Reid's grasp, and his mostly toothless mouth curved into a snarl.

"Johansson," said Reid, "hold him."

Maria stepped forward to grab him. The sheikh flailed, as if to strike her, but she caught his arm easily and twisted it behind his back. He yelped in pain. She trapped his other arm and held him firmly.

Reid grabbed a fistful of his gray, filthy beard and yanked it upward, forcing Mustafar to look toward the ceiling. "Where is it?" Reid growled. He pulled left and right, the sheikh's head lolling on his thin neck.

"What are you doing?" Maria asked.

Reid didn't answer. *He's not… the sheikh.* That's what the Amun member had been trying to tell him as he went into shock.

Reid used both thumbs to separate the thick, wiry gray hair—and then he saw it. Just beneath the man's chin, where it met the jaw, was a brand, well concealed by his thick beard. It was the glyph of Amun.

He's not the sheikh.

They had shaved the sheikh's head, but they had not touched his beard. Many Muslim men believed it a religious obligation to maintain their beards, and despite his being a prisoner, the black-site jailers respected that. Even in Guantanamo Bay, Islamic detainees were given prayer mats and directed toward Mecca.

Amun knew it. And they had used it to their advantage to conceal the brand.

Reid took a step back. "Let him go." Maria released him, and the man fell to a heap in the dirt. "You're not him. You're not Mustafar."

Maria's mouth fell open slightly. "What are you talking about? We got him ourselves. We were the ones that came for him, brought him here…"

"And they were a step ahead of us." Reid sighed in frustration. "The mole in the agency must have caught wind that we were going after the sheikh. They tipped off Amun, who replaced the sheikh with a doppelganger. This man is not Mustafar. He's Amun."

"I don't believe it," Maria murmured.

"Think about it. The real Mustafar was wealthy and powerful, but he wasn't Amun. If we had brought him here he would have cracked under the pressure immediately. He had *everything* to lose. Besides, he was their bankroll; the sheikh is funding Amun's plot. They couldn't risk him being captured, knowing what he must know. And they couldn't stand to lose their piggy bank."

"Christ." Maria paced the short concrete room twice. "But we still have this guy. He's Amun. He must know something."

Reid shook his head. "Not likely. Knowing what I know about them, they wouldn't have told this guy anything worth knowing. They would know we were going to torture him for intel." Otets was right; the "sheikh" was just a scapegoat. He didn't know anything. Just not in the way that Reid had expected.

He knelt so that he was nearly face-to-face with the ersatz sheikh. "Isn't that right?"

In reply, the man grinned his leering, gaping grin. He chuckled softly.

"Something funny?" Maria snapped. "You're still going to spend the rest of your short, miserable life in that hole."

His chuckle became a laugh, which grew to a wild cackle. He rolled onto his back, laughing like a lunatic.

He began to shout. "Though it may be that the servant is justified in doing wrong, yet Amun is justified in being merciful!" He paused to laugh wildly again. "As for his anger—in the completion of a moment there is no remnant! As Amun we endure!"

Maria delivered a swift kick to his ribs. The man grunted and rolled over, clutching his midsection.

"Kent, this was a dead end," she muttered. "We need to go elsewhere, find a new lead."

He was beyond discouraged. He was crestfallen. He felt defeated. They had come all this way only to learn that they had made a grievous mistake well over a year ago.

"You're right. Let's go." Reid headed toward the door, about to call for Flagg, when the Amun prisoner on the ground called out to him in his croaking voice.

"Agent Zero," he said roughly. "Wait one moment."

Reid paused, turning slowly.

"That man you spoke with. He wasn't lying. I do know something that I haven't told you."

Reid took a cautious step toward him. This was a trick, he was certain. There was no way any Amun member would willingly give up knowledge. "What do you know?"

The false sheikh rolled over and, with a groan, hefted himself to his knees. "They told me that one day you might come back. I didn't believe them..."

"What do you know?" Reid demanded.

"They said that if you did, I should tell you what I know…"

Reid grabbed him by the collar of his filthy tunic and hauled him upright. "Tell me!" he shouted in the man's filthy face.

The Amun man grinned wide, displaying the empty sockets in his mouth.

"I know, Agent Zero, that you have two daughters. And we know how to find them."

CHAPTER TWENTY NINE

Reid saw red. He lost control.

Later, when asked to recount the event, he wouldn't remember what happened next. It wasn't that Kent took over. It was blind fury blacking out his memory. It was Kent's strength and skill, Reid's protective nature, and both their love and devotion to their children that galvanized into a burning, unadulterated hatred for the leering, cackling, emaciated prisoner.

At the mention of his daughters, Reid threw a hard right cross that landed solidly across the fake sheikh's jaw. Even as he laughed, teeth skittered into the dirt. Reid brought his right knee up, into the man's concave torso. Ribs gave way beneath the crushing blow.

The man tried to fall but Reid grabbed him around the throat, held him up easily, and delivered a vicious head-butt with the top of his cranium. The Amun member's broad nose exploded in a cascade of blood. Reid released him, brought his elbow up, and then slammed it down into his suprasternal notch, snapping both collarbones.

Hands wrapped around him. He was vaguely aware of shouting, of a familiar scent, but his mind was blurry. He lashed out at whoever was trying to pull him off.

Maria caught his arm and pulled it with her, using his momentum to throw Reid to the ground. He landed hard on his back in the dirt, panting.

She stood over him, her expression both stern and anxious at the same time.

"Stop," she told him firmly. "That won't help them."

Reid closed his eyes and struggled to calm himself. *We know where they are.* He wanted to leap to his feet and kill the man before him.

"Don't," Maria said, as if she could see it in his eyes. "Killing him will do nothing for the girls. We have to go *now.*"

She's right. Get up. Find them.

Maria helped him to his feet. The non-sheikh lay in the dirt, struggling to breathe through his broken nose and the blood in his mouth. Reid had to tear his gaze away before the urge to stomp his head flat grew too strong.

He pulled open the door to the steel domed structure to find Flagg just outside.

"Your prisoner needs medical attention," Reid muttered.

"Thank you, Sergeant," Maria said quickly. "We need to go immediately."

As the two agents hurried toward their waiting jet, Flagg peered into the dim room, wondering just what the hell had happened.

On their approach back to the Gulfstream, Maria called Cartwright and put him on speaker. She spoke rapidly. "It's not the sheikh. The prisoner we have is not Mustafar. They knew we were coming for him and they swapped him out with someone from Amun, someone willing to take the fall for their cause. He said they know where Kent's girls are …"

"Whoa, whoa, hang on," said Cartwright. "He's *not* the sheikh?"

"Try to keep up!" Maria snapped. "Amun told him that if Kent ever came back, he should tell him they know where his girls are. They're not safe, Cartwright."

They climbed the short stairs and entered the plane. The pilot was waiting for them in the cockpit, the door closed and secured. Reid paced the short span of the jet and breathed into his hands. All he could think about was Sara and Maya. If anything happened to them, anything at all, he would never forgive himself. If only he could warn them. He could send a message, but it would be about four in the morning on the US East Coast. Besides, he didn't know if they were safer where they were or on the move. Was Amun watching them right that moment? Had they been keeping tabs on them the whole time? His blood ran cold with the prospect.

"This guy's been in a hole in the ground for twenty months," said Cartwright. "How the hell would he know where the kids are? He's bluffing."

"No," said Reid suddenly, "I don't think he is. And even if he was, I'm not willing to take that chance." They had known about his girls all along. But they didn't take them when they came for him—they only wanted Kent Steele. He was supposed to die in that basement in Paris.

But why now? he thought. *If they didn't harm the girls earlier because they wanted to use them as leverage, why wait until now, when I discovered the prisoner wasn't Mustafar?*

"This is their ace in the hole," he said breathlessly. "They never thought I would get this far, but they planned for it in case I did."

"Look, Watson and Carver are on their way," said Cartwright. "In about five hours —"

"Anything could happen in five hours!" Maria argued.

"Amun must have people in the US, people nearby," said Reid.

"How would they even find them?" Cartwright asked.

"Maybe they've been watching the whole time. Ever since I was taken. They could have been following them ever since then..." Reid trailed off. Given the dedication he had seen from Amun so far, it was entirely possible that they had been staking out his home, had followed the girls to a hotel, and then to wherever they were now. The very thought of it turned his stomach.

"You said that you've been communicating with them through online messages, right?" asked Cartwright. "Here's what we can do: give me the account information. I'll have my tech guys trace the IP on their last message. We'll alert local PD, and I'll dispatch a squad immediately. We'll have them safe in the next thirty minutes, all right? Just stay calm."

Stay calm. Reid almost scoffed. He was nearly four thousand miles away and had no idea precisely where his girls might be. Hopefully they were asleep somewhere, safe in their beds. His mind involuntarily flashed on dark figures roaming a hotel's halls while his girls slumbered.

He shook his head violently, forcing the thought out of his mind.

"Kent? Did you hear me? I need the account info."

"Right. Sorry. We've been using Skype." He gave Cartwright the account and the password. "It's the only contact I have in there, under the name Katherine Joanne."

"Stay near the phone. In the meantime, have the pilot return to Zurich, so we can reassess this situation with the sheikh and determine our next move." Cartwright hung up.

Reid covered his face with his hands. He was growing nauseous. He couldn't think straight.

Maria instructed the pilot to return to them to Zurich. Then she sat beside Reid, put her hand on his back, and rubbed gently. "They'll find them," she said confidently. "I know they will. We just have to wait a little."

"Wait a little," Reid repeated quietly. He had never felt so powerless.

The next half hour felt like an eternity. As soon as the jet was in the air again, he rose from his seat and paced its length. He sat, then stood, then sat again. He went into the bathroom and splashed cold water on his face. Every time he tried to think clearly, his mind went to the darkest of places. He thought of all he had been through in the past few days—the basement torture, the office with Otets's thugs, the subway bathroom with the Amun assassin, the dingy warehouse in Slovenia. But in every instance he imagined his girls in those places, going through what he went through. Horrifying images swirled in his mind's eye uncontrollably. Try as he might, he couldn't jar them loose.

He tried to log into his Skype account in the desperate hope that somehow Maya was awake, sitting in front of the computer, waiting to hear from him. But the account was locked, likely by the CIA's tech team as they traced the messages to their source.

Thirty minutes passed. Then forty-five. Reid tried twice to call Cartwright, but the deputy director didn't answer.

Finally, at nearly the one-hour mark, the cell phone rang. Reid snatched it up and answered as quick as he could. "Cartwright? Do you have them?"

The long, wretched pause said everything.

"Kent," he said carefully, "we traced the IP to a Holiday Inn in New Jersey. Local police and firefighters evacuated the building under the pretense of a fire alarm. They checked every guest, searched every room. Kent... they're not there."

Reid's hands shook. A pit of despair formed in his stomach, threatening to work its way up his throat. He couldn't form words.

"Kent?" Maria's voice sounded distant, hollow. "Kent..."

"We have to go," Reid said suddenly. "We have to go back. We have to go, go to New Jersey." It was the only thing that made sense to him in the moment. Get to the girls. Find them somehow. Keep them safe. He shoved the phone into Maria's hands and strode quickly to the cockpit door, slapping it with the flat of his palm. "Hey!" he shouted to the pilot. "We need to go back!"

"Kent, we don't have the fuel for that kind of trip," said Maria gently.

"Then find some!" he shouted angrily.

"They would have an eight-hour lead on us, at least..." she said.

"What are we supposed to do, Maria?! Just sit in a conference room in goddamned Zurich while my girls are being tortured or killed?" He was screaming now, his face turning red.

"I've already dispatched a team," said Cartwright through the speakerphone. "We're cross-referencing every guest who's been in the hotel in the last three days against current guests, and we'll use those leads to search the area—"

"And while that's happening, my girls are being taken further and further from there! These people do not waste time, Cartwright! They took me to France in a fucking cargo plane! I can't..." His mind latched onto the vision of Sara and Maya, hoods over their heads, hands bound, jouncing in the hold of a plane.

Reid slapped the cockpit door again. "Hey! I know you're in there!" He hadn't even realized he had pulled his Glock, but suddenly it was in his right hand as his left pounded on the door.

"Kent, put the gun away," Maria said cautiously.

"Jesus." Cartwright sighed. "This is what I was afraid of," he murmured. "Johansson… Protocol Delta."

"Sir—" she started to say.

"That's an order, Johansson," Cartwright snapped.

Reid spun. "What's Protocol Delta?"

Maria sighed. "It's… a stopgap."

"What the hell does that mean?"

She spoke slowly. "It's a measure to prevent what happened last time from happening again."

"What? What are you talking about?" Reid was beyond confused. They needed to get to his girls—why couldn't anyone else see that? "What happened last time?"

She shook her head and stared at the floor. "Kent, when your wife died, you… that's when you went wild. You went rogue. It was a horrible, bloody trail. We can't have that happen again."

His nostrils flared as he shouted. "What is Protocol Delta, Maria?"

She reached into a side compartment next to her seat and pulled out a file folder. "Here, see for yourself."

He snatched the file folder from her and opened it. He frowned; she had handed him the transcript of the sheikh's interrogation from twenty months earlier. "What is this? What am I look f—?"

He felt the sharp stab of a needle in his neck.

Reid instinctively lashed out, spinning and backhanding Maria across the mouth. Her head whipped to the side. She didn't cry out; she simply stared at him dolefully and wiped a small amount of blood from the corner of her lip.

Reid's vision blurred. His stomach tied itself in knots. His breathing grew labored and slow. She had drugged him.

"I'm sorry," she said. "I'm so, so sorry, Kent."

The edges of his vision blackened. His knees weakened and buckled.

His last thought before he hit the carpet was of his girls, their smiling, beautiful faces, and the fact that he would never see them again.

CHAPTER THIRTY

A phone rang.

"Mm." Maya groaned as she rolled over to answer it.

"Miss Bennett?" said a cheerful young woman—too cheerful for this early in the morning. "This is your seven a.m. wake-up call."

"Thanks," she muttered, and hung up. Beside her on the king-size bed, Sara stirred.

"Come on, Squeak," Maya prodded. "We got to get up."

"Don't call me that," Sara murmured as she stuck her head under a pillow.

Maya rose and went into the bathroom. She squinted; the fluorescent lights were harsh and uninviting. She used the toilet, washed her hands and face, and brushed her teeth. Then she returned to the bedroom and poked Sara again with two fingers. "Hey. Up. We have to go soon."

"But we just got here," Sara groaned.

The night prior, at nearly ten o'clock, they had been at the Holiday Inn six miles away. Maya had decided to check the computer in the lobby just once more before bed—and was glad she did, since she had received the strange message from her dad about meeting two men who would take them somewhere safe.

Even though her dad had proved it was him, something about it still hadn't felt right to her. She already didn't feel safe, and with the news that they might need to be protected, Maya's instincts told her they should move again. She packed up their bags and her sister, and they took a taxi to a Hampton Inn a bit further down the highway. She paid in cash and checked in using a fake ID under the name Miranda Bennett, age eighteen. She had gotten it only a few months earlier under peer pressure from her friends, but she had never used it before. If her dad had found out that she had a fake ID last week, he would have hit the roof and grounded her for a month—but given the current circumstances, she had to imagine he might actually be glad for it.

"Squeak, if you don't get out of bed in the next thirty seconds, I'm dragging you out," Maya said sternly. "I need you showered, dressed, and packed. Let's go." She hated sounding like a mom— after all, she was only two years older than Sara—but sometimes it was necessary.

Wonderland Pier was a thirty-minute ride from their hotel. Maya had asked at the front desk the night before. There was a bus stop about a quarter mile away that would drop them right at the pier. There they would wait for the two men, Watson and Carver, as her dad had instructed.

She assumed that the two men they would be meeting were police officers. She had no idea what sort of trouble her dad had gotten into; at first, she had been scared for him, especially that first morning when she came downstairs to find both the front and back doors wide open and her dad gone.

But she hadn't called the police. She called Aunt Linda instead.

Maya wasn't stupid—quite the opposite. Ever since she was little she had been far more astute than the average kid her age. She knew that her dad used to travel a lot for work, claiming to be a professor ... and then coming home with scars, with bandages, sometimes with splints. He would say things like, "Daddy's just really clumsy and tripped on some stairs." One time he actually tried to say that he was sideswiped by a car.

But she wasn't stupid. She didn't know what her dad used to do and she knew better than to ask, but she assumed that it was more than giving guest lectures and attending seminars. Then, after Mom died, they moved away from Virginia to New York. He stopped traveling and started teaching full time. Life was good— she missed her mother desperately, but life in New York had been kind to them, right up until four days ago when their father went missing.

Still, she knew better than to call the police. Aunt Linda, on the other hand, did not.

Maya had spent most of the last few days staying indoors and watching television. She and Sara heeded their father's instructions and left their cell phones and tablets at home. Without the Internet, there was little to do but watch TV. Luckily, the Winter Olympics were on, and that was usually enough to distract them, at least for a little while. Maya also kept an eye on the news as often as possible, hoping to find some indication of what her dad might be doing, but there were no reports that she could connect to him.

She was a little surprised, however, to tune into the news two nights ago and see her own face, and Sara's, staring back. Aunt Linda had listened to her and not called the police when her dad went missing, but as soon as Maya and Sara left their first hotel without telling her, it seemed their aunt called the authorities immediately. Linda had provided the cops with a photo of the two of them from the previous summer, at a barbecue, sitting side by side at a picnic table and smiling over plates of food.

Maya and her sister were officially considered missing persons.

It had frightened her, at first; they were two teenagers, still children, on the lam without a single adult knowing where they were. They were potentially in danger from an unknown threat. But then Maya thought about her parents—what would they do? Her dad would likely alert the authorities, regardless of the warning. He had a tendency to be overprotective (though before he disappeared, it seemed like he was working on that).

Her mother, on the other hand... her mom would have kept her cool in this situation. She would have done what was necessary. So that's what Maya decided she would do too. She had to think responsibly, be an adult, and keep her younger sister safe.

At long last Sara rolled out of bed and dragged herself into the bathroom for about thirty minutes, eventually emerging showered, dressed, and mostly ready.

"Where are we going?" she asked. Maya had avoided telling her younger sister more than she needed to know. "And when do we get to go home?"

"Soon," Maya assured her. "We'll go home soon, I promise. But first we're going to meet up with a couple of people that can help us, okay? Dad sent them. They'll keep us safe."

Sara frowned. "Why did Dad send them? And safe from what?"

I wish I knew, Maya thought. But she forced a smile and said, "Just safe in general, so we don't have to be alone. It's going to be okay, Squeak... uh, Sara."

Another half hour later they were packed—they each carried only a backpack stuffed hastily with a few changes of clothes—and then they checked out of their room, paid in cash, and found the bus stop that would take them to the pier.

Maya was very much aware that Wonderland, the small amusement park on the pier, would not be open in February, but some of the other shops and attractions would be. In hindsight, she wished she had chosen a different location. The pier was perfectly public, but there wouldn't be many people out. Though, she thought, it would make it easier for the two men to find them.

The girls disembarked from the bus at the end of Sixth Street in Ocean City, about a three-block walk down the pier to the meeting place. Maya checked her watch; it was a quarter to nine. The two men would be there soon.

She was right. There weren't many people out. Not only was it early, and on a weekday, but it was freezing cold out and the breeze that swept in from the ocean made the air feel thick and damp. She put her arm around her sister's shoulders as they walked briskly from the bus stop to the pier. Most of the small, squat buildings that lined the boardwalk—souvenir shops, pizza places, ice cream parlors, miniature golf courses—were closed, but a handful of hopeful businesses were open. It gave Maya some small sense of relief to know that there were at least a few people around, within earshot.

They were nearly at the entrance to Wonderland when she saw him. A man walked briskly down the pier, his hands stuffed into the pockets of his black leather jacket. He was about her dad's age, tall, white, with square shoulders and a five o'clock shadow. His hair was dark and cropped close to his scalp.

Maya kept her arm around Sara's shoulders but slowed her pace as the man approached. He was definitely looking directly at them, though every now and then he glanced left and right.

When he was close enough, he said, "Hello, girls. I'm glad to see you made it here safely. My name is Watson. I believe you've been told to come with me."

Maya said nothing. There was something strange about his voice; he spoke plain English, but it sounded strange, almost strained…as if he was trying to affect an accent. But then again, her dad hadn't specifically mentioned that the men coming for them would be American.

She had an excellent memory, and remembered her dad's instructions word for word. *Be there by 9 a.m.*, he had said. *Don't wait for more than an hour. Don't look for them. They'll look for you. Their names are Watson and Carver.*

"There were supposed to be two of you," said Maya.

"Yes." The man who called himself Watson smiled placidly. "My partner got held up. But I promise, this is fine. We will meet with him. Please, we must hurry. Come." He gestured with his head down the pier, back the way they had come. "My car is this way." He led the way, glancing back over his shoulder to make sure the girls were following.

Maya hesitated. Much like the hotel the night before, something didn't feel quite right, but she couldn't put her finger on it.

They'll ask for your Skype ID, her dad had said in his message. *If anyone approaches you by any other name, you run and get help.*

Maya began to follow the man, nudging Sara along with her but walking sluggishly, deliberately slowing his pace. "You were supposed to give us a name," she said.

The man paused and smiled again. "I told you. It is Watson."

"No, you were supposed to give me my name."

"Give you your name?" Watson chuckled. "You are Maya. And that is Sara. Yes? Can we go?"

Maya's throat felt tight. Alarm bells screamed in her brain. This was not right at all.

"And my father? His first name?"

The man sighed impatiently, but maintained his cheerful (and thoroughly fake) smile. It was not at all lost on Maya that he had not yet taken his hands out of his coat pockets.

"Your father's name," the man said, "is Kent."

Maya's jaw clenched so hard she was afraid she'd crack a molar, but she forced her sweetest smile. "Okay then. Lead the way."

They had to get away from this man, and fast.

She let him lead them for a short way down the pier before she spoke up again. "Wait, wait. I'm sorry. I need to use the bathroom."

A hiss of exasperation escaped Watson's throat. "There will be bathrooms where we go—"

"It's an emergency," Maya insisted. "Look, they're right there." She pointed to the nearby building that housed a pair of public restrooms. "We'll be fast, okay? Thirty seconds." She grabbed her sister by the hand and pulled her toward the bathroom before the man could respond. He let out a grunt, but did not try to argue. Instead he resumed his lookout, glancing about anxiously.

As soon as the door was closed behind them, Maya quickly checked the stalls to make sure they were alone.

"Maya, I don't like this," Sara said softly.

"I know. Me neither. Sara, I need you to listen to me *very* carefully." She held her sister by one shoulder and looked her right in the eye. "You're going to go out the back window..."

"What?" Sara's eyes went wide.

"Just listen! I'm going to help you out the back window. I want you to run as fast as you can, two blocks down that way. Remember the alien-themed mini golf, with the lasers and UFOs and stuff?"

Sara nodded, her mouth slightly open.

"Good. Last year there was a hole in the back fence. If they haven't fixed it yet, you can slip inside. Go to the twelfth hole and hide there. Do not come out for anyone or anything but me. Understand? Run there, hide, and stay there until I come for you."

The color ran from Sara's face. Maya could tell she was petrified. "What's happening?" she asked timidly. "Who is that man?"

"We don't have time for that. You need to go. Wait for me …"

"What if you don't come?"

Maya bit her lip. "I will. I promise. You stay there until I do. Got it?" Her sister said nothing. "Sara, you got it?"

"Got it." Sara's voice was almost a whisper.

Maya kissed her on the forehead and then helped hoist her up to the height of the window, where Sara unlatched the lock and swung the pane outward. It took almost a full minute, but she managed to wriggle her way outside.

"Okay," Maya said to herself. She had no idea what she was going to do from there, but at least Sara would be safe. She put on her best fake smile and headed back outside to the waiting "Watson."

"So sorry," she said brightly. "My sister is having some stomach problems. She's really anxious and scared right now. She'll be out in just a minute …"

"We do not have a minute!" the man growled. "Do you have an idea of what danger you're in?"

"I have an idea, yeah," Maya muttered.

The man narrowed his eyes. He was catching on. He took his left hand out of his jacket, grabbed Maya by the arm, and pulled her toward the bathroom.

"Hey, let go!" she shouted. "What are you doing?"

The man grunted something under his breath—something harsh, guttural, and unintelligible to her. It wasn't English. He shouldered open the bathroom door and yanked Maya with him as he checked the empty stalls.

He cursed loudly in a foreign tongue. "Where is she?!" he demanded, hissing in Maya's face.

"Wait, wait, I'll tell you," she said desperately. "Just don't hurt me. She went out the window."

"The window?" the man glanced quizzically over his shoulder at the small rectangular portal, perhaps wondering how Sara could have squeezed through it.

Maya reared back and kicked out as hard as she could, landing the toe of her sneaker right into the man's crotch.

Breath and spittle exploded out of him with the force of the blow. He doubled over immediately, his face turning bright red as he sank to his knees. Maya didn't see any of that, though—as soon as her kick landed, he released his grip on her, and she took off running. She threw the door open and sprinted out onto the pier, pumping her legs as fast as she could.

She had been on the girls' track team for the past two years, by no means a star but still light on her feet. She wasn't great at distances, but short spans were her specialty. Her long legs propelled her forward with every bound as she demanded them to go faster.

She heard panting behind her and hazarded a glance over her shoulder. Panic wedged itself deep in her stomach; the man had recovered quickly, or was running through the pain. His face was still bright red, but now it was a mask of anger, making him look almost demonic.

He was fast, and closing the gap between then quickly.

She stared ahead again, not daring to look back at him, as she tried to will herself to speed up. She felt fingers in her hair. She couldn't outrun him...

Then stop trying, her brain told her.

She skidded to a sudden halt and at the same time dove into a crouch. Her pursuer didn't see that coming. He collided with her hard, tripped over her crouched body, and went flying through the air. For a brief moment he was soaring over her.

Then he hit the planks of the pier, face-first, with a sickening crash.

Maya stood again. Her ribs ached where he had run into her, but she ignored it as best she could and took off in the opposite direction.

I can't keep running, she told herself. *Need to find a place to hide.* One of the open shops would be ideal. The man wouldn't dare to assault her in front of someone else...would he?

I can't do that, she thought. *I can't put someone innocent in harm's way because of me.* She slowed her pace and looked to her left. She was near the entrance to Wonderland... the animatronic monkeys. She glanced back to see the man about fifty yards down the pier. He was only just now stirring, struggling to get up. He wasn't looking her way.

She quickly skirted toward the display of instrument-playing monkeys and hid behind it. He would expect her to run, to find someone and call the police. He wouldn't expect her to hide in the same place she was supposed to already be.

Maya struggled to control her ragged, panting breaths as she dared to peek around the edge of the small bandstand. The man staggered past, mere feet from her. His face was still red—dark red now, as blood ran from a wide cut near his hairline, down his cheek and neck. His eyes were furious and wild. In his right hand, he held...

Maya froze in terror. For a moment, she forgot to breathe. The man held a silver gun, a pistol, keeping it tight to his side but his finger on the trigger.

She had never seen a real gun before, and the very sight of it made her tremble. She couldn't move, didn't dare to breathe...

Suddenly a hand grabbed her roughly by the hair. She yelped and instinctively tried to squirm away, but the hand held fast, yanking her head back violently.

There was a second man, with deep mocha-colored skin. She could see his large frame, but not his face. He forced her head forward and her body followed, stumbling as he shoved her out from behind the display.

"I've got her," he called out to the first attacker. He spun, half-hiding his gun behind his body. The collar of his white shirt was soaked with blood. He leered at her murderously. "Where is the other?" the new assailant grunted.

"Escaped," said the one with blood on his face. "I can find her. We can make this one talk—"

"No," said the second man. "We have wasted enough time. We must go, now. We have one. She will suffice."

Suffice for what? Maya thought, panicked. She tried to squirm out of his grip. Her scalp burned as several hairs were pulled out by the root, but the man held her firmly. He began to drag her down the pier, in the direction the man had said his car was waiting. She had the distinct feeling that once she was in that car, there would be no coming back. She saw no other choice.

"Help!" she screamed. As loud as she could, she shouted, "I'm being kidnapped!"

The man holding her reached for something—then he showed it to her. A knife with a wickedly curved blade reached for her throat. "Shut up, girl," he hissed, "unless you want to be opened."

Maya sucked in a breath and held it. She didn't dare call out again. But she didn't have to. From the nearest shop, a store that sold novelty T-shirts, a portly woman emerged, her brow knitted in the center with concern. She folded her thick arms against the winter cold and peered at the two men holding a teenage girl by the hair.

"My god!" she exclaimed. "Let go of that girl right now, or I will call the police!" Even as she said it, the woman pulled a phone from her back pocket and had a thumb on the keypad.

The man with the gun grunted again in a foreign language. He took the pistol from behind his back, raised it—

"No, wait!" Maya heard herself shout.

Two thunderous claps split the air, louder and more real than she ever would have imagined. Blood misted into the air from two holes in the woman's chest. The cell phone clattered to the pier, followed a moment later by the woman's body thudding dully to the planks—but Maya didn't hear it. Her ears rang with the sudden, deafening gunshots.

"Idiot!" hissed the man holding her.

"She was going to call the police!" the first man said in defense.

"Now they will come anyway! Come. Hurry up!" He tugged again on Maya's hair, forcing her forward, but she barely felt it. Her legs were rubbery. They didn't want to work properly.

She had just witnessed a murder. An innocent person. And it was her fault.

Her throat was tight and her face felt numb. An awareness spawned at the back of her mind—these two men were willing to do whatever they had to do to take her away from here. No police were coming for her. No one was here to save her.

Her one saving grace, her only thought of solace, was that at least Sara was safe. Maya hoped against hope that her sister would stay there, hidden in the large plastic UFO of the twelfth hole...

"Move!" the man barked in her ear. Her feet dragged uselessly against the pier. "Walk, or else I will—"

Two more intense cracks pealed over the Wonderland pier. The body of the man holding the gun jerked and fell backward. Maya blinked in shock. She had no idea what had just happened, but the man holding her seemed to know. He waved the knife back and forth, looking around wildly.

"Don't!" he shouted. "I'll cut her open, I will—" He moved to press the knife to Maya's throat, but before the blade reached her a third gunshot split her eardrums. The man's head jerked back. The fingers in her hair spasmed, pulling more follicles out by the roots... then they slackened and fell away.

Maya's breath came raggedly. Tears stung her eyes. Through her blurry vision she saw a shape, climbing up onto the pier from the beach side. She wiped at her eyes. It was an African-American man, holding a gun up with both hands, the barrel of it pointed downward as he hurried over to her, looking left and right as he did.

"Katherine Joanne," he said to her.

"Wh-what?" she stammered. Her brain felt like it had short-circuited.

"Maya, I'm Agent Watson. Katherine Joanne—that's the account you contacted your father with. Are there more?"

"A-agent?" *Agent of what?*

"Maya." Watson looked her right in the eye. "Are there more, or did you only see two?"

"Two," she said shakily. "Only two."

"Okay." Watson knelt beside the body of the tan-skinned man that had been holding her. He tugged the collar of the man's coat and inspected his neck. Then Watson pressed a finger to his ear and spoke. "I've got Maya. Two assailants down. They're not Amun; they must be from one of the factions under their thumb." He glanced up at Maya again. "Where is your sister?"

"She's … hiding …"

"Where?"

Maya pointed. "That way. About two blocks that way."

"Okay. I need you to show me where." He pressed his finger to his ear again—Maya could see that he was wearing a wire, a transparent lead trailing down into his collar. "Carver, bring the car around to the Ninth Street entrance. We'll meet you there." He took Maya gently by the shoulder. "I need you to show me, okay? Don't worry. You're safe now."

Maya flinched at his touch. Her eyes threatened more tears. She had just seen three people shot in the span of a minute. This new person—*Agent* Watson?—said she was safe, but as long as he was holding a gun, she didn't feel all that safe.

They both turned suddenly to the sound of a pained groan. The first assailant, the one with the gun, wasn't quite dead. He lay on his back, bleeding out onto the planks, squirming in agony. He coughed flecks of blood onto his shirt.

"Does not matter," he murmured. "You will still be too late."

Agent Watson aimed his gun at the downed assailant, though it didn't seem like the man was ever getting up again. "Too late for what?" Watson demanded.

The man somehow managed a grin. "The ground will split open … with the heels … of their feet." He laughed, and then winced in pain.

While Maya watched, the man's muscles slackened. He stopped moving. His eyes, though, stayed wide open, and the hint of a grin remained on his lips as he died.

She shuddered and looked away.

"Come on," Watson said quietly. "Show me where your sister is, and we'll get out of here."

Maya nodded and led the way down the pier toward the mini-golf course where Sara was hiding. She still wasn't entirely sure what was going on. But as her brain started churning again, recovering from the shock of what she had just seen, she began to form a much better idea of what her dad might be involved in.

They would definitely have a lot to talk about when she saw him again—though if what she had been through with the two would-be kidnappers was any indication, she couldn't be certain that she *would* ever see her father again.

CHAPTER THIRTY ONE

Reid regained consciousness slowly. There was an intense head-ache at the front of his skull and he wasn't sure where he was. He had been dreaming—if he could call it that. He had heard his daughters' voices, happy and giggling. He'd heard sounds of waves gently crashing on the surf. He heard Kate's light, wonderful laugh-ter, and then a slight nervous edge to her voice as she called out to Maya to watch her footing on the breakwater. He heard all the sounds of a family outing to the shore from years earlier, but he saw nothing. Only darkness. It was as if he was blind. He desperately wished to see the delighted faces of his girls, the content smile on Kate's lips. But he saw nothing, just black.

Then he woke, and his head throbbed, and he forgot for a moment where he was. He was seated in a cream-colored seat in a narrow cabin—right. He was aboard the Gulfstream. They were still in the air, he could tell by the pressure in his ears. He tried to rub his head, but his right wrist snapped taut after only a few inches.

He was handcuffed to the plush armrest.

His vision was fuzzy and he felt mildly nauseous. Despite the many questions on his mind, he rested back in the seat for a moment and closed his eyes, waiting for the feeling to pass.

"Here." Maria's voice. He opened his eyes slightly to see her holding out a bottle of water. "The nausea will pass." She spoke quietly. She almost sounded ashamed.

He took the water with his uncuffed left hand, opened it, and drained half the bottle. Then he asked, "Why?"

"Believe me," she said, "it was the last thing I wanted to do. And as much as I don't care much for Cartwright at the moment, he was right. We couldn't have you losing control again. Protocol Delta was necessary."

His mouth felt like it was full of cotton. He drank the rest of the water. His head began to clear, and he suddenly remembered the peril that had caused Maria to drug him in the first place. He sat up quickly, ignoring a fresh wave of headache pain. ""The girls? What have you heard?"

"They're safe, Kent. We found them."

He breathed an enormous sigh of relief. "Tell me what happened."

"They met Watson and Carver at the rendezvous point. There were…complications, but neither of them was harmed," Maria explained. "They're in a safe house in northeastern Maryland."

"I want to talk to them."

"I just sent a message to Cartwright that you're awake," she said. "He has to patch you in via a secure line that goes through Langley. It'll just be a minute." Then she added, "But they're safe, Kent."

Reid took several deep breaths. The nausea was passing. His vision was clearing too. He wanted to be angry at Maria, but he couldn't find the energy or, frankly, the motivation. "I wasn't losing control," he said simply. "I'm not that guy anymore. I was just doing what any parent would do." He looked her in the eye. "Do you have children? In your…other life?"

She shook her head. "No."

Then you wouldn't understand, he wanted to say.

Instead he asked, "How long have I been out?"

"About five hours," Maria told him. "We're still en route to return to Zurich. We should be there soon." A cell phone rang. Maria answered it, murmured a few words, and then handed it to Reid. "Someone wants to talk to you."

He put the phone to his ear.

"Dad?"

Reid closed his eyes in an effort to extinguish the threat of tears. That one word, just the sound of Maya's voice, and it was as if all his worry and mental anguish was exhaled from him. "It is so good to hear your voice, sweetheart. You okay?"

She was silent for a long moment. "I... don't know. I think I will be. I... saw some things."

"I'm so sorry, baby." He wanted to ask her what she'd seen, but now wasn't the time. They would talk later, when they were together again. She deserved that much.

"When will you get home?" Her voice cracked as she asked the question, and his heart broke anew.

"I don't know," he said honestly. "Soon, I hope. But you're safe, and that's what matters most to me. Can I talk to your sister?"

"She's sleeping," said Maya. "The, uh, events of the morning really drained her."

"Let her sleep," said Reid. "Put Watson on the phone, would you?"

"Sure." She added tightly, "I love you, Dad."

"I love you too, Maya."

A moment later, a deep male voice answered. "It's Watson."

"What can you tell me?" Reid asked.

Watson lowered his voice—for Maya's benefit, Reid guessed. "Two assailants, both dead. We ran recognition on them. One was Turkish, the other Afghani. Neither was Amun, but I'm sure they were working with them."

"Do you know how they got to the girls?" Reid asked. "Were they watching the whole time, or were they sent?"

"That's the strange part," said Watson. "The first one approached the girls and tried to gain their trust... posing as me."

Reid understood immediately what that meant. Amun had people in the United States, but more than that, whoever was leaking information from the CIA was still doing so somehow. It was the only explanation for how Amun would have known that Watson and Carver were being sent to the pier that morning. "I see," he said. "Stay on your toes. If they knew about that, they may know the location of the safe house."

"No one's getting in," Watson assured him. "We've got a whole squad at our backs."

Reid nodded. "Thank you for taking care of them."

"Wait, Zero, there's one more thing," Watson said. "The Turkish guy, before he kicked it, he said something. It wouldn't have stuck out to me if it wasn't so odd. He said, 'The ground will split open with the heels of their feet.' Does that mean anything to you?"

Reid blinked. There was a glimmer of recognition in the words, as if he had heard them somewhere before, but he couldn't immediately place it. "Not really," he said. "But I'll look into it. Thanks again, Watson." He hung up, his brow furrowed.

Maria noticed. "You don't look very at ease for a guy who just found out his daughters are safe."

Reid shook his head. "It's not that. It's..." He trailed off. Where had he heard that strange phrase before? *The ground will split open with the heels of their feet.* It sounded like something he had read before, or maybe even cited in a classroom.

The phone rang in his hand. He answered.

"It's Cartwright," the deputy director greeted. "You okay, Zero? You calm?"

"I'm fine," Reid said shortly. He had several choice words he wanted to share with Cartwright about his Protocol Delta, but he held his tongue. "You heard Watson's report?"

"I did," Cartwright said dejectedly.

"Then you know what it means. Someone is still leaking intel to Amun. Has the NSA started tracking CIA correspondence?"

The deputy director scoffed. "I imagine they have by now, but it's not like they're going to tell us, 'Hey, we started listening in on your private conversations.'"

"Well, whoever it is has found another way to get information out. We need to let Directors Mullen and Hillis know. We need to look closer at the higher-ups. And Johansson and I may have to go dark."

The ground will split open with the heels of their feet. He couldn't get it out of his head. He had definitely heard it before. But where?

Cartwright sighed. "Let's not jump to anything hastily. Come back to Zurich, and we'll figure this out."

Reid shook his head. "There's nothing for us to do in Zurich. We need to find our next lead." The only problem was that they had failed with the fake Sheikh Mustafar, and he had no idea where to go next. He didn't want to return to Zurich empty-handed and start anew from square one. He didn't want to sit in a conference room and debate options with superiors. He wanted to find Amun and discover their plot, but the only possible surviving lead he had was finding the assassin, the blond stranger who had attacked him in the Rome subway station. If there was a way to draw the assassin out of hiding, Reid would risk it. But he had no clue where the man might be or what channels he got his information through.

The CIA mole, perhaps, Reid thought. If Cartwright helped him make his whereabouts known, maybe that could flush the assassin out of hiding. It would be extremely risky and require making himself vulnerable…

The ground will split open with the heels of their feet. It tugged again at the back of his mind.

"Agent Steele," Cartwright said sternly. "I am giving you a direct order to return to Zurich, so unless you can give me a good reason why you wouldn't—"

"You want a good reason?" Reid interrupted. "Because I'm not entirely sure the leaks aren't coming from you." He hung up.

Maria blinked at him, the hint of a smirk on her lips. "I bet that felt pretty good," she said. "Do you really think it could be him?"

Reid shook his head. "I suppose it's possible, but it wouldn't add up." He certainly didn't trust Cartwright, but the deputy director had tried to get him kicked off the case, had told Hillis that Zero was compromised. That didn't seem like the kind of play he would do if he was working with Amun.

The ground will split open with the heels of their feet. It could have been a reference to a god, or a titan ... something from mythology, perhaps?

Maria frowned. "What's wrong? You look pensive."

"I just need some time to think." Reid paced the small cabin. "The ground will split open," he murmured. "With the heels of their feet..."

Gods. Titans. Deities. He ran through basic word association in his head, trying to jar the memory loose. *Demigods. Heroes. Epics...*

Suddenly it clicked.

As they whirled in circles, Mount Hermon and Lebanon split.

"Mount Hermon," he muttered.

"What?"

"Mount Hermon!" he nearly shouted. "Listen, tell me if this tracks. One of the goons that Amun sent after my girls, as he was dying, he said 'The ground will split open with the heels of their feet.' I thought it sounded familiar." He spoke a mile a minute, gesticulating with his hands as he did. "It's a line from the *Epic of Gilgamesh*, the Sumerian poem ... The rest of it goes, 'As they whirled in circles, Mount Hermon and Lebanon split.' It's referring to Gilgamesh's battle with Humbaba." *Thank you, Professor Lawson*, he thought. The reason it had sounded so familiar was because he had taught it once, years ago, when he was an adjunct professor at George Washington University.

Maria simply shook her head. "I'm sorry. I don't get it."

"It was a taunt," said Reid, excited now. "As he was dying, the terrorist recited a line from the epic—probably one that he had heard from a member of Amun. It sounds like a threat, but it's a taunt, and one that points directly to Mount Hermon, a mountain that straddles the border between Syria and Lebanon. At the top of it is a, uh, a UN buffer zone, an outpost..."

"And you think they plan to attack the UN post?"

"I don't know. But I know it's a lead. We need to get there, now."

"To Syria?" Maria looked dubious. "It sounds like a stretch, but ... all right. We'll need to refuel first." She strode quickly to the front of the cabin and picked up a plastic corded telephone, a direct line to the cockpit. She told the pilot their plan, and then listened as he relayed a message back.

"He said it'll be at least thirty minutes until we can land and refuel," Maria reported to Reid. "We're too close to the no-fly zone, so we'd have to circumvent it and go to Bern to refuel—"

"What no-fly zone?"

"Over Sion, for the winter games."

"Oh, right." The Winter Olympics were being held in the southwestern Swiss city of Sion. He had completely forgotten they were happening. "Wait a second…" *Sion.* The word stuck in his mind as if it had been nailed in place. He paced the jet again, up and back, while Maria stared at him blankly.

"What now? Are we landing, or …?"

Reid's mouth fell partially open as a new realization struck him like a bolt of lightning. "The Olympics are in Sion," he said quietly.

"Yeah, we know that." Maria was getting impatient. "What about it?"

"In the original Hebrew Bible," he explained slowly, "Mount Hermon was called something else. It was called Mount Tzion— spelled with a t-z, but translators later dropped the t and just called it Zion. But that original spelling, in Hebrew, would have been pronounced like …"

A gasp of astonishment caught in Maria's throat. "Like Sion."

"Exactly. The taunt wasn't a clue about Mount Hermon. Maria, it was a direct clue about the pending attack. Sion is the target. The Winter Olympics."

He bolted for the white phone at the front of the cabin.

"Wait! How can we be sure?"

"We can't," he said, "but think about it. It's a densely packed area, thousands of people from almost every nation on the planet. It could easily be the biggest terror attack in history."

"Jesus," Maria breathed. "We should have seen this sooner."

Reid grabbed up the phone. "Don't land in Italy," he told the pilot urgently. "We need to land in Sion."

"Agent, I can't land in Sion," the pilot said. "We're not cleared for that—"

"Then you need to get clear, *now*," Reid warned. The terrorist that had assaulted his girls never would have given them that clue if the attack wasn't already in motion. "Something terrible is about to happen, and we may already be too late to stop it."

CHAPTER THIRTY TWO

"We have to tell Cartwright," Maria said urgently. "Get all available agents to Sion, lock down the location, assess for threats—"

"No," Reid interrupted, "I don't think that's the right move." He was fairly sure that Cartwright wasn't the one leaking intel, but either way, the CIA mole would be on high alert the second the Olympics were locked down. "Amun still knew where my girls were, and the names of the agents that were coming for them. Even if it's not Cartwright, then it's someone close to him, someone close enough to have caught wind of our plan. If we loop the agency in on this, there's nothing keeping that from happening again."

Maria shook her head. "We're talking about the potential for hundreds, maybe thousands of lost lives, on an international scale. We have to tell someone. We have to warn them."

"Interpol," said Reid suddenly. "We alert Interpol, and have them notify Swiss officials and the Olympic Committee. Tell them to start evacuation protocols. Make the call, Maria."

"And what do we tell them about us? We're two CIA agents that can't report to their own bosses because of suspected leaks?"

Reid thought quickly, his eyes flitting back and forth. "No ... We go over the agency's head. Contact your father and the National Security Council. Tell him that whoever's supplying information to Amun is still finding a way to do it. We need the DNI's sanction to act on this."

"Even so, the CIA could lose credibility ..." Maria began.

"Like you said, we're talking about hundreds, maybe thousands of lives. I think that's worth a little credibility."

Reid could tell that Maria did not at all like keeping the CIA out of the loop, but she nodded tightly and pulled out her phone. She made two calls; the first was to Interpol to alert them of the possible threat and put the Olympic security into motion. Reid heard the taut anxiety in her voice as she mentioned that the CIA was potentially compromised. The second call she made was to her father, to keep the National Security Council and Director of National Intelligence abreast of the situation and get their consent to act.

Almost as soon as she hung up, the intercom crackled to life in the cabin. "We've been cleared to land and we're going in fast," the pilot announced. "Buckle up, Agents. Ten minutes to landing."

Maria took the seat beside Reid and strapped herself in. "So," she said, trying, and failing, to keep the unease out of her voice, "just to be clear here, we're about to interrupt what is arguably the biggest sporting event in the world and bring it to a grinding halt, likely costing millions of dollars in revenue, to look for a needle in a haystack on a hunch from a terrorist that died in New Jersey, and we're doing all of this without the knowledge of the agency that gives us license to do things like this."

"Yes," Reid confirmed. "That pretty much sums it up."

"Just like old times." He felt her fingers close around his. They were warm and welcome; familiar, yet foreign. It was such a strange feeling to be near her, to simultaneously feel as if she was an old friend while also feeling the electric tingle of something new and exciting.

He almost missed not trusting her.

Reid felt it in his belly as the Gulfstream dropped a few hundred feet. Maria squeezed his hand tighter.

"Before we do this," he said, "there's something I want to know. It's about what happened before, the reason you and Cartwright thought that Protocol Delta was necessary."

"You want to talk about that *now*?" Maria asked incredulously.

"It's important to me," he insisted. "All I know is that Kent went...no, that's not right. *I* did it. You said that I went wild. That

I left a horrible, bloody trail. But I can't remember it, and I don't know why I did it. I can't shake the feeling that there's more, there's something I'm not being told." He glanced over and looked her in the eye, still holding her hand. "I trust you, Maria. I can say that now. Please, tell me what happened."

She shook her head. "I really don't think this is the right time, Kent..."

"Look, if I've learned anything from teaching history, it's that we're doomed to repeat the mistakes of the past unless we learn from them. I can't learn from something that I don't remember, and I don't want to be that guy again. I don't want to put anyone in harm's way, and I don't want to jeopardize everything that's at stake here. We only have a few minutes until we land, and I don't know what's going to happen. This may be the only chance that I get to find out why I stopped being Kent Steele."

Maria sighed evenly. "All right," she said. "I'll tell you." She sucked in a breath as the Gulfstream dropped several hundred more feet, descending rapidly. "When Kate died, you were inconsolable. You were on an op when it happened. You weren't there, and you blamed yourself. More than that... you were certain that Amun had something to do with it."

Reid frowned. "But she died of an embolism," he said. "It caused a stroke. There was nothing anyone could do, not even the paramedics."

"We tried to tell you there was nothing you could have done, but you wouldn't hear it. You went hunting for Amun. You were obsessed. The agency tried to call you back, but you went dark. They sent the rest of us—me and Morris and Reidigger—after you. I split off from them to follow another lead..."

"And you found me?"

"Yes," she said. "That's when we... spent our time together. When the agency found out, they threatened to disavow us both. I went back. You didn't. And a few weeks later, you were announced KIA."

A vision flashed in Reid's mind—*a bridge. Darkness. Water rushing far below. The sensation of falling...*

The Gulfstream dipped again. Through the window Reid could see an airport coming into view, the city of Sion beyond it. There were no skyscrapers, no buildings of glass or brightly lit main avenues; Sion looked as if an ancient village had spread like a puddle, nestled at the base of a mountain range and dwarfed by the peaks.

Far in the distance, on the opposite side of the city, he could see the grand Olympic Village that had been constructed specifically for the games. Huge domed structures housed indoor events while a luge track and ski slopes had been carefully erected around a pair of smaller mountains, atop which were perched stone castles built hundreds of years earlier. The dichotomy was astounding.

He still very much had the feeling that Johansson wasn't telling him everything, but it was too late to question it. They would be on the ground in moments.

"Thank you," he said. "For being honest."

She looked away.

"Wheels down in two minutes," the pilot announced over the intercom.

"God, I hope we're not too late," Johansson murmured.

"Whatever there is to find, we'll find it," Reid said. He tried to sound as confident as possible, but his voice wavered.

The door to the Gulfstream was open before the plane came to a complete stop on the runway. Waiting on the tarmac of Sion Airport were three Swiss police cars, their lights flashing. Reid and Maria were ushered into the back of one and the motorcade departed immediately, swinging onto the highway and speeding toward the Olympic Village.

A man in a charcoal gray suit twisted around to address them from the passenger seat. "My name is Agent Vicente Baraf, with Interpol," he said as he flashed his badge. His accent was Italian, and he sported a pencil-thin black mustache. "My superiors have been in touch with your Director of National Intelligence. We understand the situation and have been instructed not to communicate with your CIA, beyond the two of you."

"We appreciate the cooperation, Agent Baraf," Maria said diplomatically. "Can you tell us what measures are currently being taken?"

"Interpol is sending more than a dozen of our agents from an economic forum in Davos to come here," Baraf told them. "But even by plane, that will take a couple of hours. In the meantime, we must work with what we have. Olympic security and Swiss police are evacuating the entire park. However, we're talking about thousands of people. It is a slow process."

"Slow is no good," said Reid. "We don't want Amun getting anxious and doing something rash."

Maria's cell phone rang from her pocket. She didn't answer it; in fact, she didn't even look at it. They both knew it was likely Cartwright. By now the CIA would have caught wind of what was happening. In fact, with the sheer volume of media coverage at the Olympics, there was a good chance that most of the developed world was aware.

Agent Baraf fiddled with the touchscreen panel in the dash of the police car. "I'm going to patch you in to a briefing," he said. "We don't have time for an in-person meeting, so in a moment you'll be addressing a room full of Interpol agents, Olympic security officials, and the Swiss Federal Office of Police." He switched on the car's Bluetooth and a murmur of voices was suddenly audible through the car stereo's speakers. "Attention, everyone," said Baraf loudly. "I've got CIA Agents Steele and Johansson en route, and they're going to share what they know, so listen carefully." The murmurs fell silent.

Reid glanced over at Johansson, who nodded. He was suddenly aware that he had never had to brief a room of agents before—at least not that he could remember—and was keenly grateful that he wasn't there in person.

He cleared his throat, leaned forward, and said loudly, "This is Agent Steele with the CIA." Once the words started, they came to him as if he had done this a hundred times before—and it was not lost on him that he likely had. "As you know, we have strong reason to believe that a terrorist organization is plotting an attack on the Winter Olympics. Our intel suggests they've been planning this for some time, so it's likely that we're not talking about an isolated occurrence, but something intended to target the widest area and largest amount of people possible."

He thought back to Otets's facility, the bombs he had seen. "All available bomb units and canines should be focused on detecting dinitrotoluene, the chemical compound being used as the active incendiary. These bombs will each have a blast radius of about forty to sixty feet, but as I said, we should not believe that this will be isolated; I expect there will be several sites, possibly intended as a chain reaction so that a single detonation can affect a large area.

"Agent Baraf has informed us that evacuation procedures have already begun. Continue those efforts, but proceed with caution. We don't want to incite a panic or give the insurgents a reason to detonate early."

A male voice spoke up over the speaker. "Sir, is there a specific nationality to which this organization belongs that we should be looking for?"

"Unfortunately, no," Reid responded. "This particular group has members from all over the world, and they're well trained. It's unlikely they'll look the part, and they won't be acting in a way that'll arouse suspicion."

Maria tapped his shoulder and pointed to her neck.

Right, Reid thought. *The brand.*

"As you empty the park, make it mandatory that every evacuee shows their face and neck," Reid told the briefing room. "This organization is called Amun, and their members are marked with a brand, a rectangular burn, in the shape of an Egyptian hieroglyph. Detain anyone with any suspicious markings on their face or neck." He was very much aware that Amun might not have sent their own members to do the detonating; it was more likely that they had recruited some suicide-bombing faction to do it for them, but it was the only thing he had to go on.

"ETA is eight minutes," Baraf announced.

"One last thing," Reid told the room. "Proceed with extreme caution. These people, Amun, will not hesitate to take lives—their own and others'—for their cause. They are to be considered extremely dangerous. If the perpetrators are positively identified, do not hesitate to use lethal force."

"Thank you, Agent," said Baraf. "You all have your assignments. Dismissed." He switched off the speakerphone.

Through the windshield, the Sion Olympic Park came into view; the tall artificial slopes, the twisting luge track, the enormous domed building that likely housed the ice skating rinks. Despite their flashing lights and whooping sirens, the three-car police motorcade was forced to slow as they drew nearer with the astounding flux of people.

Baraf was right; there were thousands, of every nationality and ethnicity, most sporting the colors of their home country, faces painted with the colors of their banner and holding small flags. They milled about just outside the Olympic Park in huge clusters, blocking streets and sidewalks. Most were confused and looked annoyed at the evacuation. Many were downright irate, waving their arms or shouting at Swiss police.

"Agent Baraf," Maria spoke up, "we should get these people a safe distance from the park and the buildings. Amun is smart enough to realize that we might evacuate, and may have taken measures against it."

Baraf nodded and relayed the message into a radio. "The problem," he told them, "is manpower. We have a full security staff and every available agent, but there are simply too many people."

Outside the car, Reid could see at least a dozen news crews, maybe more, filming live with the Olympic attractions at their back. He was right; the world was aware that a terrorist attack was pending at the Winter Games … which meant that Amun knew as well.

The thought had crossed his mind that they could detonate their bombs remotely. After all, that's what he had done at Otets's facility, using the suitcase bomb. They didn't necessarily need a man at the site of the attack. The most important question on his mind, however, wasn't how they would do it—it was why they hadn't done it yet. The stadiums and sites were being emptied. It looked as if most of the spectators were already out. Any athletes and heads of state would have been among the first to be escorted from the premises.

What was Amun waiting for? he wondered. The illusion of safety? Or would they give up on their plan if it had been foiled?

No, he thought. *They wouldn't give up. They spent too long on this. They would have planned for this eventuality. But how?*

His gaze scanned the crowds, the structures, the news cameras, for anything that might seem amiss, as the motorcade inched closer.

"What can we do to help?" Maria asked Baraf.

"For one," the Interpol agent replied, "we can get these media crews out of here. They can report from elsewhere. Their presence is making people believe their proximity is safe. Then we can establish barricades a suitable distance away..."

Baraf continued talking, but Reid barely heard him. He was staring intently, his eyes narrowed as he scrutinized for any detail he might find that could help them.

He found none.

"Agent Steele?" Baraf was twisted in his seat, staring right at him. "How wide did you say potential blast radius was?"

"Oh, um, sorry. Approximately forty to sixty feet, based on the explosives I saw being manufactured."

"So twenty-five meters minimum," Baraf said to Maria. "Barricades on all three streets surrounding the entrance to the Olympic Park..."

Again the Interpol agent's voice became background noise to Reid's thoughts.

There's something here.

No—not something. Someone. Amun wouldn't entrust their master stroke to some other faction. They wouldn't remote detonate. They'd have someone here, maybe more than one, to ensure things were done properly.

"I need to get into the park," he said aloud.

"Into the park? Why?" Maria asked. "Bomb units are inside, doing their sweeps. We'd be more useful out here..."

"Stop the car," he insisted. They didn't have time to crawl through the people-choked streets.

Baraf nodded to the driver and the motorcade stopped, right in the middle of the street and half a block from the entrance to the Olympic Park. Reid pushed his door open and got out. For a moment he stood beside the car, his gaze darting carefully as he picked apart the crowd.

"Kent?" Maria got out as well. "What's the plan?"

He didn't answer. He simply stared at a point in the crowd.

For the briefest of moments, he could have sworn that he saw a glimpse of bleached blond hair, an angular chin—a familiar face.

"Kent, what's wrong?" Maria insisted.

"I don't know." He shook his head. "I could have sworn I saw..."

The Amun assassin from the subway in Rome. But maybe his eyes were playing tricks on him, making him see what he wanted to see. If he truly had seen him, the assassin was gone, vanished into the crowd.

He was vaguely aware that Maria had continued speaking. "Kent? Did you hear what I just said?"

"Sorry, no..." He had zoned out, staring at the throngs of people, searching for the blond head.

"I said, we should split up, take different sides of the park, and..."

There.

Reid did a double-take. He hadn't been imagining things at all.

Standing about fifty yards away, leaning against a telephone pole and smirking directly at him, was the Amun assassin.

As Reid stared back in disbelief, the blond man turned and began shoving his way through the crowd, back the way he had come—back into the Olympic Park.

He was daring Kent Steele to come after him.

And he did.

Chapter Thirty Three

"**S**tay with Baraf!" Reid shouted to Maria. "Help him!"

"Where are you go—Kent, wait!" Maria yelled after him, but her words were quickly drowned out as he sprinted forward, shoving people aside and edging through the crowd as best he could.

He had spotted the assassin. He was certain of it.

The only general admission entrance to the Olympic Park was a single double-lane road that cut directly through its center, between a tall sky-blue contemporary sculpture that had been erected for the occasion and a welcome center. Reid spotted a glimmer of blond hair vanishing behind the sculpture and pursued. His right hand kept instinctively reaching for the gun holstered beneath his jacket, and he had to remind himself that he was in a dense crowd and trying not to incite panic.

Just beyond the entrance road were four checkpoints, hastily organized by the Federal Office of Police and Interpol, with lengthy lines of people filing out—at each checkpoint, officers briefly inspected the face and neck of each guest as they left the facility, many of them dour or sullen.

He wouldn't have tried to go right through a checkpoint with armed guards, Reid reasoned. To his left, around the huge blue wire sculpture, was the side employee entrance to a small stadium that housed the skating rinks.

It was the only other way he could have gone.

He hurried over and tugged on the door. It was open, but beyond it was darkness.

Reid ventured inside. As soon as the door was closed behind him, he pulled out the Glock 27 from his shoulder holster and carefully stepped down a dim hallway. Compared to the daylight outside, it was dark, but emergency lights near the floor lit his way.

The sounds of disgruntled spectators were all but drowned out from inside the building. It was almost entirely silent. His breathing was too loud, he thought, a dead giveaway to his location. Every footstep might as well be an earthquake to an assassin lying in wait.

I should have told Maria to follow. I should have backup. I shouldn't have come in here alone. There would be a hundred places for the assassin to hide, to lie in wait for Reid to wander into.

Despite all these thoughts, he kept going further down the access corridor until it opened onto the main floor. To his left and right were the foremost rows of seats, arranged in a large oval around an ice rink. Center ice was illuminated overhead by powerful fluorescent lamps, casting the rink in eerie blue light. Everything else, however, was dark.

The ice was empty; that much he could see. The only way to go was up. He took the stairs carefully, slowly, one at a time, with his gun leveled at a presumed center mass on the assassin.

"That's far enough." The voice boomed, echoing over the rows of seats in such a way that Reid couldn't tell what direction it came from. "Put the gun down."

Reid resisted the urge to whip around, to attempt to track the voice. Instead he kept his hand steady as his gaze flitted left and right for any sign of movement.

"Why would I do that?" he called back. "So you can shoot me?"

"I could shoot you now," the voice said matter-of-factly. "I have a clear line of sight."

"Then why don't you?" Reid challenged.

A soft chuckle. "Because twice now I've tried to kill you with a gun, and both times some stroke of fortune saved you from me." The assassin paused briefly. "You opened me with a knife and left me for dead. I think I ought to return the favor."

Reid scoffed. "You're a lunatic."

"No, Agent. I'm much more than that. Now...put the gun down."

Reid swore softly under his breath. He saw no other option—either he could keep the gun, try to find the assassin, and possibly get shot...or he could put his gun down and possibly get shot.

Slowly he lowered himself into a crouch and set the Glock down on the step.

"And the other one," said the echoing voice.

"I don't have another—"

"Do *not* lie to me!" the assassin barked loudly. "You owe me more than that."

"I don't owe you anything," Reid growled back.

The assassin chuckled again. "Where is it? Ankle holster? Jacket pocket? Out with it."

Reid grunted in frustration, but he crouched again and pulled his second pistol, the small LC9, from his ankle holster. He set it beside the Glock and rose.

"Good. Now, up the stairs."

Reid did so, until he came to a wide center aisle about halfway up the stadium, a thoroughfare between sections of the rink.

"Stay right there," said the assassin.

From the darkness a silhouette took form. At first, in the dim lighting, it was just a shape, but as Reid's eyes adjusted it became a man, and then a man with blond hair, a sharp chin, square shoulders. He was holding something aloft—a pistol.

Reid didn't need to see it to know that it was a silenced Sig Sauer.

The assassin had him dead to rights for the second time that he could remember. If he pulled the trigger, there would be no more confusion between Reid Lawson and Kent Steele, because they would both cease to exist.

"I figured you out," Reid said, trying to sound confident. "Your plan is going to fail. How long did your people plot this out? Two years? Maybe more?"

"Nothing has failed," the assassin said calmly.

"Is that so? Then why didn't you detonate yet?"

"Oh, we will," the blond stranger replied. "Very soon. Just … not where you think."

Reid's expression fell slack. He felt that now-familiar ball of dread curdle in his stomach.

"What are you talking about?"

Reid couldn't see his smile, but he could hear it in the assassin's voice. "You took the bait. We led you here. Amun has given you to me."

I was wrong. Sion isn't the target at all.

The terrorist in New Jersey, his dying words weren't a clue. They were a distraction, a way to incite an international panic while the real threat loomed elsewhere, ignored—and a trap, to get Kent Steele there alone.

He had failed.

The sick, tight sensation in his stomach worsened at the assassin's hoarse chuckle. "You're putting it together," he taunted. "You see, Agent, Amun teaches us that every man has a purpose. We do many things in our lives, but we all have a singular reason for being. We can choose to ignore our purpose—but to do so is not to serve Amun. I have been given a purpose. And my purpose, simply put, is to kill you."

This man is psychotic, Reid thought. *Or just completely indoctrinated.*

He shook his head slowly. "If this is my end, it's yours too. There's no way out of this for you. This place is crawling with agents and police and security. Even if you do kill me, you'll never make it out."

"Agent, that's the point. I kill you. I am killed in return. I will not accept being taken prisoner. I will serve Amun in my highest purpose." The assassin held the gun up, showing it to Reid, and then set it down on the nearest seat. "Don't you see? You are my destiny. And I … I am your reckoning." He reached into his jacket and unsheathed a curved hunting knife. The blade glinted silver in the dim light.

Now that the gun was off of him, Reid's first instinct was to run, to make a dash for the exit, to warn Baraf and Maria that Sion was not the intended target at all. But the Sig Sauer was still within the assassin's reach. Reid wouldn't make it five yards before being shot in the back. He had to get the stranger away from the gun, at least enough so that he could make a break for it.

"My reckoning? Is that what you think you are?" Reid forced a laugh. "I don't even remember you. Whatever happened between us, you must not have left much of an impression. You're not my reckoning. You're just one more body I'll have to leave along the way."

His ridicule did the trick. The assassin let loose a guttural yell as he lunged at Reid. He flipped the knife around and swung down in an overhand stab. Reid instinctively blocked it with a forearm, twisted his body as he crouched, and flung the assassin over his shoulder.

The blond man landed on one knee and propelled himself back up, swinging the knife in a wide backwards arc. Reid leapt back, barely avoiding the blade—and tripped, toppling over the row of seats in front of the aisle. He hit the ground hard. Pain shot up his elbow.

The assassin was on him again in an instant. There were fingers in his hair. His head was yanked back. Any second, he knew, the knife would be at his neck.

Reid put up his hand to block it and caught the blade in his palm. He shouted in pain as his palm was slit open—but it was preferable to his throat. He shoved the blade up as he ducked beneath it, and then he planted both hands flat on the ground and kicked backward with as much force as he could muster.

The blond assassin grunted as he took the mule-kick to the chest. His body left the ground for a moment, and then crashed over two rows of hard plastic seats. He groaned, pulling himself up slowly.

Reid saw his chance. He dashed down the row toward the stairs and took them two at a time. He needed to get back outside, out in the open, back to Maria, tell her what he now knew…

He glanced over his shoulder just in time to see the assassin standing on the stairs, rearing back with the hunting knife, aiming to throw it.

Reid tucked into a roll.

The knife sailed just barely over his head, but he miscalculated the steepness of the stairs and lost control, tumbling down head over heels. His ribs hit the edge of a step and he lost his breath.

The hunting knife clattered onto the ice and skidded to a stop.

Reid winced in pain and tried to catch his wind again. The assassin had lost his knife, for the moment, but he might still be armed. Reid glanced up to see the blond man limping down the stairs after him. The tumble over the seats must have injured him.

Good. That'll slow him down. Though I'm not faring much better.

His ribs were most certainly bruised. His palm was bleeding amply. His left knee throbbed. He wasn't sure he could outrun the assassin down the access corridor through which he had entered the building, and that was the only sure exit he knew of.

The knife. Get to the knife.

Reid forced himself to stand, bounded down the last few steps, and leapt out onto the ice. He slid on his knees across the recently resurfaced rink and grabbed the hunting knife by its ivory handle.

The assassin wavered at the threshold to the rink. Reid hoped he wasn't sure-footed enough to take the fight onto the ice. He stood carefully, maintaining his footing, daring the assassin to come join him.

The blond stranger took a cautious step forward. He wobbled slightly, holding his arms out for balance. Reid could see his face clearly under the powerful overhead lights that lit the ice. Again a strange familiarity struck him, though he couldn't quite place it.

Then he looked the assassin in the eyes.

Curious—Reid was certain they had been a cold, icy blue back in the subway in Rome. But now they were green, a deep green, like the color of a dense forest.

The recognition struck him like a high-voltage shock to the brain. A vision flashed—a face, that same face he was staring at, but with dark hair, the shadow of a beard, the angular chin, and those green eyes.

A train station in Denmark.

A name came to him. "Rais," he murmured aloud.

The assassin smiled wide. It was neither pleasant nor threatening; if anything, it was triumphant. "You remember, Agent."

Rais. A new vision flashed: the assassin standing over him, gleeful, pointing the barrel of a gun at Reid's forehead.

"My face was different then," said Rais. "But I knew you would remember."

"You're the one I was after," Reid said quietly. "When I...back when ..."

Back when he was on the warpath, shortly after Kate's death. When Agent Kent Steele went on his spree, leaving a trail of bodies in his wake, grief-stricken and desperate to lose himself in the hunt. Memories flooded back to him, and with them came an intense headache at the front of his skull. He tortured anyone who might have information. He promised them amnesty for intel, and then he killed them anyway.

The agency had tried to call him back in. He ignored them.

He had been chasing the assassin, and ...

Another vision—a train station in Denmark. He had tracked the assassin and found him just before he boarded a train bound for Munich. They fought. They were both bloodied; they beat each other half to death. But ultimately Rais had him on his back with a gun to his head.

The assassin had pulled the trigger, but the gun misfired. Kent slipped a knife from his boot. Stabbed his would-be assassin in the gut and dragged the knife up, splitting him open.

He left Rais there to die.

"I found you ... I *killed* you."

But it had brought him neither satisfaction nor answers, and Rais had not died.

A satisfied smirk played on the assassin's lips. That was all he wanted, for Reid to remember him.

"As Amun, we endure," Rais said. "As I said, it is my destiny to kill you."

"You'll try."

Reid's grip tightened around the hunting knife as the assassin surged forward. He expected Rais to waver on the ice, but his boots somehow gave him purchase on the slick surface.

Reid realized it too late. Rais had planned for this, had specifically lured him here, to the rink. The assassin wore some sort of traction boots, while Reid was hopelessly unsteady.

He swung the knife upward as Rais drew near, but his movements were jerky. His swing went wide and Rais blocked it easily. The assassin's fist connected with Reid's jaw in a vicious uppercut. Stars swam in his vision. He had barely seen the blow coming, being too distracted by maintaining his balance.

Reid barely felt the second fist connect with his cheek. He heard a clatter—the knife slipping from his grip.

The blow sent him reeling, so he went with it, pushing with his heels and propelling himself backward. He hit the ice hard and slid about ten feet. Rais had been prepared to throw a third punch, but it hit nothing, and his momentum drove him forward. He staggered and fell to his limbs on the ice.

I need to bring this fight to solid ground if I'm ever going to get an upper hand. He rolled over, got to his feet, and pushed himself forward into a baseball-style slide just as Rais was regaining his footing. Reid collided with the assassin and tackled him onto the level platform where the stairs began. The two men tumbled in a tangle of limbs.

Rais ended up on top. He straddled Reid and swung his fists downward, one after another, pummeling him. Reid put both hands up to try to block the blows, but they kept coming, again and again. The assassin's face was red, his expression pure ire, as he swung over and over. A fist glanced off his arm and split his lips. Another connected with his right temple. Reid's vision swam. If he didn't do something, he would lose consciousness. He tried to squirm away, but Rais squeezed his hips together, trapping Reid beneath him.

The assassin grabbed both sides of Reid's head and tried to press his thumbs into his eyes. Reid bucked his hips as hard as he could, throwing Rais off balance. The assassin faltered, and Reid shot a fist straight out and struck the assassin in the throat. A wet choking sound escaped his lips. Reid shoved him aside and rolled over, out of the way.

He winced as something dull and rigid jammed into his side.

He had forgotten all about it. He wasn't unarmed at all.

Reid reached into his jacket pocket and swiftly pulled out the Swiss Army knife. He flicked out the three-inch blade. Rais was struggling to regain his breath, but rising to his feet at the same time.

Before he could, Reid buried the knife into the assassin's side, all the way to its red hilt.

Rais threw his head back and shrieked in pain as the knife pierced his kidney. Reid tugged the blade loose and let loose a primal shout as he stabbed again, this time in the muscles of his back. Rais howled and fell to all fours.

Rais tried to crawl away, but Reid grabbed him by the back of his belt and yanked him backward. Then he jammed the thin blade into his side again.

Rais screamed with each stab. The strength drained from his limbs. He couldn't crawl forward. He could barely move.

Reid stabbed once more, into his lower back, and twisted the blade. "Give Amun my regards," he hissed into the assassin's ear. "Maybe this time he'll let you stay dead."

Rais couldn't even scream anymore; his mouth yawned silently, etched with agony.

Reid suddenly felt exhausted. He let himself slump backward into a plastic seat as Rais collapsed onto his elbows. He hurt everywhere. He wasn't sure he could muster the strength to stand again, let alone to kill this man.

We're doomed to repeat the mistakes of the past unless we learn from them.

The words that he had said to Maria less than thirty minutes earlier ran through his head. He now knew the mistakes of his past; at least some of them. Killing Rais before, or thinking he had killed Rais, had brought him no closure, no satisfaction.

But this was no longer about satisfaction. He was going to kill Rais. He couldn't let someone like that live.

And yet, he understood now what he had failed to understand before.

"Nnggh…" The assassin moaned in soft whimpers as he futilely flailed out an arm, as if he could crawl away, but he was weak and losing blood fast. There was nowhere he could go. With a sustained grunt, he rolled himself over onto his back. He stared up at Reid, his forest-green eyes wide and fearful.

"I get it now," Reid told him. "I understand. You…your people…your whole organization, Amun…you're afraid of me. You're afraid of Agent Zero. It's never been just about the plot."

Amun had discovered that Kent Steele was alive, and they dispatched the Iranians to find and kill him. They sent Morris after him. They sent Rais after him. They tried to get to his girls. And now the false lead about an attack on the Olympics.

It wasn't just about the plot—it was about him. So much of what he had been through was to keep him from getting to where he was supposed to be. They were afraid of Agent Zero, because they knew from previous experience that he was capable of stopping them. They went to great lengths to try to kill him or, at the very least, keep him at bay. Agent Zero was their ghost, a haunting specter that they couldn't rid themselves of.

Reid maintained eye contact with Rais. He wanted to watch the life drain from his eyes.

"You goddamn fool," Reid said softly. "This was never about destiny. To them, you're just a pawn. Someone to do their dirty work."

With a grunt, he got down from the chair and sank to his knees. He leaned forward, close to Rais's face. He smelled the ample blood staining the floor beneath them. He saw the abject fear of death— or more likely of failure—in his adversary's eyes.

"Before you die," Reid told him, "I want your last thought to be this: no matter what passed between us, no matter what you believe about destiny or reckoning, to me you're still just one more body I'll have to leave along the way."

He slipped the knife between Rais's ribs, aimed at his heart.

The assassin gasped a breath, his eyes wide and bloodshot. Slowly he exhaled as his eyelids fluttered closed.

Reid left the knife there, buried in Rais's chest, and stood. He didn't know if Rais was the one who had taken Reidigger's life, but still it felt like some form of poetic justice.

Reid was in bad shape. He hurt everywhere, but he had to move.

The fact that the false lead sent him to the Winter Olympics had to mean that the attack was not only elsewhere, but imminent. It was about to happen, if it wasn't happening already.

Chapter Thirty Four

"Jesus, Kent, what happened to you?" Maria spotted him as he limped out of the steel door to the skating rink. She hurried over and slung his arm over her shoulders to help steady him.

"It's not Sion," he said breathlessly. After killing Rais, Reid had retrieved his guns and then made his way back down the dark access corridor as quickly as he was able—which was not all that quick at all. His knee was more pained with each step; he must have torn something when he tumbled down the stairs. His right eye was swollen anew. Both lips were split and puffy. His left hand was covered in blood where his palm was sliced open—and all of that only accounted for the visible cuts and bruises. He knew there would be much more beneath his clothes.

He had shoved open the employee exit of the skating rink and blinked in the sudden brightness of day, agitatedly eager to warn Maria and Baraf.

"It's not Sion," he repeated. "This was a distraction, another false lead. To incite panic, to create a sensational worldwide news story. Get people looking the wrong way..."

Maria blinked in astonishment. "That doesn't explain what happened to you!"

"Well, it was also an attempt to kill me." He grunted in pain as she helped him toward the park's exit.

Maria pulled out her phone and hit a button with her free hand. "Baraf," she said quickly, "I found him. Meet us at the entrance."

"Think about it," Reid said once she had hung up. "Every news outlet in the developed world is covering this story right now. No one is paying any attention elsewhere. Maria, the attack is happening today—but not here."

She groaned in frustration. "How can we stop it if we don't know where?"

The Italian Agent Baraf trotted over to them, his frown deepening when he saw Reid's state. "Oh, *Dio*," he murmured. "What happened...?"

"There's a body in the stadium," Reid said by way of explanation. "You'll want to let security know before anyone else goes in there."

"What?" Baraf's eyes widened in shock.

"The attack isn't happening here," Maria told him. "This was a distraction."

"It's not Amun's style," Reid said quickly, before the Interpol agent could ask anything. He scolded himself for not thinking of it before. He got so caught up in his conviction that he had solved the puzzle, that it had to be the Winter Olympics, he didn't stop to think about what Amun was really after. "An attack here could have been large-scale, but they're after much more than something as simple as a high body count. If this group is basing their ideology on the same cult of Amun that existed before, then they don't just want to kill people. They want to sow political dissent with the intention of eventual control. They want to take out *specific* people, for a specific goal; people like leaders, heads of state, lawmakers..."

But where would that be happening?

Agent Baraf threw his hands up in frustration. "So all of this was for nothing? I cannot believe this! We have evacuated thousands! And now the entire world believes that terrorists were targeting the Olympics!"

"Hey," Maria shot back, "we had a responsibility to see this through! What if there had been an attack and we had done nothing?"

Their heated voices became little more than background noise as Reid attempted to reason it out. *Why a distraction in Switzerland?* The Olympics were likely the biggest stage that Amun could ask for.

With hundreds of members of the media present, word would get out quickly. But there had to be more to it than that. They could have simply set off a few bombs anywhere and created a temporary distraction.

Sion was a fake target intended to mislead them, to obfuscate the real intended target. He chided himself for not recognizing it; the tactic of deception was one used frequently throughout history. His mind drifted to World War II, to the 1944 invasion of Normandy—more specifically, Operation Bodyguard, one of the largest military deceptions of all time. Allied forces appeared to make the Pas de Calais their primary target, forcing German troops to defend the location, and then took the Axis armies by surprise when they instead invaded France from the northern coast.

"The same country," Reid murmured. The Allies had planned Operation Bodyguard and targeted a location that was not only within the same country, but not all that distant from their intended target. "It was the same country." His murmurs were lost over the veritable shouting match between Maria and Baraf.

"...Pulled more than a dozen agents from an international summit!" Baraf was saying as Reid snapped back to reality. "Not to mention the Swiss Federal Police, and—"

"Baraf!" Reid interrupted. The Interpol agent blinked in surprise at the sudden outburst. "What international summit? You said your agents were pulled from a forum?"

"Yes, the World Economic Forum in Davos."

Reid had heard of it before. It was an annual gathering of world leaders and captains of industry, held at a mountain resort in the Swiss Alps, in the town of Davos.

Baraf's frown slackened. He seemed to forget all about his anger. "You don't believe...?"

"How many people are in attendance," Reid demanded, "and who?"

"Uh...almost two thousand guests total. Approximately seventy are heads of state, and the others are business leaders from all over the world. In addition, somewhere between four and five hundred members of the media."

Reid spun toward Maria. "We need to go, right now."

"You think it's the forum?" Baraf shook his head. "Amun would be foolhardy to try anything there. Security has been heightened in light of recent attacks—"

"Amun has been planning this for more than two years," Reid interrupted. "There's plenty of historical precedent for something like this. Creating a distraction this close to the forum would pull Swiss forces away from a Swiss event. Don't you see? Amun isn't foolhardy. They're ready."

Maria supported him under one shoulder as they hurried out of the park through the entrance, cutting a swath through still-waiting Olympic spectators, toward the police car that had carried them here from the nearby airstrip. Reid's knee throbbed angrily, but he did his best to ignore it.

"Agents, wait!" Baraf called out as he rushed after them. "The forum does not even begin until tomorrow. We should alert the security personnel in Davos; they can assess the situation, and—"

"We don't have time for assessments," Reid interjected. "Amun won't wait. They have their window of opportunity today, while all eyes are on the Olympics." His mind was working a mile a minute. Amun had incited a panic and created a distraction in the very same country that they planned to carry out their attack. It was bold, but he understood why; whatever resources Davos could spare would have been sent to Sion. The World Economic Forum had not yet begun; no one would suspect any threat at the moment. Amun would carry out their attack soon, likely that same evening, when the majority of heads of state had arrived at the alpine resort.

"Even if the forum doesn't start until tomorrow," he continued, "you're talking about two thousand people—I imagine most of them have already arrived or are en route."

"Well, yes," Baraf confirmed, "they would likely be at the resort by now, in their suites, and…" He trailed off as the realization struck him.

"Exactly." Anyone who would imagine a strike on the World Economic Forum would guess it would happen *during* the three-day forum—not the day before.

They reached the police car and climbed in, Agent Baraf riding shotgun and Reid and Maria behind him. "Take us back to the airstrip as quick as you're able," Reid asked the officer.

"Agent, that would do us little good," said Baraf. "Davos has no airport, and it is more than four hundred kilometers away. The nearest airport is Zurich, and even then it is an hour-long helicopter ride."

"Just get us to the airstrip," Reid insisted.

The officer switched on the car's lights and sirens and sped back toward the waiting Gulfstream.

"Agent Baraf," he said, "can you get on the phone with Interpol and tell them to send their agents back?"

"Of course," he replied. "Should I alert Davos's security?"

"Yes, right away," Reid replied. Then a thought occurred to him. "But... don't relate the nature of the threat."

Baraf blinked at him in surprise.

"I'm sure they have their own security protocols for instances like this," Reid explained, "and I'm guessing it involves swift and immediate evacuation. We need them to handle this carefully. Otherwise, it could cast suspicion and cause Amun to act earlier." He knew it was extremely risky—possibly a deadly gamble, but Amun had a plan, and he was confident they would stick to it unless they were given any inkling that they shouldn't. "If they must start evacuation, they need to do it slowly. Make it seem natural. Put people in cars and send them away. For the sake of everyone there, it cannot *look* like an evacuation."

Baraf understood. "I will relate it."

"Maria." Reid turned to her. "We're going to need all hands on deck for this."

She nodded as she pulled out her phone and made the call, putting it on speaker.

"You two had better have a *hell* of a good explanation for what you're pulling." Cartwright's voice was tight and angry and more than a little distraught. "Director Mullen wants your heads on a plate for going over him again. Not to mention causing one of the biggest false alarms in recent history! What were you think—"

"Cartwright, we've got bigger problems right now," Reid interrupted. He quickly recounted his theory about the new target: the guests of the World Economic Forum.

"How can you be sure?" Cartwright asked. "We need evidence, not hunches. We've already got an international crisis on our hands, and you want to create a second one?"

"It fits perfectly," Reid said firmly. "We're not just talking about political leaders here, but heads of industry, CEOs, senior executives... we're talking about the opportunity for them to eliminate hundreds of the world's most powerful people."

Cartwright was silent for a long moment. Reid knew precisely what the deputy director was thinking: if he ignored Reid and passed it off as a hunch, and there *was* a legitimate threat, the fallout could be astronomical.

"Christ," he muttered. "Zero, you had better be sure about this..."

"I am sure." Reid tried to sound as confident as possible. "This isn't a lead from Amun. This is learning from the mistakes of the past. Sion was a deception. Davos is the target."

Cartwright groaned. "What do you need?"

"Zurich is an hour away by helicopter," Reid said. "I need you to send any available agent you can, immediately. We'll meet them there."

"Kent," Maria spoke up, "we can't get to Davos in less than an hour."

"Yes, we can," Reid told her. "And Cartwright?" he said into the phone. "We need to keep this as quiet as we can. If Amun gets any idea that we're on to them, they may do something rash."

"Something rash seems like an incredible understatement," Cartwright said. "All right, Zero. I'll have them wheels-up in ten minutes."

Maria hung up. "You're not thinking what I think you're thinking… are you?"

"Yeah," Reid said, "I think I am."

Baraf twisted in his seat. Beyond him, through the windshield, the airstrip came into view. "Interpol agents are back en route to Davos," he confirmed. "We can fly directly to Zurich, and I can have a helo waiting for us to take us—"

"We're not going to Zurich," Reid said.

"What?" Baraf glanced quizzically at Reid, then Maria, and then back to Reid. "Then where?"

The police car screamed onto the airstrip and the pilot, in a white uniform and aviator shades, descended the plane's stairs to greet them. His smile faded, however, as he saw the three agents racing toward him.

"You fueled up?" Reid asked.

"Yes sir, ready whenever you are."

"We need you to take us to Davos."

The pilot frowned. "Sir, there's no airport in Davos."

"I know." Reid dashed up the stairs and into the Gulfstream, followed closely by Maria and Baraf. The confused pilot trailed after them.

"What's the max speed on a G650? About six hundred miles an hour?" Reid asked.

"Six-ten." The pilot might have guessed what Reid was after, since he looked a little ill.

"So you could get us there in, what, thirty minutes?"

"Sir—"

"And how much room would you need to land?"

"I… I'd need a runway. Sir."

"And if you didn't have one?"

The pilot blanched. "… Sir? You can't be serious."

"Maria, phone." She slapped the cell into Reid's hand and he showed it to the pilot. "Your orders were to take us wherever we wanted to go. If you'd prefer, I can get the Director of National Intelligence on the phone right now and we can explain to him that you're wasting time and potentially compromising literally thousands of lives. Or, you can take us where we want to go."

The pilot gulped. "Uh...four," he said meekly. "Four hundred feet, give or take. Five to be safe."

"Thank you. Wheels up, now."

As the pilot scurried away, Reid gave the phone back to Maria. The hint of a smirk played on her lips, but she was doing her best to hide it.

"What?" he asked.

"I know this is a very grave situation, but...you are one hundred percent Agent Zero right now."

He didn't say it aloud, but the strange thing about it was that he *wasn't* all Zero. If not for Professor Lawson, he wouldn't have interpreted the dying terrorist's taunt about Sion. And he doubted he would have given the World Economic Forum a second thought. He was both—or rather, they were him.

And he was fully aware that he would simply have to live with that.

Maria retrieved a first-aid kit from an overhead compartment and opened it on a fold-out table in front of him. "Let me see that hand," she said. He put out his bloodied left hand, palm-up, to show the long slice where Rais's knife had opened it. "I don't have much to work with, but we can at least bandage it."

"Thanks," he said quietly as she cleaned the blood away from the wound. Her touch sent a pleasant tingling sensation up and down his arm, very nearly numbing the pain.

"Don't mention it."

"No, I mean for..." He didn't know quite how to articulate his thoughts to her—mostly because he was having trouble sorting them out for himself. For someone he had distrusted only two days earlier, he was now seeing her more like a partner. A friend. No, it was more than that. At least he thought it could be.

She glanced up at him, her slate-gray eyes patiently meeting his as she waited for him to finish his sentiment.

"For everything," he said finally. "I wouldn't have gotten this far without you."

"Like I said." She smiled. "Don't mention it."

The phone rang again as soon as the Gulfstream was in the air.

"Agents are on a chopper," Cartwright said. "But Jesus, Zero, I'm looking at this guest list, and it's staggering. Kent, the Vice President is there. Our own VP. Not to mention the President of the People's Republic of China. The Prime Minister. More than a hundred of the world's billionaires." Cartwright heaved a sigh before adding, "This is so much more than a matter of national security. I need to report this up the chain immediately."

"Deputy Director," Reid said, "I understand your position, but if word gets out at all—if the media starts reporting on it, or Amun has any reason to believe their plan won't work…"

"…Then bombs start going off," Cartwright finished with a defeated sigh.

"Amun is watching. Trust me on that." He thought back to his own experiences. Amun had been there every step of the way. In the basement with the Iranians, he had first seen the brand of Amun on the Middle Eastern brute's neck. In Otets's facility, two more members of Amun, each with the glyph scorched into their skin. And when Morris failed to kill him, the Amun assassin Rais was there.

"Amun is watching," he said again. "This is their grand scheme, and if they get any idea that we're onto them, they're going to know that we're aware of their plot. If Davos starts a hasty evacuation, or if any media is alerted to this…"

"Kent, this is a lot more than our jobs at stake here," Cartwright argued. "The NSA is likely recording this call. If this goes south, they'll know that we knew. Do you know where they put people like us in that situation?"

"I do." *Hell Six*, he thought. *In a hole in the ground for the rest of our lives.* "Just stay calm a minute and stay on the phone." He put Cartwright on speaker and set the cell down. "Baraf, you said security has been heightened in Davos. How long has this security detail been working onsite?"

Agent Baraf shook his head. "I'm not entirely sure, but at least two weeks."

"Okay. Then that means Amun placed their bombs before then, which means that they're not likely on timers." The bombs he had seen in Otets's facility had a capacity of double-digit hours, minutes, and seconds—but not days. And there was no way that Amun would compromise the position of their explosives in order to set timers. "Equally unlikely is a dead man's switch—no one is going to hold a trigger for two weeks. So they must be on remote detonation. From what I saw, these are not complex devices; they're a fairly simple bypass to a remote transmitter."

"And the transmitter's range would have to be close," said Maria. "Within, what, a quarter mile?"

Reid nodded. "Maybe even less, if they want to ensure everything goes off without a hitch. But considering the sprawl of the resort, we need to consider anywhere within a quarter mile of the suites. That's our perimeter." He turned to the Interpol agent. "Baraf, tell Davos security that they need to focus their efforts on locating the bombs. If they're going to start evacuating, it needs to be done slowly, carefully. There cannot be a panic."

Baraf nodded tightly. "Davos will have done thorough sweeps prior to guests arriving. Wherever Amun has concealed their explosives may be more difficult to find than we have time for."

"I know." Reid tried to put himself in Amun's shoes. *Where would I hide them?* He thought back to Reidigger's apartment in Zurich, when he did the same thing to find the bug-out bag beneath the floorboards.

But before that, he had checked the walls for any sign of disturbance.

"Before anyone arrived," he said suddenly, "I bet the resort did some upkeep, right? Any necessary repairs would have been completed..."

"You would be correct," Baraf told him. "In fact, a renovation was completed only a few weeks ago."

"That must be it. I bet that's how they hid their bombs—they could have sent members in, posing as construction crews. It would have given them access to any part of the resort."

"That's true," said Maria, "but any work they did would have had to be inspected and approved afterwards, right? So Davos should have a log, or some sort of record..."

Baraf's eyes widened. "Which would mean that with any luck, they've given us the locations of their bombs!"

Hiding in plain sight, Reid thought. If it was true, it would be the cruelest taunt possible. If their attack was able to go off, Davos would eventually realize that they had had everything they would have needed to prevent it.

"Baraf, can you relate all that to Davos security?" Reid asked.

The Interpol agent nodded. The phone was already to his ear. "Cartwright, you still with us?"

"I'm here." The deputy director's voice sounded exhausted.

"We need a favor. Davos doesn't have an airport. We need you to get on the phone with the Swiss Federal Office of Police and see if we can clear about five hundred yards of highway, outside the city and at least a mile from the resort. We don't want to be seen coming in."

"Just like old times," Cartwright sighed. "All right, I'll make it happen."

Twenty-three minutes later, the Gulfstream G650 alit on the Parsenbahn thoroughfare, on a straight stretch of highway that the Federal Office of Police had quickly and temporarily blockaded. As soon as the three agents disembarked, the small jet turned on the highway, with some difficulty, and took off again, to avoid any scrutiny from the media. They were just far enough from the alpine resort to avoid being seen, but it was entirely possible, Reid realized, that someone had witnessed their rapid descent. Without an airport, it would be very strange to see any plane flying low over Davos.

He could only hope that Amun hadn't noticed.

He, Maria, and Baraf were ushered into a waiting police car. "No lights, and no sirens," he told the officer in the driver's seat. "And if there's a back way in, take us there."

It took them less than two minutes to get from the Parsenbahn to the alpine mountain resort. Reid couldn't help but admire the beauty of it; the site of the World Economic Forum in Davos looked more like a sprawling village of low-rise condos and villas, each roof capped in snow and surrounded by tall fir trees that downright dwarfed the buildings they encircled. The entire resort was nestled in the shadow of the Swiss Alps. It was picturesque, serene—and very likely about to be destroyed.

They disembarked from the police car and were immediately greeted by a thin, keen-eyed man with black hair and a well-tailored black suit. He did not waste any time expressing his displeasure.

"Agents," he said in harsh German-accented English, "I am Burkhalter, general manager of the resort. I do not appreciate being kept in the dark regarding the safety of my guests."

"We sincerely apologize, sir," Baraf offered diplomatically, "but there is little time for that. If I can brief your security team, we can assess—"

Burkhalter interrupted with a sharply raised hand. "I must insist that you share the details and legitimacy of any potential threat immediately!"

"And we will," Reid cut in. "We can talk as we walk. Can you show us to the closest structures that have been recently renovated?"

The manager opened his mouth to speak—likely to argue Reid's request—when a phone chimed from his inner coat pocket. He plucked it out and held up one finger to signal them to wait.

"Burkhalter," he answered. His exasperated expression slackened, the corners of his mouth dragged into a dumbfounded frown. "I…I understand," he murmured. "Stand by for instructions." He lowered the phone and stared at Reid. "It would seem your tip is correct, Agent. My security team has discovered an incendiary device."

CHAPTER THIRTY FIVE

Reid's stomach tightened instinctively. They had found a bomb—but only one, and he had the feeling there were many more hidden in the resort.

"Where?" he demanded.

"Guest quarters," Burkhalter told them. The color had drained from the manager's face. "A chalet, recently renovated."

Reid snatched the cell from him and put it on speaker. "This is Agent Kent Steele with the CIA. With whom am I speaking?"

A gruff voice came through the phone. "This is Captain Hegg, head of security."

"What can you tell us?"

"The device was sealed inside a wall, as suspected," Hegg said. "They appear to have used a lightweight wood-pulp composite material, rather than plaster."

"Maximum damage," said Maria knowingly. "So the blast radius isn't as affected."

Burkhalter's shock finally seemed to wane as he waved a hand impatiently. "None of that is important. This is officially a crisis situation, which calls for immediate evacuation protocol."

"Wait," Reid insisted. Burkhalter blinked at him in astonishment. "Just wait. Listen to me. The people that did this have been planning this for a long time. I have no doubt that they've acquired information on which heads of state are staying in which suites. They are here. They are watching. And if we give them any reason at all to believe that we're aware of them—they will detonate."

Burkhalter scoffed loudly. "Then what would you have us do, Agent? This staggered evacuation could take hours. Some of our guests will insist on knowing the nature of the threat. And if you are wrong and these terrorists set off their bombs anyway, we could be responsible for hundreds of lost lives. Important lives." He shook his head. "Davos will not bend to the whims of fanatics. We must get people to safety."

"I believe he is right, Agent Steele," Baraf agreed quietly. "It is, as you might say, a catch-22."

Reid ran his hands through his hair as he thought desperately of a potential solution. He had no idea how many bombs might be onsite. It could take days to locate them all. They couldn't evacuate everyone before Amun caught on. They were here somewhere, at least one of them, maybe more, with their finger on the trigger, waiting for their moment. And they could be anywhere…

"Wait," Reid murmured. *That's it*, he thought. Someone here had their finger on the bombs' trigger—but they *couldn't* be anywhere.

"This is quite enough," Burkhalter grumbled. "We are getting these people to safety immediately—"

"Burkhalter," he said harshly, "you *will* continue a careful evacuation of the resort. Do not incite a panic. Do *not* attract media attention. The bomber is here somewhere, on the premises, and there are limited places they can be. If you start emptying this place, deaths will be on *your* shoulders. Do you understand?"

Burkhalter set his jaw firmly. He looked as if he might have some choice words for Reid, but instead he nodded once, tightly.

"Captain Hegg," Reid said into the phone. "Your team is currently sweeping for bombs?"

"That is correct, sir," Hegg confirmed. "We've called in bomb squads from the Federal Office to assist—"

"I'm afraid we don't have time for that," Reid interrupted. "I understand it's very dangerous, but we need to locate as many of the devices as we can. These particular bombs are activated by a radio transmitter. It's a small black box about the size of a matchbook with a single blue wire from it. If they remove that, it should render the bombs useless to Amun..."

"Should?" Hegg asked.

"It's the best chance we've got. Inform your team: remove the transmitters immediately from any discovered devices. Keep Burkhalter updated on your progress."

"I will." Hegg ended the call and Reid handed the phone back to the manager.

"Do you want to clue us in on what you're thinking?" Maria asked.

"Whoever is controlling the bombs must be stationary," Reid said. "They have to be set up somewhere. They're not mobile."

"What makes you think that?" Baraf asked.

"Each bomb requires its own detonator," Reid explained, recalling the devices he had seen in Otets's facility, "unless they're physically linked, and this place is too sprawled for that. Even remotely, if all the bombs were on a single detonator, it could potentially weaken the signal to a degree that would impede their potential success."

Burkhalter looked like he might be sick. "How many devices do you believe are hidden?"

Reid shook his head. "We don't know."

"All right," said Baraf, "then we're looking for someone who has established a temporary base of operations somewhere they would be uninterrupted."

"Staff quarters, perhaps?" Burkhalter offered. "Basement levels?"

"There are far too many places that could be," said Baraf disdainfully.

"Hang on," Maria said suddenly. "We're at the base of the Swiss Alps." She pointed upward toward the enormous mountain beyond Davos. "Mountains wreak havoc on radio reception."

"You're right," Reid agreed. "The thicker the material, the higher the chance it'll absorb radio waves...which means the bomber would need some elevation, a place with a clear enough signal to transmit across the resort." He spun on Burkhalter. "Where would someone be able to be isolated while still getting clear signals?"

"I...um..." The thin manager rubbed his chin. "The crow's nest, I suppose?"

"What's the crow's nest?"

"It's a nickname for the former control room in the conference center," Burkhalter explained quickly. "The equipment grew obsolete years ago. Now we only use it as a broadcast booth, since it overlooks the main auditorium..."

"And no one would be using it yet because the forum hasn't begun," Maria finished.

"I know how to get there," said Baraf urgently. "Follow me. Mr. Burkhalter, if you would, please gather whatever security personnel are not working directly with Captain Hegg on locating the bombs and have them start searching any isolated areas of the premises. We'll need all the help we can get."

"But again," Reid reminded him, "make sure they go about it carefully. We can't have it be obvious."

"I shall." The general manager nodded again and hurried away toward the staff headquarters to gather what Reid hoped would be enough manpower to find the bomber in time. The three agents headed the opposite direction, Baraf leading the way. The Italian agent sprinted ahead, with Maria and Reid on his heels. (It was fairly impressive to him how quickly Baraf could move in leather loafers.) They crossed a snowy courtyard and cut between a row of A-framed chalets and a blocky three-story building of suites.

Reid's knee throbbed angrily as he limped along as quickly as he could. Despite his best efforts, his pace slowed, and soon Maria and Baraf had gained a lead on him.

"Kent!" she called back. "Are you all right?"

"Just keep going," he panted. "Don't wait for me. We need to..." He caught sight of an object in his periphery and glanced upward, between the chalets. "Baraf, wait. What is that?" He pointed toward the horizon.

Baraf slowed to a jog and gazed in the same direction, toward a four-story white spire behind the A-framed structures. "That? It is a, uh, how do you say … a steeple. Of a church."

"Is it in use?"

Baraf stopped and frowned. "It is a landmark, centuries old. The resort was built around it, and …" He groaned. "No. It is not used."

Reid caught his breath as he weighed their options. Burkhalter's crow's nest theory fit the bill perfectly—just as perfectly as an unused steeple in an ancient church would.

"We split up," he instructed. "Baraf, can you take the control room?"

The agent nodded. "It would be my pleasure."

"Maria, go with him. I'll check the steeple."

She scoffed. "You're going in alone, on a bum leg? No way. You need me more than he does."

"Baraf?" Reid questioned.

He grinned fiercely. "Do not let the suit fool you. I am quite capable on my own. Good luck, Agents." He sprinted off again, heading toward the conference center.

Maria took one of Reid's arms and slung it around her shoulders. "Come on," she said. "You're not getting anywhere fast, and I'm not waiting around for you."

He couldn't help but chuckle as she helped him along as quickly as they could. "Is this what it was like in the old days? You picking up my slack?"

"Oh, definitely. Picking up your slack, cleaning up your messes … you have no idea how much you owe me."

"If I can't remember it, it didn't happen." He grunted softly as they grew close to the church. The pain in his knee was getting worse.

Baraf was right; the church must have been hundreds of years old, but it looked sturdy, the stone façade barely weathered. Clearly the people of Davos took good care of the landmark.

Maria drew her Glock and shoved open the doors. She cleared the nave and then ushered Reid inside. "You're not going to like this," she said.

The interior of the church was surprisingly small—it was doubtful that more than fifty people could have fit in the pews. At the rear of the building, just beyond the transept, was the onset of the steeple's tower, and a spiraling wooden staircase that led to the top.

Of course there are stairs, Reid thought bitterly. In his haste to find the bomber, he hadn't considered that four stories stretched between them and the peak, and suddenly he wished he had opted to take the control room instead.

He glanced upward, but he couldn't see anything beyond the wooden ceiling at the top of the stairs that would serve as the floor for the small, circular room at the top. It was a small blessing—it meant that if the bomber was up there, he wouldn't see them coming either.

Maria must have been thinking the same, because she glanced upward dubiously. "Only one way up," she said quietly. "We could really use a diversion right about now."

"No time," Reid said, though he agreed that going in blind was less than ideal. "Besides, any diversion we might make could cause them to act early. If he's up there, he won't have line of sight on us. Let's just get it done."

He went first. Even the initial few wooden steps made his knee burn with pain. He put a finger to his lips to warn Maria to stay quiet; every small sound seemed to echo up the tower. In response, she rolled her eyes, having already ascertained that.

As they ascended carefully, trying not to make any noise that might serve as a warning up the cavernous spire, Reid's leg felt as if it was on fire. What he first thought was a severely pulled muscle he now realized was more likely a tear. Before they had even reached the halfway point his leg began to tremble with the threat of giving out.

Push through it, he insisted to his body. *Lives are at stake.*

It certainly didn't help that he could barely support himself on the banister—it was on his left side, the hand that Rais had sliced open. He began to lag again behind Maria.

About two-thirds of the way up the spiral staircase leading to the top of the steeple, his leg folded beneath him, threatening to give out. He clutched at the banister for support and kept himself from falling.

Maria reached out instinctively and grabbed his arm. "You okay?"

"Go on without me," he whispered. "I'll be right behind you."

"Are you sure?"

"I'll be fine. Just... be careful."

She hesitated a moment, but then nodded and hurried upward, doubling her pace, stepping heel-to-toe on each stair in an attempt to minimize any noise she might make. Reid followed as best he could, but she soon vanished from sight around the next curve of the spiral staircase. In just a few moments, he thought, she would be in the small round room overhead at the steeple's peak.

"Come on," he grunted to his knee as he pulled himself up yet another stair.

A sharp crack split the air and echoed down the length of the steeple, startling him. A single gunshot.

Reid held his breath. *It was Maria,* he told himself. *She got him. She shot the bomber, and any moment now she'll call out the all-clear.*

He did not hear any shouts. Instead he heard a booming thud hit the wooden ceiling mere feet over him.

There was no mistaking it. A body had just hit the floor.

Reid gritted his teeth and forced himself higher. He hadn't even realized that he had drawn his Glock, but there it was, gripped in his good right hand, doing his best to ignore the scorching pain in both his leg and his slashed hand as he supported half his weight on the banister.

Please hold out, he begged of his body.

Mercifully, it did. He made it to the end of the staircase, where an open arched doorway led into the small round chamber. With his gun aloft, he took a breath and entered, immediately tracking the barrel left and right.

His gaze caught several things at once: Maria, down. Blood on her. A light-haired man. A gun in his hand. Aimed at Reid.

He didn't have time to process everything. He quickly took aim and fired.

The bomber did too.

In that same instant, Reid's knee decided it had finally had enough. Just before his finger squeezed the trigger, his left leg went out from under him and he fell in a half-spin to the floor. His own shot went wild and hit the ceiling.

The bomber's shot missed his head by inches.

Reid winced in pain as he collapsed to the floor beneath his bum leg. The bomber was on him in an instant, crossing the span of the room in two long strides. He kicked at Reid's hand and the Glock flew from it, clattering down the wooden stairs.

Reid glared up at him as he leered down. In his fist he held an ugly black pistol—a Luger P08. The bomber was unassumingly short with sandy hair. His dark eyes, notable overbite, and sharp nose that hooked slightly at the tip gave him an overall resemblance to a rat. On his neck, Reid could clearly see the branded glyph of Amun.

"Agent Zero," he said in a hiss. "I must say, this meeting is bittersweet." His English was just barely tinged with a Swiss German accent. "On the one hand, it is an honor to meet such a legend. However, I have to assume that our mutual friend failed in Sion."

Reid ignored him and turned to Maria, who groaned in pain as she propped herself on one elbow. Her hand held the opposite shoulder, where the bomber had shot her.

"You okay?" he asked.

"Bastard had the drop on me," she grunted. "But I'll live."

"Is that so?" said the rat-faced bomber with a sneer.

"Others will come," Reid told him. "They would have heard the shots." "Undoubtedly. And I'll see them coming." He motioned toward the table behind him, where three flat-screen monitors sat side by side, black-and-white images on each. Reid recognized one as the church entrance, and another as the inside of the church. The last monitor had a downward-angle view of the spiral stairs leading up to the steeple.

"You saw us," he murmured. "You were watching the whole time."

"Hidden cameras. Very small, and very discreet. Amun thought of everything, Agent Zero. The time that it would take anyone to reach us up here is more than enough time for me to detonate, if necessary."

On the table next to the monitors was Maria's gun, and next to that was a trapezoidal black box, a few inches thick, with more than two dozen chrome toggle switches in rows. Each switch had a small red LED beside it. From the back of the box were a multitude of wires, each ending in a smaller black rectangular box—radio transmitters, Reid knew, a unique one for each bomb hidden throughout Davos.

He was watching us, Reid thought, *but he didn't detonate. Why?*

"You saw that I was injured," he reasoned aloud.

The bomber grinned viciously. "I took a risk, yes. My brothers would likely not approve. But I saw an opportunity, and I couldn't resist. Soon, Agent Zero, you will die. Before that, however, you are going to watch the destruction of Davos and hundreds of world leaders." He gestured to the only window in the steeple, a large keyhole-shaped frame with dark iron-framed glass. "We have the perfect vantage point for it."

Reid pulled himself up into a seated position. The bomber leapt back, the Luger pointed, clearly not interested in taking any more chances. Reid's knee screamed in protest at the movement; there was no way he was getting back up onto it.

Though maybe I don't have to, he thought. He still had the small silver and black LC9 strapped to his ankle. Agent Baraf would certainly have reached the control room by now and realized that it was a dead end. He would either double back to the church or try to contact them by phone, and when that failed, he would come looking.

As soon as anyone else entered the church and the bomber's attention was diverted, he would go for his ankle holster, he decided. He would have only a sliver of an opportunity, but he had to try.

The bomber glanced at his wristwatch. "I'm afraid our timetable has moved up a few hours," he sighed, "but you have forced our hand, Agent Zero. Now, if you will please direct your attention to the resort below…" His hand hovered dangerously over the toggle switchboard.

"Wait!" Reid exclaimed. "Amun didn't think of everything." He had to buy some time, somehow, and there was only one way he could think of doing that—prove to the bomber that Amun was not as flawless as he perceived.

The rat-faced man raised an eyebrow. "There is no flaw in our plan."

"There's one. You underestimated me. I figured out the locations of your bombs."

The bomber's face spread slowly into a wide grin. "You're stalling."

"I'm not. You sent people in as construction workers during the resort's renovation. They hid the bombs behind walls and covered them with a light composite material that wouldn't hinder the explosion."

The bomber's grin collapsed. "How…?"

"You're not as smart as you think you are," Reid said simply.

"They've already…found a few," Maria added slowly. Reid noticed with mild panic that her face was ashen; she was losing blood fast.

Come on, Baraf.

"No." The bomber shook his head vigorously. "No, they haven't found any." His lips trembled in anger and trepidation. He took another step back, and again his hand hung in the space above the toggled switches. "If they had, then I suppose there's a chance this would do nothing." He locked his gaze on Reid's as his finger touched a random toggle.

"No, don't—!" Reid heard himself shout.

The bomber flicked the switch.

Reid held his breath, waiting to hear an explosion, to feel the detonation beneath, to see an orange fireball rise into the sky through the keyhole window.

Nothing happened.

The small red LED light beside the toggle went out with the flick of the switch, but otherwise, silence reigned in the small round room at the top of the steeple.

Reid breathed a sigh of relief. The triggered bomb must have been one that Hegg's team had already found and disarmed. But his solace was short-lived.

The bomber's hands shook with silent fury as his face reddened in outrage. He spun on Reid. "You've ruined everything!" he screamed. His eyes were wild and murderous as he leveled the trembling Luger—but not at him.

He pointed it at Maria.

"Choose," he hissed. "Either I shoot this woman right before your eyes, or I flip another switch. Choose."

"What?" Reid exclaimed in horror. "I...no. I can't. I won't."

"Choose!" the bomber shouted. He reached out with his left hand and rested a finger on a toggle.

Reid stared in disbelief. Where Rais and the fake sheikh were dangerous fanatics, this man was simply a monster. There was no way he could make that choice. He refused.

"Choose."

"Listen to me," Reid said quickly. "*You're* the one who has a choice. Amun's plot has failed, whether you realize it or not. You can still walk away from this. Give us information, and we'll grant you amnesty. You have my word."

The bomber shook his head slowly. "As Amun," he said quietly, "we endure."

He flicked the switch.

Reid winced.

Nothing happened. No detonation occurred. *Thank God*, he thought.

"Again," the bomber declared. "Choose."

You've got to be kidding me. There were still nearly two dozen switches on the board. There was no way Davos would continue to get that lucky.

"I won't," Reid insisted. "I won't choose."

"I will." Maria's voice was weak, her eyes half-closed, all color drained from her face. Reid glanced over at her in surprise. Most of her shirt was soaked in blood, and she was no longer holding her wound—she had lost the strength to keep her arm up. "I'll choose."

"Maria…" he started.

"It's okay, Kent." A smile twitched on her lips. "We had a real good run, you and me." Tears brimmed in her eyes. "I really loved you. You know that?"

Reid nodded as he felt a sting in his own eyes. He wanted to say something, anything, but instead he stared at the floor. He couldn't watch Maria die in front of him.

The bomber leaned over her. "It is not your choice to make," he said venomously. "It is his." He wanted to shame Agent Zero, to torture him before he killed him. Reid was well aware that this madman would kill him, and Maria, and set off the bombs—just not necessarily in that order.

And then a thought occurred to him. Maria was well aware of that as well. There was no reason for her to sacrifice herself.

"I know that," she told the bomber weakly. "I'm…stalling." She gestured with her chin toward the monitors behind them.

On the center monitor, Baraf and three security officers stormed into the church, transitioning to the rightmost monitor as they barreled up the spiraling stairs.

"No!" the bomber screamed. He dropped the Luger to the floor and lurched for the switchboard.

A burst of adrenaline coursed through Reid, numbing his pain as he saw his opportunity. He pitched forward, yanked the LC9 free of his ankle holster, and aimed it at the bomber. He popped off two shots, center mass, into the man's back as he reached for the triggers.

The bomber's body racked with a violent spasm as the bullets struck him. He overshot the switchboard and fell across the table, sharply coughing blood onto the keyhole-shaped window.

As his legs weakened and gave out beneath him, his hands grasped desperately for something, anything, to hold onto.

A finger found purchase on a switch, and pulled it.

CHAPTER THIRTY SIX

Reid felt the thunderous explosion shake the boards beneath him. He heard the astonishingly loud detonation. He closed his eyes so he wouldn't see the plume of gray smoke that rose against the otherwise blue sky over Davos, but it did nothing to drown out the screams and cries of those outside.

He had failed. Even a single detonation was still a terrorist attack. He had failed to stop it.

When he opened his eyes again, Maria was lying on her side, unmoving. He crawled over to her and checked her pulse. She was alive, though her breathing was shallow.

"Hang on," he told her. "Just hang on."

Feet pounded the stairs outside the room. Seconds later, Baraf and the three officers poured in, guns aloft, and more than a little shocked at what they found.

"She needs medical attention right away," Reid demanded.

None of the security officers moved. They seemed as if they were trying to piece together what had happened up in the church steeple.

"Help her!" Baraf barked at them. Two of the officers hurried forward, lifting Maria gingerly and carrying her briskly down the stairs.

The third officer checked on the bomber. "He is alive, sir."

"Good," Reid said dispassionately. "Make sure he stays that way. I want to know everything he knows. And I want to make damn sure he knows what he did here today."

The officer immediately got on the radio to request a medical airlift.

Baraf extended a hand and carefully helped Reid to his feet. He winced at the scorching pain in his knee and leaned on the Italian agent's shoulder. They stood like that for a moment, side by side, both staring out the keyhole window as thick gray smoke continued to roil upward into the air.

"The conference center," Baraf said quietly. "Lives were certainly lost." He turned to face Reid. "But you should be proud of what you were able to accomplish. You saved hundreds today—probably thousands."

"Still not enough," Reid murmured. He didn't feel like a hero, and he certainly didn't want to stand there and stare out at the smoke, or hear the sirens that began to wail from somewhere nearby as emergency vehicles roared toward the location. Despite everything he had gone through, everything he had done, in some way—perhaps a very small way, but a way nonetheless—it still felt as if Amun had won.

Agent Zero indeed, he thought bitterly as he turned and limped painfully out of the room to begin his slow trek down the stairs.

Deputy Director of Special Operations Group Steve Bolton was out to lunch when he heard the news. There was a sports bar less than ten minutes from Langley that served excellent cheesesteaks, and at least once a week he would skip the cafeteria and treat himself.

The television behind the bar was playing highlights from the previous night's hockey game, the Washington Capitals' four-to-one victory over the Buffalo Sabres, when it was interrupted by a breaking news story out of Davos, Switzerland.

Bolton stopped chewing and simply stared.

The plot had failed. Zero must have figured it out. Only a single bomb had detonated.

He felt a tight knot of panic in his chest. The half-eaten cheesesteak threatened to come back up.

He knew all too well what Amun did to people who failed them.

They wouldn't dare, he thought. He was a CIA official. They needed him. Besides, wasn't he the one who had given them Alan Reidigger?

Alan had made a grave error. Several months ago, he had used the CIA database to check up on someone named Reid Lawson. Bolton tracked the activities of all his field agents; to an outside observer, it would look like he was just being a thorough boss, but his propensity for following up on his agents was a byproduct of his own paranoia. At the time, however, he had thought little of it. Reidigger was on a human trafficking op. It had nothing to do with Amun.

But then Alan checked up again on the same name just a few months earlier. Bolton grew suspicious; Reidigger left the name out of his report, despite having checked up on this person twice now. What was stranger still was that the database contained no information on the man—no background, no address, no phone number, nothing. Merely a name.

It was odd that the CIA would have an empty data file on someone, but it was more so that Alan would continuously look it up with no note in his briefing. And when Reidigger searched the database for a third time only a few weeks ago, Bolton decided to look into it himself. An Internet search for Reid Lawson came up with dozens of results; there was no way to tell for sure which one was Reidigger's Lawson.

Then Bolton realized: that was exactly the point. Reidigger wasn't checking the database to find Reid Lawson. He was checking it to make sure there was no information available. Someone had altered the file, obfuscated the data, and Bolton was fairly certain it was Reidigger himself. A deletion from CIA records would certainly raise some eyebrows, but files were altered or amended on a daily basis.

Bolton hated the idea that any of his agents might be keeping secrets from him—ironic, since his own secrets could get himself and others killed—so he dug deeper, checking into the CIA archives for any mention of a Reid Lawson.

And he found one.

Deputy Director Steve Bolton was shocked to discover that Reid Lawson was the birth name of one Agent Zero. Not only was Kent Steele alive, but he had eluded the CIA under the one alias that no one ever thought he would actually use...his real name. And Reidigger knew it.

Bolton had given Reidigger, his own agent, to Amun. They had tortured him for the whereabouts of Kent Steele, and then they killed him.

The deputy director had done everything they had asked. They wouldn't dare touch him.

Even so, he took a pen from his jacket pocket as he slid his iced tea off the coaster, flipped it over, and jotted out a quick note. Cartwright had let it slip that the NSA was monitoring all members of the CIA in supervisory roles, so he had to be careful with his correspondence.

I didn't know, he wrote. *They went dark.*

It was a poor excuse, but it was an excuse nonetheless. It's the only thing that made sense to him; Cartwright and Zero must have gone dark. As the head of Special Operations Group, he should have been privy to the knowledge of a strike on Davos, but he had heard nothing beyond the potential attack on the Winter Olympics.

Somewhere in the sports bar with him was a member of Amun. Bolton had no idea who it might be or if there was more than one, but he knew they were watching him, following him, and picking up his correspondence as he left them. They would intercept the coaster and see his note. And then...Well, he had no idea what might happen from there.

But he did know that he had left his sidearm in his desk drawer when he left for lunch.

His phone rang, but he ignored it. Instead he dropped a twenty on the bar, rose from his stool, and pulled on a coat. He strode quickly to the door, and as he pushed it open, he saw movement in his periphery. He didn't turn. He knew.

Someone was following him. They ignored his message, the coaster, and followed him out into daylight. They didn't bother trying to hide the fact that they were tailing him.

His throat ran dry. *They wouldn't dare*, he told himself.

Steve Bolton stepped out into the afternoon daylight, and the man from Amun followed.

CHAPTER THIRTY SEVEN

"Agent Steele? Did you hear what I said?"

Reid snapped out of his thoughts and glanced over at the young agent sitting at his bedside. She was one of Cartwright's, one of the agents he had sent by helicopter to assist with Davos. She couldn't have been more than twenty-five. Davos had likely been her first major op.

She had also told him her name twice and he still hadn't retained it. Not from lack of regard. He just had a lot weighing on him.

"Um, sorry. I was ... distracted. Can you repeat that?"

"I said that Agent Johansson is improving," the agent replied. "She received a blood transfusion and her vitals are steady."

"Great. When can I see her?"

"Soon," the agent promised. "She's not yet awake."

Reid nodded his thanks. In the wake of the explosion at the World Economic Forum in Davos, he and Maria had been taken immediately by chopper to a hospital in Zurich, where she landed in the ICU and he in general admission. He'd been right about his leg—a partially torn meniscus. It would be at least a few weeks of getting around slowly.

But that wasn't why he was lost in his thoughts. That wasn't why he hadn't been able to sleep through the night, even with the pain meds they gave him. It was the other news, the report that he had insisted on staying abreast of, despite being in another city and away from the site.

The single explosion at the alpine resort had claimed the lives of nine people and injured seventeen more. Among the deceased were delegates from Brazil, Japan, and Mexico; an executive of a clean emissions initiative; and three members of the media.

After his and Maria's hasty departure, Baraf and Interpol took over the investigation, with aid from the agents sent by Cartwright. With the bomber's receiver disabled, the rest of the explosives were located quickly and fully disarmed—twenty-three in all.

By most accounts, Amun's attack was a failure. They had only managed to detonate a single bomb. But to Reid, they had still managed to detonate a single bomb.

A phone call from Cartwright earlier that morning had informed him that the ensuing media frenzy had begun before the dust even settled, before security personnel finished a complete evacuation of the resort. Within minutes of the explosion, the world was aware. The pending attack on the Winter Olympics was a distraction from the real target, an economic forum in the Swiss Alps that hosted dozens of world leaders and industry titans.

"And the bomber?" Reid asked the young agent.

"He's alive," she told him, "and talking."

Reid struggled to sit up in his hospital bed. "Saying what?"

She looked away. "The deputy director said you would ask. He also said you should rest..."

"Please," he insisted. "It's important to me."

She nodded slowly. "All right. His interrogation led to the location of three men posing as doctors in a Swiss hotel. Federal law enforcement arrived this morning as they were trying to flee. Two of them were apprehended—one a German surgeon whose medical license had been stripped due to criminal allegations, and the other identified as Sheikh Mustafar of Tehran."

Reid breathed a small, satisfied sigh. The sheikh—the *real* sheikh—would undoubtedly spend the rest of his days in a similar hole as his deranged doppelganger at Hell Six.

"And the third?" he asked.

"The third man managed to evade authorities long enough to reach the roof," the agent told him. "He...jumped."

"He jumped?" Reid stared blankly. "Jesus. Is he dead?"

She nodded. "It gets worse. A police body cam captured the whole thing, as well as his final words. He said, 'As Amun, we endure.' Then he jumped. That footage has already been leaked to the press."

"So the world knows about Amun," he said slowly. "And if they don't, they will soon."

"Yes. And you know how mainstream media is. It's the top story everywhere. So … the agency has decided to roll with it. The glyph of Amun is being disseminated to law enforcement agencies around the world, with the warning to be watchful for anyone with the mark branded on their skin."

Reid knew he should have been at least mildly content with the results. Soon everyone would know about the terrorist organization, and its members would have nowhere to run. But even so, Amun's goal of inciting fear in the world had worked, in some way, even if their larger plan had failed.

The agent rose from her seat. "I'll have the nurses let you know when you can visit Agent Johansson."

"Thank you," he told her as she left his room.

"Oh, there's one more thing." She paused at the door. "It sort of got lost in the shuffle of everything that's happened, but still, you should know. That man, the one in Sion, was found alive."

"The man in Sion?" It took Reid a moment to register what she was telling him. Sion already felt like ages ago. "What man in …" He trailed off as it him in. "The assassin? The blond one?"

She shrugged. "If that's the guy, then yes. He's not in good shape, but he's alive. Don't worry about him, though. He's under heavy guard, and he'll be taken into custody as soon as he's well enough."

Reid couldn't believe what he was hearing. He was certain he had pierced the assassin's heart—yet Rais had *survived* that somehow.

"Agent?" he said. "Please do me a favor and get a message over there. That man is not to be underestimated, no matter what. He is extremely dangerous."

She smiled. "I'll tell them, Agent Steele. But trust me. He's not going anywhere anytime soon."

Rais could not move.

He could not speak. He could not even breathe on his own. He was useless, defeated, and utterly alone.

The assassin lay in a hospital bed in Sion, Switzerland. There was a breathing tube down his throat, a feeding tube in his stomach, and a catheter in his urethra. Even the most basic of bodily functions were impossible for him in his state. The doctors dosed him with so much pain medication that he slept twenty hours that first day.

But there was still life in him. There was still fury in him.

Kent Steele had now eluded him three times. The first time, when Steele had opened his gut and left him to die, the German surgeon repaired Rais's fractured ribs with screws and a small steel plate.

That small plate, just a little less than two inches wide, had ultimately saved his life. Where Steele had evaded his attempts in the first two instances by a stroke of fortune, this time it had been Rais who had serendipity on his side. When Steele had slipped the small knife between his ribs, aiming for his heart, that narrow metal plate redirected the blade just slightly away. A mere quarter inch to one direction, and the blade would have pierced his left atrium.

Back in the Olympic Park, in the darkness of the skating rink stadium, Rais had regained consciousness to find Steele gone and the small red knife jutting from his chest. He did not believe he would survive, but he was not about to give up on his destiny, either.

He knew what he had to do if there was to be any chance of survival and escape. With his very last ounce of strength, he tugged the knife loose and used it to cut the glyph of Amun from his arm. He pressed his arm against his body to pinch the puckered, raised skin of the brand and, in three strokes, sliced it off.

Mere minutes later, he heard voices. Two security officers entered the stadium on the CIA tip that there was a body inside. Rais called out to them weakly, more moans than words, but in the empty, echoing chamber they heard him.

"Good lord," one of them had exclaimed. "Is he alive?"

Then Rais lost consciousness again.

When he woke, he was in a hospital, hooked up to machines. Tubes in his body cavities. His head swimming with drugs. His right arm was handcuffed to the bed's steel railing.

Coherent thoughts came slowly, as if floating on a breeze: he was alive. Swiss police were posted outside his door in pairs. Every time he woke, there were different faces, new shifts.

He knew that once he was well enough to speak, the police would want to interrogate him—or worse, hand him over to the CIA. He could not allow that to happen. As soon as he had even a modicum of strength back, he would have to try to escape this place.

News came over the course of two days, pieced together from conversations in the hall or from the medical staff. With each new piece of information, his wrath and indignation grew.

Amun's plot had failed.

The bomber was in custody.

The Egyptian, his point of contact with Amun, was dead.

The sheikh and the German doctor were arrested.

Everything Rais had worked for in the past several years was gone. Everything except one crucial factor—Kent Steele was still alive.

And so was he.

On the third day of his hospitalization, his doctor, a short white man with spectacles and a shiny bald patch, entered the room to check his wounds. He methodically peeled back the dressings and gently prodded at the raw, painful sutures.

"You're healing nicely," he told Rais flatly. The doctor knew all too well who his patient was and his association with what had happened. "I'm sure you remember little of the past few days. We've removed one of your kidneys, and performed surgery to extract a lacerated portion of your liver." He spoke dispassionately. "There will be some long-term nerve damage, but nothing that should hinder quality of life." He paused a moment, considering the implication of what he'd just said. "Though, I imagine that wherever you end up for the rest of your life will be somewhat lacking in 'quality.'"

With the tube in his throat, Rais could say nothing in response.

"Once your respiratory rate improves, we'll remove the tubes, scale back your medication, and move you out of the ICU," the doctor continued. "But your recovery will still take some time before you can be discharged. And then ..." His gaze flitted toward the two police officers posted outside the door of the room. He didn't need to say anything further; Rais knew that "and then" meant he'd be detained—or, more likely, he'd be interrogated and tortured for information, and then sent to some hellish hole to wither and die.

He could not allow that to happen.

Night fell and Rais struggled to sleep. His limbs felt heavy and his wounds pained him with every slight movement. The doctor had decreased his medication; whether it was to wean him from the painkillers or purposely vindictive, he didn't know, but the pain was more intense now. He tried to ignore it, but when it didn't abate, he instead used it to fuel his anger as he tried to devise an escape plan. It would have to be under the cover of night, past visiting hours and when the staff was at a minimum. He was on the fourth floor, so windows were not an option. He would have to take his two guards by surprise without making any noise, as not to alert nearby staff. Then he would need clothes; they had to cut his off of him when they brought him in. He couldn't very well leave in a police uniform. That would be far too suspicious.

He had time to plan his escape, even if it meant pulling out the catheter and IV lines himself and fighting his way out. He could only hope that he would regain enough strength to do it. He was not yet sure where he would go or what he could do. Only one thing was clear in his mind: it was no longer solely his destiny to rid the world of Kent Steele.

It was now a necessity.

CHAPTER THIRTY EIGHT

"Hey." Maria snapped her fingers twice in front of his face. "Earth to Kent."

He blinked up at her. "Sorry. I was, uh, just thinking."

"Penny for your thoughts?"

He was silent a long moment. "People still died, Maria. We tried our best, did everything we could, and people still died."

The two of them sat across from each other in a conference room in CIA headquarters in Zurich, waiting for Cartwright and debriefing. The first thing that Reid had done upon returning to HQ was to get on the secure line to the safe house and make sure his girls were all right. Despite being several thousand miles away from the economic forum and the explosion, the experience had jarred him. Amun had very nearly won.

But his daughters were safe, if not a bit afflicted with cabin fever and eager to go home. For the first time since he had disappeared from the house in New York, Reid was able to honestly promise them that he was safe and would be home to them soon.

Maria had spent the rest of the previous day and the night in the hospital. After her wound was treated and she received a blood transfusion, she was deemed well enough to be released, though her right arm would be in a sling for the next two weeks.

She reached over the table and took his hand in hers. "You're right," she said, "people still died. Not just in Davos, either. We lost friends. Innocent bystanders caught in crossfire. Unfortunately, Kent, that's the job. As long as there are people like Amun out there, willing to do horrible things to try to impose their will, people will die. As cynical as it may sound, putting a stop to it is an overly idealistic goal. Our job is about controlling it, stifling it, and trying our damnedest to prevent it whenever possible. Sometimes... it's just not possible."

He smirked. "Funny. I took you for a glass-half-full kind of woman." His smile faded. "This time last week, I never would have imagined I'd be cut out for this sort of work. I'm still not really sure." He sighed. "I think I have a long road ahead of me. There's a lot I don't remember."

"Maybe that's not such a bad thing," Maria suggested. "Maybe without some of those memories, you can be a new person. Maybe you can be all the best parts of Kent, and all the best parts of Reid."

"Yeah. Maybe." Reid smiled. "And don't think for a second I've forgotten what you said up in that steeple."

"I don't know what you're talking about," she said coyly.

"No? Do I need to refresh your memory...?"

She scoffed. "I was stalling a terrorist, Kent. It's called subterfuge. You *used* to know what that meant."

"Yeah, and apparently you *used* to love me."

Maria blushed fiercely. "I... yeah. Maybe. Though I think... I think we were both different people then."

"Yeah," he agreed quietly. The tension in the air grew thick, so he quickly changed the subject. "But no more secrets, all right? Not between us. I think I can safely say that aside from my girls, you might be the only person in the world I feel I can trust. I'd like to keep it that way."

"Agreed." Maria winced. "But... can I get away with just one more little secret?"

Reid smirked. "What now?"

She reached into her back pocket and pulled out a folded white envelope. "I didn't tell you about this before because I wasn't sure if you were telling the truth. And then we got separated, and then... well, you know."

"What is it?"

"A few weeks ago, this came in the mail to the safe house in Rome. It was sent by Alan Reidigger. He didn't know that I was there." She slid the envelope across the table to him. "It's yours. I haven't opened it."

Reid unfolded the envelope. Sure enough, it was addressed to him—*c/o Reid Lawson* was written on the front, along with the address to the apartment in Rome. He turned it over and saw that on the back flap were six words, neatly written in small letters: *In the event of my death.*

Maria was right. The envelope was still sealed.

"I bet you might find a few answers in there," she said.

Reid turned the envelope over in his hands. He very much wanted answers—but at the same time, he wasn't sure he'd like them. It didn't feel like the right time to open it, not there, sitting in a conference room.

He wasn't sure it would ever be the right time.

The door swung open and Deputy Director Cartwright entered, carrying a brown file folder. Reid folded the envelope and stuck it in his pocket. *Later,* he thought.

"Agents," Cartwright greeted tightly. "We did a good thing today." Even as he said it, he did not look pleased.

Maria frowned. "You're sending some mixed signals, sir."

"There's still a lot of confusion," Cartwright said. "A lot of people want to ask you a lot of questions. Not just the CIA, but Internal Affairs, the Swiss government, the National Security Council, possibly even Interpol. The most important thing we can do right now is be completely honest about the events of the last five days."

Both agents nodded their agreement.

"There's more," said Cartwright. "I have strong reason to believe that the mole within the CIA is Steve Bolton."

The name barely registered any effect in Reid—he had only heard it in passing as another official within the CIA—but Maria looked up sharply. "How can you know?" she asked.

"I had my suspicions earlier, when we sent Carver and Watson for your girls," Cartwright explained. "Bolton was the only one I told, and the terrorist identified himself as Agent Watson. But I didn't act on it; I wasn't sure, and to make an accusation like that with so little evidence would not have reflected well on me if it wasn't true." He shook his head. "I should have gone with my instinct then."

"It's not too late…" Maria offered.

"Bolton is missing," the deputy director told them. "He went to lunch just before the attack on Davos, and never returned. His cell phone was found about a block from a bar he liked. No one has seen or heard from him."

"Then that's it," said Reid. "If he was supplying them with intel, then the leaks should stop."

"We can only hope, Zero." The deputy director shook his head. "I'd really like to consider today a win—and for all intents and purposes, it was. But we may still have problems in the agency, and Amun is still out there."

"True," Reid agreed, "but Amun has made a fatal flaw." He turned to Maria. "Remember your analogy back in Rome, about their chain? Someone to the left and someone to the right? We've broken their chain. We have the bomber, the German doctor, and the real sheikh. Rais is dead, and so is the Egyptian. They're disrupted. I don't know how long that'll last, but hopefully long enough for us to get a jump on them."

"Us?" Maria asked.

Reid bit his lip. With everything that had happened, he hadn't really given any thought to what would happen next. Strange, he thought, that his instinct was to continue on, keep going. If he thought about it for even a moment, all he really wanted was to get home to his daughters.

"Johansson, would you give us a minute?" Cartwright asked.

"Of course." Maria rose and left the conference room.

Once she was gone, the deputy director took her seat across from Reid. He set the brown folder between them and folded his hands atop it.

"I don't like to mince words," he said. "You've already been reinstated for this case. I've spoken to Directors Mullen and Hillis, and in light of what you've done, we can maintain that reinstatement—pending a psych eval, MRIs, a few other tests. You could come back, full-fledged." Cartwright paused a moment. "Or, you could choose not to." He tapped the brown folder with an index finger. "In here is your full debrief from this case. Once this mess is wrapped up, Zero's files have to go somewhere. Either the archives... or the active database."

Reid was silent for a long moment. He desperately missed his quiet life with his girls, their game nights, his lectures and classes... but on the other hand, he found himself yearning for the thrill of the chase, the feel of cold steel in his hand, and the exhilaration he got from the recoil of a gun.

"Thanks," Reid said, "but I think I need some time. I'm not sure if I'm ready for that. I still need to figure out who I am."

Cartwright chuckled. "You haven't realized that yet?" The deputy director leaned forward. "Don't kid yourself into thinking you're some big mystery, Zero. It's quite simple. You *are* Reid Lawson. You were born as Reid Lawson. It's not an alias. That's why we never found you in our follow-up after your alleged death; we thought you were smart enough not to use your real name. Who would do that? Turns out you were hiding in plain sight all along."

Reid felt a wave of relief wash over him. He was Reid Lawson. His wife had been Kate Lawson. His children were Maya and Sara Lawson. That's who they were, who he was.

"But you're also Kent Steele," Cartwright said. "Yes, it's an alias, made for your protection, but it's no less who you are."

Reid nodded. "I understand. But until I regain my memories and sort them out, there still feels like there's a Reid side and a Kent side. My brain is a bit of a mess."

"We... may have a guy that can help," the deputy director said thoughtfully. "He's a... well, I'm not sure how to describe him. He's a tech guy—at least that's his job description—but he's very brilliant. A little strange, too, but brilliant. I know this is your head we're talking about, but if anyone could figure this out, it'd be him. If you come back, you could sit with him. Maybe he could shed some light on what's going on in your attic." When Reid was silent, he continued, "Take some time. Figure it out. But don't take too long. This offer won't be on the table forever, and I'd hate to lose an asset like you."

Reid smirked. "Yesterday you told Director Hillis I was compromised."

Cartwright shrugged a shoulder. "Yeah, well, I guess I can be wrong sometimes." He stood and buttoned his jacket. "Now come on, Zero. You've got a lot of questions to answer before we can get you home to your girls."

"Zero," Reid repeated thoughtfully. "I suppose I'm that, too."

"Yes," Cartwright agreed. "No matter what name you go by, or who anyone thinks you are, you'll always be Agent Zero. Outside of a handful of people, no one will know what you did today. You've done it before, and no one knew. If you do it again, no one will know that either. It's part of the job. Zero is nothing, nobody. Zero is a ghost." With his hand on the door, he added quietly, "I suppose we all are."

EPILOGUE

Three days after the explosion at Davos, a Cessna Citation X flew the transatlantic flight from Zurich Airport to Dulles International in Virginia. Inside the jet, Reid drummed his fingers against the leather armrest eagerly. The past few days had been grueling, seemingly endless hours of conferences, meetings, debriefings, telling and retelling his story over and over for various men in suits whose faces and names blurred together after a while.

But he was finally going home.

"Kent, you okay?" Maria sat beside him across the narrow aisle. "You look like a kid waiting for Christmas morning."

"Yeah." He smiled. "I'm great. I'm just excited to see them again." Even the Cessna's seven-hundred-mile-per-hour top speed wasn't nearly fast enough to get him home to his girls, and now that they were nearly there, his impatience grew exponentially. "You know, it's funny," he mused. "I'm kind of ... nervous, actually. It feels like it's been so long."

Maria grinned. She opened her mouth to reply, but her cell phone rang. "It's my dad," she said. "Probably wondering how close we are. Excuse me." She rose from her seat and went to the rear of the cabin to answer it. "Hey, Dad. Yeah, almost home ..."

Reid's fingers drummed again on the armrest. He didn't even realize his left knee was bouncing in anticipation. *I need to relax,* he told himself. He grabbed the black nylon bag at his feet— Reidigger's GOOD bag—and tugged it open, reaching for a bottle of water he'd stowed inside.

His fingers brushed against something else. It was the still-sealed envelope addressed to him, from Alan, marked for the event of his death.

Reid hadn't opened it yet. There had been so much going on, and…and if he was being honest with himself, that was an excuse. He had some trepidation about reading its contents. He was concerned he might learn something about his past that he'd later regret. He also wanted to be alone when he read it, and the past few days had been a whirlwind of activity.

He could hear Maria a short distance behind him, speaking with her father, recounting the meetings and conferences they'd had, and he knew he had some time to himself.

No more excuses, he thought. *No time like the present.*

He worked his thumb under the flap and tore the envelope open.

He wasn't sure what he had expected, but was a little surprised to find only a single sheet of paper in the envelope—and on it, a fairly short, neatly written letter in a familiar hand, the same handwriting he had seen once before on the note he found in Reidigger's passport.

Hey Zero, the letter began.

If you're reading this, I'm probably dead (or maybe you're just really impatient). Either way, it means that you made it to the safe house, which means that things probably went sideways on us. I'm sorry about that. I want you to know that I only did what I felt I had to do.

Before you read the rest of this, I need you to remember something. I need you to remember the Hohenzollern Bridge. The doc said that if the suppressor was ever removed, saying it aloud should help recall the memory, so go ahead. Give it a whirl. Then maybe the rest of this letter will make a little more sense.

Reid blinked at the page for several seconds. He knew the Hohenzollern; it was a railway bridge in Germany that spanned the river Rhine. It was inaugurated in 1911 by Kaiser Wilhelm. He knew the facts, but he didn't know the significance.

"Hohenzollern Bridge," he murmured aloud.

A vision instantly flashed through his mind.

It's night. You stand on the footpath of the bridge, leaning against the railing and staring down at the darkness of the rushing river below. The eighty-foot drop would certainly injure, possibly even kill, the average person. But not you.

If only.

Footsteps approach. You glance up slowly, not the least bit surprised to see Alan Reidigger approaching. He's cautious, moving slowly, apprehensive.

"Hey, Zero," he says. He's trying to sound cheerful, but his voice is strained. "You've been busy."

Over his shoulder, about fifty yards down the footpath, is Agent Morris. Alan didn't come alone.

"Are you here to kill me, Alan?"

Reidigger leans against the railing with his forearms, staring out alongside you.

"Yes," he says.

That was nineteen months ago, Reid knew, almost to the day. That was after Kate's death, after Kent's vicious spree, after he was called back in by the CIA and chose to ignore it. Reidigger had found him in Cologne, Germany, and had come to him on the bridge. He told him he was there to kill him.

"Yes," he had said.

They both stood there in silence for a long time, staring out over the water.

"I found him," Kent said finally. "The Amun assassin I was chasing. His name is Rais. I opened him up and left him to die." He looked skyward. "Do you know what happened next?"

Reidigger did know. "Nothing," he said quietly.

"That's right. Nothing. I felt nothing. I got nothing out of it. No satisfaction. No vindication. No new leads. No direction." Kent paused for a long moment. "Alan, I took this too far. I don't think there's any coming back." He glanced over at his friend and added, "I assumed the agency would send someone. I just didn't think it would be you."

"I volunteered," Alan told him. "If anyone was going to do it, it was going to be me."

"And Morris?"

"He's here for backup, if I need it."

"You won't," Kent assured him. "I won't move against you."

Alan sighed. "Kent, you're damn foolish, you know that? You've been blinded by grief. Have you forgotten that you've got two girls at home? They love you. Their mother just died, and they haven't seen their father in weeks. They need you. And frankly, you need them."

Kent looked up again, this time in confusion. "You said you were here to kill me."

"I am," said Alan, "in a manner of speaking. I'm here to kill Kent Steele."

"I don't understand."

"You say there's no coming back, but I don't think that's true," Alan explained. "Listen to me carefully. The CIA has been developing a highly experimental device—a microchip that is capable of suppressing memory. I'm pretty sure I can get my hands on a prototype."

"Memory suppression? Alan, what the hell are you talking about?"

"Before I was a field agent, I worked in R&D. I saw some things. I've still got friends there. This chip is tiny, no bigger than a grain of rice. If I can get to it, I know a neurosurgeon in Zurich that will install it, no questions asked. We can suppress these memories, Kent. You'll forget about the assassin and the Fraternity. You'll forget you ever worked for the CIA. You would have no memory of being Zero. You'll go and live a quiet life with your girls somewhere. I've plotted a lot of it out. But I need your help—and obviously, your head."

Kent was struck speechless. He had heard the stories, of course; legend had it that the CIA had been experimenting with the human brain for decades, but he had never seen anything legitimate come of it. He'd always chalked it up to urban myth.

345

But if what Reidigger was saying was true, then … maybe it was possible to come back from all this.

"You'll need to say yes now," Alan told him, "because I'm sure in a minute or two Morris is going to get impatient. He's going to come down this way, and the only thing he's got for you is a bullet."

"What if it doesn't work? What if they find out?"

Reidigger scoffed lightly. "I don't know, Kent," he said impatiently. "Like I said, it's experimental. And if the agency finds out, then they'll kill you, and probably me too. We don't have time to work out logistics. The only alternative is that you die on this bridge tonight."

Kent thought of his girls. Strange, it had felt like so long since he'd thought of them, and he was suddenly aware of how much they needed him, how scared they probably were. He had sent them to New York to stay with Kate's sister, and he hadn't so much as called them in a while. They needed him—and he needed them.

"Thank you, Alan."

"Thank me later. Meet me in Zurich. You know the place," Alan said. "Then there's just one more thing."

Alan pulled out his gun and pointed it at Kent. "I need you to fall." He fired once.

The bullet missed him by less than two inches, whizzing so close to his ear that he felt a breeze from it. Kent staggered against the railing and tipped over the side.

A bridge. Darkness. Water rushing far below. The sensation of falling…

Reid took a deep breath. The memory had been so vivid, so lucid, that it was like he was there. He had to remind himself that he was on the Cessna, en route to the United States and his girls.

He touched the scar on his neck where the memory suppressor had been torn from him. He had done this willingly, for his girls—and for himself, to end his self-destructive warpath. Suddenly the words from Reidigger's note, the one he had found in Zurich, made a lot more sense: *If you're reading this, it's because what we did came back to bite us in the ass. I always thought it might, which is why I've been carrying this around ever since.*

Reidigger had suspected that the suppressor might not last forever, or that someone would find out that Kent Steele was still out there—and he had planned for it. He had risked his life to help his friend. He had died for his friend. And even after his death he had continued to help keep his friend Zero alive.

Reid opened the letter once more. There were two more paragraphs below the memory trigger of the bridge.

I hope you remember, the letter continued, *because what I'm going to tell you next is extremely important. Kent, before they sent me, the CIA wanted to bring you in, but you wouldn't listen. It wasn't just because of your warpath. There was something else, something you were close to finding—too close. I can't tell you what it was because even I don't know. You wouldn't tell me, so it must have been heavy.*

Whatever it was, it's still there, locked away in your brain somewhere. If you ever need it, there is a way. The neurosurgeon that installed the implant, his name is Dr. Guyer. He was last practicing in Zurich. He could bring back everything, if you choose. Or he could suppress them all again, if you wanted to do that. The choice is yours. Godspeed, Zero.—Alan

Reid stared at the letter for a long moment, rereading it twice more before he fully grasped what Reidigger was telling him. He could bring it all back, if he wanted. He could know everything. Or he could suppress it again.

Neither of those choices was very appealing.

He had suppressed the memories once before out of desperation and necessity. There was no way he could return to ignorance after everything that had happened, especially if it meant compromising the safety of his daughters.

But remembering was an equally disturbing option. If he unlocked all of his memories as Kent Steele, would he return to being that person and fall back into old habits? Would Reid Lawson, or the personality that he had developed as Reid, cease to exist?

And most unnerving of all was Reidigger's vague allusion to "something else." Something he was close to finding. What if he remembered something that he wasn't meant to remember—or something dangerous that Kent Steele had been so desperate to forget?

"All right, Dad," he heard Maria say behind him. "Yup, see you real soon. Love you too." As she ended the call, Reid folded the note and tucked it back into the envelope. She dropped into the seat beside him. "Everything okay?" she asked, noticing the envelope in his hand.

"Yeah." He forced a smile. "Everything's great." His first instinct was to share the letter with her, but something in the back of his mind kept him from doing so. It was meant for him, and no one else. Besides, they had just gone through hell to solve one mystery. There was no immediate need to launch into a new one.

Instead he told her, "It was a farewell letter. I think he knew Amun was on his trail and wanted closure. I wish I could remember more of him; he seemed like a good guy."

"The best," Maria agreed quietly.

Before tucking the letter back into the bag, he took something else out—the photo of him and Reidigger standing in front of the fountain in Rome. It was well worn and creased down the center. In the picture, they were both smiling, and seemed very much at ease with each other.

I hope I do remember you someday, he thought. Alan had been a better friend to him than he could ever hope to have been in return, and he wanted to honor the man's memory as best he could. He tucked the photo into the envelope, with the letter, and put it back in the bag.

The overhead intercom came to life as the pilot announced, "We'll be landing in just a few minutes. Buckle in, Agents."

With that brief statement, the eagerness suddenly returned and Reid forgot about the letter. He would be seeing his girls again in mere minutes.

He cleared his throat as the plane dipped in altitude. "So, uh, you'll be heading back to Baltimore then?"

"Yeah. For the time being, until the next assignment." She smiled. "It'll be nice. I haven't been home in a long time. What about you? Have they told you where you're going yet?"

Director Mullen had informed him that regardless of whether or not he took their offer, the CIA would be relocating him and his girls. Other members of Amun might be aware of his address in New York and they didn't want to take any chances.

"Alexandria," he told her. "I'll be taking an adjunct position at Georgetown."

"Virginia, huh?" She shrugged. "You know, that's only about an hour or so from me."

He smiled. "I, uh...yeah. That's close." He looked at her gray eyes, her vibrant smile. She was more familiar to him now, and not just because of what they had been through in the last few days. It was like reuniting with a childhood friend after decades apart; the memories were fuzzy, perhaps even lost, but there was a closeness, a kinship—maybe more than that. Something bordering on intimacy.

She wanted him to say more, he could tell. *Just ask her,* his brain prodded his mouth.

"It, um, would be nice to see you again," he offered.

She leaned over the aisle and kissed him, only briefly, but meaningfully. Her lips felt inviting and familiar against his.

"Definitely would be nice," he said sheepishly.

"And, uh..." She paused a moment. "I know you've got a lot to do, and two girls to take care of. But it would be good to have you back."

Reid glanced at the floor and nodded. She was right; he had a lot to do, and a lot to think about. But there was only one thing on his mind at the moment—no, two things, and they were both in the back of a black town car at that very moment, heading toward the airport to greet him. There would be time to weigh his options and sort things out later.

It was time to go home.

Maya didn't even realize that her left knee was bouncing in anticipation. She was seated behind Agents Carver and Watson in the back of a sleek black luxury sedan with her sister beside her as they drove down the tarmac of a small runway at Dulles. There was a second black car driving parallel to them; she had no idea who might be in that one and the windows were tinted too dark to see. But it didn't matter. They were about to see their father, and then they would go finally home.

"You excited, Squeak?" she asked her sister.

Sara smiled wide and nodded eagerly. If her younger sister was at all affected by the events of the past week, she didn't show it. She was resilient—and she hadn't seen what Maya had witnessed.

The mostly-silent Agent Carver drove, with Watson in the passenger seat in front of them. He had been very kind to them the past few days that they had spent in the safe house. He made sure they were well fed and had everything they needed. Admittedly, Maya had gone a little stir-crazy at the safe house. They had to maintain the rules of no cell phones, no computers, and no tablets. There was, thankfully, a television—which meant that she was able to watch the news.

It was not at all lost on Maya that the two major international events, first the false alarm at the Winter Olympics and then the explosion at Davos, both occurred in the same day, and that the very next afternoon their father had announced his homecoming.

That fact, combined with the safe house, the armed guards, the two men that had assaulted them on the boardwalk, and Watson's honorific of "Agent" meant that Maya had put together a pretty good idea of what her father might have been spirited away for. At least, she believed she did, but she didn't try to vocalize it or even ask any questions. She was smart enough to know that none of the men protecting them would give her an honest answer.

The one conclusion that she had definitively come to, however, in the time spent at the safe house, was that she was not okay. She had been nearly kidnapped, threatened with a gun, had a knife held to her throat, and witnessed two men and an innocent woman shot dead.

Despite how jubilant she was that her dad was coming home alive and well, there were some things they would have to discuss. She felt he owed her that much.

"Hey, take a look!" Agent Watson pointed upward, through the windshield, as a small white twin-engine jet descended from the sky toward them.

Sara craned her neck and her smile grew. "Is that him?"

"That's him," Watson confirmed.

Maya felt a tinge of nervous excitement run down her spine. The wheels of the Cessna touched down gently a few hundred yards from them, and it taxied a short distance down the runway. The two black sedans slowed as they approached the plane.

The door swung open from the inside and a short set of steel stairs were lowered by a man in a white uniform shirt—presumably the pilot—as Agent Carver stopped the car and parked.

At first, no one emerged. Neither of the girls moved from their seats, though Sara squirmed anxiously. Then a shape filled the doorway... but it wasn't their father. It was a woman—a tall, stunning woman with blonde hair cascading around her shoulders and, curiously, her right arm in a white sling. She exited the plane and strode quickly toward the other waiting black car. She pulled open the rear passenger-side door, but just before entering the vehicle, she glanced over at their car and flashed a warm smile. Maya didn't think the woman could see beyond the tinted windows—could she?

Then she got in, closed the door, and the other black car departed almost immediately. Maya was so confused by the beautiful woman and her strange smile that she didn't even notice the plane's other passenger disembarking until Sara tapped her suddenly on the shoulder and pointed.

"Maya, look!" she practically shrieked. Sara turned to Agent Watson. "Can we...?"

"Of course." Watson grinned. "What are you waiting for?"

The girls leapt out of the car, leaving both rear doors open as they ran to him.

"Daddy!" Sara jumped into his arms and he caught her, squeezing her tightly and swinging her back and forth.

"God, it's so good to hug you again," he said, his voice muffled as he buried his cheek in her hair. He held Sara for several seconds, and then set her down and turned to Maya.

His wide smile faded.

She had run for him, same as her sister, but she stopped a few paces short and simply stared. Over the last few days, she had spent a lot of time imagining what their reunion might be like, particularly at night as she was trying to fall asleep. Sometimes she dreamed about it. But she had never expected this.

One side of his face was badly bruised, the eye still purple and swollen. There was a butterfly bandage across his forehead and a larger one at his neck. He was clearly limping on one knee, and his left hand was wrapped in thick, mitten-like gauze.

His expression slackened. He knew exactly what she was thinking. "Maya ..." he started.

He had very clearly been in danger, which meant that they too had been in real danger. The reality of it, his bandages and bruises and limp, struck her hard.

She tried to keep the tears at bay, but she couldn't. All of her emotions came bubbling to the surface, all at once—not just her joy at seeing her father alive, but her alarm at seeing him in such a state, the fear she had squelched so she could keep her sister safe, the horror of seeing the scene at the boardwalk. All of it came on like a burst dam, as if her brain had decided it was finally safe to relent, and the tears came liberally.

Her father wrapped her in a hug and held her. He didn't say anything—he didn't have to. He just held her as she sobbed into his shoulder.

"Hey," he said at last. His voice cracked. "I'm here now." He squeezed her again and told her, "It's going to be okay."

She wanted to tell him that it wasn't okay, that it never would be okay ... but right then, in that moment, it felt like it almost might be.

Maya sniffled and took a step back to wipe her eyes. She laughed at herself a little—she had always felt self-conscious about crying in front of anyone, even her dad.

"We have a lot to talk about," she said.

"Yeah," he agreed. "We do."

Her dad put one arm around her, and the other around Sara, and the three of them headed toward the waiting car. Somewhere, toward home.

NOW AVAILABLE!

TARGET ZERO
(An Agent Steele Spy Thriller—Book #2)

"One of the best thrillers I have read this year."
—Books and Movie Reviews (re Any Means Necessary)

In this follow up to book #1 (AGENT ZERO) in the Agent Zero spy series, TARGET ZERO (Book #2) takes us on another wild, action-packed ride across Europe as elite CIA agent Kent Steele is summoned to stop a biological weapon before it devastates the world—all while grappling with his own memory loss.

Life returns only fleetingly back to normal for Kent before he finds himself summoned by the CIA to hunt down terrorists and stop another international crisis—this one even more potentially devastating than the last. Yet with an assassin hunting him down, a conspiracy within, moles all around him and with a lover he can barely trust, Kent is setup to fail.

Yet his memory is quickly returning, and with it, flashes into the secrets of who he was, what he'd discovered—and why they are after him. His own identity, he realizes, may be the most perilous secret of all.

TARGET ZERO is an espionage thriller that will keep you turning pages late into the night.

"Thriller writing at its best."
—Midwest Book Review (re *Any Means Necessary*)

Also available is Jack Mars' #1 bestselling LUKE STONE THRILLER series (7 books), which begins with Any Means Necessary (Book #1), a free download with over 800 five star reviews!

TARGET ZERO
(An Agent Steele Spy Thriller—Book #2)

Made in the USA
Las Vegas, NV
05 April 2022

46914684R10215